Peter Pan Must Die

Also by John Verdon

Think of a Number
Shut Your Eyes Tight
Let the Devil Sleep

John Verdon

Peter Pan Must Die

A novel

Crown Publishers

NEW YORK

Copyright © 2014 by John Verdon

All rights reserved.
Published in the United States by Crown Publishers,
an imprint of the Crown Publishing Group,
a division of Random House LLC,
a Penguin Random House Company, New York.
www.crownpublishing.com

Crown and the Crown colophon are registered trademarks of
Random House LLC.

Library of Congress Cataloging-in-Publication Data
is available upon request.

ISBN 978-0-385-34840-9
eBook ISBN 978-0-385-34841-6

Printed in the United States of America

Book design based on design by Lynne Amft
Jacket design: Eric White
Jacket photograph: Marcia Lippman

2 4 6 8 10 9 7 5 3 1

First Edition

For Naomi

Long Before the Killing Began

There was a time when he dreamt of being the head of a great nation. A nuclear power.

As the president, he would have his finger on the nuclear trigger. With a twitch of that finger he could launch nuclear missiles. He could obliterate huge cities. He could put an end to the human stink. He could wipe the rotten slate clean.

With maturity, however, had come a more practical perspective, a more realistic sense of what was possible. He knew that the nuclear trigger would never be within his reach.

But other triggers were available. One day at time, one trigger-pull at a time, much could be accomplished.

As he thought about it—and through his teenage years he'd thought about little else—a plan for his future slowly took shape. He came to know what his specialty would be—his art, his expertise, his field of excellence. And that was no small thing, since previously he had known almost nothing about himself, had no sense of who or what he was.

He had so few memories of anything before he was twelve.

Only the nightmare.

The nightmare that came again and again.

The circus. His mother, smaller than the other women. The terrible laughter. The music of the merry-go-round. The deep, constant growling of the animals.

The clown.

The huge clown who gave him money and hurt him.

The wheezing clown whose breath smelled like vomit.

And the words. So clear in the nightmare that their edges were as jagged as ice smashed against stone. "This is our secret. If you tell anyone, I'll feed your tongue to the tiger."

Part One
An Impossible Murder

Chapter 1

The Shadow of Death

In the rural Catskill Mountains of upstate New York, August was an unstable month, lurching back and forth between the bright glories of July and the gray squalls of the long winter to come.

It was a month that could erode one's sense of time and place. It seemed to feed Dave Gurney's confusion over where he was in his life—a confusion that had begun with his retirement from the NYPD three years earlier, after twenty-five years on the job, and had intensified when he and Madeleine had moved out to the country from the city where they'd both been born, raised, educated, and employed.

At that moment, a cloudy late afternoon in the first week of August, with low thunder grumbling in the distance, they were climbing Barrow Hill, following the remnant of a dirt road that linked three small bluestone quarries, long abandoned and full of wild raspberry brambles. He was trudging along behind Madeleine as she headed for the low boulder where they normally stopped to rest, doing his best to take her frequent advice: *Look around you. You're in a beautiful place. Just relax and absorb it.*

"Is that a tarn?" she asked.

Gurney blinked. "What?"

"That." She inclined her head toward the deep, still pool that filled the broad hollow left years ago by the removal of the bluestone. Roughly round, it stretched from where they sat by the trail to a row of water-loving willow trees on the far side—a glassy expanse perhaps two hundred feet across that mirrored the weeping branches of the trees so precisely, the effect resembled trick photography.

"A *tarn*?"

"I was reading a wonderful book about hiking in the Scottish Highlands," she said earnestly, "and the writer was forever coming upon 'tarns.' I got the impression that it was some kind of rocky pond."

"Hmm."

His nonresponse led to a long silence, broken finally by Madeleine. "See down there? That's where I was thinking we should build the chicken coop, right by the asparagus patch."

Gurney had been staring bleakly at the reflection of the willows. Now he followed her line of sight down a gentle slope through an opening in the woods formed by an abandoned logging road.

One reason that the boulder by the old quarry had become their habitual stopping place was that it was the only point on the trail from which their property was visible—the old farmhouse, the garden beds, the overgrown apple trees, the pond, the recently rebuilt barn, the surrounding hillside pastures (long untended and full this time of year with milkweed and black-eyed Susans), the part of the pasture by the house that they mowed and called a lawn, the swath up through the low pasture that they mowed and called a driveway. Madeleine, perched now on the boulder, always seemed pleased at this uniquely framed view of it all.

Gurney didn't feel the same. Madeleine had discovered the spot herself shortly after they'd moved in, and from the first time she had shown it to him all he could think of was that it was the ideal location for a sniper to target someone entering or leaving their house. (He had the good sense not to mention this to her. She did work three days a week in the local psychiatric clinic, and he didn't want her thinking he was in need of treatment for paranoia.)

The need to build a chicken coop, its projected size and appearance, and the site where it should be built had become daily topics of conversation—obviously exciting to her, mildly irritating to him. They had acquired four chickens in late May at Madeleine's urging and had been housing them in the barn—but the idea of moving them up to new quarters by the house had taken hold.

"We could build a nice little coop with an enclosed run between the asparagus patch and the apple tree," she said brightly, "so on hot days they'd have shade."

"Right." The word came out more wearily than he'd intended.

The conversation might have deteriorated from there had Madeleine's attention not been diverted. She tilted her head.

"What is it?" asked Gurney.

"Listen."

He waited—not an unusual experience. His hearing was normal, but Madeleine's was extraordinary. A few seconds later, as the breeze rustling the foliage subsided, he heard something in the distance, somewhere down the hill, perhaps on the town road that dead-ended into the low end of their pasture "driveway." As it grew louder, he recognized the distinctive growl of an oversized, undermuffled V8.

He knew someone who drove an old muscle car that sounded exactly like that—a partially restored red 1970 Pontiac GTO—someone for whom that brash exhaust note was the perfect introduction.

Jack Hardwick.

He felt his jaw tightening at the prospect of a visit from the detective with whom he had such a bizarre history of near-death experiences, professional successes, and personality clashes. Not that he hadn't been anticipating the visit. In fact, he'd known it was coming from the moment he'd heard about the man's forced departure from the State Police Bureau of Criminal Investigation. And he realized that the tension he felt now had a lot to do with what had happened prior to that departure. A serious debt had been incurred, and some kind of payment would have to be made.

A formation of low dark clouds was moving quickly over the far ridge as though retreating from the violent sound of the red car—now visible from where Gurney was sitting—as it made its way up the mowed pasture swath to the farmhouse. He was briefly tempted to stay on the hill until Hardwick left, but he knew that would accomplish nothing—only extend the period of discomfort before the inevitable meeting. With a small grunt of determination he got up from his place on the boulder.

"Were you expecting him?" asked Madeleine.

Gurney glanced down the slope. The GTO came to a stop by his own dusty Outback in the little makeshift parking area by the side of the house. The big Pontiac engine roared louder for a couple of seconds as it was revved prior to being shut down.

"I was expecting him in a general way," said Gurney, "not necessarily today."

"Do you want to see him?"

"I'd say he wants to see me, and I'd like to get it over with."

Madeleine nodded and stood up, pushing her short brown hair back from her forehead.

As they turned to start down the trail, the mirror surface of the quarry pool shivered under a sudden breeze, dissolving the inverted image of the willows and the sky into thousands of unrecognizable splinters of green and gray.

If Gurney were the kind of man who believed in omens, he might have seen the shattered image as a sign of the destruction to come.

Chapter 2

The Scum of the Earth

When he was halfway down Barrow Hill, deeper in the woods, out of sight of the house now, Gurney's phone rang. He recognized Hardwick's number.

"Hello, Jack."

"Both your cars are here, but no one's coming to the door. You hiding in the basement?"

"I'm very well, thanks. And how are you?"

"Where the hell are you?"

"Coming down through the cherry copse, quarter mile to your west."

"Hillside with all the yellow leaf blight?"

Hardwick had a way of getting under Gurney's skin. It wasn't just the little jabs themselves, or the pleasure the man seemed to take in delivering them; it was the uncanny echo of a voice from Gurney's childhood—the relentlessly sardonic voice of his father.

"Right, the one with the blight. What can I do for you, Jack?"

Hardwick cleared his throat with disgusting enthusiasm. "Question is, what can we do for each other? Tit for tat, tat for tit. By the way, I noticed your door is unlocked. Mind if I wait for you in the house? Too many fucking flies out here."

Hardwick, a solidly built man with a ruddy complexion, a prematurely gray crew cut, and the disconcertingly blue eyes of an Alaskan sled dog, was standing in the center of the big open room that composed half of the lower floor. At one end was a country kitchen.

A round pine breakfast table was tucked in a nook next to a pair of French doors. At the far end was a sitting area, arranged around a massive fieldstone fireplace and a separate woodstove. In the middle was a plain Shaker-style dining table and half a dozen ladder-back chairs.

The first thing that struck Gurney as he entered the room was that something in Hardwick's expression was slightly off.

Even the leer in his opening question—"And where might the delectable Madeleine be?"—seemed oddly forced.

"I'm right here," she said, coming in from the mudroom and heading for the sink island with a half-welcoming, half-anxious smile. She was carrying a handful of asterlike wildflowers she'd picked on their way down from Barrow Hill. She laid them by the dish drainer and looked at Gurney. "I'm leaving these here. I'll find a vase for them later. I need to go upstairs and practice for a while."

As her footsteps receded to the upper floor, Hardwick grinned and whispered, "Practice makes perfect. So what's she practicing?"

"Cello."

"Ah. Of course. You know why people love the cello so much?"

"Because it has a nice sound?"

"Ah, Davey boy, now there's the kind of direct no-nonsense insight you're famous for." Hardwick licked his lips. "But do you know what it is *exactly* that makes that particular sound sound nice?"

"Why don't you just tell me, Jack?"

"And deprive you of a fascinating little puzzle to solve?" He shook his head with theatrical resoluteness. "Wouldn't dream of it. A genius like you needs challenges. Otherwise he goes to pot."

As Gurney stared at Hardwick, it dawned on him what was wrong, what was *off.* Underneath the prickly banter, which was the man's customary approach to the world, there seemed to be a not-so-customary tension. Edginess was part of Hardwick's personality, but what Gurney detected in his expression now was more nervousness than edginess. It made him wonder what was coming. The man's unsettledness was contagious.

It didn't help that Madeleine had chosen a rather jittery piece for her cello practice.

Hardwick began walking around the long room, touching the backs of chairs, corners of tables, potted plants, decorative bowls and bottles and candlesticks that Madeleine had picked up in the area's inexpensive antique shops. "Love this place! Just love it! It's so fucking *authentic*!" He stopped and ran his hands back through his bristly crew cut. "You know what I mean?"

"That it's fucking authentic?"

"The whole deal here—it's pure *country*. Look at that cast-iron woodstove, made in America, as American as fucking pancakes. Look at you—lean, all-American, Robert Redford kind of guy. Look at them wide floorboards, straight and honest as the trees they came from."

"Those."

"Beg your pardon?"

"*Those* wide floorboards. Not *them* wide floorboards."

Hardwick stopped pacing. "The fuck are you talking about?"

"Is there a point to this visit?"

Hardwick grimaced. "Ah, Davey, Davey—all business, as usual. You dismiss my attempt at a few pleasantries, my efforts at social lubrication, a few friendly compliments on the puritan simplicity of your home decor—"

"Jack . . ."

"Right. Fuck the pleasantries. Where do we sit?"

Gurney motioned to the small round table by the French doors.

When they were seated across from each other, Gurney leaned back and waited.

Hardwick closed his eyes, massaging his face roughly with his hands as though trying to eradicate some deep itching under the skin. Then he folded his hands on the table and began speaking. "You ask if there's a point to my visit. Yes, there is. An opportunity. You know that thing from *Julius Caesar* about a tide in the affairs of men?"

"What about it?"

Hardwick leaned forward, as though the words contained life's ultimate secret. The chronic mockery had disappeared from his voice. "*There is a tide in the affairs of men / Which, taken at the flood leads on to fortune. / Omitted, all the voyage of their life / is bound in shallows and in miseries.*"

"You memorized that just for me?"

"Learned it in school. Always stayed with me."

"Never heard you mention it before."

"The right situation never came up before."

"But now . . . ?"

A tic yanked at the corner of Hardwick's mouth. "Now the right moment has arrived."

"A tide in your affairs——?"

"In *our* affairs."

"Yours and mine?"

"Exactly."

Gurney said nothing for a while, just gazed at the excited, anxious face across from him. He found himself far more uncomfortable with this suddenly raw and earnest version of Jack Hardwick than he'd ever been with the perennial cynic.

For a few moments the only sound in the house was the sharp-edged melody of an early-twentieth-century cello piece that Madeleine had been struggling with for the past week.

Almost imperceptibly, Hardwick's mouth twitched again.

Seeing this a second time, and waiting for it to happen a third time, was getting to Gurney. Because, to him, it suggested that the payment about to be demanded for the debt incurred months earlier was going to be substantial.

"You plan on telling me what you're talking about?"

"What I'm talking about is the Spalter murder case." Hardwick enunciated those last three words with a peculiar combination of importance and contempt. His eyes were fixed on Gurney's, as if searching for the appropriate reaction.

Gurney frowned. "The woman who shot her rich politician husband up in Long Falls?" It had been a sensational news item earlier in the year.

"That's the one."

"As I recall, that was a slam-dunk conviction. The lady was buried under an avalanche of evidence and prosecution witnesses. Not to mention that special little extra—her husband, Carl, dying during the trial."

"That's the one."

The details began coming back to him. "She shot him in the cemetery as he was standing at his mother's grave, right? The bullet paralyzed him, turned him into a vegetable."

Hardwick nodded. "A vegetable in a wheelchair. The vegetable the prosecution wheeled into court every day. God-awful sight. Constant reminder for the jury while his wife was being tried for doing it to him. Until, of course, he died halfway through the trial and they had to stop wheeling him in. They went on with the trial—just switched the charge from attempted murder to murder."

"Spalter was a wealthy real estate guy, right? Had just announced a third-party run for governor?"

"Yep."

"Anticrime. Anti-mob. Ballsy slogan. *'Time to get rid of the scum of the earth.'* Or something like that."

Hardwick leaned forward. "Those were the precise words, Davey boy. In every speech he managed to talk about 'the scum of the earth.' Every goddamn time. 'The scum of the earth have risen to the top of our nation's cesspool of political corruption.' The scum of the earth this, the scum of the earth that. Carl liked to stay on message."

Gurney nodded. "I seem to recall that the wife was having an affair, and that she was afraid he might divorce her, which would end up costing her millions, unless he should happen to die before he changed his will."

"You got it." Hardwick smiled.

"I got it?" Gurney looked incredulous. "This is the high-tide opportunity you were talking about? The Spalter case? In the event you hadn't noticed, the Spalter case is done, closed, over. If memory serves, Kay Spalter is doing twenty-five to life in max security at Bedford Hills."

"All true," said Hardwick.

"So what the hell are we talking about?"

Hardwick indulged in a long, slow, humorless smile—the kind of dramatic pause he was fond of and Gurney hated. "We're talking about the fact that . . . the lady was framed. The case against her was total bullshit, start to finish. Pure . . . unadulterated . . . bullshit." Again, at the corner of the smile, the tic. "Bottom line, we're talking about getting the lady's conviction overturned."

"How do you know the case was bullshit?"

"She got screwed by a dirty cop."

"How do you know that?"

"I just know things. Also, people tell me things. The dirty cop has enemies—with good reason. He's not dirty, he's filthy. The ultimate piece of shit." Now there was a new fierceness in Hardwick's eyes.

"Okay. Let's say she was framed by a dirty cop. Let's even go so far as to say she was innocent. What's that got to do with you? Or me?"

"Besides the minor issue of justice?"

"That look in your eyes has nothing to do with justice."

"Sure it does. It has everything to do with justice. The organization fucked me. So I'm going to fuck the organization. Honestly, legally, and totally on the side of justice. They forced me out because they always wanted to. I got a little sloppy about a few files on the Good Shepherd case that I passed along to you, bureaucratic bullshit, and that gave the scumbags their excuse."

Gurney nodded. He'd been wondering if the debt would be mentioned—the benefit delivered to Gurney, the career-ending expense paid by Hardwick. Now he didn't have to wonder anymore.

Hardwick went on. "So now I'm entering the PI business. Unemployed detective for hire. And my first client is going to be Kay Spalter, through the lawyer who'll be handling her appeal. So my first victory's gonna be a very big one."

Gurney paused, thought about what he'd just heard. "And me?"

"What?"

"You said this was an opportunity for both of us."

"And that's exactly what it is. For you, it could be the case of a fucking lifetime. Get into it, and tear it to pieces, put it back together the right way. The Spalter case was the crime of the decade, followed by the frame of the century. You get to figure it out, set it straight, and kick some nasty bastards in the balls along the way."

"You didn't drive all the way over here today just to give me an opportunity to kick bad guys in the balls. Why do you want me involved in this?"

Hardwick shrugged, took a deep breath. "Plenty of reasons."

"And the biggest would be . . . ?"

For the first time it looked like he was having trouble getting the words out. "To help turn the key another quarter inch and lock up the deal."

"There's no deal yet? I thought you said Kay Spalter was your client."

"I said she's *going to be* my client. Some legal details need to be signed off on first."

"Details?"

"Believe me, everything's lined up. Just a matter of pushing the right buttons."

Gurney saw the tic again and felt his own jaw muscles tightening.

Hardwick went on quickly. "Kay Spalter was represented by a court-appointed asshole who's still technically her attorney, which weakens an otherwise powerful set of arguments for having the conviction reversed. One potential bullet in the appeal gun would be incompetent representation, but the current guy can't really make that argument. You can't say to the judge, 'You have to free my client because I'm an asshole.' Someone else has to call you an asshole. Law of the land. So, bottom line—"

Gurney broke in. "Wait a second. There's got to be a ton of money in that family. How did she end up with a court-appointed—?"

"There *is* a ton of money. Problem is, it was all in Carl's name. He controlled everything. Tells you something about the kind of guy he was. Kay lived like a very rich lady—without actually having a cent to her name. Technically, she's indigent. And she got assigned the kind of attorney indigents usually get. Not to mention a tight budget for defense out-of-pockets. So, as I was saying: Bottom line, she needs new representation. And I have the perfect man all lined up, sharpening his fangs. Smart, vicious, unprincipled fucker—always hungry. She just needs to sign a couple of things to make the switch official."

Gurney wondered if he was hearing right. "You expect *me* to sell her that idea?"

"No. Absolutely not. No selling required. I'd just like you to be part of the equation."

"What part?"

"Hotshot homicide detective from the big city. Successful murder investigations and decorations up the kazoo. Man who turned the Good Shepherd case inside out and embarrassed the shit out of all the fuckheads."

"You're saying you want me to play the role of a bright, shiny front man for you and this 'vicious, unprincipled fucker' of yours?"

"He's not really unprincipled. Just . . . aggressive. Knows how to use his elbows. And no, you wouldn't just be a 'front man' for anyone. You'd be a player. Part of the team. Part of the reason Kay Spalter should hire us to reinvestigate the case, engineer her appeal, and get her bullshit conviction reversed."

Gurney shook his head. "I'm not following this at all. If there wasn't any money for a hotshot attorney to begin with, how come there is now?"

"To begin with, looking at the surface strength of the prosecution's case, there wasn't much hope that Kay would prevail. And if she couldn't prevail, there'd be no way for her to pay a significant legal bill."

"But now——?"

"But now the situation is different. You, me, and Lex Bincher are going to make sure of that. Believe me, she will prevail, and the bad guys will bite the dust. And once she prevails, she will be entitled to inherit a huge chunk of cash as Carl's primary beneficiary."

"Meaning this Bincher guy is working on a contingency fee in a criminal case? Isn't that semi-illegal, or at least unethical?"

"Don't sweat it. There's no actual contingency clause in the agreement she'll sign. I guess you could say that Lex getting paid will sort of depend on the success of the appeal, but there's nothing in writing that makes that connection. If the appeal fails, technically Kay will just owe him a lot of money. But forget about all that. That's Lex's problem. Besides, the appeal will succeed!"

Gurney sat back, stared out through the door at the asparagus patch at the far side of the old bluestone patio. The asparagus ferns had grown much taller than in either of the previous two summers. He reckoned a tall man could stand in their midst and not be seen. Normally a soft bluish green, now, under an unsettled gray sky, they appeared colorless.

He blinked, rubbed his face roughly with both hands, and tried to refocus his mind on reducing the tacky mess being placed before him to its essentials.

The way he saw it, he was being asked to launch Hardwick in his new PI business—by helping to ensure his first major client commitment. And this was to be the repayment for the regulation-skirting favors Hardwick had done for him in the past, at the cost of Hardwick's career with the state police. That much was clear, as far as it went. But there was a lot more to consider.

One of Hardwick's distinctive traits had been a bold independence, the kind of let-the-chips-fall-where-they-may independence that comes from not being too attached to anything or anybody or any predetermined goal. But the man sure as hell was attached to this new project and its intended outcome, and the change didn't strike Gurney as all that positive. He wondered what it would be like working with Hardwick in this altered state—with all his abrasiveness intact, but now in the service of a resentful obsession.

He turned his attention from the asparagus ferns to Hardwick's face. "So, what does that mean, Jack—'part of the team'? What, specifically, would you want me to do, other than look smart and rattle my medals?"

"Whatever the hell you feel like doing. Look, I'm telling you—the prosecution's case was rotten start to finish. If the chief investigating officer doesn't end up in Attica at the end of this, I'll . . . I'll become a fucking vegan. I absolutely guarantee you that the underlying facts and narratives will be full of disconnects. Even the trial transcript is full of them. And, Davey boy, whether you admit it or not, you know damn well that no cop ever had a sharper eye and ear for disconnects than you do. So that's the story. I want you on the team. Will you do this for me?"

Will you do this for me? The plea echoed in Gurney's head. He didn't feel capable of saying no. Not right at that moment, anyway. He took a deep breath. "You have the trial transcript?"

"I do."

"With you?"

"In my car."

"I'll . . . take look at it. We'll have to see where we go from there."

Hardwick stood up from the table, his nervousness now looking more like excitement. "I'll leave you a copy of the official case file, too. Lots of interesting shit. Could be helpful."

"How'd you get the file?"

"I still have a few friends."

Gurney smiled uncomfortably. "I'm not promising anything, Jack."

"Fine. No problem. I'll get the stuff from the car. You take your time with it. See what you think." On the way out, he stopped and turned back. "You won't be sorry, Davey. The Spalter case has everything— horror, gangsters, politics, big money, big lies, and maybe even a little bit of incest. You're gonna fuckin' love it!"

Chapter 3

Something in the Woods

Madeleine cooked a simple dinner and they ate with little conversation. Gurney kept expecting her to engage him in an exhaustive discussion of his meeting with Hardwick, but she asked only one question.

"What does he want from you?"

Gurney described the nature of the Kay Spalter case, Hardwick's new PI status, his evidently huge emotional investment in getting Kay's conviction overturned, his request for assistance.

Madeleine's only reaction consisted of a small nod and a barely audible "Hmm." She stood up, cleared the dishes and silverware from the table, and took them to the sink island, where she proceeded to wash them, rinse them, and stack them in the drainer. Then she got a pitcher from the cupboard and watered the plants that stood on the sideboard below the kitchen windows. Each minute that she failed to pursue the subject exerted a stronger tug on Gurney to add a few additional words of explanation, reassurance, justification. Just as he was about to do so, she suggested they take a stroll down to the pond.

"It's too nice an evening to stay inside," she said.

Nice was not a word he would have used to describe the uncertain sky with its scuttling clouds, but he resisted the urge to debate the point. He followed her to the mudroom off the kitchen, where she put on one of her tropically bright nylon jackets. He slipped into an olive-drab cardigan he'd had for nearly twenty years.

She squinted at it doubtfully. "Are you trying to look like someone's grandfather?"

"You mean stable, trustworthy, and lovable?"

She raised an ironic eyebrow.

Nothing else was said until they'd made their way down through the low pasture and were seated on the weathered wooden bench beside the pond. She appeared, as she often did, in a static position, not quite relaxed. It was as if her slim, naturally athletic body craved movement in the way that some bodies crave sugar.

Except for a grassy opening between the bench and the water, the pond was ringed by tall bulrushes, where redwing blackbirds built nests and fended off intruders with aggressive swoops and screeches through late spring and into the summer.

"We have to start pulling out some of those giant reeds," said Madeleine, "or they'll take over completely."

Each year the encircling band of bulrushes had grown thicker, inching farther out into the water. Pulling them out, Gurney had discovered the one time he'd tried it, was a muddy, tiresome, frustrating job. "Right," he said vaguely.

The crows, settling in the tops of the trees up along the edge of the pasture, were in full voice now—a sharp, continuous chattering that each evening reached a peak at sunset, then diminished into silence as dusk fell.

"And we really have to do something with that thing." She pointed at the warped and tilting trellis a former owner had erected at the beginning of the path around the pond. "But it'll have to wait until after we build the coop with a nice big fenced run. The chickens should be able to run around outside, not just sit in that dark little barn all the time."

Gurney said nothing. The barn had windows—it wasn't all that dark inside—but that was a line of argument guaranteed to go nowhere. It *was* smaller than the original building, which had been destroyed in a mysterious fire several months earlier, in the middle of the Good Shepherd case, but surely it was big enough for a rooster and three hens. To Madeleine, however, enclosed places were at best temporary resting areas and the open air was heaven. It was clear that she empathized with what she imagined to be the imprisonment of the chickens, and it would be as easy to convince her that the barn was a reasonable home for them as it would be to persuade her to live in it herself.

Besides, they hadn't come down to the pond to debate the future of bulrushes or trellises or chickens. Gurney felt certain that she'd return to the matter of Jack Hardwick, and he began to prepare a line of argument defending his potential involvement in the case.

She'd ask if he was planning to take on yet another full-scale murder investigation in his so-called retirement, and if so, why had he bothered to retire?

He'd explain again that Hardwick had been forced out of the NYSP partly as a result of the assistance he'd provided at Gurney's request on the Good Shepherd case, and providing assistance in return was a simple matter of justice. A debt incurred, a debt paid.

She'd point out that Hardwick had undermined himself—that it wasn't the passing along of a few restricted files that got him fired; it was his long history of insubordination and disrespect, his adolescent relish in puncturing the egos of authority figures. That kind of behavior carried obvious risks, and the ax had finally fallen.

He'd counter with an argument about the fuzzier demands of friendship.

She'd claim that he and Hardwick had never really been friends, just uneasy colleagues with occasional common interests.

He'd remind her of the unique bond that was formed in their collaboration years earlier on the Peter Piggert case, when on the same day in jurisdictions a hundred miles apart they each found half of Mrs. Piggert's body.

She'd shake her head and dismiss the "bond" as a grotesque coincidence in the past that was a poor reason for any present action.

Gurney leaned back against the bench slats and looked up at the slate sky. He felt ready, if not entirely eager, for the give-and-take that he expected would begin momentarily. A few small birds, singly and in loose pairs, passed high overhead, flying rapidly, as if late for their roosting commitments.

When Madeleine finally spoke, however, her tone and angle on the subject were not what he'd expected.

"You realize that he's obsessed," she said, looking out over the pond. Half a statement, half a question.

"Yes."

"Obsessed with getting revenge."

"Possibly."

"*Possibly?*"

"Okay. Probably."

"It's a horrible motive."

"I'm aware of that."

"And you're also aware that it makes his version of the facts unreliable?"

"I have no intention of accepting his version of anything. I'm not that naive."

Madeleine looked over at him, then back out in the direction of the pond. They were silent for a while. Gurney felt a chill in the air, a damp, earthy-smelling chill.

"You need to talk to Malcolm Claret," she said matter-of-factly.

He blinked, turned, and stared at her. "What?"

"Before you get involved in this, you need to talk to him."

"What the hell for?" His feelings about Claret were mixed—not because he had anything against the man himself or doubted his professional abilities, but the memories of the occasions that prompted their past meetings were still full of pain and confusion.

"He might be able to help you . . . help you understand why you're doing this."

"Understand why I'm doing this? What's that supposed to mean?"

She didn't answer immediately. Nor did he press the question—taken aback momentarily by the sudden sharpness in his own voice.

They'd been through this before, more than once—this question of why he did what he did, why he'd become a detective in the first place, why he was drawn to homicide in particular, and why it continued to fascinate him. He wondered at the defensiveness of his reaction, given that this was well-trod ground.

Another pair of small birds, high in the darkening sky, were hurrying to some more familiar, perhaps safer, place—most likely the place they considered home.

He spoke in a softer voice. "I'm not sure what you mean by 'why you're doing this.'"

"You've come too close to being killed too many times."

He drew back a little. "When you're dealing with murderers—"

"Please, not now," she interrupted, raising her hand. "Not the Dangerous Job speech. That's not what I'm talking about."

"Then what—"

"You're the smartest man I know. The smartest. All the angles, possibilities—nobody can figure it out better or faster than you can. And yet . . ." Her voice trailed off, suddenly shaky.

He waited a long ten seconds before prompting her gently. "And yet?"

It was another ten seconds before she went on. "And yet . . . somehow . . . you've ended up face-to-face with an armed lunatic on three separate occasions in the past two years. An inch from death each time."

He said nothing.

She stared sadly out over the pond. "There's something wrong with that picture."

It took him a while to reply. "You think I want to die?"

"*Do* you?"

"Of course not."

She continued looking straight ahead.

The hillside pasture and the woods beyond the pond were all growing darker. At the edge of the woods the gold patches of ragweed and lavender sprigs of grape-hyacinth had already faded to shades of gray. Madeleine gave a little shiver, zipped her windbreaker up to her chin, and folded her arms across her chest, pulling her elbows tightly against her.

They sat in silence for a long while. It was as if their conversation had come to a strange stopping place, a slippery declivity from which there was no clear way up and out.

As a quivering spot of silver light appeared in the center of the pond—a reflection of the moon, which had emerged at that moment through a break in the clouds—there was a sound deep in the woods behind the bench that made the hairs stand up on Gurney's arms. A keening note, a not-quite-human cry of desolation.

"What the . . . ?"

"I've heard it before," said Madeleine. "On different nights it seems to come from different places."

He listened, waiting. A minute later, it sounded again, weird and plaintive.

"Probably an owl," he said, without having any reason to believe it.

What he avoided saying was that it sounded to him like a lost child.

Chapter 4

Pure Evil

I t was past midnight, and Gurney's efforts to fall asleep had been as unsuccessful as if he'd had half a dozen cups of coffee.

The moon, glimpsed briefly at the pond, had disappeared behind a thick new blanket of clouds. Both windows were open at the top, letting a humid chill into the room. The darkness and the touch of the damp night air on his skin formed a kind of enclosure, giving him a creeping sense of claustrophobia. In that small, oppressive place he found it impossible to put aside his uneasy thoughts about the suspended but hardly completed death-wish discussion with Madeleine. But the thoughts went nowhere, led to no conclusions. The frustration persuaded him to abandon the bed.

He got up and felt his way to the chair where he'd left his shirt and pants.

"As long as you're up, you might want to close the upstairs windows." Madeleine's voice from the far side of the bed sounded surprisingly wide awake.

"Why?" he asked.

"The storm. Haven't you heard the thunder getting closer?"

He hadn't. But he trusted her ears.

"Shall I close these by the bed too?"

"Not yet. The air feels like satin."

"Wet satin, you mean?"

He heard her sigh, give her pillow a few pats, and resettle herself. "Wet earth, wet grass, wonderful . . ." She yawned, made a contented little sound, and said no more. He marveled at how she could find such restorative power in the very elements of nature he instinctively fled from.

He put on his pants and shirt, went upstairs, and closed the windows in the two spare bedrooms and in the room that Madeleine devoted to sewing, crocheting, and cello practice. He came back downstairs, went into the den, and got the plastic shopping bag full of the Spalter case materials Hardwick had left for him, and brought it out to the dining room table.

The heaviness of the bag bothered him. It seemed to be a crude warning.

He began spreading its contents out on the table. Then, remembering Madeleine's unhappy reaction the last time he took over that table to examine the paperwork documenting the progress of a murder case, he picked everything up and carried it to the coffee table in front of the fireplace at the other end of the room.

The individual items included a full printed transcript of *State of New York v. Katherine R. Spalter* trial proceedings; the NYSP Bureau of Criminal Investigation case file on the Spalter homicide (including the multisection original incident report with photos and drawings, crime scene inventories, forensic lab reports, interview and interrogation reports, investigatory progress reports, the autopsy report and photos, the ballistics report, and scores of miscellaneous memos and phone call reports); a list of pretrial motions (all perfunctory, all cut-and-pasted out of the capital case motions manual) and their dispositions (all denied); a folder with articles, blog printouts, broadcast transcripts, and a list of links to online coverage of the crime, arrest, and trial phases of the story; a manila envelope containing a set of DVDs of the trial itself, provided by the local cable station that apparently had been granted Court TV–style access to the proceedings; and, finally, a note from Jack Hardwick.

It was a kind of road map—Hardwick's suggested route through the daunting heap of information spread out on the coffee table.

Gurney had good and bad feelings about this. Good, because directions and prioritization could be time-savers. Bad, because they could be manipulative. Often they were both. But they were hard to ignore—as were the opening sentences of Hardwick's note.

"Follow the sequence I've laid out here. If you depart from the path you'll drown in a data shit-swamp."

The rest of the two-page note consisted of a series of numbered steps on the route.

"Number one: Get a taste of the case against Kay Spalter. Get the DVD marked 'A' from the envelope and check out the prosecutor's opening statement. It's a classic."

Gurney retrieved his laptop from the den and inserted the disk.

Like some other recordings of courtroom proceedings he'd seen, this one began with an image of the prosecutor standing in the open area in front of the judge's bench, facing the jury box, clearing his throat. He was a small man with close-cropped dark hair, maybe in his mid-forties.

There were background noises of papers rustling, chairs moving, a jumble of indistinguishable voices, someone coughing—most of which subsided after a few sharp raps of the judge's gavel.

The prosecutor glanced at the judge, a heavyset black man with a dour expression, who gave him a perfunctory nod. He took a deep breath and stared at the floor for several seconds before looking up at the jury.

"Evil," he finally announced in a strong, formal voice. He waited for absolute silence before continuing. "We all think we know what evil is. History books and news reports are full of evil deeds, evil men, evil women. But the scheme you are about to be exposed to—and the ruthless predator you will convict at the end of this trial—will bring the reality of evil home to you in a way you'll never forget."

He glared at the floor, then went on. "This is the true story of a woman and a man, a wife and a husband, a predator and a victim. The story of a marriage poisoned by infidelity. The story of a homicidal plot—an attempted murder that produced a result you may well conclude was worse than murder itself. You heard me right, ladies and gentlemen. *Worse than murder.*"

After a pause during which he seemed to be trying to make eye contact with as many jurors as possible, he turned and walked to the prosecution table. Directly in back of the table, in front of the area assigned to courtroom spectators, sat a man in a large wheelchair—an elaborate device that reminded Gurney of the kind of thing in which Stephen Hawking, the paralyzed physicist, made his rare public appearances. It seemed to be providing support for all parts of the occupant's body, including his head. There were oxygen tubes in his nose and no doubt other tubes in other places, out of sight.

Although the angle and lighting left much be desired, the image on the screen conveyed enough of Carl Spalter's situation to make Gurney grimace. To be paralyzed like that, trapped in a numb, unresponsive body, unable even to blink or to cough, dependent on a machine to keep from drowning in your own saliva . . . Christ! It was like being buried alive, with your body itself the grave. To be trapped inside a half-dead mass of flesh and bones struck him as the ultimate claustrophobic horror. Shuddering at the thought, he saw that the prosecutor had resumed addressing the jury, with his hand extended toward the man in the wheelchair.

"The tragic story whose terrible climax brought us to this courtroom today began exactly a year ago when Carl Spalter made the bold decision to run for governor—with the idealistic goal of ridding our state of organized crime once and for all. A laudable goal, but one that his wife—the defendant—opposed from the beginning, as the result of corrupt influences you'll learn about during this trial. From the moment Carl set foot on the path of public service, she not only ridiculed him in public, doing everything she could to discourage him, but she also withdrew from all marital contact with him and began cheating on him with another man—her so-called personal trainer." He raised an eyebrow at the term, sharing a sour smirk with the jury. "The defendant revealed herself as a woman hell-bent on getting her own way at any cost. When rumors of her infidelity reached Carl, he didn't want to believe it. But finally he had to confront her. He told her she had to make a choice. Well, ladies and gentlemen, she made a choice, all right. You'll hear convincing testimony concerning that choice— which was to approach an underworld figure—Giacomo Flatano, or 'Jimmy Flats' —with an offer of fifty thousand dollars to kill her husband." He paused, deliberately looking at each member of the jury.

"She decided she wanted out of the marriage, but not at the expense of losing Carl's money, so she tried to hire a hit man. But the hit man turned down the offer. So what did the defendant do next? She tried to talk her lover, the personal trainer, into doing it in return for a life of leisure with her on a tropical island, financed by the inheritance she'd receive at Carl's death—because, ladies and gentlemen, Carl still had hopes for the marriage and still hadn't changed his will."

He extended his hands forward in a kind of supplication for the jury's empathy. "He had hopes of saving his marriage. Hopes of being with a wife he still loved. *And what was that wife doing?* She was conniving—first with a gangster, then with a cheap Romeo—to get him killed. What kind of person—?"

A new voice was heard, out of the video frame, whiny and impatient. "Objection! Your Honor, Mr. Piskin's emotional conjecture is way beyond anything that—"

The prosecutor calmly interrupted. "Every word I'm saying will be supported by sworn testimony."

The jowly judge, visible in an upper corner of the screen, muttered, "Denied. Proceed."

"Thank you, Your Honor. As I was saying, the defendant did everything in her power to persuade her young bedmate to kill her husband. But he refused. Well, guess what the defendant did then. What do you think a determined would-be killer would do?"

He stared inquiringly at the jury for a good five seconds before answering his own question. "The petty gangster was afraid to shoot Carl Spalter. The personal trainer was afraid to shoot Carl Spalter. *So Kay Spalter began taking shooting lessons herself!*"

The out-of-frame voice was heard again. "Objection! Your Honor, the causal link in the prosecution's use of the word 'So' implies an admission of motive by the defendant. There is no such admission anywhere in—"

The prosecutor broke in. "I'll restate the narrative, Your Honor, in a way fully supported by testimony. The gangster declined to shoot Carl. The trainer declined to shoot Carl. *And at that point* the defendant began taking shooting lessons herself."

The judge shifted his bulk with apparent physical discomfort. "Let the record show Mr. Piskin's restatement. Proceed."

The prosecutor turned to the jury. "Not only did the defendant take shooting lessons, but you'll hear testimony from a certified fire-arms instructor concerning the remarkable level of skill she acquired. Which brings us to the tragic culmination of our story. Last November, Carl Spalter's mother, Mary Spalter, passed away. She died alone, in the kind of accident that is all too common—a fall in her bath-tub in the senior residential community where she had spent the final years of her life. At the funeral service that was conducted at the Willow Rest cemetery, Carl rose to deliver a eulogy at her grave. You'll hear how he took a step or two, suddenly pitched forward, and hit the ground face-first. He didn't move. Everyone *thought* he had tripped, and that the fall had knocked him unconscious. It took a few moments before anyone saw the trickle of blood on the side of his forehead—a trickle of blood coming from a tiny hole in the temple. A subsequent medical examination confirmed what the initial investigating team suspected—that Carl had been struck by a high-powered small-caliber rifle bullet. You'll hear from the police experts who reconstructed the shooting that the bullet was fired from an apartment window approx-imately five hundred yards from the point of impact on the victim. You'll see maps, photographs, and drawings illustrating exactly how it was done. It will all be abundantly clear," he said with a reassuring smile. He checked his watch before going on.

As he spoke again, he paced back and forth in front of the jury box. "That apartment house, ladies and gentlemen, was owned by Spalter Realty. The apartment from which the bullet was fired was vacant, awaiting renovation, as were most of the apartments in that building. The defendant had easy access to the keys. But that's not all. You'll hear damning testimony that Kay Spalter . . ." He stopped and pointed toward a woman seated at the defense table with her profile to the camera. ". . . that Kay Spalter was not only in that building the morn-ing of the shooting, but was in the very apartment from which the bullet was fired at the exact time Carl Spalter was shot. Furthermore, you'll hear eyewitness testimony that she entered that empty apart-ment alone and that she left it alone."

He paused and shrugged, as if the facts of the case and the convic-tion those facts demanded were so obvious that there was no more to say. But then he continued. "The charge is *attempted murder*. But what does that legal term really mean? Consider this. The day before Carl was shot, he was full of life, full of wholesome energy and ambition. The day after he was shot . . . Well, just look. Take a good look at the man stuck in that wheelchair, propped up and held in place with metal braces and Velcro straps because the muscles that should be doing that job for him are now useless. Look into his eyes. What do you see? A man so battered by the hand of evil that he might be wishing he were dead? A man so devastated by the treachery of a loved one that he might be wishing he'd never been born?"

Again the off-screen voice broke in. "Objection!"

The judge cleared his throat. "Sustained." His voice was a weary rumble. "Mr. Piskin, you're over the line."

"I apologize, Your Honor. I got a little carried away."

"I suggest you carry yourself back."

"Yes, Your Honor." After seeming to gather his thoughts for a moment, he turned to the jury. "Ladies and gentlemen, it's a sad fact that Carl Spalter can no longer move or speak or communicate with us in any way, but the horror in that fixed expression on his face tells me that he's fully aware of what happened to him, that he knows who did this to him, and that he has no doubt that there is in this world such a thing as Pure Evil. Remember, when you find Kay Spalter guilty of attempted murder, as I know you will, this—what you see here before you—this is the real meaning of that colorless legal phrase 'attempted murder.' This man in this wheelchair. This life crushed beyond hope of repair. Happiness extinguished. This is the reality, dreadful beyond words."

"Objection!" cried the voice.

"Mr. Piskin . . ." rumbled the judge.

"I'm finished, Your Honor."

The judge called for a half-hour recess and summoned the prosecutor and defense attorney to his chambers.

Gurney replayed the video. He'd never seen an opening statement quite like it. It was a lot closer in emotional tone and content to a closing argument. But he knew Piskin by reputation, and the man was no amateur. So what was his purpose? To act as though Kay Spalter's conviction was inevitable, that the game was over before it began?

Was he that sure of himself? And if that was just his opener, how was he going to top an accusation of "Pure Evil"?

Speaking of which, he wanted to see the expression on Carl Spalter's face that Piskin had focused the jury on but the courtroom video had failed to capture. He wondered if there might be a photograph in the voluminous material delivered by Hardwick. He picked up the sequenced guide, looking for a hint.

Perhaps not accidentally, it was the second item on the list.

"Number two: Check out the damage. BCI case file, third graphics tab. It's all in those eyes. I never want to see whatever put that look on his face."

A minute later Gurney was holding a full-page head-and-shoulders photo printout. Even with all the preparation, the horror in Spalter's eyes was shocking. Piskin's final rant had not been exaggerated.

There was indeed in those eyes the recognition of a terrible truth—a reality, as Piskin had put it, dreadful beyond words.

Chapter 5

Bloodthirsty Weasels

The scraping squeak of the right-side French door being pulled from its sticking point against the sill woke Gurney from a surreal dream that slipped away as soon as he opened his eyes.

He found himself slouched down in one of the two armchairs at the fireplace end of the long room, the Spalter documents spread out on the coffee table in front of him. His neck ached when he raised his head. The light coming through the open door had a dawn faintness about it.

Madeleine stood there silhouetted, breathing in the cool, still air.

"Can you hear him?" she asked.

"Hear who?" Gurney rubbed his eyes, sitting up straighter.

"Horace. There he goes again."

Gurney listened halfheartedly for the crowing of the young rooster but heard nothing.

"Come to the door and you'll hear him."

He almost replied that he had no interest in hearing him but realized that would be a poor way to start the day. He pushed himself up from the chair and went to the door.

"There," said Madeleine. "You heard him that time, right?"

"I think so."

"He'll be a lot easier to hear," Madeleine said brightly, pointing to the expanse of grass between the asparagus patch and the big apple tree, "as soon as we build the coop over there."

"No doubt."

"They do it to announce their territory."

"Hmm."

"To ward off other roosters, let them know, 'This is my yard, I was here first.' I love it, don't you?"

"Love what?"

"The sound of it, the *crow*."

"Oh. Yes. Very . . . rural."

"I'm not sure I'd want a lot of roosters. But one is really nice."

"Right."

"*Horace*. At first I wasn't sure, but now it seems the perfect name for him, doesn't it?"

"I guess." The truth was that the name Horace, for no reason that made sense, reminded him of the name Carl. And the name Carl, the instant it came to mind, came complete with the stricken eyes in the photograph, eyes that appeared to be staring at a demon.

"What about the other three? Huffy, Puffy, and Fluffy—do you think those names are too silly?"

It took Gurney a few seconds to refocus his attention. "Too silly for chickens?"

She laughed and shrugged. "As soon as we build their little house, with a nice open-air pen at one end, they can all move up from the stuffy barn."

"Right." His lack of enthusiasm was palpable.

"And you'll make the pen predator-proof?"

"Yes."

"The director of the clinic lost one of his Rhode Island reds last week. The little thing was there one minute, gone the next."

"That's the risk of letting them out."

"Not if we build the right kind of pen. Then they can be out, running around, pecking in the grass, which they love, and still be safe. And it'll be fun watching them—right over there." She pointed again with an emphatic little jab of her forefinger at the area she'd chosen.

"So what does he think happened to his missing chicken?"

"Something grabbed it and carried it off. Most likely a coyote or an eagle. He's pretty sure an eagle, because when we have the kind of drought we've had this summer they start looking for things other than fish."

"Hmm."

"He said if we're going to build a pen we should be sure the wire mesh goes over the top and down at least six inches into the ground. Otherwise things can burrow underneath it."

"*Things?*"

"He mentioned weasels. Apparently they're really awful."

"Awful?"

Madeleine made a face. "He said if a weasel gets in with the chickens, he'll . . . bite their heads off—all of them."

"Not eat them? Just kill them?"

She nodded, her lips pressed tightly together. More than a wince, it was an expression of empathic misery. "He explained that some kind of frenzy comes over a weasel . . . once he tastes blood. Once he does, he won't stop biting until all the chickens are dead."

Chapter 6

Ants

A little after sunrise, feeling that he'd made a sufficient gesture in the direction of solving the chicken problem—by drawing a construction diagram for a coop and fenced run—Gurney put away his pad and settled down at the breakfast table with a second cup of coffee.

When Madeleine joined him, he decided to show her the photograph of Carl Spalter.

From her triage and counseling work at the local mental health crisis center, she was accustomed to being in the presence of the extremes of negative feelings—panic, rage, anguish, despair. Even so, her eyes widened at the vividness of Spalter's expression.

She laid the photo on the table, then pushed it a few inches farther away.

"He knows something," she said. "Something he didn't know before his wife shot him."

"Maybe she didn't. According to Hardwick, the case against her was fabricated."

"Do you believe that?"

"I don't know."

"So maybe she did it, and maybe she didn't. But Hardwick doesn't really care which, does he?"

Gurney was tempted to argue the point, because he didn't like the position it put him in. Instead, he just shrugged. "What he cares about is getting her conviction thrown out."

"What he *really* cares about is *getting even*—and watching his former employers twist in the wind."

"I know."

She cocked her head and stared at him as if to ask why he'd let himself be drawn into such a fraught and nasty undertaking.

"I haven't promised anything. But I have to admit," he said, pointing to the photograph on the table, "I am curious about *that.*"

She pursed her lips, turned to the open door, and gazed out at the thin, scattered fog illuminated by the sideways rays of the early sun. Then something caught her attention at the edge of the stone patio just beyond the doorsill.

"They're back," she said.

"Who? What?"

"The carpenter ants."

"Where?"

"Everywhere."

"Everywhere?"

She answered in a tone as mild as his was impatient. "Out there. In here. On the windowsills. By the cupboards. Around the sink."

"Why the hell didn't you mention it?"

"I just did."

He was about to ride the argument over a self-righteous cliff, but sanity prevailed and all he said was "I hate those damn things." And hate them he did. Carpenter ants were the termites of the Catskills and other cold places—gnawing away the inner fiber of beams and joists, in silence and darkness converting the support structures of solid homes to sawdust. An exterminating service sprayed the outside of the foundation every other month, and sometimes they seemed to be winning the battle. But then the scout ants would return, and then . . . battalions.

For a moment he forgot what he and Madeleine had been talking about before the ant tangent. When he remembered, it was with the sinking feeling that he'd been straining to justify a questionable decision.

He decided to try for as much openness as he could. "Look, I understand the danger, the less-than-virtuous motive driving this thing. But I believe I owe Jack something. Maybe not a lot, but certainly something. And an innocent woman may have been convicted on evidence manufactured by a dirty cop. I don't like dirty cops."

Madeleine broke in. "Hardwick doesn't care whether she's innocent. To him, that's irrelevant."

"I know. But I'm not Hardwick."

Chapter 7

Mick the Dick

"So everyone thought he tripped, until they found a bullet in his brain?" asked Gurney.

He was sitting in the passenger seat of Hardwick's roaring GTO—not a traveling option he'd normally choose, but the trip from Walnut Crossing to the Bedford Hills Correctional Facility would take close to three hours, according to Google, and it seemed a good opportunity to ask questions.

"The little round entry wound was kind of a hint," said Hardwick. "But the CAT scan left no doubt. Eventually a surgeon retrieved most of the bullet fragments."

"It was a .220 Swift?" Gurney had managed to review half the trial transcript and a third of the BCI case file before Hardwick arrived to pick him up, and he wanted to be sure of his facts.

"Yep. Fastest bullet made. Flattest trajectory in the business. Put it in the right rifle with the right scope, you can blow the head off a chipmunk a quarter mile away. Definitely a precision item. Nothing quite like it. Add a silencer to that package, and you've got—"

"A silencer?"

"A silencer. Which is why no one heard the shot. That, and the firecrackers."

"Firecrackers?"

Hardwick shrugged. "Witnesses heard anywhere from five to ten packs of firecrackers go off that morning. Over in the direction of the building where the shot came from. The last pack around the time Spalter was hit."

"How'd they know which building it was?"

"On-site reconstruction. Witness descriptions of the victim's position when he was hit. Followed by a door-to-door search of the possible sources."

"But nobody caught on right away that he *was* hit, right?"

"They just saw him falling. As he was walking toward a podium at the head of the grave, he was hit in the left temple and fell forward. At the moment he was hit, his left side was exposed to an empty stretch of the cemetery, the river, a busy county highway, and beyond that a row of partially gutted apartment buildings owned by the Spalter family."

"How'd they identify which apartment the shooter used?"

"Easy enough. She ... I mean, the shooter, whoever ... left the gun behind, mounted on a nice tripod."

"With a scope?"

"Top-of-the-line."

"And the silencer?"

"No. The shooter removed that."

"Then how do you know——"

"The end of the barrel was custom-threaded for one. And the firecrackers alone couldn't have covered the report of an unsuppressed .220 Swift. It's a seriously powerful cartridge."

"And the silencer alone would only deal with the muzzle blast, which would have left an audible supersonic report, which would explain the need for the firecracker distraction. So——cautious approach, thorough planning. Is that the way it's being understood?"

"That's the way it *should* be understood, but who the fuck knows what they understand? It never came up in the trial. Lot of shit never came up in the trial. Lot of shit that should have come up."

"But why leave the gun and remove the silencer?"

"No fucking idea. Unless it was one of those super-sophisticated five-thousand-dollar jobs——too good to leave behind?"

Gurney found that hard to digest. "Of all the ways a vindictive wife might kill her husband, the prosecution narrative is that Kay Spalter chose to take the most complicated, expensive, high-tech——"

"Davey boy, you don't have to convince me that the narrative sucks.

I know it sucks. More holes in it than an old junky's arm. That's why I picked it for my kickoff case. It's got major reversal potential."

"Okay. So there was a silencer, but the silencer was taken. Presumably by the shooter."

"Correct."

"No prints left on anything?"

"No prints, no nothing. Latex glove job."

"This rotten-apple detective—he didn't plant anything in the apartment to incriminate Spalter's wife?"

"He didn't know her then. He didn't decide to put her in the frame until he met her and decided he hated her and she had to be the shooter."

"This guy is the CIO named in the case file? Senior Investigator Michael Klemper?"

"Mick the Dick—that's our boy. Shaved head, small eyes, big chest. Temperament of a rottweiler. Martial arts fanatic. Likes breaking bricks with his fists, especially in public. A *very* angry man. Which brings us back to the timing issue. Mick the Dick was divorced by his wife a few years back. Super-ugly divorce. Mick . . . Well, now we get into some . . . some unsubstantiated hearsay. Libel, slander, lawsuit territory, you get what I mean?"

Gurney sighed. "Go on, Jack."

"According to rumor, Mick's wife was doing the deed with a certain influential organized crime figure she happened to meet because Mick happened to be—so the rumor goes—on the take from the aforesaid crime figure." Hardwick paused. "You see the problem?"

"I see several."

"Mick found out she was fucking the major wiseguy, but that left him with a dilemma. I mean, that's not a can of worms you want opened in divorce court, or anywhere else. So he couldn't take the normal legal steps. However, he used to talk privately about wanting to strangle the bitch, twist her head off, feed it to his dog. Apparently, he would also say this to *her* from time to time. One of those times, she made a video of him telling her in colorful detail, after a few drinks, how he was going to feed her sensitive body parts to his pit bull. Guess what happened then?"

"Tell me."

"The next day she threatened to put the video on YouTube and flush his career and pension down the toilet if he didn't give her a quiet divorce on her terms with a very generous settlement."

Hardwick's thin grin conveyed a kind of perverse admiration. "That was when the homicidal hate started oozing out of old Mick the Dick like pus. He would have gladly killed her at that point, wiseguy connection or no wiseguy connection, if she hadn't ensured that the tape would go viral if anything happened to her. So he was forced to give her the divorce. And the money. And ever since then he's been taking it out on every woman who even remotely reminds him of his wife. Mick was always a little touchy. But after he got that divorce deal rammed up his ass, he turned into two hundred and fifty pounds of pure vengeance, searching for targets."

"You're telling me he framed Kay Spalter just because she was fucking around like his wife?"

"Worse than that. Crazier than that. I think his blind hatred for anyone like his wife made him believe that Kay Spalter actually *did* murder her husband, and that it was his duty to see that she paid for it. She was guilty in his fucked-up mind, and he was determined to put her away at any cost. He wasn't going to let another unfaithful bitch get off scot-free. If that meant suborning a little perjury here and there in the interest of justice, so what?"

"You're telling me he's a psycho."

"Mild way of putting it."

"And you know all this how, exactly?"

"I told you. He has enemies."

"Could you be more specific?"

"Someone close enough to the man to hear things gave me the details of his bile and bullshit on the job, snippets of phone calls, comments here and there, what he said about women in general, about his ex-wife and Kay Spalter in particular. The Dick got carried away sometimes, wasn't as careful as he should have been."

"This 'someone' have a name?"

"Can't reveal that."

"Yes you can."

"No way."

"Listen up, Jack. You keep secrets, and there's no deal. I get to know everything you know. Every question answered. That's the deal. Period."

"Christ, Davey, you're not making this easy."

"Neither are you."

Gurney glanced over at the speedometer and saw that it was creeping toward eighty. Hardwick's jaw muscle was tight. So were his hands on the wheel. A good minute passed before he said simply, "Esti Moreno." Another minute passed before he went on. "She worked under Mick the Dick from the time of his divorce right up through the end of the Spalter trial. Finally managed to get reassigned—same barracks, but a different reporting line. Had to accept an office job, all paperwork, which she hates. But she hates the paperwork less than she hates the Dick. Esti's a good cop. Good brain. Good eyes and ears. And principles. Esti's got principles. You know what she said about the Dick?"

"No, Jack, what did she say?"

"She said, 'You do some kind of shit, some kind of karma is coming around to bite your ass.' I love Esti. She's a real pisser. Also, did I mention that she's a Puerto Rican bombshell? But she can be subtle, too. A subtle bombshell. You should see her in one of those trooper hats." Hardwick was smiling broadly, his fingers tapping out a Latin rhythm on the steering wheel.

Gurney was quiet for long while, trying to absorb what he was being told as objectively as possible. The goal was to take it all in and at the same time to keep it at arm's length, much as one might absorb crime scene details that could have different interpretations.

He pondered the odd shape the case was beginning to take in his mind, including the ironic parallel between the conviction-at-any-cost pursued by Klemper and the reversal-at-any-cost pursued by Hardwick. Both efforts seemed to provide further evidence that man is not primarily a rational species, and that all our so-called logic is never more than a bright facade for murkier motives.

Thus occupied, Gurney was only half aware of the landscape of hills and valleys they were passing through—rolling fields of overgrown weeds and starved saplings, expanses of drought-faded greens and yellows, the sun coming and going through an intermittent pale haze, the unprofitable farms with their barns and silos unpainted for decades, the sadly weathered villages, old orange tractors, rusted plows and hay rakes, the quaint and quiet rural emptiness that was Delaware County's pride and curse.

Chapter 8

Coldhearted Bitch

Far from the gritty-beautiful, economically battered, depopulated counties of central New York State, northern Westchester County had the casual charm of country money. In the midst of this postcard landscape, however, the Bedford Hills Correctional Facility seemed as out of place as a porcupine in a petting zoo.

Gurney was reminded once again that the actual security paraphernalia of a maximum-security prison covers a broad spectrum of sophistication and visibility. At one end are state-of-the-art sensors and control systems. At the other end are guard towers, twelve-foot chain-link fences, and razor wire.

Surely technology would one day make razor wire obsolete. But for now it was the thing that made the clearest demarcation between inside and outside. Its message was simple, violent, and visceral. Its presence would easily overwhelm any effort to create an atmosphere of normalcy—not that any serious efforts in that direction were made at correctional facilities. In fact, Gurney suspected, razor wire might very well outlive its practical containment function, purely on the basis of its message value.

Inside, Bedford Hills was fundamentally similar to most places of incarceration he'd visited over the years. It looked as bleakly institutional as its purpose. And despite the thousands and thousands of pages written on the subject of modern penology, that purpose—that essence—came down to one thing.

It was a cage.

It was a cage with many locks, security checkpoints, and procedures aimed at ensuring that no one entered or departed without proper evidence of their right to do so. Lex Bincher's office had seen to it that Gurney and Hardwick were on Kay Spalter's approved-visitors list, and they were admitted without difficulty.

The long, windowless visiting room that they were led to for their meeting resembled rooms like it throughout the system. Its primary structural feature was a long counterlike divider separating the room into two sections—the inmate side and the visitor side, with chairs on both sides and a chest-high barrier in the center. Guards stood at either end with a clear view down the length of the barrier, aimed at preventing any unauthorized exchanges. The room was painted, not recently, an institutional noncolor.

Gurney was relieved to see that there were only a few visitors present, allowing for more than adequate space and the possibility of some privacy.

The woman who was brought into the room by a stocky black guard was short and slim with dark hair in a pixie style. She had a fine nose, prominent cheekbones, and full lips. Her eyes were a startling green, and beneath one of them there was a small bluish bruise. There was a hard intensity in her expression that made her face more arresting than beautiful.

Gurney and Hardwick stood up as she approached. Hardwick was the first to speak, eyeing her bruise. "Jesus, Kay, what happened to you?"

"Nothing."

"Doesn't look like nothing to me."

"It's been taken care of," she said dismissively. She was talking to Hardwick but looking at Gurney, examining him with a frank curiosity.

"Taken care of how?" persisted Hardwick.

She blinked impatiently. "Crystal Rocks. My protector." She flashed a quick humorless smile.

"The lesbian meth dealer?"

"Yes."

"Big fan of yours?"

"A fan of who she thinks I am."

"She likes women who kill their husbands?"

"Loves 'em."

"How's she going to feel when we get your conviction thrown out?"

"Fine—so long as she doesn't think I'm innocent."

"Yeah, well ... that shouldn't be a problem. Innocence is not the issue in the appeal. The issue is due process, and we aim to prove, in your case, that the process was in no way due. Speaking of which, I'd like to introduce you to the man who's going to help us show the judge just how un-due it was. Kay Spalter, meet Dave Gurney."

"Mr. Supercop." She said it with a touch of sarcasm, then paused as if to see how he'd react. When he showed no reaction at all, she went on. "I've read all about you and your decorations. Very impressive." She didn't look impressed.

Gurney wondered if those coolly assessing green eyes ever looked impressed. "Nice to meet you, Mrs. Spalter."

"Kay." There was nothing cordial in her tone. It sounded more like a pointed correction, a way of conveying distaste for her married name. She continued to look him over, as though he were a piece of merchandise she was considering purchasing. "You married?"

"Yes."

"Happily?"

"Yes."

She seemed to be turning this information over in her mind before asking her next question. "Do you believe I'm innocent?"

"I believe that the sun rose this morning."

Her mouth twitched into something resembling a split-second smile. Or maybe it was just a tremor created by all the energy contained in that compact body. "What's that supposed to mean? That you only believe what you see? That you're a no-bullshit guy who bases everything on facts?"

"It means that I just met you, and I don't know enough to have an opinion, much less a belief."

Hardwick cleared his throat nervously. "Maybe we ought to sit down?"

As they took their places at the small table, Kay Spalter kept her eyes on Gurney.

"So what do you need to know to have an opinion about whether I'm innocent?"

Hardwick broke in, leaning forward. "Or about whether you got a fair trial, which is the real issue."

She ignored this, stayed focused on Gurney.

He sat back and studied those remarkable unblinking green eyes. Something told him that the best preamble would be no preamble. "Did you shoot Carl Spalter, or cause him to be shot?"

"No." The word came out hard and fast.

"Is it true you were having an extramarital affair?"

"Yes."

"And your husband found out about it?"

"Yes."

"And he was considering divorcing you?"

"Yes."

"And a divorce under those circumstances would have had a major negative effect on your economic status?"

"Absolutely."

"But at the time he was fatally wounded, your husband hadn't yet made a final decision on the divorce, and hadn't changed his will—so you were still his chief beneficiary. Is that right?"

"Yes."

"Did you ask your lover to kill him?"

"No." An expression of distaste came and went in an instant.

"So his story at the trial was a complete fabrication?"

"Yes. But it couldn't have been *his* fabrication. Darryl was the lifeguard at our club pool and a so-called personal trainer—million-dollar body and a two-cent brain. He was just saying what that piece of shit Klemper told him to say."

"Did you ask an ex-con by the name of Jimmy Flats to kill your husband?"

"No."

"So his story at the trial was a fabrication too?"

"Yes."

"Klemper's fabrication?"

"I assume so."

"Were you in that building where the shot came from, either the day of the shooting or any time prior to that?"

"Definitely not on the day of the shooting."

"So the eyewitness testimony that you were there in the building, in the actual apartment where the murder weapon was found—that's also a fabrication?"

"Right."

"If not on that particular day, then how long before?"

"I don't know. Months? A year? Maybe I was there two or three times altogether—occasions when I was with Carl when he stopped to check on something, work being done, something like that."

"Most of the apartments were vacant?"

"Yes. Spalter Realty paid next to nothing to buy buildings that needed major renovations."

"Were the apartments locked?"

"Generally. Squatters would sometimes find ways in."

"Did you have keys?"

"Not in my possession."

"Meaning?"

Kay Spalter hesitated for the first time. "There was a master key for each building. I knew where it was."

"Where was it?"

She seemed to shake her head—or, again, maybe it was just an infinitesimal tremor. "I always thought it was silly. Carl carried his own master key for all the apartments, but he kept an extra one hidden in each building. In the utility room in each basement. On the floor behind the furnace."

"Who knew about the hidden keys, besides you and Carl?"

"I have no idea."

"Are they still there, behind the furnaces?"

"I assume so."

Gurney sat quietly for several seconds, letting this curious fact sink in before going on.

"You claimed that you were with your boyfriend at the time of the shooting?"

"Yes. In bed with him." Her gaze, locked on Gurney, was neutral and unblinking.

"So when he testified he was alone that day—that was one more fabrication?"

"Yes." Her lips tightened.

"And you believe that Detective Klemper manufactured and directed this elaborate web of perjury ... why? Just because you reminded him of his ex-wife?"

"That's your friend's theory," she said, indicating Hardwick. "Not mine. I don't doubt that Klemper's a woman-hating asshole, but I'm sure there's more to it."

"Like what?"

"Maybe my conviction was convenient for someone beyond Klemper."

"Who, for example?"

"The mob, for example."

"You're saying that organized crime was responsible for—?"

"For the hit on Carl. Yes. I'm saying that it makes sense. More sense than anything else."

"*For the hit on Carl.* Isn't that a pretty cold—"

"A pretty cold way of discussing my husband's death? You're absolutely right, Mr. Supercop. I'm not going to shed sweet public tears to prove my innocence to a jury, or to you, or to anyone else." She eyed him shrewdly. "That makes it a little harder, doesn't it? Not so easy to prove the innocence of a coldhearted bitch."

Hardwick drummed his fingers on the table to get her attention. Then he leaned forward and reiterated with slow intensity, "We don't have to prove you didn't do it. *Innocence is not the issue.* All we have to prove is that your trial was seriously, purposely fucked up by the chief investigator on the case. Which is exactly what we will do."

Again Kay ignored Hardwick and kept her gaze fixed on Gurney. "So? Where do you stand? You have an opinion yet?"

Gurney responded only with another question. "Did you take shooting lessons?"

"Yes."

"Why?"

"Because I thought I might have to shoot someone."

"Who?"

"Maybe some mob guys. I had a bad feeling about Carl's relationship with those people. I saw trouble coming and I wanted to be ready."

Formidable, thought Gurney, searching for a word to describe the small, bold, unflinching creature sitting across from him. And maybe even a little *frightening*.

"Trouble from the mob because of Carl starting an anticrime political party? And making his 'These Are the Scum of the Earth' speeches?"

She gave a little snort of ridicule. "You don't know a damn thing about Carl, do you?"

Chapter 9

Black Widow

Kay Spalter's eyes were closed in apparent concentration. Her full mouth was compressed into a narrow line, and her head was lowered, with her hands clasped tightly under her chin. She'd been sitting like that across the table from Gurney and Hardwick without saying a word for a good two minutes. Gurney guessed that she was wrestling with the question of how much to confide in two men she didn't know, whose real agenda might be hidden—but who, on the other hand, might be her last chance at freedom.

The silence seemed to be getting to Hardwick. The tic reappeared at the corner of his mouth. "Look, Kay, if you have any concerns, let's get them out on the table so we can—"

She raised her head and glared at him. *"Concerns?"*

"What I meant was, if you have any questions—"

"If I have any questions, I'll ask them." She turned her attention to Gurney, studying his face and eyes. "How old are you?"

"Forty-nine. Why do you ask?"

"Isn't that early to be retired?"

"Yes and no. Twenty-five years in the NYPD—"

Hardwick broke in. "The thing of it is, he never really retired. Just moved upstate. He's still doing what he always did. He's solved three major murder cases since he left the department. Three major murder cases in the past two years. That not what I'd call *retired*."

Gurney was finding Hardwick's sweaty-salesman assurances hard to take. "Look, Jack—"

This time it was Kay who interrupted Gurney. "Why are you doing this?"

"Doing what?"

"Getting involved in my case."

Gurney had a hard time coming up with an answer he was willing to give. He finally said, "Curiosity."

Hardwick jumped in again. "Davey is a natural-born onion peeler. Obsessive. Brilliant. Peeling away layer after layer until he gets to the truth. When he says 'curiosity' he means a hell of a lot more than—"

"Don't tell me what he means. He's here. I'm here. Let him talk. Last time, I heard what you and your lawyer friend had to say." She shifted in her chair, pointedly focusing her attention on Gurney. "Now I want to hear what *you* have to say. How much are they paying you to work on this case?"

"Who?"

She pointed at Hardwick. "Him and his lawyer—Lex Bincher of Bincher, Fenn, and Blaskett." She said it as if it were a vile-tasting but necessary medicine.

"They're not paying me anything."

"You're not getting paid?"

"No."

"But you expect to get paid sometime in the future, if your effort produces the desired result?"

"No, I don't."

"You don't? So, apart from that crap about onion peeling, why are you doing this?"

"I owe Jack a favor."

"For what?"

"He helped me with the Good Shepherd case. I'm helping him with this one."

"Curiosity. Payback. What else?"

What else? Gurney wondered if she knew that there was a third reason. He sat back in his chair, thinking for a moment about what he was going to say. Then he spoke softly. "I saw a photograph of your late husband in his wheelchair, apparently taken a few days before he died. The photograph was mainly of his face."

Kay finally showed some sign of an emotional reaction. Her green eyes widened, and her skin seemed a shade paler. "What about it?"

"The look in his eyes. I want to know what that was about."

She bit down on her lower lip. "Maybe it was just . . . the way a person looks when he knows he's about to die."

"I don't think so. I've seen a lot of people die. Shot by drug dealers. By strangers. By relatives. By cops. But never before have I seen that expression on anyone's face."

She took a deep breath, let it out shakily.

"You all right?" asked Gurney. He'd observed hundreds, maybe thousands, of examples of faked emotion in his career. But this looked real.

She closed her eyes for a few seconds then opened them. "The prosecutor told the jury that Carl's face reflected the despair of a man who'd been betrayed by someone he loved. Is that what you're thinking? That it might be the look of a man whose wife wanted him dead?"

"I think that's a possibility. But not the only possibility."

She reacted with a small nod. "One last question. Your buddy here keeps telling me the success of my appeal has nothing to do with whether or not I shot Carl. It just depends on showing 'a substantive defect in due process.' So tell me something. Does it matter to *you personally* whether I'm guilty or innocent?"

"To me, that's the *only* thing that matters."

She held Gurney's gaze for what seemed like a long time before clearing her throat, turning to Hardwick, and speaking in a changed voice: crisper, lighter. "Okay. We have a deal. Ask Bincher to send me the letter of agreement."

"Will do," said Hardwick with a quick, serious nod that barely concealed his elation.

She looked at Gurney suspiciously. "Why are you staring at me like that?"

"I'm impressed with the way you make decisions."

"I make them as soon as my gut and brain agree. What's the next item on our list?"

"You said earlier that I didn't know a damn thing about Carl. Educate me."

"Where shall I start?"

"With whatever seems important. For example, was Carl involved in anything that might have led to his murder?"

She flashed a quick, bitter smile. "It's no surprise he was murdered.

The only surprise was that it didn't happen sooner. The cause of his death was his life. Carl was ambitious. Crazy with ambition. Sick with ambition. He inherited that gene from his father, a disgusting reptile who'd have swallowed the world whole if he could have."

"When you say Carl was 'sick,' what do you mean?"

"His ambition was destroying him. More, bigger, better. More, more, more. And the *how* didn't matter. To get what he wanted, he was dealing with people you wouldn't want to be in the same room with. You play with rattlesnakes . . ." She paused, her eyes bright with anger. "It's so damn absurd that I'm locked up in this zoo. *I'm* the one who warned him to back away from the predators. *I'm* the one who told him he was in over his head, that he was going to get himself murdered. Well, he paid no attention to me, and he got himself murdered. And *I'm* the one convicted for it." She gave Gurney a look that seemed to say, *Is life a fucked-up joke or what?*

"You have any idea who shot him?"

"Well, that's another little irony. The guy without whose approval nothing happens in upstate New York—in other words, the snake who either ordered the hit on Carl or at least okayed it—that snake was in our house on three occasions. I could've popped him on any one of those occasions. In fact, I came very close to it the third time. You know what? If I'd done it then, when I had the urge, Carl wouldn't be dead now, and I wouldn't be sitting here. You get the picture? I was convicted for a murder I didn't commit—because of a murder I should have committed but didn't."

"What's his name?"

"Who?"

"The snake you should have killed."

"Donny Angel. Also known as the Greek. Also known as Adonis Angelidis. Three times I had a chance to take him out. Three times I let it go by."

This narrative direction, Gurney noted, had illuminated another piece of Kay Spalter. Inside the smart, striking, fine-boned creature, there was something very icy.

"Back up for a minute," said Gurney, wanting a clearer sense of the world the Spalters lived in. "Tell me more about Carl's business."

"I can only tell you what I know. Tip of the iceberg."

Over the next half hour Kay covered not only Carl's business and its strange corporate structure, but his strange family as well.

His father, Joe Spalter, had inherited a real estate holding company from *his* father. Spalter Realty ended up owning a huge chunk of upstate New York's inventory of rental properties, including half the apartment houses in Long Falls—all of this by the time that Joe, close to death, transferred the company to his two sons, Carl and Jonah.

Carl took after Joe, had his ambition and money-hunger, squared. Jonah took after his mother, Mary, an aggressive pursuer of many hopeless causes. Jonah was a utopian dreamer, a charismatic New Age spiritualist. As Kay put it, "Carl wanted to own the world, and Jonah wanted to save it."

The way their father saw it, Carl had what it took to "go all the way"—to be the richest man in America, or maybe the world. The problem was, Carl was as uncontrolled as he was ruthless. There was nothing he wouldn't do to get what he wanted. As a child he'd once set fire to a neighbor's dog as a distraction so he could steal a video game. And that wasn't a one-time instance of craziness. Things like that happened regularly.

Joe, as ruthless as he was himself, saw this trait as a potential problem—not that he cared about setting fire to dogs or about stealing. It was the lack of *prudence*, the lack of an appropriate risk-reward calculus, that bothered him. His ultimate solution was to bind Carl and Jonah together in the family business. Jonah was supposed to be a moderating influence, a source of the caution that Carl lacked.

The vehicle for this supposedly beneficial combining of their personalities was an unbreakable legal agreement that they both signed when Joe handed the corporation over to them. All of its provisions were designed to ensure that no business could be done, no decisions taken, and no changes made to the corporation without Carl and Jonah's *joint* approval.

But Joe's fantasy of merging the opposite inclinations of his sons into a single force for success was never realized. All that came of it was conflict, the stagnation of Spalter Realty, and an ever-growing animosity between the brothers. It pushed Carl in the direction of politics as an alternate route to power and money, with backdoor help from organized crime, while it pushed Jonah in the direction of religion and the establishment of his grand venture, the Cyberspace Cathedral, with backdoor help from his mother, whom Joe had left exceedingly well-off. The mother at whose funeral Carl was fatally wounded.

When Kay finally concluded her recounting of the Spalter family saga, Gurney was the first to speak. "So Carl's Anticrime Party and his 'Scum of the Earth' speeches about smashing organized crime in New York were nothing but—"

She finished his thought. "A lie, a disguise. For a politician secretly in bed with the mob, what better cover could you have than an image as the state's most aggressive crime fighter?"

Gurney nodded, trying to let the twisty soap opera narrative sink in. "So your theory is that Carl eventually had some kind of falling-out with this Angel character? And that's the reason he was killed?"

"Angel was always the most dangerous player in the room. Carl wouldn't have been the first or even the tenth of Angel's business associates to end up dead. There's a saying in certain circles that the Greek only puts two offers on the negotiating table: 'Do it my way. Or I blow your fucking head off.' I'd bet anything that there was something Carl refused to do Donny's way. And he did end up getting his head blown off, didn't he?"

Gurney didn't answer. He was trying to figure out who the hell this brutally unsentimental woman really was.

"By the way," she added, "you ought to look at some pictures of Carl taken before this thing happened."

"Why?"

"So you understand what he had going for him. Carl was made for politics. Sold his soul to the devil—with a smile made in heaven."

"How come you didn't leave him when things got ugly?"

"Because I'm a shallow little gold digger, addicted to power and money."

"Is that true?"

Her answer was a brilliant, enigmatic smile. "You have any more questions?"

Gurney thought about it. "Yeah. What the hell is the Cyberspace Cathedral?"

"Just another God-free religion. Type the words into a search engine, you'll find out more than you ever wanted to know. Anything
else?"

"Did Carl or Jonah have any kids?"

"Not Jonah. Too busy being spiritual. Carl has one daughter, from
his first marriage. A demented slut." Kay's voice sounded as flatly fac-
tual as if she'd been describing the girl as "a college student."

Gurney blinked at the disconnect. "You want to tell me more
about that?"

She looked like she was about to, then shook her head. "Better that
you look into it yourself. I'm not objective on that subject."

After a few more questions and answers and after arranging a time
for a follow-up phone call, Hardwick and Gurney stood to leave. Hardwick made a point of looking again at Kay's bruised cheek. "You sure
you're all right? I know someone here. She could keep an eye on you,
maybe separate you from the general population for a while."

"I told you, I've got it covered."

"Sure you're not putting too many eggs in Crystal's basket?"

"Crystal's got a big, tough basket. And my nickname helps. Did I
mention that? Here in the zoo it's a term of great respect."

"What nickname?"

She bared her teeth in a quick, chilly smile. "The Black Widow."

Chapter 10

The Demented Slut

Once they'd put the Bedford Hills Correctional Facility behind them and were heading for the Tappan Zee Bridge, Gurney brought up the subject that was eating at him. "I get the impression you know some significant things about this case that you haven't told me."

Hardwick gunned the engine and veered around a slow-moving minivan with an expression of disgust. "Obviously this asshole has no place to get to and doesn't care when he arrives. Be nice to have a bulldozer, push him into a ditch."

Gurney waited.

Hardwick eventually responded to his question. "You've got the outline, ace—key points, main actors. What more do you want?"

Gurney thought about this, thought about the tone. "You seem more like yourself than you did earlier this morning."

"Fuck's that supposed to mean?"

"You figure it out. Remember I can still walk away from this, which I will do if I don't get the feeling that I know everything you know about the Spalter murder case. I'm not playing front man just to get that woman to sign on with your lawyer. What did she say his name was?"

"Take it easy. No sweat. His name is Lex Bincher. You'll meet him."

"See, Jack, that's the problem."

"What problem?"

"You're assuming things."

"Assuming what things?"

"Assuming that I'm on board."

Hardwick fixed a concentrated frown on the empty road ahead of them. The tic was back. "You're not?"

"Maybe I am, maybe I'm not. The point is, I'll let you know."

"Right. Good."

A silence fell between them that lasted until they were across the Hudson and speeding west on I-287. Gurney had spent the time reflecting on what it was that had him so upset, and had come to the conclusion that the problem wasn't Hardwick. It was his own dishonesty.

In fact, he *was* on board. There were aspects of the case—beyond the appalling photograph of Carl Spalter—that had him intrigued. But he was pretending to be undecided. And the pretense had more to do with Madeleine than with Hardwick. He was pretending—and letting on to her—that this was a rational process he was conducting according to some objective criteria when, truth be told, it wasn't anything like that. His involvement was no more a matter of rational choice than the idea that he might choose to be, or not to be, affected by gravity.

The truth was that a complex murder case attracted his attention and curiosity like nothing else on earth. He could make up reasons for it. He could say it was all about justice. About rectifying an imbalance in the scheme of things. About standing up for those who had been struck down. About a quest for truth.

But there were other times when he considered it nothing but high-stakes puzzle-solving, an obsessive-compulsive drive to fit all the loose pieces together. An intellectual game, a contest of mind and will. A playing field on which he could excel.

And then there was Madeleine's dark suggestion: the possibility that he was somehow attracted by the terrible *risk* itself, that some self-hating part of his psyche kept drawing him blindly into the orbit of death.

His mind rejected that possibility even as his heart was chilled by it.

But ultimately he had no faith in anything he thought or said about the *why* of his profession. They were just ideas he had about it, labels he was sometimes comfortable with.

Did any of the labels capture the essence of the gravitational pull? He couldn't say.

The bottom line was this:

Rationalize and temporize as he might, he could no more walk away from a challenge like the Spalter case than an alcoholic could walk away from a martini after the first sip.

Suddenly exhausted, he closed his eyes.

When he finally opened them, he caught a glimpse of the Pepacton Reservoir dead ahead. Meaning they'd passed through Cat Hollow and were back in Delaware County, less than twenty minutes from Walnut Crossing. The water in the reservoir was depressingly low, the result of a dry summer, the kind of summer likely to produce a drab autumn.

His mind returned to the meeting at Bedford Hills.

He looked over at Hardwick, who appeared to be lost in his own unpleasant thoughts.

"So tell me, Jack, what do you know about Carl Spalter's 'demented slut' daughter?"

"You obviously skimmed past that page in the trial transcript— where she testified to hearing Kay on the phone with someone the day before Carl got hit, saying that everything was arranged and that in twenty-four hours her problems would be over. The lovely young lady's name is Alyssa. Think positive thoughts about her. Her demented sluttiness could be the key that springs our client."

Hardwick was doing sixty-five on a winding stretch of road where the posted limit was forty-five. Gurney checked his seat belt. "You want to tell me why?"

"Alyssa is nineteen, movie-star gorgeous, and pure poison. I've been told she has the words 'No Limits' tattooed in a special place." Hardwick's expression exploded into a manic grin that faded as quickly as it appeared. "She's also a heroin addict."

"How does this help Kay?"

"Be patient. Seems Carl was very generous with little Alyssa. He spoiled her rotten, maybe worse than rotten—as long as he was alive. But his will was another matter. Maybe he had a moment of insight into what his junkie daughter could do with a few million bucks at her disposal. So his will provided that everything would go to Kay. And he hadn't changed the will at the time of the shooting—maybe because he hadn't made up his mind about the divorce, or just hadn't gotten around to it—a point the prosecutor kept highlighting as Kay's main motive for the murder."

Gurney nodded. "And after the shooting, he wasn't capable of changing it."

"Right. But there's another side to that. Once Kay was convicted, it meant she couldn't inherit a cent—because the law prevents a beneficiary from receiving the assets of a deceased person whose death the beneficiary has facilitated. The assets that would have gone to the guilty party are distributed instead to the next of kin—in this instance, Alyssa Spalter."

"She got Carl's money?"

"Not quite. These things move slowly at best, and the appeal will stop any actual distribution until there's a final resolution."

Gurney was starting to feel impatient. "So how is Miss 'No Limits' the key to the case?"

"She obviously had a powerful motive to see that Kay was found guilty. You might even say she also had a powerful motive for committing the murder herself, so long as Kay was blamed for it."

"So what? The case file doesn't mention any evidence that would connect her to the shooting. Did I miss something?"

"Not a thing."

"So where are you going with this?"

Hardwick's grin widened. Wherever he was going, he was obviously getting a kick out of the ride. Gurney glanced at the speedometer needle and saw that it was now hovering around seventy. They were heading downhill past the west end of the reservoir, approaching the tight curve at Barney's Kayak Rentals. Gurney's jaw tightened. Old muscle cars had plenty of horsepower, but the handling in fast turns could be unforgiving.

"Where am I going with this?" Hardwick's eyes were gleaming with delight. "Well, let me ask you a question. Would you say there might be a slight conflict-of-interest issue ... a slight due-process issue ... a slight tainted-investigation issue ... if a potential suspect in a murder case was fucking the chief investigating officer?"

"What—Klemper? And Alyssa Spalter?"

"Mick the Dick and the Demented Slut herself."

"Jesus. You have proof of that?"

For a moment, the grin grew bigger and brighter than ever. "You know, Davey boy, I think that's one of those little things you can help us with."

Chapter 11

The Little Birds

Gurney said nothing. And he continued to say nothing for the next seventeen minutes, which is how long it took them to drive from the reservoir to Walnut Crossing, and then up the winding dirt and gravel road from the county route to his pond, pasture, and farmhouse.

Sitting next to the house in the roughly idling GTO, he knew he had to say something, and he wanted it to be unambiguous. "Jack, I have the feeling we're on two different paths with this project of yours."

Hardwick looked as if there were something sour in his mouth. "How so?"

"You keep pushing me toward the tainted-investigation issues, the due-process defects, et cetera."

"That's what appeals are all about."

"I understand that. I'll *get* there. But I can't *start* there."

"But if Mick Klemper—"

"I know, Jack, I know. If you can show that the CIO ignored an avenue of investigation because—"

"Because he was fucking a potential suspect, we could get the conviction reversed on that alone. Bingo! What's wrong with that?"

"There's nothing wrong with that. My problem is how I'm supposed to get from here to there."

"A smart first step would be to have a chat with the breathtaking Alyssa, get a sense of who we're dealing with, the pressure points that could turn her our way, the angles that—"

"You see, that's exactly what I mean by two different paths."

"The hell are you talking about?"

"For me, that chat could be a smart tenth or eleventh step, not a first step."

"You're making a bigger deal out of this than it needs to be."

Gurney gazed out the car's side window. Over the ridge beyond the pond, a hawk was slowly circling. "Apart from getting Kay Spalter to put her name on the dotted line, what am I supposed to be bringing to this party?"

"I told you already."

"Tell me again."

"You're part of the strategy team. Part of the firepower. Part of the ultimate solution."

"That so?"

"What's wrong with that?"

"If you want me to contribute, you need to let me do it my way."

"What are you, Frank fucking Sinatra?"

"I can't help you if you want me to put the tenth step ahead of the first."

Hardwick uttered what sounded like a bad-tempered sigh of surrender. "Fine. What do you want to do?"

"I need to start at the beginning. In Long Falls. In the cemetery. In the building where the shooter stood. I need to be where it happened. I need to *see* it."

"What the fuck? You want to reinvestigate the whole goddamn thing?"

"Doesn't seem like such a bad idea."

"You don't need to do that."

He was about to tell Hardwick that there was a bigger issue involved here than the pragmatic appeal goal. An issue of truth. Truth with a capital T. But the pretentious ring of that sentiment kept him from stating it. "I need to get grounded, literally."

"I don't know what you're talking about. Our focus is on Klemper's fuck-ups, not the fucking graveyard."

They went back and forth for another ten minutes.

In the end, Hardwick capitulated, shaking his head in exasperation. "Do whatever you want to do. Just don't waste a shitload of time, okay?"

"I don't plan to waste *any* time."

"Whatever you say, Sherlock."

Gurney got out of the car. The heavy door closed with a louder impact than he'd heard from a car door in decades.

Hardwick leaned over toward the open passenger-side window. "You'll keep me informed, right?"

"Absolutely."

"Don't spend too much time in that graveyard. That is one seriously peculiar place."

"Meaning what?"

"You'll find out soon enough." Scowling, Hardwick revved his obnoxiously loud engine, stirring it up from a bronchial rumble to a full roar. Then he eased out the clutch, turned the old red GTO around on the yellowing grass, and headed down the pasture trail.

Gurney looked up again at the hawk, gliding with elegant ease above the ridge. Then he went into the house, expecting to see Madeleine or to hear the sound of cello practice upstairs. He called her name. The interior of the house, however, communicated only that odd sense of emptiness it always seemed to have when she was out.

He thought about what day of the week it was—whether it was one of the three days she worked at the mental health clinic, but it wasn't. He searched his memory for any trace of her mentioning one of her local board meetings, or yoga classes, or volunteer weeding sessions at the community garden, or shopping trips to Oneonta. But nothing came to mind.

He went back outside, looked up and down the gently sloping terrain on both sides of the house. Three deer stood watching him from the top of the high pasture. The hawk was still gliding, now in a wide circle, making only small adjustments in the angle of its outstretched wings.

He called out Madeleine's name, this time loudly, and cupped his ears for a reply. There was none. But as he was listening, something caught his eye—below the low pasture, through the trees, a glimpse of fuchsia by the back corner of the little barn.

There were only two fuchsia objects he could think of that belonged in their secluded end-of-the-road world: Madeleine's nylon jacket and the seat of the new bicycle he'd bought her for her birthday—to replace the one lost in the fire that had destroyed their original barn.

As he strode down, ever more curious, through the pasture, he called her name once more—sure now that what he was looking at was in fact her jacket. But again there was no reply. He passed through the informal row of saplings that bordered the pasture, and as he entered the open mowed area surrounding the barn, he saw Madeleine sitting on the grass at the far corner of the building. She appeared to be intent on something just out of his line of sight.

"Madeleine, why didn't you—" he began, his annoyance at her lack of response coming through clearly in his voice. Without looking at him, she raised one of her hands toward him in a gesture that meant he should either stop approaching or stop speaking.

When he stopped both, she motioned him forward. He came up behind her and peered around the corner of the barn. And there he saw them—the four chickens, sitting placidly in the grass, their heads lowered, their feet tucked under their breasts. The rooster sat on one side of Madeleine's outstretched legs, and the three hens sat on the other side. As Gurney stared down at this odd tableau, he could hear the chickens making the same low, peaceful cooing sounds they made on their roost when they were ready for sleep.

Madeleine looked up at Gurney. "They need a little house and a safe fenced yard to run around in. So they can be out as much as they want in the air and be happy and safe. That's all they want. So we have to do that for them."

"Right." The reminder of the construction project ahead irritated him. He looked down at the chickens on the grass. "How are you going to get them back in the barn?"

"It's not a problem." She smiled, more at the chickens than at him. "It's not a problem," she repeated in a whisper. "We'll go into the barn soon. We just want to sit in the grass for a few more minutes."

Half an hour later, Gurney was sitting in front of his computer in the den, making his way through the website of the Cyberspace Cathedral, "Your Portal to a Joyful Life." Predictably perhaps, given the name of the organization, he could find no physical address, no picture of any brick-and-mortar headquarters.

The only option offered on the Contact page was email. When Gurney clicked on it, the actual email form that popped up was addressed to Jonah himself.

Gurney thought about that for a while—the disarming, almost intimate suggestion that one's comment, inquiry, or plea for help would go directly to the founder. That in turn made him wonder what sort of comments, inquiries, or pleas for help the website might be generating; looking for the answer kept him scrolling through the site for another twenty minutes.

The eventual impression he got was that the promised joyful life was a vaguely New Age state of mind, full of soft-focus philosophy, pastel graphics, and sunny weather. The whole enterprise seemed to be proffering the sweetness and protection of baby powder. It was as if Hallmark had decided to start a religion.

The object that held Gurney's attention longest was a photograph of Jonah Spalter on the Welcome page. High-resolution and seemingly unretouched, it had a kind of directness that contrasted sharply with the surrounding fluff.

There was something of Carl in the shape of Jonah's face, the full dark hair with a slight wave, the straight nose, the strong jaw. But there all resemblance ended. While Carl's eyes at the end were full of the most extreme despair, Jonah's seemed to be fixed on a future of endless success. Like the classic masks of tragedy and comedy, their faces were remarkably similar and totally opposite. If these brothers had been locked in the kind of personal battle that Kay had indicated, and if Jonah's photograph truly represented his current appearance, there was no doubt which brother had emerged victorious.

In addition to Jonah's picture, the Welcome page included a long clickable menu of topics. Gurney chose the one at the top of the list: "Only Human." As a page with a border of entwined daisies came up on the screen, he heard Madeleine's voice calling to him from the other room.

"Dinner's on the table."

She was already seated at the small round table in the nook by the French doors—the one at which they ate all their meals, except when they had guests and used the long Shaker table instead. He sat across from her. On each of their plates were generous portions of sautéed haddock, carrots, and broccoli. He poked at a slice of carrot, speared it with his fork, began chewing it. He discovered he wasn't very hungry. He continued eating anyway. He didn't care much for the haddock. It reminded of the tasteless fish his mother used to serve.

"Did you get them back in the barn?" he asked with more irritation than interest.

"Of course."

He realized he'd lost track of the hour and glanced over at the clock on the far wall. It was six-thirty. He turned his head to look out the glass door and saw the sun glaring back at him from just above the western ridge. Far from any romantic notions of a pastoral sunset, it reminded him of a movie-cliché interrogation lamp.

That association carried him back to the questions he'd posed at Bedford Hills just a few hours earlier, and to those uncannily steady green eyes that seemed more suited to a cat in a painting than a woman in prison.

"You want to tell me about it?" Madeleine was watching him with that knowing look that sometimes made him wonder if he'd been unconsciously whispering his thoughts.

"About . . . ?"

"Your day. The woman you went to see. What Jack wants. Your plan. Whether you believe she's innocent."

It hadn't occurred to him that he wanted to talk about that. But perhaps he did. He laid his fork down. "Bottom line, I don't know what I believe. If she's a liar, she's a good one. Maybe the best I've ever seen."

"But you don't think she's a liar?"

"I'm not sure. She seems to want me to believe she's innocent, but she's not going out of her way to persuade me. It's as though she wants to make it difficult."

"Clever."

"Clever or . . . honest."

"Maybe both."

"Right."

"What else?"

"What do you mean?"

"What else did you see in her?"

He thought for a moment. "Pride. Strength. Willfulness."

"Is she attractive?"

"I don't think 'attractive' is the word I'd choose."

"What, then?"

"Impressive. Intense. Determined."

"Ruthless?"

"Ah. That's a tough one. If you mean ruthless enough to kill her husband for money, I can't say yet one way or the other."

Madeleine echoed the word "yet" so softly, he hardly heard her.

"I intend to take at least one more step," he said, but even as he was saying it he recognized its subtle dishonesty.

If the skeptical glint in Madeleine's eye was any indication, so did she. "And that step would be . . . ?"

"I want to look at the crime scene."

"Weren't there pictures in the file Jack gave you?"

"Crime scene photos and drawings capture maybe ten percent of the reality. You have to stand there, walk around, look around, listen, smell, get a feel for the place, a feel for the possibilities and limitations—the neighborhood, the traffic, a feel for what the victim might have seen, what the killer might have seen, how he might have arrived, where he might have gone, who might have seen him."

"Or *her*."

"Or her."

"So when are you going to do all this looking, listening, smelling, and feeling?"

"Tomorrow."

"You do remember our dinner?"

"Tomorrow?"

Madeleine produced a long-suffering smile. "The members of the yoga club. Here. For dinner."

"Oh, right, sure. That's fine. No problem."

"You're sure? You'll be here?"

"No problem."

She gave him a long look, then broke it off as though the subject was closed. She stood, opened the French doors, and took a long deep breath of the cool air.

A moment later, from the woods beyond the pond came that strange lost cry they'd heard before, like an eerie note on a flute.

Gurney rose from his chair and stepped out past Madeleine onto the stone patio. The sun had dipped below the ridge, and the temperature felt like it had dropped fifteen degrees. He stood quite still and listened for a repetition of that unearthly sound.

All he could hear was a silence so deep it sent a shiver through his body.

Chapter 12

Willow Rest

When Gurney came out to the kitchen the next morning, he was ravenously hungry.

Madeleine was at the sink island, shredding bits of bread onto a large paper plate, half of which was already covered with chopped strawberries. Once a week she gave the chickens a plate of something special in addition to the packaged feed from the farm supply store.

Gurney was reminded by her more-conservative-than-usual outfit that it was one of her work days at the clinic. He looked up at the clock. "Aren't you running late?"

"Hal is picking me up, so . . . no problem."

If he remembered rightly, Hal was the clinic director. "Why?"

She stared at him.

"Oh, right, yes, your car, in the shop. But how come Hal—?"

"I mentioned my car problems at work the other day, and Hal said he passes our road anyway. Besides, if I'm late because he's late, he can hardly complain. And speaking of being late, you won't be, will you?"

"Late? For what?"

"Tonight. The yoga club."

"No problem."

"And you'll think about calling Malcolm Claret?"

"*Today?*"

"Good a time as any."

At the sound of a car coming up the pasture lane, she went to the window. "He's here," she said breezily. "Got to go." She hurried over to Gurney, kissed him, and then picked up her bag from the sideboard with one hand and the plate of bread and strawberries with the other.

"You want me to take care of that chicken stuff for you?" asked Gurney.

"No. Hal can stop at the barn for two seconds. I'll take care of it. Ta-ta." She headed through the hallway past the mudroom and out the back door.

Gurney watched through the window as Hal's gleaming black Audi crept slowly down toward the barn and around to the far side where the door was. He watched until the car reappeared from behind the barn a minute or two later and headed down the road.

It was barely eight-fifteen in the morning, and already his day was congested with thoughts and emotions he'd rather not have.

He knew from experience that the best remedy for dealing with an unsettled state of mind was to take some sort of action, to move forward.

He went to the den, got the Spalter case file and the thick packet of documents describing Kay's journey through the legal system after her arraignment—the pretrial motions, the trial transcript, copies of the prosecution's visual aids and items of evidence, and the routine post-conviction appeal filed by the original defense attorney. Gurney carried it all out to his car, because he had no idea which specific items he might need to refer to in the course of the day.

He went back in the house and got a plain gray sport jacket out of his closet, the one he'd worn hundreds of times on the job, but maybe only three times since he'd retired. That jacket with his dark slacks, blue shirt, and simple military style shoes screamed "cop" as loudly as any uniform. He was guessing that the image might prove useful in Long Falls. He made one last glance around, went out to his car again, and entered the address of the Willow Rest cemetery in the portable GPS on the dashboard.

A minute later he was on his way—and feeling better already.

L ike so many old cities on rivers and canals of fading commercial utility, Long Falls seemed to be struggling against a persistent current of decline.

There were scattered signs of attempted revitalization. An abandoned fabric mill had been converted into professional offices; a cluster of small shops now occupied a former casket factory; a block-long
building of sooty bricks the color of old scabs, with the name CLOVER-
SWEET CREAMERY etched on a granite lintel over the entrance door,
had been relabeled NORTHERN ART STUDIOS & GALLERIES on a wider
and brighter sign affixed above the lintel.

As he drove along the main artery, however, Gurney counted at
least six derelict buildings from a more prosperous time. There were
a lot of empty parking spaces, too few people on the streets. A thin
teenager, wearing the loser's uniform of sagging jeans and an oversized baseball hat worn sideways, stood on an otherwise deserted corner with a muscular dog on a short leash. As Gurney slowed for a red
light, he could see that the young man's anxious eyes were scanning
the passing cars with an addict's characteristic combination of hope
and detachment.

It sometimes seemed to Gurney that something in America had
gone terribly wrong. A large segment of a generation had become
infected with ignorance, laziness, and vulgarity. It no longer seemed
unusual for a young woman to have, say, three small children by three
different fathers, two of whom were currently in prison. And places
like Long Falls, which once may have nurtured a simpler kind of life,
were now depressingly similar to everywhere else.

These thoughts were interrupted by his GPS announcing in an
authoritative voice, "Arriving at destination on your right."

The sign, next to a spotless blacktop driveway, said only WILLOW
REST—leaving the nature of the enterprise unspecified. Gurney turned
in and followed the driveway through an open wrought-iron gate in a
yellow brick wall. Well-tended landscape plantings on each side of the
entrance conveyed the impression not of a cemetery but of an upscale
residential development. The driveway led directly to a small, empty
parking area in front of an English-style cottage.

Window boxes overflowing with purple and yellow pansies below
old-fashioned small-paned windows reminded him of the weird-cozy
esthetic of a wildly popular painter whose name he could never recall.
There was a VISITOR INFORMATION sign alongside a flagstone pathway
that extended from the parking area to the cottage door.

As Gurney was heading up the path, the door opened and a woman who seemed not to notice him emerged onto a broad stone step. She was casually dressed, as if for some light gardening, a notion under-scored by a small pruning scissors in her hand.

Gurney guessed her age to be mid-fifties. Her most noticeable feature was her hair, which was pure white and arranged in a short layered style, ending in choppy little points around her forehead and cheeks. He recalled his mother having that hairdo when it was first fashionable in his childhood. He even recalled its name: the artichoke. That word in turn produced a fleeting feeling of unease.

The woman glanced with surprise at Gurney. "Sorry, I didn't hear you drive up. I was just coming out to take care of a few things. I'm Paulette Purley. How can I help you?"

During his drive to Long Falls, Gurney had considered various ways of answering questions about his visit and had decided on an approach that he labeled in his own mind "minimal honesty"—which meant telling enough of the truth to avoid being caught in a lie, but telling it in a way to avoid setting off unnecessary alarms.

"I'm not sure yet." He smiled innocently. "Would it be all right for me to take a stroll around the grounds?"

Her unremarkable hazel eyes seemed to be appraising him. "Have you been here before?"

"This is my first visit. But I do have a satellite map I printed out from Google."

A cloud of skepticism crossed her face. "Wait just a moment." She turned and went into the cottage. A few seconds later she returned with a colorful brochure. "Just in case your Google thing isn't entirely clear, this may be useful." She paused. "May I direct you to the resting place of a specific friend or relative?"

"No. But thank you. It's such a lovely day, I think I'd prefer to find my own way."

She cast a worried look at the sky, which was half blue, half clouds. "They've been talking about the possibility of rain. If you'd tell me the name—"

"You're very kind," he said, backing away, "but I'll be fine." He retreated to the small parking area and saw on the opposite side of it a flagstone pathway passing under a rose-covered trellis beside which a sign read PEDESTRIAN ENTRANCE. As he walked through it, he glanced back. Paulette Purley was still standing in front of the cottage, watching him with a look of anxious curiosity.

It didn't take Gurney long to realize what Hardwick had meant when he referred to Willow Rest as "seriously peculiar." The place bore little resemblance to any cemetery he'd ever seen. Yet there also was something familiar about it. Something he couldn't put his finger on.

The basic layout consisted of a gently curving cobblestone lane that paralleled the low brick wall surrounding the property. Smaller lanes branched from it in toward the center of the cemetery grounds at regular intervals amid a profusion of lush rhododendrons, lilacs, and hemlocks. These lanes had offshoots of still smaller lanes, each of which terminated like a driveway at a mowed grassy area the size of a small backyard, separated from its neighbors by rows of waist-high spireas and beds of daylilies. In each of the grassy areas he entered, there were several marble grave markers, flush with the ground. In addition to the name of the interred, each marker bore only a single date instead of the traditional birth and death dates.

Next to each "driveway" was a plain black mailbox with a family name stenciled on the side. He opened a few of the mailboxes as he made his way along the lanes, but found nothing in any of them. About twenty minutes into his exploration, he came upon a mailbox that bore the name Spalter. It marked the entrance to the largest of the plots he'd encountered so far. The plot occupied what seemed to be one of the higher points in Willow Rest, a gentle rise from which the narrow river was visible beyond the perimeter wall. Beyond the river was the state highway that bisected Long Falls. On the far side of the highway a block of three-story apartment buildings faced the cemetery.

Chapter 13

Death in Long Falls

Gurney was already familiar with the basic topography, structures, angles, and distances. All of that had been documented in the case file. But actually seeing *the* building, and then pinpointing *the* window, from which the fatal bullet was fired—fired toward the area where he was now standing—had a jarring effect. It was the effect of reality colliding with preconception. It was an experience he'd had at countless crime scenes. That gap between the mental picture and the actual sensory impact was what made *being there* so important.

A physical crime scene was concrete and unfiltered in a way that no photo or description ever could be. It held answers you could find if you looked with open eyes and an open mind. If you looked carefully, it could tell you a story. It gave you, quite literally, a place to stand, a place from which you could survey the real possibilities.

After conducting a preliminary 360-degree examination of his general surroundings, Gurney focused on the details of the Spalter plot itself. More than twice the size of the next largest he'd come upon, he estimated the dimensions of the central mowed area as fifty by seventy feet. A low border of well-kept rosebushes surrounded it.

He counted eight flat marble grave markers lying just below the height of the grass, arranged in rows that allocated a space of approximately six feet by twelve feet for each burial. The earliest date, 1899, appeared on marker that bore the name Emmerling Spalter. The most recent date, 1970, was on a marker that bore the name Carl Spalter. The edges of the letters on the glossy surface of the marble were distinctly sharp and freshly carved. But obviously the date was not of his death. His birth, then? Probably.

As Gurney gazed down at the marker he saw that it was next to one for Mary Spalter, the mother at whose funeral Carl had been fatally wounded. On the other side of Mary Spalter's grave was a marker bearing the name Joseph Spalter. Father and mother and murdered son. A peculiar family gathering, in this thoroughly peculiar cemetery. Father and mother and murdered son—the son who hoped to be governor—all reduced to nothing at all.

As he was pondering the sad smallness of human lives, he heard a low mechanical hum behind him. He turned to see an electric golf cart coming to a silent stop at the rose border of the Spalter plot. The driver was Paulette Purley, smiling inquisitively.

"Hello, again, Mr. . . . ? Sorry, but I don't know your name."

"Dave Gurney."

"Hello, Dave." She stepped out of the cart. "I was about to make my rounds when I noticed those rain clouds getting closer." She gestured vaguely toward some gray clouds in the west. "I thought you might need an umbrella. You don't want to be out here in a downpour without one." As she was speaking, she took a bright blue umbrella from the floor of the cart and brought it to him. "Getting wet is fine if you're swimming, but otherwise not so pleasant."

He took the umbrella, thanked her, and waited for her to segue to her real purpose, which he was sure had nothing to do with keeping him dry.

"Just drop it off at the cottage on your way out." She started back to the cart, then stopped as though another thought had just occurred to her. "Were you able to find your way all right?"

"Yes, I was. Of course, this particular plot would—"

"Property," she interjected.

"Beg pardon?"

"At Willow Rest we prefer not to use the vocabulary of cemeteries. We offer 'properties' to families, not depressing little 'plots.' I take it you're not a member of the family?"

"No, I'm not."

"A family friend, perhaps?"

"In a way, yes. But may I ask why you're asking?"

She appeared to be searching his face for a clue on how she should proceed. Then something in his expression seemed to reassure her. Her voice dropped into a confidential register. "I'm sorry. I certainly didn't mean any offense. But the Spalter property, you can understand I'm sure, is a special case. We sometimes have a problem with ... what shall I call them? Sensation seekers, I suppose. *Ghouls,* when you come right down to it." She curled her lips in an expression of distaste. "When something tragic occurs, people come to gawk, take pictures. It's disgusting, isn't it? I mean, it's a *tragedy.* A horrible family *tragedy.* Can you imagine? A man is shot at his own mother's funeral? Shot in the brain! Crippled! A completely paralyzed cripple! A vegetable! Then he dies! And his own wife turns out to be the murderer! That's a terrible, terrible *tragedy!* And what do people do? They show up here with cameras. *Cameras.* Some of them even tried to steal our rosebushes. As souvenirs! Can you imagine that? Of course, as resident manager, it all ends up being *my* responsibility. It makes me sick talking about it. Sick to my stomach! I can't even ..." She waved her hand in a gesture of helplessness.

The lady doth protest too much, thought Gurney. *She sounds every bit as enlivened by the "tragedy" as the people she's condemning.* But, he reflected, that wasn't unusual. Few behaviors of other people are more irritating than those that display our own faults in an unattractive way.

His next thought was that her apparent appetite for drama might give him a useful opening. He looked into her eyes as if he and she were having a deep meeting of the minds. "You really care about this, don't you?"

She blinked. "Care? Of course I do. Isn't that obvious?"

Instead of answering, he turned away thoughtfully, walked toward the rose border, and poked absently in the mulch with the tip of the umbrella she'd handed him.

"Who are you?" she finally asked. He thought he heard a touch of excitement in the question.

He continued prodding the mulch. "I told you, my name is Dave Gurney."

"Why are you here?"

Again he spoke without turning. "I'll tell you in a minute. But first let me ask you a question. What was your reaction—the very first thing you felt—when you found out that Carl Spalter had been shot?"

She hesitated. "Are you a reporter?"

He turned toward her, took out his wallet, and held it up, displaying his gold NYPD detective's shield. She was standing far enough away that the word "Retired" at the bottom of the shield would not be legible, and she didn't come any closer to examine it. He closed his wallet and put it back in his pocket.

"You're a detective?"

"That's right."

"Oh . . ." She looked alternately confused, curious, excited. "What . . . what would you want here?"

"I need to get a better understanding of what happened."

She blinked rapidly several times. "What is there to understand? I thought everything was . . . resolved."

He took a few steps closer to her, spoke as if he were sharing privileged information. "The conviction is being appealed. There are some open questions, possible gaps in the evidence."

She wrinkled her brow. "Aren't all murder convictions appealed automatically?"

"Yes. And the vast majority of the convictions are upheld. But this case may be different."

"Different?"

"Let me ask you again. What was your reaction—*the very first thing you felt*—when you found out that Carl had been shot?"

"Found out? You mean, when I noticed it."

"*Noticed* it?"

"I was the first one to see it."

"See what?"

"The little hole in his temple. At first I wasn't sure it was a hole. It just looked like a round red spot. But then a tiny red trickle started down the side of his forehead. And I knew, I just *knew*."

"You pointed it out to the first responders?"

"Of course."

"Fascinating. Tell me more."

She pointed at the ground a few feet from where Gurney was standing. "That's where it was, right there—where the first drop of blood from the side of his forehead fell onto the snow. I can almost see it now. Have you ever seen blood on snow?" Her eyes seemed to widen at the memory. "It's the reddest red you can imagine."

"What makes you so sure it was in that precise—"

She answered before he could finish. "Because of *that.*" She indicated another point on the ground, a foot or so farther away.

It wasn't until Gurney took a step toward it that he saw a small green disc below the grass level. It had pinhole perforations around its circumference. "A watering system?"

"His head was face down just a few inches short of it." She stepped over to the spot and placed her foot next to the watering head. "Right there."

Gurney was struck by the coldness, the hostility, of the gesture.

"Do you attend all the funerals here?"

"Yes and no. As the resident manager, I'm never far away. But I always maintain a discreet distance. Funerals, I believe, are for invited family and friends. Of course, in the case of the Spalter funeral, I was more present."

"More present?"

"Well, I didn't feel it was appropriate to sit with Mr. Spalter's family and personal associates, so I remained a bit to the side—but I was certainly more present than at other interments."

"Why was that?"

She looked surprised at the question. "Because of my relationship."

"Which was what?"

"Spalter Realty is my employer."

"The Spalters own Willow Rest?"

"I thought that was common knowledge. Willow Rest was founded by Emmerling Spalter, the grandfather of ... the recently deceased. Didn't you know that?"

"You'll have to be patient with me. I'm new to the case, and I'm new to Long Falls." He saw something critical in her expression, and he added with the hint of a conspiratorial tone, "You see, I was brought here for a completely fresh perspective." He gave her a moment or two to absorb the implications of that statement, then went on. "Now let's go back to my question about the feeling you had when you realized—*noticed*—what had happened."

She hesitated, her lips tightening. "Why is that important?"

"I'll explain in a minute. In the meantime, let me ask you another question. What did you feel when you learned that Kay Spalter had been arrested?"

"Oh, God. Disbelief. Shock. Complete shock."

"How well did you know Kay?"

"Obviously not as well as I thought I did. Something like this makes you wonder how well you know anyone." After a pause, her expression morphed into a kind of shrewd curiosity. "What's this all about? These questions—what's going on here?"

Gurney gave her a long, hard look, as if he were assessing her trustworthiness. Then he took a deep breath and spoke in what he hoped would come across as a confessional tone. "There's a funny thing about cops, Paulette. We expect people to tell us everything, but we don't like to reveal anything ourselves. I understand the reasons for it, but there are times ..." He paused, then took a deep breath and spoke slowly, looking her in the eye. "I have the impression that Kay was a much nicer person than Carl. Not the sort of person who'd be capable of murder. I'm trying to find out if I'm right or wrong. I can't do that alone. I need the insight of other people. I have a strong feeling you may be able to help me."

She stared at him for several seconds, then gave a little shiver and wrapped her arms around her body. "I think you should come back to the house with me. I'm sure it's going to rain any minute now."

Chapter 14

The Devil's Brother

The cottage wasn't nearly as kitschy as Gurney had expected. Despite its storybook facade, the interior was rather restrained. The front door opened onto a modest entry hall. On the left he saw a sitting room with a fireplace and several traditional landscape prints on the walls. Through a doorway on the right, he glimpsed what appeared to be an office with a mahogany desk and a large painting of Willow Rest behind it. It reminded him of one of those sprawling nineteenth-century macroviews of a working farm or village. Straight ahead on the left was a staircase to an upper floor and on the right a door that presumably led to another room or two at the back of the house. It was where Paulette Purley had gone to make coffee after taking Gurney into the sitting room and steering him to a wing chair by the fireplace. On the mantel was a framed photograph of a lanky man with his arm around a younger Paulette. Her hair was a bit longer then, fluffed up as though caught in a breeze, and honey blond.

She reappeared with a tray on which there were two cups of black coffee, a small pitcher of milk, a sugar bowl, and two spoons. She placed the tray on a low table in front of the hearth and sat in a matching chair facing Gurney's. Neither spoke as they added milk and sugar, took a first sip, then sat back in their chairs.

Paulette, he noted, was holding her cup in both hands, perhaps to steady it, perhaps to take a chill out of her fingers. Her lips were pressed together but making tiny nervous movements. "Now it can rain all it wants," she said with a sudden smile, as though trying to dispel the tension with the sound of her own voice.

"I'm curious about this place," said Gurney. "Willow Rest must have an interesting history." It wasn't a history he cared about. But he thought that getting her talking about something easy might provide a bridge to something more difficult.

For the next fifteen minutes she explained Emmerling Spalter's philosophy, which struck Gurney as escapist nonsense, cannily packaged. Willow Rest was one's final *home,* not a cemetery. Only the date of birth, not the date of death, was engraved on a marker, because once we are born we live forever. Willow Rest provided not gravesites but homesites, a piece of nature with grass and trees and flowers. Every property was scaled to accommodate a multigenerational family rather than an individual. The mailbox at each property was an encouragement to family members to leave cards and letters for their loved ones. (These were gathered once a week, burned in a little portable brazier at each site, and raked into the soil.) Paulette explained earnestly that Willow Rest was all about life, continuity, beauty, peace, and privacy. As far as Gurney could see, it was about everything except death. But he was not about to say that. He wanted her to keep talking.

Emmerling and Agnes Spalter had three children, two of whom died of pneumonia before they were out of their cribs. The survivor was Joseph. He married a woman named Mary Croake.

Joseph and Mary had two sons, Carl and Jonah.

The mention of these names, Gurney noticed, had an immediate effect on Paulette's tone and expression, bringing back to her lips an almost imperceptible twitching.

"I've been told they were as different as two brothers could be," he said encouragingly.

"Oh, yes! Black and white! Cain and Abel!" She fell silent, her eyes fixed in anger on some memory.

Gurney prompted her. "I imagine Carl could be a difficult person to work for."

"*Difficult?*" A bitter one-syllable laugh erupted from her throat. She closed her eyes for a few seconds, seemed to reach a decision, and then the words came rushing out.

"*Difficult?* Let me explain something to you. Emmerling Spalter became a very wealthy man buying and selling large tracts of land in upstate New York. He passed his business, his money, and his talent for making it along to his son. Joe Spalter was a bigger, tougher version of his father. He wasn't someone you'd want for an enemy. But he was rational. You could talk to him. In his hard-as-nails way, he was fair. Not nice, not generous. But fair. It was Joe who hired my husband as the Willow Rest resident manager. That was ..." She looked lost for a moment or two. "Oh, my, time is becoming so difficult. That was fifteen years ago. Fifteen." She looked at her coffee cup, seemed surprised that it was still in her hands, and laid it down carefully on the table.

"And Joe was Carl and Jonah's father?" prompted Gurney.

She nodded. "Joe's dark side all went to Carl, and everything that was decent and reasonable went to Jonah. They say there's some good and bad in all of us, but not in the case of the Spalter brothers. Jonah and Carl. An angel and a devil. I believe Joe saw that, and the way he tied them together as a condition for inheriting the business was his attempt at solving the problem. Maybe hoping for some kind of balance. Of course, it didn't work."

Gurney sipped his coffee. "What happened?"

"After Joe passed away, they went from being opposites to being enemies. They couldn't agree on anything. All Carl was interested in was money, money, money—and he didn't care how they made it. Jonah found the situation unbearable, and that's when he set up the Cyberspace Cathedral and disappeared."

"Disappeared?"

"Pretty much. You could reach him through the Cathedral website, but he had no real address. There was a rumor that he was always on the move, living in a motor home, managing the Cathedral project and everything else in his life by computer. When he made an appearance here in Long Falls for his mother's funeral, that was the first time anyone had seen him in three years. And even then, we didn't know he was coming. I believe he wanted to make a total break from everything connected with Carl." She paused. "He might even have been afraid of Carl."

"Afraid?"

Paulette leaned forward and picked up her coffee, holding it again in both hands. She cleared her throat. "I don't say this lightly. *Carl Spalter had no conscience.* If he wanted something, I don't think there would be any limit to what he might do."

"What's the worst thing——"

"The worst thing he ever did? I don't know, and I don't want to know. But I do know what he did to *me*—or what he *tried* to do to me." Her eyes brightened with anger.

"Tell me."

"My husband, Bob, and I had lived in this house for fifteen years, ever since he accepted his position here. The downstairs always served as the Willow Rest business office, and the little upstairs apartment went with the job. We moved in right after Bob was hired. It was our home. And, in a way, we both did his job. We did it together. We felt that it was more than a job; it was a commitment. A way of helping people through terrible times in their lives. It wasn't just a way of making a living—*it was our life.*"

Tears were welling in her eyes. She blinked hard and went on. "Ten months ago, Bob had a massive coronary. In that hallway." As she looked toward the doorway, she closed her eyes for a moment. "He was dead by the time the ambulance arrived." She took a deep breath. "The day after his funeral, I received an email from Carl's assistant at Spalter Realty. *An email.* Telling me that a *cemetery management company*—can you image such a thing?—*a cemetery management company* would be taking over responsibility for Willow Rest. And, for an efficient transition, it would be necessary for me to vacate the cottage within sixty days."

She stared at Gurney, erect in her chair, full of fury. "What do you think of that? After fifteen years! The day after my husband's funeral! An email! A goddamn, wretched, disgusting, insulting email! *Your husband's dead, now get out of here.* Tell me, Detective Gurney—what kind of man does something like that?"

When it appeared that her emotion had subsided, he said softly, "That was ten months ago. I'm glad to see you're still here."

"I'm here because Kay Spalter did me—and everyone else in the world—a giant favor."

"You mean Carl was shot before your sixty days were up?"

"That's right. Which proves there's some good in the world after all."

"So you still work for Spalter Realty?"

"For Jonah, really. When Carl was incapacitated, full control of Spalter Realty passed to Jonah."

"Carl's fifty percent ownership didn't become part of his own estate?"

"No. Believe me, Carl's estate was big enough without it—he was involved in so many other things. But when it came to the holdings of Spalter Realty, the corporate agreement Joe made them sign included a provision that transferred everything to the surviving brother at the death of either one."

That certainly seemed to Gurney like a fact significant enough to have made its way into the case file, but he hadn't seen any mention of it. He made a mental note to ask Hardwick if he was aware of it.

"How do you know about this, Paulette?"

"Jonah explained it to me the day he took over. Jonah is very open. You get the impression that he really and truly has no secrets."

Gurney nodded, tried not to look skeptical. He'd never met a man with no secrets. "I gather, then, that Jonah canceled Carl's plan to outsource the management of Willow Rest?"

"Absolutely. Immediately. In fact, he stepped right in and offered me the same job Bob had, at the same salary. He even told me that the job and the house would be mine to keep as long as I wanted either one of them."

"He sounds like a generous man."

"You know those empty apartments over there across the river? He told the Spalter Realty security guard to stop chasing the homeless people out of them. He even got the electricity turned back on for them—the electricity that Carl had turned off."

"He sounds like he cares about people."

"*Cares?*" An otherworldly smile changed her expression completely. "Jonah doesn't just *care*. Jonah is a *saint*."

Chapter 15

A Cynical Suggestion

L ess than five hundred yards from the manicured enclave of Willow Rest, Axton Avenue provided a dose of upstate economic reality. Half the street-level shops were run-down, the other half boarded up. The apartment windows above them looked forlorn if not entirely abandoned.

Gurney parked in front of a dusty-looking electronics store that, according to the case file, occupied the ground floor of the building from which the bullet had been fired. A logo showing through a poorly overpainted sign above the display window indicated it had once been a RadioShack franchise.

Next to the store, the entry door for the residential floors was a few inches ajar. Gurney pushed it open and entered a small, dingy lobby. What little light there was came from a single bulb in a caged ceiling fixture. He was greeted by the standard odor of derelict urban buildings: urine enhanced with touches of alcohol, vomit, cigarette smoke, garbage, and feces. And there were the familiar auditory inputs. Somewhere above him two male voices were arguing, hip-hop music was playing, a dog was barking, and a small child was screaming. All that was missing to turn it into a clichéd movie scene was the slam of a door and the clatter of feet on the stairs. Just then Gurney heard a shouted "Fuck you, you stupid fuck!" from an upper floor, followed by the sound of someone actually coming down the stairs. The coincidence would have made him smile if the stench of the urine wasn't making him nauseous.

The descending footsteps grew louder, and soon a young man

appeared at the top of the shadowy flight that led down into the lobby. Spotting Gurney, he hesitated for a second, then hurried down past him and out onto the street, where he stopped abruptly to light a cigarette. He was scrawny with a narrow face, sharp features, and stringy shoulder-length hair. He took two deep, desperate drags on his cigarette, then walked quickly away.

Gurney considered going down into the basement for the master key that Kay had told him was secreted behind the furnace. But he decided instead to give the building a once-over and get the key later if he needed it. For all he knew, the apartment he was most interested in might be unlocked. Or occupied by drug dealers. He was no longer routinely carrying the gun he'd kept with him during the Good Shepherd case—and he didn't want to burst in, uninvited and unarmed, on a jumpy meth-head with an AK-47.

He climbed the two flights of stairs to the top floor quickly and quietly. Each floor had four apartments—two at the front of the building, two at the rear. On the third floor, gangsta rap was playing behind one door and a child was crying behind another. He knocked at each of the two silent doors and got no response beyond a hint of muffled voices behind one of them. When he knocked at the other two, the rap volume dropped a bit, the child continued to cry, but no one came to either door. He considered pounding on them, but quickly dismissed the notion. Gentler approaches tended to lead to a wider range of options down the road. Gurney was fond of options and wanted to keep them as numerous as possible.

He descended a flight to the second-floor hallway, which, like the others, was illuminated only by a single-bulb fixture in the middle of the ceiling. He oriented himself according to his recollection of the photo in the case file and approached the apartment from which the fatal shot had been fired. As he was putting his ear to the door, he heard a soft footstep—not in the apartment, but behind him. He turned quickly.

At the top of the flight of stairs that came up from the lobby stood a stocky, gray-haired man, motionless and alert. In one hand he carried a black metal flashlight. It was switched off—and being gripped as a weapon. Gurney recognized it as the grip taught in police academies.

The man's other hand rested on something affixed to his belt in the shadow of a dark nylon jacket. Gurney was willing to bet that SECURITY would be stenciled across the back.

There was a look in the man's small eyes verging on hatred. However, as he scrutinized Gurney more closely—taking in the detective-on-the-job ensemble of cheap sport jacket, blue shirt, and dark pants—the look morphed into a kind of resentful curiosity. "You looking for somebody?"

Gurney had heard that exact voice—meanness and suspicion as much a part of it as the smell of urine was part of the building—from so many cops who'd gone sour over the years, he felt he knew the man personally. It wasn't a good feeling.

"Yes, I am. Trouble is, I don't have a name. Meantime, I'd like to get a look inside this apartment."

"That so? 'A look inside this apartment'? You mind telling me who the hell you are?"

"Dave Gurney. Ex-NYPD. Just like you."

"What the hell do you know about me?"

"Doesn't take a genius to recognize an Irish cop from New York."

"That so?" The man was giving him a flat stare.

Gurney added, "There was a time when the force was full of people like us."

That was the right button.

"People like us? That's ancient history, my friend! Ancient fucking history!"

"Yeah, I know." Gurney nodded sympathetically. "That was a better time—a much better time, in my humble opinion. When did you get out?"

"When do you think?"

"Tell me."

"When they got heavy into all that diversity bullshit. *Diversity.* Can you believe it? Couldn't get promoted unless you were a Nigerian lesbian with a Navajo grandmother. Time for the smart white guys to get the hell out. Goddamn shame what this country is turning into. Goddamn joke is what it is. *America.* That's a word that used to mean something. Pride. Strength. What is it now? Tell me. What is it now?"

Gurney shook his head sadly. "I'll tell you what it's *not*. It's not what it used to be."

"I'll tell you what it is. *Affirmative fucking action.* That's what it is. Welfare bullshit. Dope addicts, pill addicts, coke addicts, crack addicts. And you want to know why? I'll tell you why. *Affirmative fucking action.*"

Gurney grunted, hoping to convey morose agreement. "Looks to me like some of the people in this building might be part of the problem."

"You got that right."

"You got a hell of a tough job here, Mr. .... Sorry, I don't know your name."

"McGrath. Frank McGrath."

Gurney stepped toward him, put his hand out. "Nice to meet you, Frank. What precinct were you assigned to?"

They shook hands.

"Fort Apache. The one they made the movie about."

"Tough neighborhood."

"It was fucking nuts. Nobody would believe how fucking nuts it was. But that was *nothing* compared to the diversity bullshit. Fort Apache I could take. For a two-month period back in the eighties I remember we were averaging a murder a day. One day we had five. It was *us* against *them*. But once that diversity bullshit started, there was no more *us*. Department turned into a muddled-up bunch of crap. You know what I'm saying?"

"Yeah, Frank, I know exactly what you're saying."

"Crying goddamn shame."

Gurney looked around the little hallway where they were standing. "So what are you supposed to do here?"

"*Do?* Nothing. Not a fucking thing. Ain't that a fucker?"

A door on the floor above them opened, and the hip-hop racket tripled in volume. The door slammed, and it dropped back down.

"Shit, Frank, how do you stand it?"

The man shrugged. "Money's okay. I make my own schedule. No lezzy bitch looking over my shoulder."

"You had one of them on the job?"

"Yeah. Captain Pussy-Licker."

Gurney forced out a loud laugh. "Working for Jonah must be a big improvement."

"It's different." He paused. "You said you wanted to get into that apartment. You mind telling me what—"

Gurney's phone rang, stopping the man in midsentence.

He checked the ID screen. It was Paulette Purley. He'd exchanged cell numbers with her, but he hadn't expected to hear from her so soon. "Sorry, Frank, I need to take this. Be with you in two seconds." He pressed TALK. "Gurney here."

Paulette's voice sounded troubled. "I should have asked you this before, but I got so angry thinking about Carl, it slipped my mind. What I was wondering is, can I talk about this?"

"Talk about what?"

"Your investigation, the fact that you're looking for a 'fresh perspective.' Is that confidential? Can I discuss any of this with Jonah?"

Gurney realized that whatever he would say needed to serve his purposes with both Paulette and Frank. It made choosing the right words tricky, but it also presented an opportunity. "I'll put it this way. Caution is always a virtue. In a murder investigation it can save your life."

"What are you telling me?"

"If Kay didn't do it, someone else did. It could even be someone you know. You won't end up saying the wrong thing to the wrong person if you don't say anything to anyone."

"You're scaring me."

"That's my goal."

She hesitated. "Okay. I understand. Not a word to anyone. Thanks." She hung up.

Gurney continued speaking as though she hadn't. "Right ... but I need to take a look at the apartment ... No, that's okay, I can get a key from the local cops or from the Spalter Realty office ... Sure ... no problem." Gurney burst into laughter. "Yeah, right." More laughter. "It's not funny, I know, but what the hell. You gotta laugh."

Long ago he'd learned that nothing makes a fake conversation sound more authentic than unexplained laughter. And nothing makes a person more willing to give you something than his believing that you can get it just as easily somewhere else.

Gurney made a show of ending the call and announced, almost apologetically, as he headed purposefully for the stairs, "Got to go to the police station. They have an extra key for me. Be back in a little while." Gurney went to the stairs and started down them in a hurry. When he was almost to the bottom, he heard Frank say the magic words:

"Hey, you don't need to do that. I got a key right here. I'll let you in. Just tell me what the hell's going on."

Gurney climbed back up to the gloomy little hallway. "You can let me in? You're sure that's not a problem? You need to check with anyone?"

"Like who?"

"Jonah?"

He unclipped a heavy set of keys from his belt and opened the apartment door. "Why would he care? As long as all the freeloading scumbags in Long Falls are happy, he's happy."

"He's got a very generous reputation."

"Yeah, another Mother fucking Teresa."

"You don't think he's an improvement over Carl?"

"Don't get me wrong. Carl was a grade-A prick. All he cared about was money, business, politics. A prick all the way. But he was the kind of prick you could understand. You could always understand what Carl wanted. Predictable."

"A predictable prick?"

"Right. But Jonah, he's a whole other animal. No way to predict Jonah. Jonah's a fucking fruitcake. Like here. Perfect example. Carl wanted all the scumbags kicked out, kept out. Makes sense, right? Jonah comes in, says no. Gotta give 'em shelter. Gotta bring the scumbags in out of the rain. Some kind of new spiritual principle, right? *Honor the scumbags.* Let 'em piss on the floor."

"You don't really buy the angel-and-devil view of the Spalter brothers, do you?"

He gave Gurney a shrewd look. "What I heard you say on the phone—is that true?"

"Is what true?"

"That maybe Kay didn't whack Carl after all?"

"Jesus, Frank, I didn't realize I was talking that loud. I need you to keep that stuff to yourself."

"No problem, but I'm just asking—is that a true possibility?"

"A true possibility? Yeah, it is."

"So that opens things up for a second look?"

"A second look?"

"At everything that went down."

Gurney lowered his voice. "You could say that."

A speculative, humorless little smile revealed Frank's yellow teeth. "Well, well, well. So maybe Kay wasn't the shooter. Ain't that something."

"You know, Frank, it sounds like maybe you have something to tell me."

"Maybe I do."

"I'd be very grateful for any ideas you might have on the subject."

Frank took a pack of cigarettes out of his jacket pocket, lit one, and took a long, thoughtful drag. Something mean and small crept into his smile. "You ever think Mr. Perfect might be a little too perfect?"

"Jonah?"

"Right. Mister Generosity. Mister Be-Nice-to-the-Scumbags. Mister Cyber-Fucking-Cathedral."

"Sounds like you saw another side of him."

"Maybe I saw the same side his mother saw."

"His mother? You knew Mary Spalter?"

"She used to visit the main office once in a while. When Carl was in charge."

"And she had a problem with Jonah?"

"Yeah. She never much liked him. You didn't know that, huh?"

"No, but I'd love to hear more about it."

"It's simple. She knew Carl was a prick, and she was okay with that. She understood tough men. Jonah was way too sweet for her taste. I don't think the old lady trusted all that *niceness*. You know what I think? I think she thought he was full of shit."

Chapter 16

Like the Knife

After unlocking the apartment and being assured that Gurney would still be there when he returned an hour later, rancorous Frank continued on his rounds—which he claimed included all of Spalter Realty's holdings in Long Falls.

The apartment was small but relatively bright compared to the dreary hallway. The front door opened into a cramped foyer with water-stained wood flooring. On the right was a galley-style kitchen, on the left an empty closet and a bathroom. Straight ahead was a medium-sized room with two windows.

Gurney opened both windows to let in some fresh air. He looked out across Axton Avenue, across the narrow river that ran beside it, and over the low brick wall of Willow Rest. There, on a gentle rise bordered by trees, rhododendrons, lilacs, and rosebushes, was the place where Carl Spalter had been shot and later buried. Wrapped by foliage on three sides, it reminded Gurney of a stage. There was even a kind of proscenium arch, an illusion created by the horizontal member of a light pole that stood on the river side of the avenue and seemed from Gurney's line of sight to curve over the top of the scene.

The stage image underscored the other theatrical aspects of the case. There was something operatic about a man's life ending at his mother's grave, a man falling wounded on the very ground where he himself would soon be buried. And something soap-operatic in the accompanying tale of adultery and greed.

Gurney was transfixed by the setting, feeling that odd tingle of excitement he always felt when he believed he was standing where a murderer had stood, seeing much of what the murderer had seen.

There had been, however, a light coating of snow on the ground that fateful day, and, according to the case-file photos, two rows of folding chairs, sixteen in all, had been set up for the mourners on the far side of Mary Spalter's open grave. To be sure that he was picturing the setting accurately, he'd need to know the position of those chairs. And the position of the portable podium. And Carl's position. Paulette had been very precise about the position of Carl's body when it struck the ground, but Gurney needed to envision everything together, everything where it was at the moment the shot was fired. He decided to go down and get the crime scene photos from his car.

As he was about to leave the apartment, his phone stopped him.

It was Paulette again, more agitated than before. "Look, Detective Gurney, maybe I'm misunderstanding this, but it's really bothering me. I have to ask you . . . Were you suggesting that somehow Jonah . . . ? I mean, what were you really saying?"

"I'm saying that the case may not be as *closed* as everyone thinks. Maybe Kay did shoot Carl. But if she *didn't*—"

"But how could you believe that Jonah, of all people—" Paulette's voice was rising.

"Hold on. All I know now is that I need to know more. In the meantime, I want you to be careful. I want you to be safe. That's all I'm saying."

"Okay. I understand. Sorry." The sound of her breathing grew calmer. "Is there anything I can do to help?"

"As a matter of fact, yes. I'm over here in the apartment where the shot came from. I want to envision what the shooter saw from this window. It would be a huge help if you could go back to where we were standing before, when you showed me the position of Carl's head on the ground."

"And the drop of blood on the snow."

"Yes. The drop of blood on the snow. Could you go there now?"

"I guess so. Sure."

"Great, Paulette. Thank you. Take that bright blue umbrella with you. It'll make a good marker. And your phone, so you can call me when you get there. Okay?"

"Okay."

Energized by this bit of progress, he hurried out to get the case file from his car. He returned minutes later with a large manila envelope under his arm—just in time to catch sight of someone stepping into the neighboring apartment.

Gurney moved quickly to the door, inserting his foot in the jamb before it could be closed.

A short, wiry man with a long black ponytail stared out at him. After a moment he began to smile a little crazily, displaying several gold teeth, like a Mexican bandit in a politically incorrect Western. There was an intensity in his gaze that Gurney figured could come from drugs, a naturally tight spring, or a mental disorder.

"Something I can do for you?" The man's voice was hoarse but not unfriendly.

"Sorry to be in your face like this," said Gurney. "This has nothing to do with you. I just need some information about the apartment next to yours."

The man looked down at the foot pressed against his door.

Gurney smiled and stepped back. "Sorry again. I'm in kind of a hurry and having a hard time finding anyone to talk to."

"About what?"

"Simple stuff. Like who's been living in this building the longest?"

"Why?"

"I'm looking for people who were here eight, nine months ago."

"Eight, nine months. Hmm." He blinked for the first time. "That'd be round about the time of the Big Bang, wouldn't it?"

"If you mean the shooting, yes."

The man stroked his chin as if he had a goatee. "You looking for Freddie?"

At first the name meant nothing. Then Gurney remembered seeing the name Frederico something-or-other in the trial transcript. "You mean the Freddie who said he saw Kay Spalter in this building on the morning of the shooting?"

"Only Freddie that ever sat his ass here."

"Why would I be looking for him?"

"'Cause of the fact he's missing. Why else?"

"Missing since when?"

"Like, you don't know that? That a joke? Man, who the fuck are you, anyway?"

"Just a guy who's taking a second look at everything."

"Sounds like a big job for 'just a guy.' "

"Big pain-in-the-ass job, actually."

"That's funny." He didn't smile.

"So when did Freddie go missing?"

"After he got the call." He cocked his head and gave Gurney a sideways look. "Man, I'm thinking you know this shit already."

"Tell me about the call."

"I don't know nothing about the call. Just that Freddie got it. Made it sound like it was from one of your guys."

"From a cop?"

"Right."

"And then he disappeared?"

"Yeah."

"And this was when?"

"Right after the lady got sent up."

Gurney's phone rang. He let it ring. "Did Freddie say the call was from a cop by the name of Klemper?"

"Could be."

Gurney's phone kept ringing. The ID said it was Paulette Purley. He put it back in his pocket.

"You live in this apartment?"

"Mostly."

"You going to be around later?"

"Maybe."

"Maybe we could talk again?"

"Maybe."

"My name's Dave Gurney. Can you tell me yours?"

"Bolo."

"Like the string tie?"

"No, man, not like the tie." He grinned, showing off the gold teeth again. "Like the knife."

Chapter 17

An Impossible Shot

Gurney stood at the window, phone in hand, gazing over the avenue and river at the Spalter crime scene and burial ground. He could see Paulette standing roughly in the middle of it, a blue umbrella in one hand, a phone in the other.

He backed away from the window several paces to the spot in the room where, according to the forensic photo, the rifle had been found on its tripod. He knelt down to lower his line of sight to the approximate height of the rifle scope, and spoke into his phone.

"Okay, Paulette, open the umbrella and place it where you remember Carl's body lying."

He watched as she did it, wishing he'd brought his binoculars. Then he looked down at the police sketch of the scene that he had on the floor in front of him. It showed two positions for Carl: the spot where he was standing when he was hit and the spot where he fell to the ground. Both positions were between his mother's open grave in front and two rows of folding chairs in back. There was a number written on the sketch by each of the sixteen chairs, presumably keying them to a separate list of the mourners who had occupied them.

"Paulette, can you recall by any chance who was sitting where?"

"Of course. I can still see it like it happened this morning. Every detail. Like that trickle of blood on the side of his head. That drop of blood on the snow. God, will that ever go away?"

Gurney had memories like that. Every cop did. "Maybe not completely. But it'll come to you less frequently." He neglected to mention that the reason some memories like that had faded in his own mind was because they'd been pushed aside by more terrible ones.

"But tell me about the people sitting in the chairs, especially those in the first row."

"Before he stood up, Carl was on the end. That would be on the right side of the row, looking from where you are now. Next to him, his daughter, Alyssa. Next to her, an empty chair. Next to that, Mary Spalter's three female cousins from Saratoga, all in their seventies. Actually triplets, and still dressing alike. Cute, or weird, depending on your point of view. Then another empty chair. And in the eighth chair, Jonah—as far from Carl as he could get. No surprise there."

"And the second row?"

"The second row was taken by eight ladies from Mary Spalter's retirement community. I believe they were all members of some organization there. Oh . . . what was it? Something odd. Elder something . . . Elder Force—that was it."

"Elder Force? What kind of organization is that?"

"I'm not sure. I spoke to one of the ladies briefly. Something about . . . give me a second. Yes. They have a motto, or saying, as I recall. 'Elder Force: It's Never Too Late to Do Good.' Or words to that effect. I got the impression that they were involved in some sort of charitable activities. Mary Spalter had been a member."

He made a mental note to look up Elder Force on the Internet. "Do you know if anyone had expected Kay to be at the funeral, or expressed surprise that she wasn't?"

"I didn't hear anyone ask about it. Most people who knew the Spalters were aware there was a problem—that Kay and Carl were separated."

"Okay. So Carl was at one end of the row, Jonah at the other?"

"Yes."

"How long after Carl got up from his chair was he hit?"

"I don't know. Four or five seconds? I can picture him standing up . . . turning to walk to the podium . . . taking one, two steps . . . and that's when it happened. As I said, everyone thought he tripped. But that's what you *would* think, isn't it? Unless you heard a gunshot, but nobody did."

"Because of the firecrackers?"

"Oh, God, yes, the firecrackers. Some idiot had been setting them off all morning. It was such a distraction."

"Okay. So you remember Carl taking one or two steps. Could you go to the spot you recall Carl reaching at the moment he started to collapse?"

"That's easy enough. He was passing directly in front of Alyssa."

Gurney could see her moving maybe eight or ten feet to the right of the umbrella on the ground.

"Here," she said.

He squinted, making sure he was seeing her position clearly. "Are you positive?"

"Positive this is the spot? Absolutely!"

"You have that much faith in your memory?"

"I do, but it's not just that. It's the way we always arrange the chairs. They're set up in rows the same length as the grave itself, so everyone can face it without turning. We add as many rows as we need, but the orientation of the chairs to the grave is always the same."

Gurney said nothing, was just trying to absorb what he was hearing and seeing. Then a question occurred to him that had been at the back of his mind ever since his first reading of the incident report. "I was wondering about something. The Spalter family had a high profile. I assume they were socially well connected. So—"

"Why was the funeral so modest? Is that what you're wondering?"

"Fourteen mourners, if I'm counting right, aren't many under the circumstances."

"That was the decedent's choice. I was told that Mary Spalter had added a codicil to her will naming the individuals she wanted with her at the end."

"You mean at her interment?"

"Yes. Her three cousins, two sons, granddaughter, and the eight women from Elder Force. I think the family—Carl, actually—was planning a much larger memorial event to occur sometime later, but ... well ..." Her voice trailed off. After a moment's silence, she asked, "Is there anything else?"

"One last question. How tall was Carl?"

"How tall? Six-one, maybe six-two. Carl could look intimidating. Why do you ask?"

"Just trying to picture the scene as accurately as I can."

"Okay. Is that it, then?"

"I think so, but . . . if you don't mind, just stand where you are for a minute. I want to check something." Keeping his eyes fixed on Paulette as best he could, Gurney rose from his kneeling position—where the rifle had been found on its tripod. He moved slowly to his left as far as he could go and still manage to maintain a line of sight to Paulette through one of the apartment's two windows. He repeated this, moving as far as he could to the right. After that he went to the windows, stepping up on each windowsill in turn, to see as much as he could see.

When he got down, he thanked Paulette for her help, told her he'd be talking to her again soon, ended the call, and put the phone back in his pocket. Then he stood for a long while in the middle of the room, trying to make sense of a situation that suddenly made no sense at all.

There was a problem with the light pole on the far side of Axton Avenue. The horizontal cross-member was in the way. If Carl Spalter was anywhere near six feet tall and had been standing anywhere near the spot Paulette had indicated, there was no way the fatal shot to his head could have come from that apartment.

The apartment where the murder weapon was found.

The apartment where the BCI evidence team found gunpowder residues that matched the factory loading of a .220 Swift cartridge—which was consistent with the recovered rifle and consistent with the bullet fragments extracted from Carl Spalter's brain.

The apartment where an eyewitness placed Kay Spalter on the morning of the shooting.

The apartment where Gurney now stood, mystified.

Chapter 18

A Question of Gender

Bafflement has the power to bring some men to a dead stop. It had the opposite effect on Gurney. An apparent contradiction—the shot could not have been fired through the window through which it must have been fired—affected him like amphetamine.

There were things he wanted to check immediately in the case file. Rather than stay in the bare apartment, he took the big manila envelope back down to the car, opened it on the front seat, and began flipping through the original incident report. It was structured in two sections, following the split location of the crime scene—the victim site and the shooter site—with separate strings of photos, descriptions, interviews, and evidence-collection reports for each site.

The first thing that struck him was a peculiar omission. There was no mention in the incident report, or in any follow-up report, of the light pole obstruction. There was a telephoto picture of the Spalter gravesite area taken through the apartment window, but in the absence of a scaled reference marker for Carl's position at the moment he was struck, the line-of-sight problem was not obvious.

Gurney soon found another equally peculiar omission. There was no mention of security videos. Surely someone had checked for their presence in and around the cemetery, as well as on Axton Avenue. It was hard to believe that such a routine procedure could have been overlooked, and even harder to believe that it had been conducted without any record of the outcome being entered in the file.

He slipped the case file under his front seat, got out of the car, and locked the doors. Looking up and down the block, he saw only three storefront businesses that appeared to actually be in business. The former RadioShack, which now seemed to have no name at all; River Kings Pizza; and something called Dizzy Daze, which had a show window full of inflated balloons but no other indication of what they might be selling.

The closest to him was the no-name electronics store. As Gurney approached it, he saw two hand-printed signs in the glass door: *"Refurbed Tablet Computers from $199"* and *"Will Return 2PM."* Gurney glanced at his watch. It was 2:09. He tried the door. It was locked. He was starting toward River Kings, with the added goal of buying a Coke and a couple of slices, when a pristine yellow Corvette pulled up to the curb. The couple who emerged from it were less pristine. The man was in his late forties, thickly built, with more hair on his arms than on his head. The woman was a bit younger, with spiky blue and blond hair, a broad Slavic face, and huge breasts straining against the buttons of a half-open pink sweater. As she struggled revealingly out of the low-slung seat, the man went to the electronics store door, unlocked it, and looked back at Gurney. "You want something?" The guttural, heavily accented question was as much a challenge as an invitation.

"Yes. But it's kind of complicated."

The man shrugged and gestured to the woman, who'd finally freed herself from the grip of the car. "Talk to Sophia. Got something I need to do." He went inside, leaving the door open behind him.

Sophia walked past Gurney into the store. "Always got something needs to do." The voice was as Slavic as the cheekbones. "What I can be helping you?"

"How long have you had this store?"

"Long? He had it years, years, years. What you want?"

"You have security cameras?"

"Secure?"

"Cameras that photograph people in the store, on the street, coming in, leaving, maybe shoplifting."

"Shoplifting?"

"Stealing from you."

"Me?"

"Stealing from the store."

"From the store. Yes. Fucking bastards try to steal the store."

"So you have video cameras watching?"

"Video. Yes."

"Were you here nine months ago when the famous Carl Spalter shooting happened?"

"Sure. Famous. Right here. Fucking bastard wife upstairs shoot him over there." Sophia gestured broadly in the direction of Willow Rest. "Mother's funeral. *Own mother.* You think of that?" She shook her head as if to say that a bad deed done at a mother's funeral should earn the doer double the pain in hell.

"How long do you keep the security tapes or digital files?"

"Long?"

"How much time? For how many weeks or months? Do you retain any of what's recorded, or is it all periodically erased?"

"Usually erase. Not fucking bastard wife."

"You have copies of your security videos from the day Spalter was shot?"

"Cop took all, nothing left. Lot of money could have been. Big fucking bastard cop."

"A cop took your security videos?"

"Sure."

Sophia was standing behind a counter display of cell phones that formed a loose U shape around her. Behind the U was a half-open door that Gurney could see led to a messy office. He could hear a man's voice on the phone but couldn't make out the words.

"He never brought them back?"

"Never. On video man got bullet in the brain. You know what money TV gives for that?"

"Your video showed the man getting shot in the cemetery across the river?"

"Sure. Camera out front sees everything. Hi-def. Even background. Best quality. All function is automatic. Cost plenty."

"The cop who took—"

The door behind her opened wider and the hairy man came out into the counter area.

His expression was deepening the lines of suspicion and resentment that shaped his features.

"Nobody took nothing," he said. "Who are you?"

Gurney gave the man a flat stare. "Special investigator looking into the state police handling of the Spalter case. Did you have any direct contact with a detective by the name of Mick Klemper?"

The man's expression remained steady. Too steady, too long. Then he shook his head slowly. "Got no memory of that."

"Was Mick Klemper the 'big fucking bastard cop' that the lady here says took your security videos and never returned them?"

He gave her a look of exaggerated confusion. "What the fuck you talking about?"

She returned his look with an exaggerated shrug. "Cops didn't take nothing?" She smiled innocently at Gurney. "So I guess they didn't. Wrong again. Very often. Maybe had too much drink. Harry knows, remembers better than me. Right, Harry?"

Hairy Harry grinned at Gurney, his eyes like gleaming black marbles. "See? Like I said: Nobody took nothing. You go now. Unless you want to buy a TV. Big screen. Internet-ready. Good prices."

Gurney grinned back. "I'll think about that. What would a good price be?"

Harry turned his palms up. "Depends. Supply and demand. Life so much fucking auction, you know this what I mean? But good price anyways for you. Always good prices for policemans."

D own the avenue, upon closer inspection, the store with the balloon display didn't seem to be in business after all. The slanting sun had illuminated the window in a way that made it seem full of bright lights. And the coverage of the single security camera at the River Kings pizzeria was limited to a ten-foot square around the cash register. So unless the killer had been hungry, there wasn't anything to be learned there.

But the electronics store situation had put Gurney's brain into overdrive. If he had to pick a best guess, it would be that Klemper had discovered something inconvenient in the security video and decided to make it disappear. If so, there could have been a number of ways of keeping Harry's mouth shut. Maybe Klemper knew the electronics store was a front for some other activity. Or maybe he knew things about Harry that Harry didn't want other people to know.

Gurney reminded himself, however, that best guesses were still only guesses. He decided to move on to the next question. If the bullet couldn't have come from that particular apartment, where might it have come from? He looked across the little river to Paulette's blue umbrella, still open to mark the spot where Carl had fallen.

Examining the facades of the buildings along the avenue, he saw that the bullet might have been fired from virtually any one of forty or fifty windows facing in the direction of Willow Rest. Without a way of prioritizing them, they'd pose quite an investigative challenge. But what was the point? If gunpowder residue consistent with a .220 Swift cartridge had been found in the first apartment, then the .220 rifle had to have been fired there. Was he to believe that it had been fired at Carl Spalter from another apartment, then brought to the "impossible" apartment, fired again, and left there on its tripod? If so, the other apartment would have to be very close by.

The closest, of course, would be the one next door. The apartment occupied by the little man who called himself Bolo. Gurney entered the building lobby, took the stairs two at a time, went directly to Bolo's door, and knocked softly.

There was a sound of feet moving quickly, something sliding— maybe a drawer opening, closing—a door being shut, then feet moving again just inside the door where Gurney stood. Instinctively he stepped to the side, standard procedure when there was reason to suspect an unfriendly welcome. For the first time since arriving in Long Falls he questioned the wisdom of coming unarmed.

He reached over and knocked again, very gently. "Hey, Bolo, it's me."

He heard the sharp clicks of two deadbolts, and the door opened about three inches—only as far as its two chains permitted.

Bolo's face appeared behind the opening. "Holy shit. You're back. Guy who came to take a look at everything. *Everything* is one big lot of shit, man. What now?"

"Long story. Can I take a look out your window?"

"That's funny."

"Can I?"

"True? No shit? You want to look out my window?"

"It's important."

"I heard a lot of hot-shit lines, man, but that's a good one." He closed the door, undid the chains, opened it again, wider. He was wearing a yellow basketball jersey that came down to his knees and maybe nothing else. " 'Can I look out your window?' I got to remember that one." He stepped back to let Gurney in.

The apartment appeared to be the twin of the one next to it. Gurney looked into the kitchen, then down the short opposite hall where the bathroom was. The door was closed.

"You have visitors?" asked Gurney.

The gold teeth appeared once more. "One visitor. She don't want nobody to see her." He pointed to the windows on the far side of the main room. "You want to look out? Go look."

Gurney was uncomfortable with the closed bathroom door, didn't want that kind of an unknown behind him. "Maybe later." He stepped back into the open doorway, positioning himself at an angle that allowed him to be equally aware of any movement in the apartment or on the landing.

Bolo nodded with an appreciative wink. "Sure. Got to be careful. No dark alley for you, man. Smart."

"Tell me about Freddie."

"Told you. He disappeared. You lie down with a fucker, you gonna get fucked. Bigger the fucker, worse you get fucked."

"Freddie testified at Kay Spalter's trial that she was in the apartment next to yours on the day her husband was shot. You knew he said that, right?"

"Everybody knew."

"But you didn't see Kay yourself?"

"Thought *maybe* I saw her, somebody *like* her."

"What does that mean?"

"What I told the other cop."

"I want to know it from you."

"I saw a small . . . small *person*, looked pretty much like a woman. Small, thin. Like a dancer. There's a word for that. *Petite*. You know that word? Some hot-shit word. You surprised I know that word?"

"You say 'looked like a woman'? But you're not sure it *was* a woman?"

"The first time, I thought it was. But hard to tell. Sunglasses. Big headband. Big scarf."

"The *first* time? How many times—"

"Twice. I told the other cop."

"She was here *twice*? When was the first time?"

"Sunday. The Sunday before the funeral."

"You're sure about the day?"

"Had to be Sunday. Was my only day off. From the fucking car wash. I am going out to Quik-Buy for cigarettes, going down the stairs. This *petite* person coming up the stairs, passes me, right? At the bottom of the stairs I think I don't have my money. I come back up to get it. Now she's standing there, outside the door, behind where you stand now. I go straight into my place for my money."

"You didn't ask her what she was doing here, who she was looking for?"

A sharp little laugh burst out of him. "Shit, man, no. Here you don't better bother nobody. Everybody got their own business. Don't like questions."

"She went into that apartment? How? With a key?"

"Yeah. A key. Of course."

"How do you know she had a key?"

"I heard it. Thin walls. Cheap. Key opening the door. Easy sound to know. Hey, that reminds me, definitely had to be Sunday. Ding-dong. Church down the river, twelve o'clock every Sunday. Ding-dong, ding-dong. Twelve fucking ding-dongs."

"You saw this small person again?"

"Yeah. Not that day. Not until shooting day."

"What did you see?"

"This time it's Friday. Morning. Ten o'clock. Before I go to the car wash. I'm out, coming back with pizza."

"At ten in the morning?"

"Yeah, good breakfast. I'm coming back, I see this little person go into this building. Same little person. *Petite*. Goes in very fast, with a box, or something bright, wrapped up. When I come in, little person is at top of the stairs, pretty sure now it's a wrapped-up box, like for Christmas. Long box—three, four feet long. Christmas paper. When I get to the top of the stairs, the little person is already inside the apartment, but the door is still open."

"And?"

"Little person is in the bathroom, I am thinking. That's why this big rush, maybe why the outside door is still open."

"And?"

"And it's true, little person is in the bathroom taking a big leak. Then I know for sure."

"Know what?"

"The sound."

"What do you mean?"

"It wasn't right."

"What wasn't right?"

"Men and women, the sound is different when they piss. You know this."

"And what you heard was . . . ?"

"Absolutely sound of pissing man. Little man, maybe. But absolutely man."

Chapter 19

Crime and Punishment

After getting from Bolo his legal name (Estavio Bolocco), as well as his cell number and a more detailed description of the petite he-she-whatever creature, Gurney went back down to his car and spent another half hour searching the case file for any record of an Estavio Bolocco having been interviewed, for any note regarding the appearance in the apartment of a possible suspect on the Sunday prior to the shooting, or for any question being raised regarding the shooter's gender.

He came up with zero on all three searches.

His eyelids were starting to feel heavy, and the burst of energy he'd felt earlier was just about expended. It had been a long day in Long Falls, and it was time to head for Walnut Crossing. As he was about to pull away from the curb, a black Ford Explorer pulled in just in front of him. Chunky Frank McGrath stepped out and walked back to Gurney's car window.

"You all done here?"

"For today, anyway. I need to get home before I fall asleep. By the way, do you recall back around the time of the shooting a guy by the name of Freddie living here?"

"Squatting here, you mean?"

"Yeah, I guess that's what I mean."

"Fre-de-ri-co." McGrath's dragged-out Spanish accent reeked of contempt. "What about him?"

"Did you know he disappeared?"

"Maybe I did. Long time ago."

"You ever hear anything about it?"

"Like what?"

"Like *why* he disappeared."

"Why the hell would I care about that? They come and go. One less sack of shit for me to deal with. Nice if they all disappeared. Make that happen, I'll owe you one."

Gurney tore half a sheet of paper out of his notebook, wrote his cell number on it, and handed it to McGrath. "If you hear anything about Freddie, any rumor of where he might be, I'd appreciate a call. In the meantime, Frank, take it easy. Life is short."

"Thank Christ for small favors!"

For most of his drive home, Gurney felt as though he'd opened a puzzle box and discovered that several large pieces were missing. The one thing he was sure of was that no round fired from the apartment in question could have struck Carl Spalter in the temple without first passing through the metal arm of that light pole. And that was inconceivable. No doubt the missing puzzle pieces would eventually resolve the apparent contradiction. If only he knew what sort of pieces he was looking for, and how many.

The two-hour drive home to Walnut Crossing was mostly over secondary roads, through the rolling patchwork landscape of fields and woods that Gurney liked and Madeleine loved. But he noticed very little of it.

He was immersed in the world of the murder.

Immersed—until, at the end of the gravelly town road, he passed his pond and turned up his pasture lane. That's when he was jarred into the present by the sight of four visiting cars—three Priuses and one Range Rover—parked in the grassy area alongside the house. It looked like a mini convention of the environmentally responsible and extravagantly countrified.

Oh, Jesus. The damn yoga club dinner!

He glanced at the time—6:49 p.m.—on the dashboard clock. Forty-nine minutes late. He shook his head, frustrated at his forgetfulness.

When he entered the big ground-floor space that served as kitchen, dining room, and sitting area, there was an energetic conversation in progress at the dining table. The six guests were familiar—they were people he'd been introduced to at local concerts and art shows—but he wasn't sure of any of their names. (Madeleine had once pointed out, however, that he never forgot the names of murderers.)

Everyone looked up from the conversation and their food, most of them smiling or looking pleasantly curious.

"Sorry I'm late. I ran into a little difficulty."

Madeleine smiled apologetically. "Dave runs into difficulty more often than most people stop for gas."

"Actually, he arrived at exactly the right time!" The speaker was an ebullient, heavyset woman whom Gurney recognized as one of Madeleine's fellow counselors at the crisis center. All he could remember about her name was that it was peculiar. She went on enthusiastically, "We were talking about crime and punishment. And in walks a man whose life is all about that very subject. What could be more timely?" She pointed to an empty chair at the table with the air of a hostess welcoming the guest of honor to her party. "Join us! Madeleine told us you were off on one of your adventures, but she was pretty stingy with the details. Might it have something to do with crime and/or punishment?"

One of the male guests jogged his chair a few inches to the side to give Gurney more room to get to the empty one.

"Thanks, Scott."

"Skip."

"Skip. Right. When I see you, the name Scott always pops into my mind. I worked for years with a Scott who looked a lot like you."

Gurney chose to think of this little lie as a gesture of social kindness. It was surely preferable to the truth, which was that he had no interest in the man and less than none in remembering his name. The problem with the excuse, to which Gurney had given no thought, was that Skip was seventy-five and emaciated, with an Einstein-like explosion of unruly white hair. In what way this cadaverous member of the Three Stooges might resemble an active homicide detective was an interesting question.

Before anyone could ask it, the heavyset woman bulldozed forward. "While Dave's getting some food on his plate, shall we fill him in on our discussion?"

Gurney glanced around, concluding that a vote on that proposition might fail, but—Bingo! Her name came to him. Filomena, Mena for short—was clearly a leader, not a follower. She went on. "Skip made the point that the only purpose of prison is punishment, since rehabilitation . . . How did you put it, Skip?"

He looked pained, as if being called on by Mena to speak brought back some dreadful embarrassment from his school years. "I don't remember at the moment."

"Ah. Now I remember! You said that the only point of prison is punishment, since rehabilitation is nothing but a liberal fantasy. But then Margo said that properly focused punishment is indispensable to rehabilitation. But I'm not sure Madeleine agreed with that. And then Bruce said—"

A stern-looking gray-haired woman interrupted. "I didn't say 'punishment.' I said 'clear negative consequences.' The connotations are quite different."

"All right, then, Margo is all for clear negative consequences. But then Bruce said . . . Oh, my goodness, Bruce, what *did* you say?"

A fellow at the head of the table with a dark mustache and a tweed jacket produced a condescending smirk. "Nothing profound. I just made a minor observation that our prison system is a wretched waste of tax revenue—an absurd revolving-door institution that breeds more crime than it prevents." He sounded like a very polite, very angry man whose preferred alternative to incarceration would be execution. It was difficult to picture him immersed in yoga meditation, breathing deeply, unified with all creation.

Gurney smiled at the thought as he spooned some of the remaining vegetarian lasagna onto his plate from a serving dish in the middle of the table. "You part of the yoga club, Bruce?"

"My wife is one of the instructors, which I suppose makes me an honorary member." His tone was more sarcastic than amiable.

Two seats away, a pale ash blonde, whose only cosmetic seemed to be a shiny, transparent face cream, spoke in a voice barely above a whisper. "I wouldn't say I'm an instructor, just a member of the group." She licked her colorless lips discreetly, as if to remove invisible crumbs. "Getting back to our topic, isn't all crime really a form of mental illness?"

Her husband rolled his eyes.

"Actually, Iona, there's some fascinating new research on that," said a sweet-looking woman with a soft round face, sitting across from Gurney. "Did anyone else read the journal article about the tumors? It seems there was a middle-aged man, quite normal, no unusual problems—until he began getting overpowering urges to have sex with small children, quite out of control, with no prior history. To make a long story short, medical tests revealed a fast-growing brain tumor. The tumor was removed, and the destructive sexual obsession disappeared with it. Interesting, isn't it?"

Skip looked annoyed. "Are you saying that crime is a by-product of brain cancer?"

"I'm just saying what I read. But the article did provide references to other examples of horrendous behavior directly linked to brain abnormalities. And it does make sense, doesn't it?"

Bruce cleared his throat. "So we should assume that Bernie Madoff's Ponzi scheme was hatched in a nasty little cyst in his cerebral cortex?"

"Bruce, for goodness' sake," interjected Mena. "Patty isn't saying that at all."

He shook his head grimly. "Strikes me as a slippery path, folks. Leads to zero responsibility, doesn't it? First it was 'Satan made me do it.' Then it was 'My deprived childhood made me do it.' Now we've got this new one: 'My tumor made me do it.' Where does the excuse-making stop?"

His vehemence created an awkward silence. Mena, in what Gurney guessed was her habitual role of social director and peacemaker, tried to divert everyone's attention to a less fraught topic. "Madeleine, I heard a rumor that you were getting chickens. Is that true?"

"It's more than a rumor. There are three lovely little hens and a charmingly arrogant young rooster living temporarily in our barn. Crowing and clucking and making all sorts of wonderful little chicken sounds. They really are amazing to watch."

Mena cocked her head curiously. "Living *temporarily* in your barn?"

"They're waiting down there for their permanent home to be built—out in back of our patio." She pointed at the area outside the French doors.

"Make sure the coop is secure," said Patty with worried smile. "Because all sorts of creatures prey on chickens, and the poor things are nearly defenseless."

Bruce leaned forward in his chair. "You know about the weasel problem?"

"Yes, we know all about that," said Madeleine quickly, as if to ward off any description of how weasels kill chickens.

He lowered his voice, seemingly for dramatic effect. "Possums are worse."

Madeleine blinked. "Possums?"

Iona stood up abruptly, excused herself, and headed for the restroom in the hallway.

"Possums," he repeated ominously. "They look like bumbling little creatures with a tendency to end up as roadkill. But let one into a chicken coop? You'll see a completely different animal—crazed by the taste of blood." He looked around the table as if he were telling a horror story to children around a midnight campfire. "That harmless little possum will tear every chicken in that coop to pieces. As though his true purpose in life was to rip every living thing around him to bloody shreds."

There was a stunned silence, broken finally by Skip. "Of course, possums aren't the only problem." This, perhaps due to its timing or tone, provoked bursts of laughter. But Skip went on earnestly. "You have to watch out for coyotes, foxes, hawks, eagles, raccoons. Lots of things out there like to eat chickens."

"Fortunately, there's a simple solution to all those problems," said Bruce with peculiar relish. "A nice twelve-gauge shotgun!"

Apparently sensing that her diversion of the conversation into the world of chickens was a mistake, Mena attempted a U-turn. "I'd like to get back to where we were when Dave walked into the room. I'd love to hear his perspective on crime and punishment in our society today."

"Me too," enthused Patty. "I'd especially like to hear what he has to say about evil."

Gurney swallowed a bite of lasagna and stared at her cherubic face. "Evil?"

"Do you believe there is such a thing?" she asked. "Or is it a fictional concept like witches and dragons?"

He found the question irritating. "I think 'evil' can be a useful word."

"So you do believe in it," interjected Margo from the other end of the table, sounding like a debater scoring a hostile point.

"I'm aware of a common human experience for which 'evil' is a useful word."

"What experience would that be?"

"Doing what you know in your heart to be wrong."

"Ah," said Patty with an approving light in her eyes. "There was a famous yogi who said, 'The handle on the razor of evil cuts more deeply than its blade.'"

"Sounds like a fortune cookie to me," said Bruce. "Try telling it to the victims of the Mexican drug lords."

Iona looked at him with no discernible emotion. "It's like a lot of those sayings. 'The harm I do to you, twice that much I do to me.' There are so many ways of talking about karma."

Bruce shook his head. "Far as I'm concerned, karma's a crock. If a murderer has already done twice as much damage to himself as to the one he's murdered—which seems like a pretty neat trick—does that mean that you shouldn't bother to convict and execute him? That puts you in a ridiculous position. If you believe in karma, there's no point in bothering to arrest and punish murderers. But if you want murderers arrested and punished, then you have to agree that karma's a crock."

Mena jumped in happily. "So we're back to the issue of crime and punishment. Here's my question for Dave. In America we seem to be losing faith in our criminal justice system. You worked in that world for over twenty years, right?"

He nodded.

"You know its weak points and strong points, what works and what doesn't. So you must have some pretty good ideas about what needs to change. I'd love to hear your thoughts."

The question was about as appealing to him as an invitation to do a jig on the table. "I don't think change is possible."

"But there's so much wrong," said Skip, leaning forward. "So many opportunities for improvement."

Patty, on a different wavelength, said pleasantly, "Swami Shishnapushna used to say that detectives and yogis were brothers in different garments, equal seekers after the truth."

Gurney looked doubtful. "I'd like to think of myself as a seeker of truth, but I'm probably just an exposer of lies."

Patty's eyes widened, appearing to find something more profound in this than Gurney had intended.

Mena tried to get things back on point. "So, if you could take over the system tomorrow, Dave, what would you change?"

"Nothing."

"I can't believe that. It's such an obvious mess."

"Of course it's a mess. But every piece of the mess benefits someone in power. And it's a mess nobody wants to think about."

Bruce waved his hand dismissively. "Eye for an eye, tooth for a tooth. Simple! Thinking's not the solution, it's the problem."

"A kick in the balls for a kick in the balls!" cried Skip with an addled grin.

Mena pursued her point with Gurney. "You said you wouldn't change anything. Why not?"

He hated conversations like this. "You know what I *really* think about our wretched criminal justice system? I think the terrible truth is that it's as good as it's going to get."

That created the longest silence of the evening. Gurney focused on his lasagna.

The pale Iona, a frown contending with her Mona Lisa smile, was the first to speak. "I have a question. One that bothers me. It's been on my mind a lot lately, and I haven't been able to decide on an answer." She was gazing down at her nearly empty plate, slowly guiding a single pea across the center of it with the tip of her knife.

"This may sound silly, but it's serious. Because I think a totally honest answer would reveal a lot about a person. So it bothers me that I can't decide. What does that kind of indecision say about me?"

Bruce tapped his fingertips impatiently on the table. "For God-sake, Iona, get to the point."

"Okay. Sorry. Here it is. Suppose you had to choose. Would you rather be a murderer . . . or his victim?"

Bruce's eyebrows shot up. "Are you asking *me*?"

"No, dear, of course not. I already know what your answer would be."

Part Two
Peter Pan

Chapter 20

Disturbing Discrepancies

After the dinner guests departed—Bruce and Iona in their massive Range Rover, the others in their silent Priuses—Madeleine began cleaning up and straightening up, and Gurney went into the den with the Spalter case file. He extracted the autopsy report, then turned on the slick retina-display tablet that his son, Kyle, had given him for Father's Day.

He spent the next half hour on a succession of neurological websites, trying to make sense of the disconnect between the nature of Carl Spalter's head wound and the ten or twelve feet that Paulette claimed he staggered before collapsing.

Gurney had the unhappy advantage of having witnessed, more closely than he would have liked, two similar head shots during his years in NYPD Homicide; in both instances the victims had fallen like axed trees. Why hadn't Carl?

Two explanations occurred to him.

One was that the ME was wrong about the extent of the brain tissue trauma, and that the motor center had not been completely destroyed by the fragmenting bullet. The second explanation was that Carl was shot not once but twice. The first bullet sent him staggering to the ground. The second bullet, to the temple, did the severe neural damage found during the autopsy. The obvious problem with that theory was that the ME found only one entry wound. Admittedly, a .220 Swift could make a very neat puncture, or a very narrow grazing line—but surely nothing subtle enough for a pathologist to miss, unless he was seriously rushed. Or distracted. Distracted by what?

As Gurney pondered this, another aspect of Paulette's mini-reenactment was eating at him—that the ultimately fatal scenario was played out within arm's reach of two individuals who could benefit enormously from Carl's death. Jonah, who would achieve full control of Spalter Realty. And Alyssa, the spoiled druggy in line to inherit her father's personal estate—assuming Kay could be gotten out of the way, as in fact she had been.

Jonah and Alyssa. He had a growing interest in meeting them both. And Mick Klemper, as well. He needed to get face-to-face with that man soon. And maybe Piskin, the prosecutor, as well—to get a sense of where he stood in this fog of contradictions, shaky evidence, and possible perjury.

There was a crash in the kitchen. He grimaced.

Funny thing about crashes in the kitchen. He once considered them an indicator of Madeleine's state of mind, until he realized that his interpretation of them was really an indicator of his own state of mind. When he believed he'd given her a reason to be less than delighted with him, he heard the crash of dishes as a symptom of her annoyance. But if he felt that he'd been behaving thoughtfully, the same dropped dishes would seem a harmless accident.

That night he wasn't comfortable with his having been nearly an hour late for dinner, or with his inability to remember the names of her friends, or with his leaving her in the kitchen and scurrying off to the den as soon as the last set of taillights receded down the hill.

He realized this last offense was still correctable. After making a few final notes from the most extensive of the neurological websites he'd come upon, he shut down the tablet, put the autopsy report away with the case file, and went out to the kitchen.

Madeleine was just closing the dishwasher door. He went to the coffeemaker on the sink island, set it up, and pushed the BREW button. Madeleine picked up a sponge and a towel and began wiping the countertops.

"Odd bunch of people," he said lightly.

" 'Interesting' people might be a nicer way to put it."

He cleared his throat. "I hope they weren't taken aback by what I said about the criminal justice system."

The coffeemaker emitted the whooshing-spitting sound that ended its cycle.

"It's not so much *what* you said. Your tone has a way of conveying a lot more than your words."

"More? Like what?"

She didn't answer right away. She was leaning over the counter, scrubbing a recalcitrant stain. He waited. She straightened up and brushed a few dangling hairs away from her face with the back of her hand. "Sometimes you sound annoyed at having to spend time with people, listen to them, talk to them."

"It's not exactly that I'm annoyed. It's . . ." He sighed, his voice trailing off. He took his cup from under the dispensing spout of the coffeemaker, added sugar, and stirred the coffee a lot longer than it needed to be stirred before completing his explanation. "When I get involved in something intense, I find it difficult to switch back to ordinary life."

"It *is* difficult," she replied. "I *know*. I think sometimes you forget what kind of work I do at the clinic, what kind of problems I deal with."

He was about to point out that those problems didn't usually involve murder, but he caught himself in time. She had the look in her eyes that meant an unfinished thought, so he just stood silently, holding his coffee cup, waiting for her to go on—expecting her to describe some of the more appalling realities of a rural crisis center.

But she took a different tack. "Maybe I can disengage more easily than you can because I'm not as good at what I do."

He blinked. "What do you mean?"

"When someone has a great talent for something, there's a temptation to focus on it to the exclusion of virtually everything else. Don't you find that to be true?"

"I suppose," he replied, wondering where this was going.

"Well, I think you have a great talent for figuring things out, for unraveling deceptions, solving complicated crimes. And maybe you're so good at it, so comfortable in that particular way of thinking, that the rest of life seems like an uncomfortable interruption." She searched his face for a reaction.

He knew there was truth in what she was saying, but all he could manage was a noncommittal shrug.

She went on in a soft voice. "I don't see myself as having a huge talent for my work. I've been told I'm good at it, but it's not the sum and substance of my life. It's not the only thing that matters. I try to treat *everything* in my life as though it matters. Because it does. You, most of all." She looked into his eyes and smiled in that odd way of hers that seemed to have less to do with her mouth than with some internal source of radiance.

"Sometimes when we talk about your absorption in a case, it turns into an argument—maybe because you feel that I'm trying to transform you from a detective into a hiking, biking kayaker. That might have been a hope or fantasy of mine when we first moved up here to the mountains, but it's not anymore. I understand who you are, and I'm content with that. More than content. I know sometimes it doesn't seem that way. It seems like I'm pushing, pulling, trying to change you. But that's not what it is."

She paused, seeming to read his thoughts and feelings more clearly than he could. "I'm not trying to turn you into someone you're not. I just feel that you'd be happier if you could let some brightness, some variety, into your life. It looks to me like you keep rolling the same boulder up the same hill again and again, without any lasting relief or reward at the end. It looks like all you want is to keep pushing, keep struggling, keep putting yourself in danger—the more danger, the better."

He was about to object to her point about danger, but decided instead to hear her out.

She looked at him, sadness filling her eyes. "It looks like you get so deeply into it, into the darkness, that it blots out the sun. It blots out everything. So I go about my life the only way I know how. I do my work at the clinic. I walk in the woods. I go to my concerts. Art shows. I read. Play my cello. Ride my bike. I take care of the garden and the house and the chickens. In the winter I snowshoe. I visit my friends. But I keep thinking—wishing—that we could be doing more of these things together. That we could be out in the sun together."

He didn't know how to respond. At some level he recognized the truth in what she was saying, but no words were attaching themselves to the feeling it generated in him.

"That's it," she concluded simply. "That's what's on my mind."

The sadness in her eyes was replaced by a smile—warm, open, hopeful.

It seemed to him that she was totally *present*—that *all* of her was

right there in front of him, with no obstructions, no evasions, no arti-
fice of any kind. He put down his cup, which he'd been holding without realizing it all the while she was talking, and stepped toward her.
He put his arms around her, feeling all her body warm against his.

Still without words, he picked her up in the clichéd manner of
new-bride-over-the-threshold—which made her laugh—and carried
her into the bedroom, where they made love with an intensely wonderful combination of urgency and tenderness.

Madeleine was up first the next morning.
        After Gurney had showered, shaved, and dressed, he found
her at the breakfast table with her coffee, a slice of toast with peanut
butter, and an open book. Peanut butter was one of her favorite things.
He went over and kissed the top of her head.

"Good morning!" she said cheerily through a mouthful of toast.
She was dressed for her work at the clinic.

"Full day today?" he asked. "Or half?"

"Dunno." She swallowed, took a sip of coffee. "Depends on who
else is there. What's on *your* agenda?"

"Hardwick. Due here at eight-thirty."

"Oh?"

"We're getting a phone call from Kay Spalter at nine, or as close to
that as she can manage."

"Problem?"

"Nothing *but* problems. Every fact in this case has a contradiction
attached to it."

"Isn't that the way you like your facts?"

"Hopelessly tangled up, you mean, so I can untangle them?"

She nodded, took a final bite of her toast, took her plate and cup
to the sink, and let the water run on them. Then she came back and
kissed him. "Running late. Got to go."

He made himself some bacon and toast and settled down in a chair
by the French doors. Softened by a thin morning fog, the view from
his chair was of the old pasture, a tumbledown stone wall along its far
side, one of his neighbors' overgrown fields, and, barely visible beyond
that, Barrow Hill.

Just as he popped the last bit of bacon in his mouth, the rumble of Hardwick's GTO became audible from the road below the barn. Two minutes later, the angular red beast was parked by the asparagus patch and Hardwick was standing at the French doors, wearing a black T-shirt and dirty gray sweatpants. The doors were open wide, but the sliding screens were latched.

Gurney leaned over and unlatched one.

Hardwick stepped inside. "You know there's a giant fucking pig strolling up your road?"

Gurney nodded. "It's a fairly frequent occurrence."

"A good three hundred pounds, I'd say."

"Tried to lift it, did you?"

Hardwick ignored the question, just looked around the room appraisingly. "I've said it before and I'll say it again. You've got a shit-load of country charm here."

"Thank you, Jack. Care to sit down?"

Hardwick picked thoughtfully at his front teeth with his fingernail, then plopped down in the chair across the table from Gurney and eyed him suspiciously. "Before we speak to the bereaved Mrs. Spalter, ace, you have anything on your mind we need to discuss?"

"Not really—apart from the fact that nothing in the case makes a damn bit of sense."

Hardwick's eyes narrowed. "These things that don't make sense . . . do they work *for* us or *against* us?"

" 'Us'?"

"You know what I mean. For or against our objective of securing a reversal."

"Probably *for* the objective. But I'm not positive. Too many things are screwy."

"Screwy? Like how?"

"Like the apartment ID'd as the source of the fatal shot."

"What about it?"

"It wasn't. It couldn't have been."

"Why not?"

Gurney explained his use of Paulette to set up the informal reenactment, and his discovery of the light pole obstruction.

Hardwick looked confused but not worried. "Anything else?"

"A witness, who claims he saw the shooter."

"Freddie? The guy who fingered Kay in the lineup?"

"No. Man by the name of Estavio Bolocco. No record of his having been interviewed, although he claims he was. He also claims he saw the shooter, but it was a man, not a woman."

"Saw the shooter where?"

"That's another problem. Says he saw him in the apartment—the apartment where the shot was supposed to have come from but couldn't have."

Hardwick made his acid-reflux face. "This is adding up to a mixed pile of good stuff and pure shit. I like the idea that your guy says the shooter was a man, not a woman. I especially like the idea that Klemper failed to keep a record of the interview. That speaks to police misconduct, possible tampering, or at least major sloppiness, all of which helps. But that crap about the apartment itself, that crap makes everything else useless. We can't present a witness who claims the shooter used a location that we then turn around and say couldn't have been used. I mean, where the fuck are we going with this?"

"Good question. And here's another little oddity. Estavio Bolocco says he saw the shooter *twice*. Once on the day of the event itself, which was a Friday. But also five days earlier. On Sunday. He says he's positive it was Sunday, because that was his only day off."

"He saw the shooter where?"

"In the apartment."

Hardwick's indigestion appeared to be increasing. "Doing what? Casing it?"

"That would be my guess. But that raises another question. Let's assume that the shooter had learned about Mary Spalter's death, discovered the location of the Spalter family plot, and figured that Carl would be front and center at the burial service. Next step would be to scout out the vicinity, see if it offered a reasonably secure shooting position."

"So what's the question?"

"Timing. If the shooter was scouting the location on Sunday, presumably Mary Spalter's death occurred Saturday or earlier, depending on whether the shooter was close enough to the family to have gotten the information directly, or had to wait for a published obit a day or two later. My question is, if the burial didn't take place until, at the earliest, seven days after her death . . . what caused the delay?"

"Who knows? Maybe some relative couldn't arrive for it any sooner? Why do you care?"

"It's unusual to delay a funeral for a whole week. *Unusual* makes me curious, that's all."

"Right. Sure. Okay." Hardwick waved his hand like he was shooing away a fly. "We can ask Kay when she calls. I just don't think her mother-in-law's funeral arrangements sound like Court of Appeals material."

"Maybe not. But speaking of that conviction, did you know that Freddie—the guy who fingered Kay at the trial—has disappeared?"

Chapter 21

An Unsettling Frankness

It was closer to nine-thirty than nine when they got Kay Spalter's call on Gurney's landline. He put it on speakerphone in the den.

"Hey, Kay," said Hardwick. "How are things in beautiful Bedford Hills?"

"Fabulous." Her voice was rough, dry, impatient. "You there, Dave?"

"I'm here."

"You said you were going to have more questions for me?"

He wondered if her abruptness was a way of feeling in control or just a symptom of prison tension. "I've got half a dozen of them."

"Go ahead."

"Last time we spoke, you mentioned a mob guy, Donny Angel, as someone we should look at for Carl's murder. The problem is, the hit on Carl seems too complicated for that."

"What do you mean?" She sounded curious rather than challenging.

"Angel knew him, knew a lot about him. He could have put together an easier hit than a sniper shot at a cemetery service five hundred yards away. So let's assume for a minute that Angel wasn't the bad guy. If you had to come up with a second choice, who would it be?"

"Jonah." She said it without emotion and without hesitation.

"The motive being control of the family company?"

"Control would allow him to mortgage enough properties to expand the Cyberspace Cathedral into the biggest religious rip-off project in the world."

"How much do you know about this goal of his?"

"Nothing. I'm guessing. My point is, Jonah's a much bigger

sleazeball than anyone realizes, and company control means big money for him. *Big.* I do know he asked Carl about mortgaging some buildings and Carl told him to go fuck himself."

"Nice brotherly relationship. Any other candidates for killer?"

"Maybe a hundred other people whose toes Carl stomped on."

"When I asked you the other day why you stayed with him, you gave me sort of a joke answer. At least, I think it was a joke. I need to know the real reason."

"Truth is, I don't know the real reason. I used to search for that mystery glue that attached me to him, but I could never identify it. So maybe I really am a cheap gold digger."

"Are you sorry he's dead?"

"Maybe a little."

"What was your day-to-day relationship like?"

"Generous, patronizing, and controlling on his part."

"And on yours?"

"Loving, admiring, and submissive. Except when he went too far."

"And then?"

"Then all hell would break loose."

"Did you ever threaten him?"

"Yes."

"In front of witnesses?"

"Yes."

"Give me an example."

"There were quite a few."

"Give me the worst."

"On our tenth wedding anniversary, Carl invited a few other couples to have dinner with us. He drank too much and got on his favorite drunk theme: 'You can take the girl out of Brooklyn, but you can't take Brooklyn out of the girl.' And that night it escalated into some grandiose bullshit about how he was going to run for president after he became governor of New York, and how I was going to be his link to the common man. He said he was going to be like Juan Peron in Argentina, and I would be his Evita. My job would be to make all the blue-collar workers love him. He added a few sexual suggestions as to how I might go about that. And then he said this really stupid thing. He said I could buy a thousand pairs of shoes, just like Evita."

"And?"

"For some reason, that was too much. Why was it too much? No idea. But it was too much. Too stupid."

"And?"

"And I screamed at him that the lady with the thousand pairs of shoes wasn't Evita Peron, it was Imelda Marcos."

"That's it?"

"Not completely. I also said if he ever talked about me like that again, I'd cut off his dick and shove it up his ass."

Hardwick, who hadn't uttered a syllable since his question about beautiful Bedford Hills, broke out into a braying laugh, which she ignored.

Gurney switched direction. "How much do you know about silencers for guns?"

"I know that cops call them suppressors, not silencers."

"What else?"

"They're illegal in this state. They're more effective with subsonic ammunition. Cheap ones are okay—expensive ones are a lot better."

"How do you know all this?"

"I asked at the firing range where I took lessons."

"Why?"

"Same reason I was there to begin with."

"Because you thought you might have to shoot someone to protect Carl?"

"Yes."

"Did you ever buy or borrow a silencer?"

"No. They got Carl before I got around to it."

" 'They' being the mob?"

"Yes. I heard what you said about the sniper route being an odd way for them to go about it. But I still think it was them. More likely them than Jonah."

He didn't see any advantage in debating the point. He decided to go down another path. "Apart from Angel, were there any other mob figures he was close to?"

For the first time in their exchange, she hesitated.

After a few seconds Gurney thought they'd been disconnected. "Kay?"

"There was someone he used to talk about, someone who was part of a poker group he played with."

Gurney noted an uneasiness in her voice. "Did he mention a name?"

"No. He just mentioned what the guy did for a living."

"Which was?"

"He arranged murders. Sort of like a broker, a go-between. If you wanted someone killed, you'd go to him and he'd get someone to do it."

"You sound upset talking about him."

"It bothered me that Carl wanted to play in a high-stakes game with someone who did that for a living. I said to him one day, 'You really want to play poker against a guy who sets up mob hits? A guy who doesn't think twice about having someone murdered? Isn't that a little nuts?' He told me that I didn't understand. He said gambling was all about the risk and the rush. And the risk and the rush were a lot bigger when you were sitting across the table from Death." She paused. "Look, I don't have much more time. Are we done?"

"Just one more thing. How come there was such a long delay between Mary Spalter's death and her burial?"

"What delay?"

"She was buried on a Friday. But it appears that she must have died a week before that—or at least before the previous Sunday."

"What are you talking about? She died on a Wednesday and was buried two days later."

"Two days? Only *two?* You're sure about that?"

"Of course I'm sure. Look up the obituary. What's this all about?"

"I'll let you know when I find out myself." Gurney glanced over at Hardwick. "Jack, you have anything you need to cover with Kay while we have her on the phone?"

Hardwick shook his head, then spoke with exaggerated heartiness. "Kay, we'll be in touch with you again soon, okay? And don't worry. We're on the right track for the outcome we all want. Everything we're discovering here is a plus for our side."

He sounded a hell of a lot surer than he looked.

Chapter 22

The Second Bouquet

fter the Kay Spalter call ended, Hardwick maintained an uncharacteristically long silence. He stood staring out the den window, seemingly lost in a series of what-if calculations.

Gurney was sitting at his desk watching him. "Spit it out, Jack. It'll make you feel better."

"We need to talk to Lex Bincher. I mean soon. Like now. We've got some shit here we need to sort out. I'm thinking that's Priority Fucking One."

Gurney smiled. "And I'm thinking Priority One is a visit to the assisted living place where Mary Spalter died."

Hardwick turned from the window to face Gurney directly. "See? That's my point. We need to get together with Lex, sit down, have a meeting of the minds before we bust our humps chasing every wild goose that flies by."

"This one may be more than a wild goose."

"Yeah? How so?"

"Whoever was casing that apartment on a Sunday—three days before Mary Spalter died—must have known she was going to be dead very soon. Meaning her accidental death was no accident."

"Whoa, Sherlock, slow down! All of that depends on the dumbest leap of faith I've heard in a long time."

"Faith in Estavio Bolocco's story?"

"Right. Faith that some car-wash jockey, squatting in a half-gutted building, high on God knows what, can remember the exact day of the week he saw someone walk through an apartment door nine months ago."

"I'll grant you there's a witness reliability issue. But I still think—"

"You call that a *'witness reliability issue'*? I call it fucking nuts!"

Gurney spoke softly. "I hear you. I don't disagree with you. However, if—and I know it's a big if—*if* Mr. Bolocco is right about the day of the week, then the nature of the crime was completely different from the narrative proposed by the prosecutor at Kay's trial. Jesus, Jack, think about it. Why would Carl's mother have been killed?"

"This is a waste of time."

"Maybe, maybe not. Let's just say, hypothetically, that her death wasn't an accident. I can think of two ways to approach the question of why she was murdered. One, that she and Carl were both primary targets—equally in the way of the murderer's goal, whatever that might have been. Or, two, that she was only a stepping-stone—a way to ensure that Carl, the primary target, would be standing out in the open, in that cemetery, at a predictable time."

The tic was back in full force at the corner of Hardwick's mouth. Twice he started to speak and stopped. On the third try he said, "This is what you wanted from the start, right? To toss the whole fucking thing up in the air and see what happened when it hit the ground? To take a straight-ahead examination of police misconduct—something as simple as Mick the Dick, CIO, screwing potential suspect Alyssa Spalter—and turn it into the reinvention of the fucking wheel? Already you want to turn one murder into two! Tomorrow it'll be half a dozen! What the fuck are you trying to do?"

Gurney's voice grew even softer. "I'm just following the string, Jack."

"Fuck the string! Jesus! Look, I'm sure that I speak for Lex as well as myself. The point is, we need to focus, focus, focus. Let me make this clear, once and for all. There are only a handful of questions that need to be answered about the investigation of Carl Spalter's murder and the trial of Kay Spalter. One: What should Mick Klemper have done that he did not do? Two: What should Klemper *not* have done that he *did* do? Three: What did Klemper keep from the prosecutor? Four: What did the prosecutor keep from the defense attorney? Five: What should the defense attorney have done that he did *not* do? Five fucking questions. Get the right answers to those questions, and Kay Spalter's conviction gets reversed. That's it, pure and simple. So tell me, are we on the same page here?" Hardwick's high-blood-pressure complexion was deepening.

"Calm down, my friend. I'm pretty sure we can *end up* on the same page. Just don't make it impossible for me to get there."

Hardwick stared hard and long at Gurney, then shook his head in frustration. "Lex Bincher is fronting the bucks for the investigatory out-of-pockets. If you're going to spend money on anything beyond getting the answers to those five questions, he's going to need to approve it in advance."

"No problem."

"No problem," Hardwick echoed vaguely, looking back out the window. "Wish I could believe that, ace."

Gurney said nothing.

After a while Hardwick sighed wearily. "I'll fill Bincher in on everything you told me."

"Good."

"For Christ's sake, just don't . . . don't let this . . ." He didn't finish the sentence, just shook his head again.

Gurney could sense the strain inherent in Hardwick's position: desperate to get to a desired destination, horrified by the uncertainties of the proposed route.

Among the various addenda to the case file was the address for the final residence of Mary Spalter—an assisted-living complex on Twin Lakes Road in Indian Valley, not far from Cooperstown, about halfway between Walnut Crossing and Long Falls. Gurney entered the address in his GPS, and an hour later it announced that he was arriving at his destination.

He turned on to a neat macadam driveway that led through a tall drystone wall, then separated at a fork with arrows indicating KEY HOLDERS one way and VISITORS AND DELIVERIES the other way.

The latter direction brought him to a parking area in front of a cedar-shake bungalow. An elegantly understated sign next to a small rose garden bore the inscription EMMERLING OAKS. SECURE SENIOR LIFE COMMUNITY. INQUIRE WITHIN.

He parked and knocked on the door.

A pleasant female voice responded immediately. "Come in."

He entered a bright, uncluttered office. An attractive woman some-where in her forties with a tanning-bed complexion was sitting at a polished desk with several comfortable-looking chairs arrayed around it. On the walls were pictures of bungalows in various color and size variations.

After giving him an assessing once-over, the woman smiled. "How can I help you?"

He returned the smile. "I'm not sure. I drove up here on an impulse. Probably just a wild goose chase."

"Oh?" She looked interested. "What wild goose are you chasing?"

"I'm not even sure about that."

"Well, then . . ." she said with an uncertain frown. "What do you want? And who are you?"

"Oh, sorry about that. My name is Dave Gurney." He took out his wallet, a little awkwardly, and stepped forward to show her his gold shield. "I'm a detective."

She studied the shield. "It says 'Retired.' "

"I *was* retired. And now, because of this murder case, it seems that I've become un-retired."

Her eyes widened. "Are you referring to the Spalter murder case?"

"You're familiar with that?"

"Familiar?" She appeared surprised. "Of course."

"Because of the news coverage?"

"That, and the personal element."

"Because the victim's mother lived here?"

"To some extent, but . . . Would you mind telling me what this is all about?"

"I've been brought in to take a look at some aspects of the case that were never resolved."

She gave him a canny look. "Brought in by a family member?"

Gurney nodded and smiled, as if to acknowledge some acuteness on her part.

"Which one?" she asked.

"How many of them do you know?"

"All of them."

"Kay? Jonah? Alyssa?"

"Kay and Jonah, of course. Carl and Mary when they were alive. Alyssa only by name."

Gurney was about to ask her how she knew them all when the obvious answer came to mind. For some reason he hadn't immediately put the name of the place, Emmerling Oaks, together with his recollection from Willow Rest that Emmerling was Carl's grandfather's name. Apparently the family company owned more than apartment houses and cemeteries. "How do you like working for Spalter Realty?"

Her eyes narrowed. "You need to answer *my* question first. Why are you here?"

Gurney had to make a decision fast, based on what his gut told him about this woman, as he weighed the potential risks and rewards of different levels of disclosure. He had little to go on. In fact, just one tiny glimpse of something that he might very well have misread. All he had was the fleeting sense that when she'd spoken the name "Carl" she'd done it with the same distaste as Paulette Purley had.

He made his decision. "Let me put it this way," he said, lowering his voice to give it the tenor of confidentiality. "There are certain aspects of Kay Spalter's conviction that are questionable."

The woman's reaction was sudden, excited, open-mouthed. "You mean she didn't do it after all? God, I knew it!"

It encouraged him to open the door a bit wider.

"You didn't think she was capable of killing Carl?"

"Oh, she was capable of it, all right. But she'd never have done it like that."

"You mean with a rifle?"

"I mean from so far away."

"Why not?"

She cocked her head, gave him a skeptical look. "How well do you know Kay?"

"Probably not as well as you do, . . . Miss? . . . Mrs.?"

"Carol. Carol Blissy."

He extended his hand over the desk. "Nice to meet you, Carol. And I really appreciate your taking the time to speak to me." She took his hand briefly but firmly. Her fingers and palm were warm. He went on, "I'm working with her legal team. I've had one face-to-face meeting with Kay and one long phone call. Our meeting gave me a good sense of her as a person, but I have the feeling you know her much better than I do."

Carol Blissy looked pleased. She absently adjusted the neckline of the black silk blouse she was wearing. She had glittery rings on all five fingers. "When I said she'd never have done it like that, what I meant was that it wasn't her style. If you know her at all, you know that she's an in-your-face kind of person. There's nothing sneaky or long-distance about Kay. If she was going to kill Carl, she wouldn't have shot him from half a mile away. She'd have walked straight up to him and split his head with an ax."

She paused, as though listening to her own words, and made a face. "Sorry, that was disgusting. But you do understand what I mean, right?"

"I understand *exactly* what you mean. I have the same feeling about her." He paused, looked admiringly at her hand. "Carol, those rings are lovely."

"Oh?" She looked down at them. "Thank you. I guess they *are* pretty nice. I think I have a good eye for jewelry." She moistened the corners of her mouth with the tip of her tongue and looked back up at Gurney from her desk. "You know, you still haven't told me why you're here."

He had to make a choice—a choice he'd been postponing—regarding how much to reveal. There were significant risks and rewards attached to various levels of candor. In this instance, the inner picture he was developing of Carol Blissy persuaded him to go a bit further than he normally would. He had a feeling that openness would be rewarded with cooperation.

"It's a sensitive issue. Not something I could just blurt out without knowing who I was talking to." He took a deep breath. "We have some new evidence suggesting that Mary Spalter's death may not have been an accident."

"Not . . . an accident?"

"I shouldn't be saying this, but I want your help, and I need to be honest with you. I think the Spalter case was a *double* murder. And I don't think Kay had anything to do with it."

It seemed to take her a few seconds to absorb this. "You're going to get her out of prison?"

"That's my hope."

"Wonderful!"

"But I need your help."

"What kind of help?"

"I assume you have security cameras here?"

"Of course."

"How long do you retain the video files?"

"A lot longer than we need to. In the old days, we had those clunky video cassettes we had to keep recycling. But the capacity of the new system is huge, and we never physically touch it. It deletes the oldest files automatically when capacity becomes an issue, but I don't think that happens for about a year—at least not with the files from the motion-activated cameras. It's different with the files created by the cameras that run continuously in the gym and in the nursing care unit. Those deletions happen quicker."

"Are you the person in charge of making sure it's all working the way it should?"

She smiled. "I'm the person in charge of *everything*." Her ringed fingers smoothed an imaginary wrinkle on the front of her silk blouse.

"I bet you do a very good job."

"I try. What is it in our video files that interests you?"

"Visitors to Emmerling Oaks on the day Mary Spalter died."

"*Her* visitors specifically?"

"No. All visitors: delivery people, repairmen, maintenance crews— anyone who came onto the property that day."

"How soon do you want it?"

"How soon do you want Kay to get out of prison?"

Gurney knew he was implying an immediacy in results that was, charitably speaking, an exaggeration, even if the video files contained the sort of smoking gun he hoped to find.

Carol set him up at a computer in a room that occupied the rear third of the bungalow. She then went to another building and emailed several large video files to Gurney's computer. When she came back she gave him some navigation instructions, leaning over his shoulder in a way that made it hard to concentrate.

As she was about to return to the front office, he asked again as off-handedly as he could, "How do you like working for Spalter Realty?"

"I probably shouldn't say anything about that." She gave Gurney the kind of playful look that suggested she probably could be talked into any number of things she shouldn't do.

"It would help me a lot to know how you feel about the Spalter family."

"I do want to help. But . . . this is just between us, right?"

"Absolutely."

"Well . . . Kay was terrific. Hot tempered but terrific. But Carl was awful. Cold as ice. All he cared about was the bottom line. And Carl was the boss. Jonah stayed away, because Jonah wanted nothing to do with Carl."

"And now?"

"Now, with Carl gone, Jonah's in charge." She looked at Gurney cautiously. "I don't know him that well yet."

"I don't know him *at all*, Carol. But I'll tell you the things I've heard. He's a saint. He's a fake. He's a fantastic person. He's a religious nut. Is there anything you can add to any of that?"

She met Gurney's inquisitive gaze and smiled. "I don't think so." She licked the corners of her mouth again. "I'm really the wrong person to ask about guys like that. I'm not what you'd call religious."

Over the next three hours Gurney reviewed the video files from the three security cameras he considered most likely to have captured something useful—the cameras positioned to provide coverage of the parking area, of the interior of Carol Blissy's office, and of vehicles utilizing the automated entry gate for residents.

The videos from the parking area and office were the most interesting. There was a painting contractor who got Gurney's attention by seeming to play the role of a cartoon painter, stopping just short of stepping in a bucket of paint and falling on his face. There was a pizza deliveryman with wild eyes who seemed to be auditioning for the role of a teen-movie psychopath. And then there was a floral delivery person.

Gurney replayed half a dozen times the two short video segments in which that individual appeared. The first showed a dark blue minivan pulling into the parking area—nondescript, except for a sign on the driver's door: FLOWERS BY FLORENCE. The second, with audio, showed the driver entering Carol's office, announcing a delivery of flowers—chrysanthemums—for a Mrs. Marjorie Stottlemeyer, and asking for and receiving directions to her condo unit.

The driver was small and frail-looking—just how small was hard to tell from the high, distorting angle of the camera—wearing tight jeans, a leather jacket, a scarf, a headband, and wraparound sunglasses. Despite repeated viewings, Gurney couldn't say for sure whether the thin little person was a man or a woman. But something else did become clearer with each viewing: despite the mention of only one name, *two* bouquets of mums were being delivered.

He went and got Carol Blissy from the front office and replayed the segment for her.

Her mouth opened in surprise. "Oh, *that* one!" She pulled a chair over and sat quite close to Gurney. "Play it again."

When he did so, she nodded. "I remember *that* one."

"You remember . . . *him?*" asked Gurney. "Or was it a *her?*"

"Funny you should ask. That's exactly what I remember, that question in my mind. The voice, the movements, they didn't seem quite like a man's *or* a woman's."

"What do you mean?"

"More like . . . a little . . . pixie. That's it—a *pixie*. That's the closest I can come to it."

The echo of Bolo's use of the word *petite* struck Gurney. "You directed this person to a particular condo, correct?"

"Yes, to Marjorie Stottlemeyer's."

"Do you know if the flowers were actually delivered to her?"

"Yes. Because she called me later about it. There was some problem about them, but I can't remember now what it was."

"Does she still live here?"

"Oh, yes. People come here to stay. The only turnover is when a resident passes away."

Gurney wondered how many of those who passed away ended up in Willow Rest. But he had more urgent questions to resolve. "How well do you know this Stottlemeyer woman?"

"What do you want to know about her?"

"How good is her memory? And would she be willing to answer a few questions?"

Carol Blissy appeared intrigued. "Marjorie is ninety-three years old, clear as a bell, and very gossipy."

"Perfect," said Gurney, turning toward her. Her perfume was subtle, with the slightest hint of roses. "It would be a big help if you could call her, tell her that a detective has been asking questions about the person who delivered those flowers to her last November, and he'd appreciate a few minutes of her time."

"I can do that." She stood, her hand just grazing his back as she passed him on her way out to the front office.

Three minutes later she returned with the phone. "Marjorie says she's just about to take a bath, and then she's going to take her nap, and after that she'll be getting ready for dinner, but she can speak to you on the phone right now."

Gurney gave Carol a thumbs-up and took the phone. "Hello, Mrs. Stottlemeyer?"

"Call me Marjorie." Her voice was high and sharp. "Carol tells me you're after that peculiar little creature who brought me the mystery bouquet. What for?"

"It could be nothing, or it could be something quite serious. When you say he brought you a 'mystery bouquet,' what did—"

"Murder? Is that it?"

"Marjorie, I hope you understand, at this point I have to be careful about what I say."

"Then it *is* murder. Oh, my Lord! I knew there was something wrong from the beginning."

"From the beginning?"

"Those mums. I didn't order anything. There was no gift card. And anyone who ever knew me well enough to send me flowers is already senile or dead."

"Was there just one bouquet?"

"What do you mean, just *one*?"

"Just one bunch of flowers, not two?"

"Two? Why in heaven's name would I get two? One was ridiculous enough. How many admirers do you think I have?"

"Thank you, Marjorie, this is very helpful. One more question. The 'peculiar little creature,' as you put it, who delivered your flowers— was it a man or a woman?"

"I'm ashamed to say, I don't know. That's the problem with getting old. In the world I grew up in, there was a real difference between men and women. *Vive la différence!* Did you ever hear that? That's French."

"Did the creature ask you any questions?"

"About what?"

"I don't know. Any questions at all."

"No questions. Didn't say much of anything. 'Flowers for you.' Something like that. Squeaky little voice. Funny nose."

"Funny how?"

"Sharp. Like a beak."

"Anything else odd that you can remember?"

"No, that's it. Hooked beak of a nose."

"How tall?"

"My height, at the most. Maybe even an inch or two shorter."

"And your height would be . . . ?"

"Exactly sixty-two inches. Five foot two, eyes of blue. My eyes, not his. His were hidden behind sunglasses. Not a speck of sun that day, mind you. But sunglasses aren't for the sun anymore, are they? They're a fashion item. Did you know that? A *fashion* item."

"Thank you for your time, Marjorie. You've been a great help. I'll be in touch."

Gurney broke the connection and handed the phone back to Carol. She blinked. "Now I remember what the problem was."

"What problem?"

"What Marjorie called me about that day. It was to ask if the delivery person had left a gift card by mistake at the desk. Because there wasn't any with the flowers. But what was that question you were asking about the number of bouquets, whether there was one or two?"

"If you look closely at the video," said Gurney, "you'll see that those chrysanthemums were in two separate wrappings. Two bouquets were being delivered here, not one."

"I don't understand. What does that mean?"

"It means that the 'little creature' made a second stop on the property after he saw Mrs. Stottlemeyer."

"Or *before* seeing her, because she said he only had one bouquet with him."

"I'd be willing to bet that the other bouquet was stashed temporarily outside her door."

"Why?"

"Because I think our little creature came here to kill Mary Spalter, and he brought the second bouquet along to give him a cover story for knocking on her door—and to give her a reason to open it."

"I don't follow you. Why not just bring one bouquet—and tell me that he was delivering it to Mrs. Spalter? Why bring Marjorie Stottle-meyer into it at all? That doesn't make sense."

"I think it does. If there was a record in your visitors' log of a delivery being made to Mary Spalter shortly before her death, the whole affair might have been looked into more carefully. It was evidently important to the killer that Mary's death appear to be accidental. And it worked. I suspect there wasn't even a thorough autopsy."

Her mouth was open. "So . . . you're saying . . . we really did have a *murderer* here . . . in my office . . . and in Marjorie's house . . . and . . ."

Suddenly she looked vulnerable, frightened. And just as suddenly, Gurney was filled with a fear that he was doing what he'd warned himself against: He was moving much too fast. He was making assumptions on top of assumptions and mistaking them for rational conclusions. And another troubling question came to mind. Why was he spelling out his murder hypothesis to this woman? Was he trying to scare her? Observe her reaction? Or did he just want to have someone ratify the way he was connecting the dots—as if that would prove he was right?

But what if he was connecting the wrong dots, creating the wrong picture entirely? What if the so-called dots were just random isolated events? At times like this he always recalled, uneasily, that everyone on earth at a particular latitude sees the same stars in the sky. But no two cultures see the same constellations. He'd seen evidence of the phenomenon again and again: The patterns we perceive are determined by the stories we want to believe.

Chapter 23

Click

In an uncertain and uncomfortable frame of mind, Gurney pulled into the first convenience store parking lot he reached after leaving Emmerling Oaks.

He bought a large strong coffee, plus a couple of granola bars to compensate for the lunch he hadn't had, and retreated to his car. He ate one of the granola bars—which turned out to be hard, tasteless, and sticky. He tossed the other one in his glove compartment for some moment of more desperate hunger and took a few swallows of lukewarm coffee.

Then he got down to business.

Before he left Carol Blissy's office, he'd downloaded the floral delivery video files to his phone, and now he sent the office segment to Bolo's cell number with a cover text message: *"Does the little person with the flowers remind you of anyone?"*

He sent the same video material to Hardwick with a message saying: *"Individual carrying the flowers may be a person of interest in the Spalter case—a possible link between the deaths of Mary and Carl. More to come."*

He watched the parking area segment of the video again, confirming his impression of the sign on the minivan door: that it wasn't painted directly on the vehicle but was the removable magnetic kind. Also, that there was only one sign and that it was on the driver's-side door rather than the passenger's-side door—an odd choice, since under most circumstances it is the passenger door that is more visible to the public. It was a choice that made sense, however, if the driver wanted to be able to remove it quickly, without having to stop.

There was no phone number on the sign. He did an Internet search for "Flowers by Florence" and found several businesses by that name, but none within a hundred miles of Emmerling Oaks. Neither fact surprised him.

He finished his coffee, now less than lukewarm, and headed for Walnut Crossing—feeling both energized and frustrated by what he viewed as the case's two main oddities: the light pole obstruction that seemed to turn the shooter's supposed location into an impossibility, and a relatively simple murder objective combined with an MO that seemed way too complicated.

Someone shot Carl the way Oswald shot Kennedy. Not the way wives shoot their husbands. Not the way mob guys settle their disputes. It seemed to Gurney that the objective could have been accomplished in a dozen easier ways—ways that would have involved a hell of a lot less planning, coordination, and precision than a five-hundred-yard sniper shot fired at a funeral ceremony across a river with a silenced rifle from inside a building full of squatters. Assuming, of course, that the shot came from somewhere in that building to begin with. From a window with a clean line of sight to Carl Spalter's temple. And speaking of complications, why kill Carl's mother first? The most obvious reason, given the outcome, would be to get Carl into the cemetery. But what if that murder was for another reason entirely?

Turning these tangled questions over in his mind on the way home made the hour-long trip disappear. Immersed in possible explanations and linkages, he was barely aware of where he was, until, at the top of the mountain road that dead-ended into his property, the text message ring of his phone brought his attention back to his surroundings. He continued up through the sloping pasture to the house before checking the screen. It was the reply from Bolo that he'd been hoping for: *"yes yes. same shades. funny noze. the pisser man."*

As questionable as the witness might be—Hardwick would surely make that point again—this confirmation (of sorts) that the odd little character had been present at both events gave Gurney his first sense of solidity about the case. It was little more than the clicking together of the first two pieces of a five-hundred-piece puzzle, but it felt good.

A click was a click. And the first click had a special power.

Chapter 24

All the Trouble
in the World

Entering the kitchen, Gurney saw a plastic shopping bag, bulging with angular objects, and a note from Madeleine on the sideboard.

> *Tomorrow is supposed to be a nice day. I picked up some things from the hardware store so we could get started on the house for the chickens. Okay? My schedule got moved around today, so I came home for a couple of hours, now have to return to the clinic. Won't be home tonight till around seven. You should go ahead and eat first. There's stuff in the fridge. Love—M.*

He looked into the bag, saw a retractable metal tape measure, a large ball of yellow nylon string, two canvas carpenter's aprons, two carpenter's pencils, a yellow legal pad, two pairs of work gloves, two bubble levels, and a handful of metal spikes for laying out corner positions.

Whenever Madeleine took a concrete step toward a project that would require his participation, his first reaction was always dismay. But due to their recent discussion of his relentless focus on blood and mayhem—or perhaps due to the intimacy they shared following that discussion—he tried to view the coop project more positively.

Perhaps a shower would put him in the right frame of mind.

Half an hour later he returned to the kitchen—refreshed, hungry, and feeling a bit better about Madeleine's eagerness to get the chicken coop started. In fact, he felt revitalized enough to take the first step. He took the hardware store items from the sideboard, got a hammer from the mudroom, and went out onto the patio. He eyed the area where Madeleine had indicated she wanted the coop and fenced-in run to be located—an area between the asparagus and the big apple tree, where Horace and his little flock of hens would be visible from the breakfast table. Where Horace could crow happily and establish his territory.

Gurney went over to the asparagus patch—a raised planting bed enclosed by four-by-four timbers—and laid Madeleine's purchases out on the grass next to it. He took the yellow pad and a pencil and roughed in the positions of the raised bed, the patio, and the apple tree. Then he paced off the approximate dimensions of the coop and run.

As he was getting the metal tape measure so he could be more precise about the distances, he heard the house phone ringing. He left his pad and pencil on the patio and went inside to the den. It was Hardwick.

"So who's the fucking midget?"

"Good question. All I can tell you is that he—I've been told it's a *he*—was in Mary Spalter's retirement community the day she died, and in that Long Falls apartment house five days before Carl Spalter was shot and again on the day he was shot."

"Is this something Klemper should have known?"

"Estavio Bolocco says he told Klemper that he saw him in the apartment on both occasions. That should have alerted Klemper to something—at least raised a question about the timing of the mother's death."

"But there's no witness to that conversation between Klemper and Bolocco, right?"

"Not unless Freddie, the trial witness, was there. But, like I told you before, he disappeared."

Hardwick sighed loudly. "Without corroboration, this supposed conversation between Klemper and Bolocco is useless."

"Bolocco's recognition of the person in the Emmerling Oaks security video connects the deaths of the mother and the son. That sure as hell isn't useless."

"By itself it doesn't prove police misconduct—which makes it useless for the purpose of the appeal, *which is our only purpose*, which is something I keep telling you, which you seem to be fucking deaf to."

"And what you're deaf to is—"

"I *know*—I'm deaf to justice, deaf to guilt and innocence. Is that your point?"

"Okay, Jack, I have to go now. I'll keep passing along whatever useless stuff I turn up." There was a silence. "By the way, you might want to check on the status of the other people who testified against Kay. Be interesting to see how many of them are locatable."

Hardwick said nothing.

Gurney ended the call.

Glancing at the clock and seeing that it was nearly six reminded him that he was hungry. He went into the kitchen and made himself a cheese omelet.

Eating calmed him. It took away most of the tension arising from the ongoing collisions between his approach to the case and Hardwick's. Gurney had made it clear from the beginning that if the man wanted his help, it was going to be provided on Gurney's terms. That aspect of the arrangement was not going to change. Neither, it seemed, was Hardwick's unhappiness with it.

As he stood at the sink washing his omelet pan, his eyes grew heavy and the idea of a quick nap became very attractive. He'd just lie down for one of those restorative twelve-minute dips into semi-sleep that he'd relied on to get through double shifts in his NYPD days. He dried his hands, went into the bedroom, put his phone on the night table, took off his shoes, stretched out on top of the bedspread, and closed his eyes.

His phone awakened him.

He sensed immediately that his nap had far exceeded its intended twelve minutes. In fact, the clock by the bed said it was 7:32 p.m. He'd been asleep for more than an hour.

The ID said it was Kyle Gurney.

"Hello?"

"Hey, Dad! You sound sleepy. I didn't wake you, did I?"

"No problem. Where are you? What's up?"

"I'm here in my apartment watching this special legal-issues interview show? *Criminal Conflict?* There's this lawyer being interviewed who keeps mentioning your name."

"What? What lawyer?"

"Some guy by the name of Bincher. Rex, Lex, something like that?"

"On television?"

"On your favorite channel. RAM-TV. Simultaneous webcast on their website."

Gurney grimaced. Even if he hadn't had such horrendous trouble with RAM-TV during the Good Shepherd investigation, the idea that anyone was talking about him on the trashiest, most slanted cable news channel in the history of broadcasting would have been repellent. And what the hell was Bincher up to, anyway?

"This thing with the lawyer is on right now?"

"As we speak. A friend of mine happened to be watching it and heard them mention the name Gurney. So he called me, and I turned it on. Just go to their website and click on the 'Live Stream' button."

Gurney got up from the bed, hurried into the den, and followed Kyle's instructions on his laptop—alternately speculating on Bincher's likely game and reliving the experience he'd had with RAM-TV's creepy programming chief just a few months earlier.

On his third try he got to the program. The screen showed two men sitting in angular chairs on opposite sides of a low table that held a pitcher of water and two glasses. At the base of the screen, white letters on a bold red stripe spelled out *CRIMINAL CONFLICT*. Below that, moving letters on a blue stripe appeared to be scrolling an endless series of panicky news flashes about every form of turmoil, disaster, and disagreement in the world—a terrorist nuclear threat, a toxic tilapia scare, a celebrity altercation involving colliding Porsches.

Holding a few sheets of paper in his hand, looking seriously concerned in the vacuous style of TV interviewers everywhere, the man on the left was leaning toward the man on the right. Gurney had tuned in as the interviewer was in midsentence:

". . . quite an *indictment* of the system, Lex, if I may use that legal term."

The man across the table, already leaning forward himself, leaned farther forward. He was smiling, but the expression appeared to be nothing more than a perfunctory baring of unfriendly teeth. His voice was sharp, nasal, and loud. "Brian, in all my years of criminal defense experience, I've never encountered a more egregious example of rotten police work. An absolute subversion of justice."

Brian looked appalled. "You'd started itemizing some of the problems just before the break, Lex. Crime scene contradictions, perjury, missing records of witness interviews—"

"And now you can add to that at least *one missing witness.* I just got a text message on that subject from a member of my investigatory team. Plus sexual misconduct with a possible suspect. Plus a gross failure to examine obvious alternate scenarios for the murder—such as a fatal falling-out with organized crime, other members of the same family with bigger and better motives for murder than Kay Spalter, or even a politically motivated assassination. In fact, Brian, I'm on the verge of requesting a special prosecutor to look into what may be a massive criminal cover-up of a tainted prosecution. It's incredible to me that the whole organized crime possibility was never pursued."

The interviewer, his face a picture of empty-headed consternation, gestured with the papers in his hand. "So what you're saying here, Lex, is that this troubling situation could be a lot bigger than anyone thought?"

"That's an understatement, Brian! I can see some major law enforcement careers going up in flames! Everyone from the state police to the DA could be heading for a legal ripsaw! And I'm not afraid to turn it on!"

"It seems like you managed to uncover a lot of damaging facts in a very short time. You mentioned earlier that you'd recruited a star detective from the NYPD, Dave Gurney, to work with you—the same detective who recently tore the official version of the Good Shepherd case to shreds. Is Dave Gurney the one responsible for your new information?"

"Let me put it this way, Brian. I'm running a powerful team. I'm calling the shots, and I've got great people executing the plays. Gurney has the best homicide clearance record in the history of the NYPD. And I have him working with the ideal partner, Jack Hardwick—a detective who was forced out of the state police for helping Gurney discover the truth about the Good Shepherd. The stuff we're coming up with is *pure dynamite*—one *bombshell* after another. Let me tell you—with their help, I plan to blow the Spalter case sky high."

"Lex, you just delivered the perfect closing line. And now we're about out of time. Thanks so much for joining us this evening. This is Brian Bork for *Criminal Conflict*, your nightly ringside seat at today's most explosive legal battles!"

A voice from behind Gurney startled him.

"What are you watching?"

It was Madeleine. She was standing in the den doorway.

"You look wet," he said.

"It just started raining. Didn't you notice?"

"I got sucked into this, in more ways than one." He gestured toward the computer.

She came into the room, frowning at the screen. "What was he just saying about you?"

"Nothing good."

"He sounded complimentary."

"Compliments are not always good things to get. Everything depends on the source."

"Who was talking?"

"The loose-cannon lawyer Hardwick got for Kay Spalter."

"What's the problem?"

"I don't like hearing my name advertised on TV, especially not by an egomaniac and not in that tone."

Madeleine looked concerned. "Do you think he's putting you in danger?"

What he was thinking, but didn't say for fear of alarming her, was that the playing field had a precarious tilt when a murderer had *your* ID before you had *his*. He shrugged. "I don't like publicity. I don't like case scenarios being blabbed to the media. I don't like wild exaggerations. And I especially don't like loudmouthed, self-promoting lawyers."

There was another aspect of his reaction that he didn't mention: an underlying sense of excitement. Although his negative comments were all true, he had to admit, if only to himself, that a loose cannon like Bincher had a way of shaking things up, of provoking revealing responses from interested parties.

"You're sure that's all that's bothering you?"

"Isn't that enough?"

She gave him a long, worried, *You didn't really answer my question* look.

Gurney had decided to wait until morning to call Hardwick about Bincher's over-the-top media performance.

Now, at 8:30 a.m., he decided to wait a little longer—at least until he had his coffee. Madeleine was already at the breakfast table. He brought his cup over and sat across from her. As soon as he did, the landline phone rang. He bounced back up and went into the den to answer it.

"Gurney here." It was his old NYPD way of identifying himself—which he thought he'd gotten over.

The hoarse, low, almost sleepy voice on the other end wasn't familiar.

"Hello, Mr. Gurney. My name is Adonis Angelidis." The speaker paused, as if expecting some word of recognition. When Gurney offered none, he went on. "I understand you're working with a man named Bincher. Is that true?"

Now he had Gurney's full attention, electrically charged by his recollection of what Kay Spalter told him about the man known as "Donny Angel."

"Why do you ask?"

"Why do I ask? Because of that TV program he was on. Bincher mentioned your name with great prominence. You're aware of this, am I right?"

"Yes."

"Good. You're an investigator, am I right?"

"Yes."

"You're a famous guy, right?"

"I wouldn't know about that."

"That's pretty funny. 'I wouldn't know about that.' I like that. Very modest man."

"What do you want, Mr. Angelidis?"

"I don't want nothing. I believe I can help you with things you need to know."

"What sort of things?"

"Things that should be discussed face-to-face. I could save you a lot of trouble."

"What sort of trouble?"

"All the trouble in the world. And time. I could save you time. A lot of time. Time is very valuable. We only got so much of it. You know what I mean?"

"Okay, Mr. Angelidis. I need to know what this is about."

"About? It's about your big case. When I listened to Bincher on the TV, I said to myself, 'This is bullshit, they don't know what the fuck they're doing.' Some of the shit he said, it's gonna waste your time, make you crazy. So I want to do you a favor, set you straight."

"Set me straight about what?"

"About who killed Carl Spalter. You want to know that, right?"

Chapter 25

Fat Gus

Gurney made his planned call to Hardwick, leaving out any assault on Bincher's personal style. After all, he was going to have a meeting with Donny Angel at two o'clock that afternoon in a Long Falls restaurant—a meeting that could change everything—and it had obviously been motivated by Bincher's performance.

After listening to Gurney's summary of the phone call from Angel, Hardwick asked without much enthusiasm if he wanted some backup or if he wanted to be wired—just in case things in the restaurant started going south.

Gurney turned down both offers. "He'll assume the possibility of backup, and the assumption is as good as the reality. As for the wire, he'll assume that too and take whatever precautions he needs to."

"You get any sense of what his game is?"

"Only that he's upset by the direction he thinks we're taking and he wants to head it off."

Hardwick cleared his throat. "An obvious concern would be Lex's suggestion that Carl might have been whacked because of a falling-out with someone in the mob."

"Speaking of which, his shotgun approach to the case seems a hell of a lot broader than your 'focus, focus, focus' advice to me."

"Fuck you, Sherlock. You're purposely not getting the point. The point is, he's bringing up scenarios that Klemper should have explored but failed to. Everything Lex said goes to the point of a dishonest, incompetent, prejudiced investigation. That's it. That's the point of the appeal. He's not saying that you should start digging into all the crap he's mentioning—only that *Klemper didn't.*"

"Okay, Jack. New subject. Your friend in BCI—Esti Moreno? Can she get a look at the autopsy report on Mary Spalter?"

Hardwick hesitated. "What do you expect it to say?"

"It'll say the cause of death was consistent with an accidental fall, but I'll bet that the description of bone and tissue damage is also consistent with the blunt force trauma you'd expect if someone grabbed her by the hair and bashed her head against the edge of the bathtub."

"Which won't prove that it *wasn't* just a hard fall. So what then?"

"Then I'll just keep following the string."

After ending the call to Hardwick, Gurney checked the time and saw that he had a couple of free hours before he'd have to leave for Long Falls. Feeling he should take some action on the chicken coop project, he put on a pair of rubber gardening boots and went out the side door to the area that he'd started measuring the previous day.

He was surprised to find Madeleine already there, holding the metal tape measure. She had one end of it hooked over the low retaining wall of the asparagus bed and was slowly backing up toward the apple tree. When she was nearly there, the end came loose and the tape went skittering along the ground, rewinding itself into the case in her hand.

"Damn!" she said. "Third time that's happened."

Gurney walked over, picked up the end, and pulled it back to the bed wall. "Is this where you want it?" he asked.

She nodded, looking relieved. "Thank you."

For the next hour and a half he assisted with measurements for the coop and the run, helped hammer in corner stakes, squared the diagonals, and only once in the course of this work did he question one of Madeleine's decisions. It was when she laid out the position of the run in a way that would result in a large forsythia bush being inside the fence instead of outside. He thought it was a mistake to let a bush take up so much of the fenced space. But she said that the chickens would *like* having a bush in their run because although they loved being outside, they were also fond of shade and shelter. It made them feel secure.

As she was explaining this, he could sense how much she cared about it. He felt a little envious of this remarkable ability of hers to focus on and care deeply about whatever was in front of her. So many different things seemed to *matter* to her. He had the rather silly-sounding thought that perhaps what mattered in life was that things mattered—a lot of things. There was something almost surreal in this thought, which he attributed partly to the odd weather. It was distinctly cool for August, with an autumnal haze in the air and an earthy fragrance rising from the wet grass. It made what was happening for that brief moment seem more like a soft-edged dream than the prickly reality of daily life.

Aegean Odyssey, the restaurant where he was meeting Adonis "Donny Angel" Angelidis, was on Axton Avenue, less than three blocks from the apartment building on which the investigation had centered. The two-hour drive from Walnut Crossing had been uneventful. Parking, as on his previous visit, was no problem. He found a spot within fifty feet of the restaurant door. He was exactly on time: two p.m.

It was quiet inside, and almost empty. Only one of the twenty or so tables was occupied, and that by a solitary old man reading a Greek newspaper. The interior decor featured the typical Greek blues and whites. The walls were accented with colorful ceramic tiles. There was a mixed aroma of oregano, marjoram, roast lamb, strong coffee.

A young waiter with dark eyes approached him. "Can I help you?"

"My name is Gurney. I'm meeting Mr. Angelidis."

"Of course. Please." He led the way to a partitioned area at the back of the room. Then he stepped aside and gestured toward a booth that could have accommodated six people but had only one occupant—a heavyset man with a large head and coarse gray hair.

The man had the flat, crooked nose of a boxer. His thick shoulders suggested he had once been quite powerful, perhaps still was. The expression on his face was dominated by deeply etched lines of sourness and distrust. He held a fat stack of dollar bills and was counting them out onto a neat pile on the table. There was a gold Rolex on his wrist. He looked up. His mouth smiled without losing any of its sourness.

"Thank you for coming. I'm Adonis Angelidis." His voice was low and hoarse, as if there were calluses on his vocal chords from a lifetime of shouting. "Forgive me for not rising to greet you, Mr. Gurney. My back is . . . not so good. Please sit." Despite his hoarseness, his articulation was oddly precise, as if he was choosing each syllable with care.

Gurney sat directly across from him. There were several plates of food on the table.

"The kitchen is closed, but I asked them to make special a few things, so you could choose. All very good. You know Greek food?"

"Moussaka, souvlaki, baklava. That's about it."

"Ah. Well. Let me explain." He laid his stack of bills on the table and began pointing at and describing in detail the contents of each dish—spanakopita, salata melitzanes, kalamaria tiganita, arni yahni, garithes me feta. There was also a small bowl of cured olives, a basket of crusty sliced bread, and a large bowl of fresh purple figs.

"I invite you to pick whatever appeals to you, or take a bit from each. All very good."

"Thank you. I'll try a fig." Gurney took one and bit into it.

Angelidis watched him with interest.

Gurney nodded his approval. "You're right. It's very good."

"Of course. You take your time. Relax. We talk when you are ready."

"We can talk now."

"Okay. I must ask you something. Somebody told me about you. You are an expert at murders. This is true? I mean, of course, *solving* murders, not *doing* them." The mouth smiled again. The heavily lidded eyes remained watchful. "This is what you care about?"

"Yes."

"Good. No Organized Crime Task Force bullshit, right?"

"My focus is homicide. I try not to let other issues get in the way."

"Good. Very good. We have common ground maybe. Maybe ground for cooperation. You think so, Mr. Gurney?"

"I hope so."

"So. You want to know about Carl?"

"Yes."

"You know Greek tragedy?"

"Excuse me?"

"Sophocles. You know Sophocles?"

"To some extent. Only what I remember from college."

Angelidis leaned forward, resting his heavy forearms on the table.

"Greek tragedy had a simple idea. A great truth: A man's strength is also his weakness. This is most brilliant. Do you agree?"

"I can see how it could be true."

"Good. Because this truth is what killed Carl." He paused, gazing hard into Gurney's eyes. "You wonder what the hell am I talking about, right?"

Gurney said nothing, took another bite of the fig, held Angelidis's gaze, and waited.

"A simple thing. A tragic thing. Carl's great strength was the speed of his mind reaching a conclusion and his willingness to act. You understand what I say? Very fast, no fear. A great strength. A man like that achieves many things, great things. But this strength was also his weakness. Why? Because this great strength has no patience. This strength must eliminate obstruction immediately. You understand?"

"Carl wanted something. Somebody got in his way. What happened then?"

"He decided, of course, to eliminate the obstruction. This was his way."

"What did he do?"

"I heard that he wanted to put out a contract through a certain individual to have the obstruction eliminated. I tell him he should wait, take smaller steps. I ask if there is anything I can do. I ask this like a father to a son. He tells me no, the problem is outside my . . . my area of business . . . and I shouldn't be involved."

"You're telling me he wanted to have someone killed, but not by you?"

"According to the rumor, he went to a man who arranges things like that."

"Did the man have a name?"

"Gus Gurikos."

"A professional?"

"A manager. A talent agent. You understand? You tell Fat Gus what you want, you agree on the price, you give him information he needs, he takes it from there. No more problem for you. He manages everything, hires the best talent—you don't need to know nothing. Better that way. Lot of funny stories about Fat Gus. Someday I tell you."

Gurney had heard enough funny stories about mob guys to last a lifetime. "So Carl Spalter paid Fat Gus to hire the appropriate talent to remove someone who got in his way?"

"That's the rumor."

"Very interesting, Mr. Angelidis. How does the story end?"

"Carl was too fast. And Fat Gus wasn't fast enough."

"Meaning what?"

"Only one thing could have happened. The guy Carl was in such a rush to have removed must have found out about the contract before Gus passed it on to the hitter. And he took action first. Preemptive strike, right? Gets rid of Carl before Carl gets rid of him."

"What does your friend Gus say about this?"

"Gus don't say shit. Gus can't say shit. Gus got hit too—that Friday, same day as Carl."

This was a big piece of news. "You're saying the target found out that Carl hired Gus to set up a hit, but before Gus could make it happen, the target turns around and hits them both?"

"You got it. Preemptive strike."

Gurney nodded slowly. It was certainly a possibility. He took another bite out of the fig.

Angelidis continued with some enthusiasm. "So this makes your job real simple. Just find out who Carl wanted hit, and you got the guy who turned around and hit Carl."

"Would you have any idea who that might be?"

"No. This is important for you to know. So you listen to me now. What happened to Carl got nothing to do with me. Got nothing to do with my business interests."

"How do you know that?"

"I knew Carl pretty good. If it was something I could take care of, he would have come to me. Point is, he went to Fat Gus. So it was a personal thing for him, nothing to do with me. Nothing to do with my business."

"Fat Gus didn't work for you?"

"Didn't work for nobody. Fat Gus was independent. Provided services to various customers. Better that way."

"So you have absolutely no idea who—"

"No idea." Angelidis gave Gurney a long, straight look. "If knew, I would tell you."

"Why would you tell me?"

"Whoever hit Carl fucked things up for me. I don't like when people fuck things up for me. Makes me want to fuck things up for them. You understand?"

Gurney smiled. "An eye for an eye, a tooth for a tooth, right?"

Angelidis's expression sharpened. "What the fuck is that supposed to mean?"

The question and its intensity surprised him. "It's a verse from the Bible, a way to achieve justice by matching——"

"I know the fucking saying. But why did you *say* it?"

"You asked me if I understood your desire to get even with whoever killed Carl and Gus."

He seemed to be thinking about this. "You don't know nothing about the hit on Gus?"

"No. Why?"

He was silent for several seconds, watching Gurney intently. "Very sick shit. You didn't hear nothing about that?"

"Zero. Didn't know the man existed, didn't know he died."

Angelidis nodded slowly. "Okay. I'll tell you this, because maybe it helps. There was a Friday-night poker game Gus always held at his house. The Friday Carl got hit, the guys show up, nobody answers the door. They ring, knock. Nobody comes. This never happens. They think maybe Gus is taking a crap. They wait. Ring, knock—no Gus. They try the door. Door's unlocked. Go in. Find Gus." He paused, looked like he was tasting something unpleasant. "I don't like talking about this. It's sick shit, you know? I believe that all business should be reasonable. Not like this crazy shit." He shook his head and adjusted the position of some of the dishes on the table. "Gus is sitting in his underwear in front of his TV. Got a nice bottle of retsina on the coffee table, half-full wineglass, a little bread, taramasalata in a bowl. Nice lunch. But . . ."

"But he was dead?" Gurney prompted.

"Dead? He was real dead. Dead with a fucking four-inch nail hammered into each eye, into each ear, right into his fucking brain, and a fifth one through his fucking throat. Five fucking nails." He paused, studying Gurney's face. "What are you thinking?"

"I'm wondering why none of this made it into the news."

"Organized Crime Task Force." Angelidis looked like the words were making him want to spit. "OCTF dropped down on it like a pile of shit. No obituary, no funeral notice, no nothing. Kept all the details to themselves. Can you believe that? You know why they keep this stuff secret?"

Gurney wasn't really being asked a question, so he didn't answer.

Angelidis sucked loudly at his teeth before continuing. "They keep it secret because it makes them feel like they know something. Like they know *secret shit* nobody else knows. Makes them feel like they got *power*. Got *classified* information. You know what they got? They got shit for brains and toothpicks for dicks." He glanced at his big gold Rolex and smiled. "Okay? It's getting late. I hope this helps you."

"It's all very interesting. I have one last question."

"Sure." Angelidis looked again at his watch.

"How well did you get along with Carl?"

"Beautiful. Like a son to me."

"No problems?"

"No problems."

"You weren't bothered by all those 'scum of the earth' speeches he made?"

"Bothered? What do you mean?"

"In press interviews he called people in your line of business the scum of the earth. And a lot of other unpleasant things. How'd you feel about that?"

"Felt it was pretty smart. Good way to get elected." He pointed at the bowl of olives. "They're very good. My cousin in Mykonos sends them to me special. Take some home to your wife."

Chapter 26

Not a Fucking Chess Match

When Gurney arrived at the end of the mountain road that led to his property, he was surprised to discover a large black SUV parked by the barn. He lowered his window at the mailbox and found that Madeleine had already emptied it. Then he drove slowly over to the shiny Escalade and stopped in front of it.

Its door opened. The man who emerged had the bulky physique of a football lineman. He also had a shaved head, unfriendly bloodshot eyes, and a rictus-like grin. "Mr. Gurney?"

Gurney returned the empty smile. "What can I do for you?"

"My name is Mick Klemper. That mean anything to you?"

"CIO on the Spalter case?"

"Right." He took out his wallet, flipped it open to his Bureau of Criminal Investigation ID. In the younger photo displayed on the laminated card, he looked like mindless muscle for the Irish mob.

"What are you doing here?"

Klemper blinked, the grin wavered. "We need to talk—before this thing you're involved in gets out of hand."

"This *thing* I'm involved in?"

"This bullshit with Bincher. Do you *know* about him?"

"Do I know *what* about him?"

"What a scumbag he is?"

Gurney thought about this for a moment. "Did someone send you here, or is this your idea?"

"I'm trying to do you a favor. Can we talk?"

"Sure. Talk."

"I mean, friendly. Like we're on the same side of the street."

The man's eyes radiated danger. But Gurney's curiosity outweighed his caution. He turned off the engine and got out of his car. "What do you want to tell me?"

"This Jew lawyer you're working for, he's made a career out of smearing cops—you aware of that?" Klemper reeked of mints overlaying a sour miasma of alcohol.

"I'm not working for anybody."

"That's not what Bincher said on TV."

"I'm not responsible for what he said."

"So the Jew scumbag is lying?"

Gurney smiled, even as he shifted his feet to get into a better position to defend himself physically, if the need arose. "How about we get back to the same side of the street?"

"What?"

"You said you wanted a friendly talk."

"My friendly point is that Lex Bincher makes money by digging up phony little glitches he can use to keep his slimebag clients on the streets. You ever see his fucking house in Cooperstown? Biggest house on the lake, every cent from drug dealers he kept out of prison with one fucking technicality after another. You know about this shit?"

"I don't care about Bincher. I care about the Spalter murder case."

"Okay, good, let's talk about that. Kay Spalter killed her husband. Shot him in the fucking head. She was tried, convicted, and sentenced. Kay Spalter is a lying, murdering cunt, doing the time she deserves. Except now your slimy little Jew friend Bincher is trying to spring her on procedural—"

Gurney interrupted him. "Klemper? Do me a favor. I'm not interested in your Jew problems. You want to talk about the Spalter case, talk."

There was a flash of hatred on the man's face, and for a moment Gurney thought their confrontation was about to become brutally simple. He closed his right hand into a fist out of Klemper's line of sight and adjusted his balance. But Klemper just produced an empty smile and shook his head. "Okay. What I'm telling you is this. There's no way she should walk on a fucking technicality. With your background, you should know better. Why the hell are you trying to spring a piece of garbage?"

Gurney shrugged, asked matter-of-factly, "Did you notice the problem with the light pole?"

"What are you talking about?"

"The light pole that made a clear shot from the apartment impossible."

If Klemper had intended to pretend ignorance, his thoughtful delay now made that position untenable. "It wasn't impossible. It happened."

"How?"

"Easy—if the victim wasn't in the exact spot where some witnesses said he was, and if the weapon wasn't fired from the exact spot where it was found."

"You mean if Carl was at least ten feet away from where everyone saw him get hit, and if the shooter was standing on a ladder?"

"It's possible."

"What happened to the ladder?"

"Maybe she stood on a chair."

"To make a five-hundred-yard head shot? With a five-pound tripod dangling from the gun?"

"Who the hell knows? Fact is, Kay Spalter was seen in the building—in that apartment. We have an eyewitness. We have dust impressions in her small shoe size in that apartment. We have gunpowder residue in that apartment." He paused, gave Gurney a shrewd look. "Who the hell told you there was a five-pound tripod?"

"That doesn't matter. What matters is you've got contradictions in your shooting scenario. Is that why you got rid of the electronics store video?"

Again Klemper's hesitation was a second too long. "What video?"

Gurney ignored the question. "Finding a piece of evidence that doesn't fit your concept means your concept is wrong. Getting rid of the evidence tends to create a bigger problem down the road—like the one you have now. What was on the video?"

Klemper didn't answer. His jaw muscles were tightening visibly.

Gurney went on. "Let me take a wild guess. The video showed

Carl getting hit standing in a spot that couldn't possibly work with the line of sight from the apartment. Am I right?"

Klemper said nothing.

"And there's another little snag. The shooter was seen casing that apartment building three days *before* Mary Spalter died."

Klemper blinked but said nothing.

Gurney continued. "The person your trial witness identified as Kay Spalter was actually a man, according to a second witness. And that same man was also captured on video in Mary Spalter's community a couple of hours before she turned up dead."

"Where's all this crap coming from?"

Gurney ignored the question. "Looks like the shooter was a hired pro with a double contract. On the mother and son. Any thoughts about that, Mick?"

That set off a twitch in Klemper's cheek. He turned away and paced slowly across the open space in front of the barn. When he reached the mailbox at the side of the road he stared for a while in the direction of the pond, then turned around and paced back.

He stopped in front of Gurney. "I'll tell you what I think. I think none of this means a fucking thing. One witness says it was a woman, another says it was a man. Happens all the time. Eyewitnesses make mistakes, contradict one another. So what? Big deal. Freddie ID'd the bitch wife in a lineup. Some other little coke-head skell didn't. So what? There's probably somebody else in that slum dump who thinks the bitch was a space alien. So fucking what? Somebody thinks they saw the same person somewhere else. Maybe they're full of shit. But let's say they're right. Did you happen to turn up the fact that Kay, the bitch wife, hated her mother-in-law even more than she hated the husband she topped? Didn't know that, did you? So maybe what we should've done was send the fucking bitch up for two murders instead of one." Pasty saliva was accumulating at the corners of Klemper's mouth.

Gurney spoke calmly. "I have the Emmerling Oaks security video of the individual who probably killed Mary Spalter. The individual on that video is definitely not Kay Spalter. And someone else who saw the video insists the same person was in the Axton Avenue building at the time the shot was fired at Carl."

"So fucking what? Even if it was a pro, even if it was a double contract, that doesn't get the bitch off the hook. All it means is she bought the hit instead of doing it herself. So it wasn't her own sweaty little finger on the trigger. So she hired the triggerman—just like she tried to do before with Jimmy Flats." Klemper suddenly looked excited. "You know what? I *love* your new theory, Gurney. It ties in with the bitch's attempt to hire Flats to hit her husband, plus her attempt to talk her boyfriend into doing it. Ties the knot tighter around her fucking neck." He stared at Gurney with a triumphant grin. "What do you got to say now?"

"It matters who pulled the trigger. It matters whether the eyewitness IDs are right or wrong. It matters whether the trial testimony is honest or perjured. It matters whether the video you buried supports or destroys the shooting scenario."

"That's the kind of shit that matters to you?" Klemper sucked a wad of mucus out of his nose and spat it out on the ground. "I expected more from you."

"More of what?"

"I came here today because I found out you worked homicide for twenty-five years in the NYPD. Twenty-five years in Sewer City. I figured anyone who spent twenty-five years dealing with every piece of shit that crawled out of a hole would understand reality."

"What reality would that be?"

"The reality that when push comes to shove, *right* matters more than rules. The reality that we're in a war, not a fucking chess match. White hats versus scumbags. When the enemy is coming at you, you stop the fucker however you can. You don't stop a bullet by waving a fucking rule book at it."

"Suppose you have it wrong."

"Suppose I have *what* wrong?"

"Suppose Carl Spalter's death had nothing to do with his wife. Suppose his brother had him shot to get control of Spalter Realty. Or the mob had him shot because they decided they didn't want him to be governor after all. Or his daughter had him shot because she wanted to inherit his money. Or his wife's lover had him shot because—"

Klemper broke in, red-faced. "That's all total horseshit. Kay Spalter is an evil, conniving, murdering whore. And if there's any justice in this fucking world, she'll die in prison with her brains bashed out on the floor. End of story!" Tiny bits of the spittle around his mouth were flying into the air.

Gurney nodded thoughtfully. "You may be right." It was his favorite all-purpose response—to the friendly and the furious, the sane and the insane. He went on calmly, "Tell me something. Did you ever run the shooter's MO through the ViCAP database?"

Klemper stared at him, blinking repeatedly, as though it would help him understand the question better. "What the hell do you want to know that for?"

Gurney shrugged. "Just wondering. There are some distinctive elements in the shooter's approach. Be interesting to see if they've popped up anywhere else."

"You're out of your mind." Klemper started backing away.

"You may be right. But if you decide to check out that MO, there's one more situation you should look into. You ever hear of an upstate Greek gangster by the name of Fat Gus Gurikos?"

"Gurikos?" Now Klemper looked honestly confused. "What's he got to do with this?"

"Carl asked Gus to take care of something for him. And then Gus just coincidentally got hit the same day Carl did—two days after Carl's mother. So maybe we're really talking about a triple hit."

Klemper frowned, said nothing.

"I'd look into it if I were you. I've been told the Organized Crime Task Force kept the Gurikos thing pretty much to themselves, but if there's a tie-in to the Spalter case you have a right to know the details."

Shaking his head, Klemper looked like he'd rather be anywhere other than where he was. He turned away abruptly and was getting into his huge SUV when he noticed that Gurney's Outback was blocking him.

"You want to get that thing out of my way?" It was a snarled order, not a question.

Gurney moved his car, and Klemper drove off without looking at him, nearly hitting the mailbox as he turned down the mountain road.

It was then that Gurney noticed Madeleine at the corner of the barn with the rooster and the three hens standing quietly in the grass behind her. The birds were strangely motionless, their heads cocked, as if aware of the approach of something they could not yet identify.

Chapter 27

A Desperate Man

After a less-than-relaxed dinner during which neither she nor Gurney said much, Madeleine began doing the dishes—a task she always insisted was hers.

Gurney went over and sat quietly on a stool at the sink island. He knew if he waited long enough, she'd get around to saying what was on her mind.

When the washed dishes had all been placed in the drainer, she picked up a towel to dry them. "I assume that was the Spalter murder investigator?"

"Yes. Mick Klemper."

"A *very* angry man."

Whenever Madeleine stated the obvious, he knew that something less obvious was being implied. In this instance it wasn't clear to him what that something was, but he did feel the need to offer some sort of explanation for what she'd apparently overheard.

"It must have been a difficult day for him."

"Difficult?"

He elaborated. "Once the Bincher accusations started shooting around the Internet, a lot of people would have been calling Klemper for clarification. BCI brass, State Police Legal Department, DA's office, Internal Affairs, attorney general's office—not to mention the media vultures."

She was holding a plate in her hand, frowning. "I find it hard to understand."

"It's simple enough. After talking to Kay Spalter, Klemper decided she was guilty. The question is, how sick was that decision?"

"How *sick*?"

"I mean, how much of it was based on Kay reminding him of his ex-wife? Also, how many laws did he break to make sure she got convicted?"

She was still holding the plate. "That's not what I mean. I'm talking about the level of rage I saw down at the barn, how close to the edge he was, how——"

"I'm pretty sure that was all coming out of fear. Fear that the evil Kay will go free, fear that his view of the case is about to be smashed, fear of losing his job, fear of going to jail. The fear of disintegrating, falling apart, losing his grasp of who he is. The fear of becoming nobody."

"So you're saying he's desperate."

"Absolutely desperate."

"Desperate. Disintegrating."

"Yes."

"Were you carrying your gun?"

For a moment the question baffled him. "No. Of course not."

"You were face-to-face with a furious lunatic—a *desperate, disintegrating* individual. But *of course* you weren't carrying your gun?" She had a look of pain in her eyes. Pain and fear. "Now do you understand why I want you to see Malcolm Claret?"

He was about to say something about not knowing that Klemper would be waiting for him, that he'd never liked carrying a gun, and that he generally didn't do so unless he was facing some known threat—but he realized that she was talking about something deeper and broader than this one incident, and for that larger subject at that moment he had no appetite.

After drying the same plate absently for another minute, she left the room and headed up the hall stairs. A minute later, he heard the initial bars of an unpleasantly jagged cello piece.

He'd avoided discussing the issue implicit in her question about Malcolm Claret, but now he couldn't help picturing the man himself—the cerebral gaze, the thinning hair over a high, pale forehead, the gestures as economical as his speech, the colorless slacks and loose cardigan, the stillness, the unassuming manner.

Gurney realized he was picturing the man as he appeared many

years ago. He altered the image in his mind as a computer aging program might—deepening wrinkles, subtracting hair, adding the wea-
rying effects of time and gravity on facial flesh. Uncomfortable with
the result, he put it out of his mind.

He thought instead about Klemper—about his obsessive negative
focus on Kay Spalter, his certainty regarding her guilt, his willingness to subvert the investigation to produce the desired conclusion as
quickly as possible.

The approach was disconcerting—not because it was completely
divorced from normal procedure, but because it *wasn't.* Klemper's
offense seemed to Gurney not a matter of kind but of degree. The
notion that a good detective always proceeds via pure logic and an
open mind to objective conclusions concerning the nature of the crime
and the identity of the perpetrator is at best a pleasant fantasy. In the
real world of crime and punishment—as in all human endeavors—
objectivity is an illusion. Survival itself demands that we leap to conclusions. Crucial action is always based on partial evidence. The hunter
who demands a zoologist's affidavit that the deer in his sights is truly
a deer will soon starve. The jungle dweller who counts all the tiger's
stripes before deciding to retreat will be killed and eaten. The genes
that urge certainty tend not to be passed into the next generation.

In the real world, we must connect the few dots we have and guess
at a pattern that makes workable sense. It's an imperfect system. So is
life itself. The danger arises not so much from the scarcity of dots as
from the unconscious personal agenda that prioritizes certain dots over
others, an agenda that *wants* the pattern to look a certain way. Our perceptions of events are warped more by the power of our emotions than
by the weakness of our data.

In this light, the situation was simple. Klemper *wanted* Kay to be
guilty and therefore came to believe that she *was.* Dots that didn't fit
the pattern were devalued or ignored. Rules that impeded a "righteous" ending were similarly devalued or ignored.

But there was another way of looking at it.

Since the process of moving to a conclusion on the basis of incom-
plete data was natural and necessary, the common warning against
doing so really amounted to no more than a warning not to leap to
the *wrong* conclusion. The truth was that any conclusion might be

premature. The final verdict on the validity of the leap would be rendered by the validity of the result.

That thought raised a disquieting possibility.

Suppose Klemper's conclusion was correct.

Suppose the hate-filled Klemper had arrived at the truth. Suppose his sloppy procedures and possible felonies constituted a rotten route to the right end. Suppose Kay Spalter was, in fact, guilty of murdering her husband. Gurney had no great appetite for helping to free a stone-cold killer, no matter how deeply flawed her trial may have been.

And there was yet another possibility. Suppose Klemper's hell-bent determination to have Kay put away had nothing to do with limited perceptions or faulty conclusions. Suppose it was a cynical and corrupt effort, bought and paid for by a third party who wanted the case closed as quickly as possible.

Suppose, suppose, suppose. Gurney was finding the echo irritating and unproductive—and the need for more facts compelling.

The dissonant chords of Madeleine's cello piece were growing louder.

Chapter 28

Like the Crack of a Whip

After listening to Gurney on the phone recounting the content of his meeting with Adonis Angelidis, including the grotesque aspects of the Gus Gurikos murder, Jack Hardwick was uncharacteristically silent. Then, instead of criticizing him once again for departing from the narrow issues that would drive the appeal process, he asked Gurney to come to his house for a more thorough discussion of the case status.

"Now?" Gurney glanced at the clock. It was nearly seven-thirty, and the sun had already slipped down behind the western ridge.

"Now would be good. This thing is getting way too weird."

As big a surprise as the invitation was, it wasn't one Gurney was going to argue with. A thorough, all-issues-on-the-table discussion was definitely needed.

Another surprise greeted him when he arrived thirty-five minutes later at Hardwick's rented farmhouse—at the lonely end of a dirt road, high in the darkening hills outside the tiny village of Dillweed. In his headlights he could see a second car parked next to the red GTO—a bright blue Mini Cooper. Evidently the man had a visitor.

Gurney was aware that Hardwick had been involved in quite a few relationships in the past, but he hadn't imagined any of those women looking quite as dramatic as the one who opened the door.

If it wasn't for her intelligent, aggressive eyes that seemed to be assessing him from the first instant, Gurney would have been easily distracted by the rest of her—a figure somewhere between athletic and voluptuous, boldly displayed in cutoff jeans and a loose scoop-neck T-shirt. She was barefoot with red toenails, caramel-tan skin, and ebony hair cut short in a way that emphasized her full lips and prominent cheekbones. She wasn't exactly pretty, but she had a definite *presence*—not unlike Hardwick himself.

A moment later the man appeared beside her with a proprietary grin.

"Come in. Thanks for making the trip."

Gurney stepped through the doorway into the front room. What he remembered from previous visits as a Spartan box of a room had acquired some warmer touches: a colorful carpet, a framed print of orange poppies bending in a breeze, a vase of pussy willow branches, a lush plant in a massive earthenware pot, two new armchairs, a nice pine sideboard, and a round breakfast table with three ladder-back chairs in the corner of the room nearest the kitchen. This woman had evidently inspired some changes.

Gurney surveyed the scene approvingly. "Very nice, Jack. Definite improvement."

Hardwick nodded. "Yeah, I agree." Then he laid his hand on the woman's half-bare shoulder and said, "Dave, I'd like you to meet BCI investigator Esti Moreno."

The introduction caught Gurney off-balance, and it showed, which prompted a bark of a laugh from Hardwick.

He recovered quickly, putting out his hand. "Nice to meet you, Esti."

"A pleasure, Dave." Her grip was strong, the skin on her palm surprisingly callused. He remembered Hardwick mentioning her name as a source of information on the original murder investigation, as well as on the shortcomings of Mick Klemper. He wondered how engaged she was in the Hardwick-Bincher project, and how she viewed it.

As if demonstrating a sense for what he was thinking, she got to the point with a remarkable lack of preamble. "I've been looking forward to meeting you. I've been trying to convince this man here to look past Kay Spalter's legal appeal issues and pay some attention to the murder itself. Now *murders*, yes? At least three? Maybe more?" Her voice was throaty, with a hint of a Spanish accent.

Gurney smiled. "Are you making any progress with him?"

"I'm persistent." She glanced at Hardwick, then back at Gurney. "I think your phone call earlier this evening about the nails in the eyes finally got to him, yes?"

Hardwick's lips tightened in an expression of distaste.

"Yes, definitely the nails in the eyes," she repeated with a conspiratorial wink at Gurney. "Everybody's got some special sensitivity, something that gets their attention, yes? So now maybe we can let Lex-the-Lawyer deal with the Court of Appeals, and we can deal with the crime—the true thing, not the *Klemper* bullshit." She articulated the man's name with evident disgust. "The issue is digging up what really happened. Putting it all together. That's what you think needs to be done, right?"

"You seem to know my thoughts pretty well." He wondered if she knew what kind of thoughts were being generated by that revealing T-shirt.

"Jack told me things about you. And I'm a good listener."

Hardwick was starting to look restless. "Maybe we ought to make some coffee, sit down, and get to it."

An hour later, at the table in the corner, their coffee cups refilled, yellow pads scribbled with notes in front of them, they were circling back through the key points.

"So we agree that the three murders must be related to one another?" said Esti, tapping the tip of her pen on her pad.

"Assuming the autopsy on the mother is consistent with murder," said Hardwick.

Esti looked at Gurney. "Just before you arrived, I reached out to someone in the ME's office. She's supposed to get back to me tomorrow. But the fact that the shooter cased the cemetery scene in Long Falls before her 'accident' is pretty suggestive. So let's agree for now we're talking about three related murders."

Hardwick was staring into his coffee cup as though it contained some unidentifiable substance. "I've got a problem with this. According to Gurney's Greek mob buddy, Carl went to Fat Gus to set up a hit on somebody—nobody knows who. The target finds out about this and, to keep it from happening, hits Carl first. Then he hits Gus, for good measure. I have this right?"

Gurney nodded. "Except for the 'buddy' part."

Hardwick ignored the objection. "Okay, so what this says to me is that Carl and his target were in, like, the ultimate high-stakes race to whack each other. I mean, the guy who makes the first hit wins, right?"

Gurney nodded again.

Hardwick went on. "So why would a guy in that situation pick such a time-consuming, pain-in-the-ass way to set Carl up? I mean, knowing there's a contract on your life creates some urgency. Wouldn't it make more sense under the circumstances to just put on a ski mask, walk into the Spalter Realty office, and pop the son of a bitch? Deal with the issue in half a day instead of a week? And the whole idea of hitting the mother first? Just to get Carl into the cemetery? That feels fucking weird to me."

It didn't feel right to Gurney either.

"Unless," said Esti, "the hit on the mother *wasn't* just a setup to put Carl in a predictable place at a predictable time. Maybe the mother was a target for another reason. In fact, maybe she was the *main* target, and Carl was secondary. You ever think of it that way?"

They paused to think about it.

"I have another problem," said Hardwick. "I get that there's a connection between the Mary and Carl murders. Got to be. And I get that there's some other kind of connection between the Carl and Gus murders—maybe what Donny Angel said, maybe not. So I'm okay with a connection between one and two, and between two and three, but somehow the one-two-three sequence all together doesn't feel so good."

Gurney felt a similar discomfort. "By the way, do we know for sure that Carl was number two and Gus was number three?"

Esti frowned. "What do you mean?"

"From the way Angelidis talked about it, I've been assuming that was the sequence, but there's no reason it *had* to be that way. All I really know is that Carl and Gus were hit the same day. I'd like to get the timing confirmed."

"How?"

"We have a precise time for Carl in the case file. But based on what Angelidis told me, I'm not so sure about Gus. There are two sources I can think of, but it'll depend on what kind of contacts we have—either with the county ME's office where the Gurikos autopsy was done, or with whoever in OCTF has access to that file."

"Let me deal with that," said Esti. "I think I know somebody."

"Great." Gurney gave her an appreciative nod. "In addition to an estimated time of death, see if you can get copies of the initial photos in the autopsy sequence."

"The shots taken before he was opened up?"

"Right—the body on the table, plus any detail shots of the head and neck."

"You want to see exactly how he was nailed?" A quirky grin revealed more relish for this kind of thing than most women would have. Or men, for that matter.

The normally impervious Hardwick grimaced in disgust. Then he turned to Gurney. "You figure that horrible shit was some kind of message?"

"Ritualistic stuff usually is, unless it's an intentional distraction."

"Which do you think this was?" asked Esti.

Gurney shrugged. "I'm not sure. But the message seems clear enough."

Hardwick looked like he was biting down on a bad tooth. "You mean like ... 'I hate you so fucking much I want to hammer spikes into your brain.' Something like that?"

"Don't forget the neck," said Esti.

"Larynx," said Gurney.

They both looked at him.

She spoke first. "What do you mean?"

"I'd be willing to bet the target of the fifth nail was Gus's larynx."

"Why?"

"It's the voice organ."

"So?"

"Eyes, ears, larynx. Sight, hearing, voice. All destroyed."

"And this means what to you?" said Hardwick.

"I may be wrong, but what comes to mind is 'See no evil, hear no evil, speak no evil.' "

Esti nodded. "That makes sense! But who's the message for? The victim? Or someone else?"

"That depends on how crazy the killer is."

"How so?"

"A psychopath who kills for an emotional release usually leaves a symbolic message that reflects the nature of his own pathology—often by mutilating some part of the victim. The message contributes to the feeling of release. It's primarily a communication between him and his victim. Probably also a communication between him and someone in his childhood, someone involved in the root of the pathology—usually one of his parents."

"You think that's what the Gurikos nails-in-the-head thing was?"

Gurney shook his head. "If the Gurikos murder was connected to the two Spalter murders, mother and son, I'd say it was driven more by a practical goal than a compulsion."

Esti looked baffled. "A practical goal?"

"It seems to me like the killer was advising someone to mind their own business, to keep quiet about something, and letting them know at the same time what would happen to them if they didn't. The big questions are, who was the *someone* and what was the *something*."

"You have some ideas about that?"

"Just guesses. The *something* may have been some fact about the first two murders."

Hardwick joined in. "Like the identity of the shooter?"

"Or the motive," said Gurney. "Or some incriminating detail."

Esti leaned forward. "Who do you think was the *someone* who was being warned?"

"I don't know enough about Gus's connections to say. According to Angelidis, Gus hosted a regular Friday-night poker game. After the murder that day, the killer left Gus's door unlocked. That could have been an oversight, or it could have been on purpose—so that someone in the poker group would find the body when they arrived for the game that evening. Maybe the 'See no evil, hear no evil, speak no evil' message was intended for someone in the group or even for Angelidis himself. OCTF might know more about the individuals involved. They may even have had Gus's house under surveillance."

Esti frowned. "I'll find out what I can from my friend, but . . . she might not have access to everything. I don't want to put her in an awkward position."

Hardwick's jaw muscles tightened. "Be careful dealing with those task force fuckers. You think the FBI is bad, they're nothing compared to the *elite* organized crime boys." He emphasized the adjective with a comical level of contempt. But there was no humor in his eyes.

"I know what they're like, and I know what I'm doing." She stared challengingly at Hardwick for a moment. "Let's go back to the beginning. How do we feel about the 'preemptive strike' explanation—that Carl was hit by his own intended victim?"

Hardwick shook his head. "Could be the truth, more likely it's crap. Nice story, but consider the source. Why should we believe anything from Donny Angel?"

She looked at Gurney. "Dave?"

"I don't think *belief* enters into it. What Angelidis *said* happened *could* have happened. It's a reasonable enough scenario. In fact, we heard another story that's consistent with it. Kay Spalter mentioned that Carl used to play poker with a guy who arranged murders for the mob."

Hardwick waved his hand dismissively. "Doesn't prove a damn thing. Sure as hell doesn't prove that Carl hired Gus to have someone killed."

Esti looked back at Gurney.

Gurney just shrugged. "Right. No proof. But still a possibility. A credible link."

"Well," said Esti, "if we think the Angelidis story is possible—that Carl's target ended up being the murderer—shouldn't we make a list of people Carl might have wanted dead?"

Hardwick uttered an incredulous little grunt.

She turned on him. "You have a better idea?"

He shrugged. "Go ahead, make a list."

"Okay, I will." She picked up her pen, held it over her pad. "Dave—any suggestions?"

"Jonah."

"Carl's brother? Why?"

"Because if Jonah were out of the way, Carl would have sole control of Spalter Realty and all its assets, which he could convert into cash to finance his political plans in a big way. Interestingly, Jonah would have the same motive to get rid of Carl—get control of Spalter Realty assets, which he could use to finance the expansion of his Cyberspace Cathedral."

Esti raised an eyebrow. "Cyber . . . ?"

"Long story. Bottom line, Jonah's got a lot of ambition and could use a lot of money."

"Okay, I'll put his name down. Who else?"

"Alyssa."

She blinked, seemed to have some unpleasant thoughts before making another note.

Hardwick's lip curled. "His own daughter?"

Esti responded first. "I overheard enough of Klemper on the phone with Alyssa to get the impression that her relationship with her father . . . wasn't what you'd call a normal father-daughter relationship. It sounded like Carl had forced her to have sex with him."

"You told me that before," said Hardwick. "I don't like thinking about shit like that."

The silence that followed was broken by Gurney. "Just look at it from a practical perspective. Alyssa was a longtime drug addict with no interest in recovery. Carl wanted to be governor of New York. He had a lot to lose—in the present and the future. If he did have an incestuous relationship with Alyssa, presumably going back into her childhood, that would create a major blackmail opportunity—a hard thing for a drug addict with an expensive habit to resist. Suppose that Alyssa's demands became exorbitant. Suppose that Carl came to view her as an unbearable threat to everything he wanted. We've heard from a few people that he was an obsessively ambitious man and capable of anything."

Hardwick had his acid-reflux expression. "You're saying that Alyssa might have discovered that he was arranging for her removal, and that she hired someone to hit him first?"

"Something like that. At least that would be consistent with the Angelidis theory. A simpler version would be that it was entirely her initiative—that Carl never made a move against her—that she was after his money, pure and simple, and had him killed."

"But according to his will, Kay was his sole beneficiary. Alyssa wasn't going to get anything. So what good would—"

Gurney broke in. "Alyssa wouldn't get anything *unless* Kay went down for the murder. Once Kay was convicted, New York law would block her inheritance and Carl's whole estate would be passed down to Alyssa."

Hardwick grinned with the dawning light of possibilities. "That could explain everything. That could explain why she was fucking Klemper, to get him to bend the case. She could even have been fucking her mother's boyfriend, to get him to perjure himself at trial. She's a stone-cold addict—she'd fuck a monkey for dope."

Esti looked troubled. "Maybe her father *wasn't* having sex with her after all. Maybe that was just a story she told Klemper. To get his sympathy."

"Sympathy, my ass! She probably figured it would turn him on."

Esti's expression moved slowly from revulsion to agreement. "Shit. Everything I think about that man keeps getting worse." She paused, made a note on her pad. "So Alyssa's a possible suspect. And so is Jonah. What about Kay's boyfriend?"

Hardwick shook his head. "Not in the preemptive strike structure we're talking about. I don't see Carl taking out a contract on him. I don't think he'd waste the money. There'd be easier ways to get rid of him. And I sure as hell can't see young Darryl in the position of discovering that he's the target of a potential hit and reacting by organizing a faster hit."

"Okay, but forget about the preemptive thing for a minute," said Esti. "Couldn't Darryl have killed Carl in the hope that his relationship with Kay might grow into something better for him once Kay had all the money? What do *you* think, Dave?"

"In the video of the trial he doesn't look like he'd have the smarts or the guts for it. A little perjury—maybe. But a well-planned triple murder? I doubt it. The guy was a minimum-wage lifeguard and pool boy at the Spalters' country club—not exactly *Day of the Jackal* assassin material. Also, I'm having a hard time picturing him smashing an old lady's head or hammering nails into somebody's eyes."

Hardwick was shaking his head. "This is fucked up. None of it feels right to me. The three murders have three completely different methods and styles. I don't see a straight line running through them. Something's missing. Anybody here share that feeling?"

Gurney offered a small affirmative nod. "There's a *lot* missing. Speaking of the MO issue, there's no record in the case file that it was ever explored through ViCAP. Am I right?"

"In Klemper's view," said Esti, "Kay shot Carl. Period. Why would he fill out the ViCAP form or look into any other databases? It's not like the bastard had an open mind."

"I get that. But it would be helpful if we could run the key data now—at least through ViCAP. And it would be nice to know if NCIC has anything on any of the key individuals, dead or alive. And Interpol, too, at least for Gus Gurikos." Gurney glanced from Esti to Hardwick and back. "Can either of you do any of that without creating a problematic trail?"

"Maybe I could get the ViCAP and NCIC parts done," said Esti after a moment. The way she said "maybe" meant she could get it done, but by a route she was not about to reveal. "For ViCAP, what data bits are you most interested in?"

"To avoid being swamped with results, concentrate on the oddities—the most peculiar elements at each of the murder sites—and use those as the search terms."

"Like '.220 Swift'—the Long Falls gun caliber?"

"Right. And 'suppressor' or 'silencer' combined with 'rifle.' "

She made some quick notes. "Okay, what else?"

" 'Firecrackers.' "

"What?"

"Witnesses at the cemetery heard firecrackers going off around the time that Carl was hit. If that was an attempt to conceal the residual sound of the suppressed muzzle blast, it may have been a technique the shooter used before, and a witness may have mentioned it to an investigator, and the investigator may have entered it on his ViCAP form."

"Jesus," said Hardwick. "That's one goddamn way-out long shot."

"It's worth a try."

Esti was tapping her pen again on her pad. "You're assuming the shooter was a pro?"

"Feels that way to me."

"Okay. Any other search terms?"

" 'Cemetery' and 'funeral.' If the shooter went to the trouble of killing someone just to set his main victim up at the grave, maybe the same thing's worked for him before."

As she was writing, Gurney added, "All the surnames connected with the case should be searched as well—Spalter, Angelidis, Gurikos. Also, we need to run Darryl's surname, the surnames of the other prosecution witnesses, and Kay's maiden name. You can find them all in the trial transcript."

Hardwick spoke with loathing in his voice. "Don't forget to include 'nails,' 'nails in eyes,' 'nails in ears,' 'nails in throat.' "

Esti nodded, then asked Gurney, "Anything from the mother's location?"

"That one's not so easy. You could look for homicides set up as bathtub falls, homicides involving floral deliveries, even the fake florist name—Flowers by Florence—but that feels like an even longer shot than the firecrackers."

"I think this is enough to keep me busy for a while."

"Jack, I recall from the Jillian Perry case that you might know somebody at Interpol. That still true?"

"Far as I know."

"Maybe you could see what they have on Gurikos?"

"I can try. No promises."

"You think you could also take a stab at tracking down the main prosecution witnesses?"

He nodded slowly. "Freddie, who testified that Kay was in the apartment building at the time of the shooting . . . Jimmy Flats, the con who said Kay tried to hire him to whack Carl . . . and Darryl, the boyfriend who said she tried the same line on him?"

"Those three at least."

"I'll see what I can do. You thinking we might squeeze a perjury admission out of one of them?"

"That would be nice. But mainly, I'd like to know that they're alive and reachable."

"Alive?" Hardwick looked like he was thinking what Gurney was thinking. If at the heart of the mystery was an individual capable of doing what was done to Gus Gurikos, then anything was possible. The possibilities were horrendous.

The notion of horrendous possibilities brought Klemper to mind. "I almost forgot to mention this," said Gurney, "but your favorite BCI investigator was waiting for me when I got home this afternoon from my meeting with Angelidis."

Hardwick's eyes narrowed. "The fuck did he want?"

"He wanted me to understand that Kay is an evil, lying, murdering bitch; that Bincher is an evil, lying Jew bastard; and that he, Mick Klemper, is a crusader in the epic struggle of Good against Evil. He admitted that he might have made an error or two, but nothing that changes the fact that Kay is guilty as sin and deserves to die in prison— preferably soon."

Esti looked excited. "He must have been in a panic to show up at your house, raving like that."

Hardwick looked suspicious. "You sure that's all he wanted? To tell you that Kay was guilty?"

"He seemed desperate to convince me that everything he'd done was legitimate in some larger context. He may also have been trying, in his bull-in-the-china-shop way, to get me to reveal how much I knew. As I see it, the unresolved question about Klemper is how *sick* is he—versus how *corrupt*."

Esti added, "Or how *dangerous*."

Hardwick changed the subject. "So I'm going to take the locate-the-three-witnesses assignment, which may turn into three mis-per traces, which may turn into God knows what. And I'm going to beg my buddy at Interpol for another favor. Esti's going to call in some favors at OCTF and get someone to run NCIC and ViCAP searches. What's on *your* plate, Sherlock?"

"First I'm going to talk to Alyssa Spalter. Then to Jonah Spalter."

"Great. But how're you going to get *them* to talk to *you*?"

"Charm. Threats. Promises. Whatever works."

Esti let out a cynical little one-syllable laugh. "Offer Alyssa an ounce of good shit, she'll follow you to the moon. Jonah you'll have to figure out for yourself."

"You know where I can get ahold of Alyssa?"

"Last time I heard, the family mansion on Venus Lake. With Carl and Kay out of the way, she has it all to herself. But watch out for Klemper. My impression is that he still sees her. He's still got a soft spot for his little monster."

Hardwick smirked. "Don't you mean a *hard* spot?"

"You're disgusting!" She turned back to Gurney. "I'll text you the address. Or, actually, I can give it to you right now. I have it in my notebook." She stood up from the table and left the room.

Gurney sat back in his chair and gave Hardwick a speculative look. "Maybe it's my imagination, but you seem to be getting an inch or two closer to my way of thinking about this case."

"The fuck are you talking about?"

"Your interest in it seems to be expanding a bit beyond the technical appeal issues."

At first Hardwick looked like he wanted to argue the point. Then he just shook his head slowly. "Those fucking nails ..." He stared down at the floor. "I don't know ... makes you wonder just how God-awful a human being can be. *How. Downright. Completely. Evil.*" He paused, still shaking his head, like someone with a kind of slow-motion palsy. "You ever come upon something that just ... just made you wonder ... what the fuck ... I mean ... if there are any limits on what a human being can do?"

Gurney didn't have to think very long about it. Images of severed heads, torn throats, bodies chopped apart. Children burned alive by their parents. The "Satanic Santa" case that involved a serial killer gift-wrapping pieces of his victims' bodies and mailing them to the local cops' homes at Christmas.

"Lots of images come to mind, Jack, but the new one that keeps disturbing my sleep is Carl Spalter's face—the photo taken of him while he was still barely alive at Kay's trial. There's something terrible about it. Maybe the look of despair in Carl's eyes affects me the way those nails in Gus's eyes affect you."

Neither of them said anything more until Esti came back with a small sheet of notepaper and handed it to Gurney. "You probably don't even need this address," she said. "I could've just told you to look for the biggest house on Lakeshore Drive."

"It'll be easier with this. Thanks."

She sat in her chair, looked back and forth curiously at the two men. "What's up? You're both looking very ... down."

Hardwick uttered a sharp, humorless bark of a laugh.

Gurney shrugged. "Every once in a while, we get a glimpse of the reality we're dealing with. You know what I'm talking about?"

Her voice changed. "Yes, of course I do."

There was a silence.

Gurney said, "We need to focus on the fact that we're making progress. We're taking the appropriate actions. Accurate data and solid logic will—"

His comment was cut short by the sound of a sudden, sharp impact against the clapboard siding of the house.

Esti tensed, looked alarmed.

Hardwick blinked. "The fuck was that?"

The sound was repeated—like the crack of the hard tip of a whip against the house—and all the lights went out.

Chapter 29

Game Changers

Reflexively, Gurney dropped from his chair to the floor. Hardwick and Esti followed immediately, in a flurry of expletives.

"I'm not carrying," said Gurney quickly. "What do you have in the house?"

"Glock nine in the bedroom closet," said Hardwick. "SIG .38 in the night table."

"Kel-Tec .38 in my shoulder bag," said Esti. "Bag's behind you, Jack, on the floor. Can you push it over to me?"

Gurney heard Hardwick moving on the other side of the table, then something sliding toward Esti on the floor.

"Got it," she said.

"Back in a sec," said Hardwick.

Gurney heard him scuttling out of the room, cursing, then the sound of an interior door squeaking open, then a drawer opening and closing. A flashlight went on, went off. He could also hear Esti's breathing, very close to him.

"There's no moon tonight, is there?" She was half whispering.

For an insane moment, in the grip of a primitive fear and the rush of adrenaline, he found her lowered voice and closeness so intensely erotic, he forgot to answer the question.

"Dave?"

"Right. Yes. No moon."

She leaned closer, her arm touching his. "What do you think is happening?"

"I'm not sure. Nothing good."

"You think we're overreacting?"

"I hope so."

"I can't see a damn thing. Can you?"

He strained his eyes in the general direction of the window by the table. "No. Nothing."

"Shit." The magnetism of her anxious, whispering voice in the darkness was becoming surreal. "You think those sounds were bullets hitting the house?"

"Could be." In fact, he was sure of it. He'd been under fire more than once in his career.

"I didn't hear any gunshots."

"Could be using a suppressor."

"Oh, shit. You really think it's sniper-boy out there?"

Gurney was pretty sure that it was, but before he could answer, Hardwick returned.

"Got the Glock and SIG. I like the Glock. How about you, ace? You okay with the SIG?"

"No problem."

Hardwick touched Gurney's elbow, found his hand, put the pistol in it. "Full clip, one in the chamber, safety on."

"Good. Thanks."

"Maybe it's time to call in the cavalry," said Esti.

"Fuck that!" said Hardwick.

"So what do we do? Sit here all night?"

"We figure out how to get the son of a bitch."

"*Get* him? That's what SWAT does. We make the call. *They* come. *They* get him."

"Fuck them. I'll get him myself. Nobody shoots at my fucking house. Fuck!"

"Jack, for Godsake, the man put a bullet through a power line. In the dark. This is a super marksman. With a night-vision scope. Hiding in the woods. How the hell are you going to *get* him? For Godsake, Jack, make sense!"

"Fuck him! He's not that fucking super—took him two shots to hit the line. I'll put my Glock up his super ass."

"Maybe it didn't take him two shots," said Gurney.

"The hell are you talking about? Lights went out on the second shot, not the first."

"Check your landline."

"What?"

"It sounded to me like the impacts were at different places on the upstairs wall. Do your power and phone lines come in together or separately?"

Hardwick didn't answer, which was answer enough.

Gurney heard him crawling from the table into the kitchen . . . then the sound of a handset being picked up, and after a moment being replaced . . . then crawling back to the table.

"It's dead. He hit the fucking phone line."

"I don't get it," said Esti. "What's the point of cutting a landline when everybody's got cell phones? He must know who Jack is, probably knows who we all are, has to assume we all have phones. You ever see a cop without a cell phone? Why cut the landline?"

"Maybe he likes to show off," said Hardwick. "Well, this fucker is fucking with the wrong guy."

"You're not the only one here, Jack. Maybe he's fucking with Dave. Maybe he's fucking with all of us."

"I don't give a fuck who he thinks he's fucking with. But it's my fucking house that he's shooting fucking bullets into."

"This is crazy. I say we get a SWAT team here, like now."

"We're not in fucking Albany. It's not like they're parked down in Dillweed, waiting for the call. Be an hour before they get here."

"Dave?" Her expression was begging for support.

Gurney couldn't provide it. "It might be better to handle this ourselves."

"Better? How the hell is it better?"

"You make this official, it's a big can of worms."

"Can of . . . what are you talking about?"

"Your career."

"*Career?*"

"You're a BCI investigator, and Jack's in the process of launching an all-out attack on BCI. How are they going to interpret your being here? You think they're not going to figure out in about two seconds how he's getting his inside information? Information he can use to ruin their lives? You think you're going to survive that—legally or otherwise? I think I'd rather deal with a sniper in the woods than be considered a traitor by people I have to work with."

Esti's voice was a bit shaky. "I don't see what they can prove. There's no reason—" She stopped abruptly. "What was that?"

"What was what?" asked Gurney.

"Out that window ... on the hill facing the house ... in the woods ... a flash of light ..."

Hardwick scrambled around the back of the table toward the window.

Peering into the darkness, Esti whispered, "I'm positive I saw some—" Again she stopped midsentence.

This time Gurney and Hardwick both saw it. "There!" cried Gurney.

"It's one of my trail cams," said Hardwick. "Motion-activated. I've got half a dozen in the woods—mainly for hunting season." Another flash occurred, seemingly higher on the hill. "Fucker's moving up the main trail. Getting away. Fuck that!"

Gurney heard Hardwick scrambling to his feet, hurrying out of the room into the kitchen, then returning with two lit flashlights in one hand, Glock in the other. He stood one flashlight in the middle of the table, beam pointing at the ceiling. "I got an idea where the son of a bitch is heading. After I leave, get in your cars, get out of here, forget you were here."

Esti's voice rose in alarm. "Where are you going?"

"I'm going to where that trail goes—to Scutt Hollow on the other side of the mountain. If I can get there before he does ..."

"We'll come with you!"

"Bullshit! You both need to get out of here—in the opposite direction—now! You get caught up in this, get questioned by the local cops—worse, by BCI—it'll be an endless mess. Take care. Got to go!"

"Jack!"

Hardwick ran out the front door. A few seconds later they heard the roar of the big GTO V8, wheels spinning, bits of gravel sprayed against the side of the house. Gurney grabbed the remaining flashlight from the table, hurried out onto the porch, saw the car's taillights speeding away around a curve in the narrow dirt road that wound down the long wooded hillside to Route 10.

"He shouldn't go alone." Esti's voice next to him was strained and ragged. "We should follow him, call it in."

She was right. But so was Hardwick.

"Jack's no fool. I've seen him in tougher situations than this. He'll be all right." Gurney's assurance sounded hollow.

"He shouldn't be chasing that maniac by himself!"

"He can make the backup call. It's up to him. As long as we're not there, he can shape the story any way he wants. If we're there, it's out of his hands. And your career is over."

"Jesus. Jesus! I hate this!" She walked in a tight, frustrated circle. "So now what? We just leave? Just drive away? Go home?"

"Yes. You first. Right now."

She stared at Gurney in the flashlight's shifting illumination. "Okay. Okay. But this is fucked up. Completely fucked up."

"I agree. But we need to preserve Jack's options. Is there anything of yours in the house?"

She blinked several times, seemingly trying to focus on the question. "My tote bag, my shoulder bag . . . I think that's it."

"Okay. Whatever you have in there—get it, and get out of here."

He handed her the flashlight and waited outside while she went into the house.

Two minutes later she was depositing her bags in the passenger seat of the Mini Cooper.

"Where do you live?" he asked.

"Oneonta."

"Alone?"

"Yes."

"Be careful."

"Sure. You too." She got in her car, backed out, turned down the dirt road, and was gone.

He switched off the flashlight and stood in the darkness, listening. He could detect no sound, no breeze, no hint of movement anywhere.

He stood there for a long minute, waiting to hear something, waiting to see something. Everything seemed unnaturally still.

Flashlight in one hand and SIG in the other, safety off, he made a 360-degree sweep of the land around him. He saw nothing alarming, nothing out of place. He pointed the beam up at the side of the house, swept it back and forth until he found a severed wire emerging from an electrical fitting by a second-floor window and, about ten feet away, a second wire emerging from a different kind of fitting by another window. He swept the light away from the house toward the road until he located the utility pole and the two loose wires he'd expected to find there, dangling down onto the ground.

He walked closer to the house, below the two severed wire ends. On the clapboards behind each, he could see a small dark hole a few inches from each fitting. He couldn't judge the diameters with any accuracy from where he stood, but he was fairly sure they couldn't have been made with a bullet any smaller than a .30 caliber or larger than a .35 caliber.

If it was the same shooter who hit Carl at Willow Rest, it would appear that he was flexible in his choice of weapons—a man who chose the tool most appropriate to the circumstances. A practical man. Or woman.

Esti's question came back to him. *What's the point of cutting a landline when everybody's got a cell phone?* From a practical perspective, cutting power and communication lines would be the preamble to an attack. But no attack had occurred. So what was the point?

A warning?

Like the nails in Gus's head?

But why the landline?

Holy Christ!

Could it be?

Power and phone. Power meant lights, which meant seeing. And the phone? What did you do with a phone—especially an old landline phone? You listened and you talked.

No power and no phone.

No seeing, no listening, no talking.

See no evil, hear no evil, speak no evil.

Or was he getting way too imaginative, way to enamored with his "message" theory? He knew damn well that falling in love with one's own hypothesis could be fatal. Still, if these weren't messages, what the hell were they?

Having switched off the flashlight, he stood again in the dark, holding the SIG Sauer pistol at his side, straining his eyes and ears. The utter silence gave him a chill. He told himself it was simply because the temperature was dropping and the air was growing damper. But that didn't make him feel any more comfortable. It was time to get the hell out of there.

Halfway to Walnut Crossing he stopped at an all-night convenience store for a container of coffee. Sitting in the parking lot, sipping the coffee, going back over what had happened at Hardwick's—what he could have done or should have done—endeavoring to organize some reasonable sequence of next steps, the thought came to him to call Kyle.

Prepared to leave a message, he was surprised to hear a live voice.

"Hey, Dad, what's up?"

"Actually, too damn much."

"Yeah? But, hell, you like it that way, don't you?"

"You think so?"

"I know so. If you're not being overwhelmed, you feel underoccupied."

Gurney smiled. "I hope I'm not calling you too late."

"Too late? It's like nine forty-five. This is New York City. Most of my friends are just going out now."

"Not you?"

"We decided to stay in tonight."

"We?"

"Long story. What's up?"

"A question, based on your Wall Street experience. Not even sure how to ask it. I spent my whole career buried in homicides, not white-collar stuff. What I'm wondering is, if an outfit was looking for major financing—let's say for expansion—is that something that would get around on the grapevine?"

"That would depend."

"On what?"

"On how 'major' a deal you're talking about. And what kind of financing. And who's involved. Lot of different factors. To get into the rumor mill, it would need to be big. Nobody on the Street talks about small stuff. What outfit are we talking about?"

"Something called the Cyberspace Cathedral—brainchild of a guy named Jonah Spalter."

"Kind of rings a bell."

"Any facts attached to that bell?"

"CyberCath . . ."

"*CyberCath?*"

"People in finance are big on abbreviations, stock-exchange names, fast talk—like they're too busy to use whole words."

"The Cyberspace Cathedral is listed on the stock exchange?"

"I don't think so. That's just the way the boys talk. What do you want to know about it?"

"Anything people say about it that I wouldn't find on Google."

"No problem. You working on a new case?"

"A murder conviction appeal. I'm trying to dig up some facts the original investigation may have ignored."

"Cool. How's it going?"

"Interestingly."

"Knowing how you talk about these things, I'd say that means that you were shot at but not hit."

"Well . . . sort of."

"Whaaat? You mean I'm right? Are you okay? Somebody tried to shoot you?"

"He was just shooting at a house I happened to be in."

"Jeez! That's part of this case you're on?"

"I think so."

"How can you be so calm? I'd be going nuts if somebody shot at a house I was in."

"I'd be more upset if he were aiming at me personally."

"Wow. If you were a comic-book hero, they'd have to call you Doctor Cool."

Gurney smiled, didn't know what to say. He didn't talk to Kyle that often, although they'd been in contact more frequently since the Good Shepherd case. "Is there any chance you might be coming up our way one of these days?"

"Sure. Why not. That'd be great."

"You still have the motorcycle?"

"Absolutely. And the helmet you gave me. Your old one. I wear it instead of my own."

"Ah . . . well . . . I'm glad it fits."

"I think we must have exactly the same size heads."

Gurney laughed. He wasn't sure why. "Well, anytime you can get away, we'd love to see you." He paused. "How's Columbia Law?"

"Busy as hell, tons of reading, but basically good."

"So you don't regret getting out of Wall Street?"

"Not for a minute. Well, maybe for an occasional minute. But then I remember all the bullshit that went with it—Wall Street is paved with bullshit—and I'm really happy not to be part of that anymore."

"Good."

There was a silence, finally broken by Kyle. "So . . . I'll make some calls, see if anyone knows anything about CyberCath, and I'll get back to you."

"Great, son. Thank you."

"Love you, Dad.

"Love you, too."

After ending the call, Gurney sat with his phone still in his hand, pondering the curious pattern of his communications with his son. The young man was . . . what? Twenty-five? Twenty-six? He could never immediately remember which. And for many of those years, especially the past ten, he and Kyle had been . . . what? Not quite estranged, that was too loaded a term for it. Distant? Separated by periods of noncommunication, certainly. But when the instances of communication did occur, they were invariably warm, particularly on Kyle's part.

Perhaps the explanation was as simple as the summation offered by Gurney's college girlfriend decades ago on the occasion of her breaking up with him: "You're just not a people person, David." Her name was Geraldine. They were standing outside the greenhouse in the New York Botanical Garden. The cherry blossoms were in full bloom. It was starting to rain. She turned and walked away, kept walking even as the rain grew heavier. They never spoke again.

He looked down at the cell phone in his hand. It occurred to him that he should call Madeleine, let her know he was on his way.

When she picked up she sounded sleepy. "Where are you?"

"Sorry, didn't mean to wake you."

"You didn't. I was reading. Dozing a little, maybe."

He was tempted to ask if the book was *War and Peace*. She'd been reading it forever, and it was a powerful soporific. "Just wanted to let you know that I'm halfway between Dillweed and Walnut Crossing. Should be home in less than twenty minutes."

"Good. How come so late?"

"I ran into some difficulty at Hardwick's."

"Difficulty? Are you all right?"

"I'm fine. Tell you all about it when I get home."

"When you get home I'll be sleeping."

"In the morning, then."

"Drive safely."

"Okay. See you soon."

He slipped the phone into his pocket, took a couple of swallows of cold coffee, dumped the rest of it in a trash bin, and drove back out onto the main road.

Hardwick was on his mind now. Along with the uncomfortable feeling that he should have ignored the man's instructions and followed him after all. Sure, there was a risk of one thing leading to another, a firefight with the shooter, official law enforcement agencies getting involved, BCI sniffing out Esti's involvement, having to fudge the facts of their meeting in order to protect her, half-true affidavits, knots and tangles and snarls. But, on the other hand, there was the possibility that Hardwick might be coming face-to-face—or muzzle-to-muzzle—with more than he could handle.

Gurney had a powerful urge to turn around and go back over the roads where Hardwick's chase was likely to have led him. But there were too many possibilities. Too many intersections. Each one would multiply the odds against duplicating the actual route the man had taken. And even if by some remarkable coincidence he made a series of accurate guesses and ended up in the right place, his unexpected arrival could create as many problems as it solved.

So he drove on, conflicted, coming eventually to the turn-off for his hilltop property. He drove slowly because deer had a way of leaping out of nowhere. He'd hit a fawn in the not-too-distant past, and the sickening feeling was still with him.

At the top of the road he stopped to let a porcupine move out of the way. He watched as it waddled off into the high grass on the rise above the barn. Porcupines had a bad reputation, earned by chewing up just about everything, from the siding on homes to the brake lines on cars. The farmer down the road had advised shooting them on sight. "They're a world of trouble and good for nothing." But Gurney had no heart for that, and Madeleine would never tolerate it.

He put the car back in gear and was about to head up the grassy lane to the farmhouse when something bright caught his eye. It was in one of the barn windows—a gleaming point of light. It occurred to him that perhaps a light in the barn had been left on—maybe by Madeleine when she last fed the chickens. But that bulb was relatively dim, with a yellowish cast, and this light in the window was sharp and white. As Gurney peered at it, it grew more intense.

He switched off his headlights. After sitting there mystified for a few more seconds, he picked up Hardwick's heavy metal flashlight from the passenger seat without turning it on, got out of the car, and walked toward the barn—guided through the darkness by that strange point of light, which seemed to move as he moved.

Then he realized with a touch of gooseflesh that the light wasn't in the barn at all. It was a reflection—a reflection on the window of a light somewhere *behind* him. He turned quickly, and there it was—a powerful light gleaming through the line of trees along the top of the ridge behind the pond. The first thought that came to mind was that it was a halogen searchlight mounted on an ATV.

In the barn behind him, perhaps in response to this illumination, the rooster crowed.

Gurney looked again at the ridge—at the swelling, brightening light behind the trees. And then, of course, it was obvious. As it should have been from the first instant. No mystery at all. No strange vehicle probing the high forest. Nothing out of the ordinary. Just a full moon rising on a clear night.

He felt like a fool.

His phone rang.

It was Madeleine. "Is that you down by the barn?"

"Yes, it's me."

"Someone just called for you. Are you on your way up?" Her voice was distinctly cool.

"Yes, I was just checking something. Who was it?"

"Alyssa."

"What?"

"A woman, by the name of Alyssa."

"Did she give you a last name?"

"I asked her for that. She said you'd probably know her last name, and if you didn't, there wasn't much point in talking to you anyway. She sounded either stoned or crazy."

"Did she leave a number?"

"Yes, it's here."

"I'll be right up."

Two minutes later, at 10:12 p.m., he was standing in the kitchen with his phone, entering the number.

Madeleine was at the sink island in her pink and yellow summer pajamas, putting away a few pieces of silverware left in the dish drainer.

His call was answered on the third ring—by a voice that was both husky and delicate. "Could this be Detective Gurney calling me back?"

"Alyssa?"

"The one and only."

"Alyssa Spalter?"

"Alyssa Spalter, who was left at the altar, just wearing a halter." She sounded like a twelve-year-old who'd been at her parents' liquor cabinet.

"What can I do for you?"

"You want to do something for me?"

"You called here a little while ago. What do you want?"

"I want to be helpful. That's all I want."

"How do you want to help?"

"You want to know who killed Cock Robin?"

"What?"

"How many murders are you involved in?"

"Are you talking about your father?"

"Who do you think?"

"Do you know who killed your father?"

"King Carl? Course I do."

"Tell me."

"Not on the phone."

"Why not?"

"Come see me, then I'll tell you."

"Give me a name."

"I'll give you a name. When I get to know you better. I give all my boyfriends special names. So when am I going to meet you?"

Gurney said nothing.

"You still there?" Her tone was wandering fluidly back and forth between clarity and intoxication.

"I'm here."

"Ah. That's the problem. You need to come *here*."

"Alyssa . . . you either know something useful, or you don't. You're either going to tell me what it is, or you're not. Up to you. Decide now."

"I know everything."

"Okay. Tell me about it."

"No way. Phone might be tapped. Such a scary world we live in. They tap everything. Tippety, tippety, tap. But you're a detective, so you know all that. Bet you even know where I live."

Gurney said nothing.

"Bet you know where I live, right?"

Again, he said nothing.

"Yeah, I bet you do."

"Alyssa? Listen to me. If you want to tell—"

She interrupted with an exaggerated, slurry seductiveness that might have been comical in other circumstances. "So . . . I'll be here all night. And all day tomorrow. Come as soon as you can. Please. I'll be waiting for you. Waiting just for you."

The connection was broken.

Gurney laid his phone down and looked at Madeleine. She was studying a fork she was about to put in the silverware drawer. She frowned, turned on the water in the sink, and began scrubbing it. Then she rinsed it, dried it, examined it again, seemed satisfied, and placed it in the drawer.

"I think you were right," said Gurney.

The frown came back, but now it was directed at him. "About what?"

"About the young woman being stoned or crazy."

She smiled humorlessly. "What does she want?"

"Good question."

"What does she *say* she wants?"

"To see me. To tell me who killed her father."

"Carl Spalter?"

"Yes."

"Are you going to see her?"

"Maybe." He paused, thinking about it. "Probably."

"Where?"

"Where she's living. The family house on Venus Lake. Out by Long Falls."

"*Venus* as in the goddess of love?"

"I guess."

"And *venereal* disease?"

"I suppose."

"Nice name for a lake." She paused. "You said 'the family house.' Her father's dead and her stepmother's in prison. Who else is in the family?"

"As far as I know, no one. Alyssa's the only child."

"Quite a *child.* You're going there alone?"

"Yes and no."

She looked at him curiously.

"Maybe with some simple electronic backup."

"You mean you're going to be wired?"

"Not like on television, with a van full of electronics geeks and satellite equipment sitting around the corner. I'm thinking a low-tech substitute. Are you going to be home tomorrow or at the clinic?"

"I'm working in the afternoon. I should be here most of the morning. Why?"

"What I'm thinking is this. When I get to Venus Lake, before I go into the house itself, I could call our landline from my cell phone. When you pick up and confirm that it's me, you just switch on the recorder. I'll leave my phone on, in my shirt pocket. It may not transmit everything with ideal clarity, but it'll provide some record of what's said in my meeting with her, which might turn out to be useful."

Madeleine looked doubtful. "That's fine for *later*, to prove whatever you want to prove, but . . . it's not exactly protection while you're there. In the two minutes Alyssa was on the phone with me, I did get a strong impression that she might be nuts. Dangerously nuts."

"Yeah, I know. But—"

She cut him off. "Don't tell me how many dangerously nutty people you had to deal with in the city. That was then, this is now." She paused, as if questioning the reality of the then/now distinction. "How much do you know about this person?"

He thought about it. Kay had said plenty about Alyssa. But how much of it was true was another question.

"How much do I know about her *for sure*? Almost nothing. Her stepmother *claims* she's a drug addict and a liar. She *may* have had sex with her father. She *may* have had sex with Mick Klemper to influence the outcome of the investigation. She *may* have framed her stepmother for murder. She *may* have been stoned out of her mind on the phone with me just now. Or she *may* have been putting on a bizarre act—for God only knows what reason."

"Do you know anything positive about her?"

"I can't say that I do."

"Well . . . it's your decision." She closed the silverware drawer a little more firmly than necessary. "But I think that meeting with her in her house by yourself is a terrible idea."

"I wouldn't do it if we couldn't set up the phone thing for protection."

Madeleine nodded ever so slightly, somehow managing to convey with that restrained gesture a clear message: *It's far too risky, but I know I can't stop you.*

Then she added something, aloud. "Have you made that appointment yet?"

He realized that she'd switched subjects, and that the segue itself was fraught with meaning, which he pretended not to grasp. "What appointment?"

She stood there by the sink, her hands resting on the rim of it, fixing him with a patient, disbelieving stare.

"Are you talking about Malcolm Claret?" he asked.

"Yes. Who did you think?"

He shook his head in a kind of helpless gesture. "There's a limit to the number of things I can keep in my mind at once."

"What time are you leaving tomorrow?"

He sensed another change of direction. "For Venus Lake? Maybe nine or so. I doubt that Miss Alyssa gets up very early. Why?"

"I want to work on the chicken house. I thought maybe if you had a few free minutes you could explain the next steps so I could make a little progress before I go to the clinic. It's supposed to be a nice morning."

Gurney sighed. He tried to focus on the chicken project—the basic geometry, how far they'd gotten with their measurements, the materials that needed to be purchased, what had to happen next—but he couldn't wrap his mind around it. It was as if the Spalter issues and the chicken issues required two different brains. And then there was the Hardwick situation. Each time his mind went back to it, he regretted his decision to do as the man had asked.

He promised Madeleine he'd deal later with the chicken house issue, went into the den, and called Hardwick's cell number.

Unsurprisingly—and frustratingly—it went directly to voice mail.

"Hardwick—leave a message."

"Hey, Jack, what's happening out there? Where are you? Let me know. Please."

Finally realizing that his brain had reached a useless point of exhaustion, Gurney joined Madeleine in bed. But sleep, when it eventually came, was hardly sleep at all. His mind was stuck in one of those feverish, shallow, circular ruts—in which the ID and the directive, *"Hardwick—leave a message,"* kept recurring in all sorts of twisted permutations.

Chapter 30

Beautiful Poison

G urney waited until the following morning to tell Madeleine about the power-line drama at Hardwick's house. When he completed his much abridged rendition of the incident, she sat quietly watching him, as if waiting for the other shoe to fall.

The other shoe was the one he was afraid to drop, but felt he had to. "I think, as a precaution—" he began, but she finished his thought for him.

"I should move out of the house for a while. Is that what you were going to say?"

"It's just to be on the safe side. Just for a few days. My feeling is that this guy made his point and isn't likely to repeat the performance, but still . . . I want you to be away from any possible danger until the issue is resolved."

Anticipating the same angry reaction she'd had to a similar suggestion he'd made a year earlier during the unnerving Jillian Perry case, he was caught off-balance by her evident lack of objection. Her first question was surprisingly practical: "How many days are we talking about?"

"I'd only be guessing. But . . . maybe three, four? Depends on how soon we can eliminate the problem."

"Three or four days starting when?"

"Hopefully by tomorrow night? I was thinking maybe you could invite yourself to your sister's place down in—"

"I'll be at the Winklers'."

"You'll be where?"

"I knew you wouldn't remember. The Winklers. At their farm. In Buck Ridge."

It rang a distant bell in his memory.

"The people with the odd animals?"

"Alpacas. And you also remember that I offered to go there to help them take care of things during the fair?"

A second distant bell. "Ah. Yes. Right."

"And that the fair starts this weekend?"

A third distant bell. "Right."

"So that's where I'll be. At the fair with them and at their farm. I was going to go the day after tomorrow, but I'm sure they won't mind me coming a day early. In fact, they had invited me to stay the whole week. I was going to take a few days off from the clinic. You know, we *did* discuss this when they first brought it up."

"I have a vague recollection. I guess it just seemed so far away at the time. But that's fine—a lot more convenient than going down to your sister's or something like that."

Her easy manner stiffened. "But what about you? If it makes sense for *me* not to be here . . ."

"I'll be fine. Like I said, the shooter was delivering a message. He seems to know that Hardwick is responsible for stirring up the Spalter case, so it makes sense that he addressed his nasty little message to him. Besides, in the highly unlikely event that he wants to make his presence known a second time, I may be able to take advantage of that."

Her face was full of anxious confusion, as if she were wrestling with a major contradiction.

He noted her expression and regretted having added an unnecessary twist, which he now tried to dance away from. "My point is that the likelihood of any real problem here is minuscule, but even if it's less than one percent, I'd like you to be as far away from it as possible."

"But again, what about *you*? Even if it is less than one percent, which I don't really believe . . ."

"Me? No need to worry. According to *New York* magazine, I'm the most successful homicide dick in the history of the Big Apple."

His tongue-in-cheek boast was supposed to relax her.

If anything, it appeared to do the opposite.

Gurney's GPS took him into the enclave of Venus Lake via a series of agrarian river valleys, bypassing the blight of Long Falls.

Lakeshore Drive formed a two-mile loop around a body of water that he estimated to be about a mile long and a quarter-mile wide. The loop began and ended in a postcard village at the foot of the lake. The Spalter home—an inflated imitation of a colonial farmhouse—stood on a formally landscaped multiacre property at the head of the lake.

He made a complete circuit of the road before stopping in front of Killington's Mercantile Emporium, which—with the meticulous rusticity of its facade and window display of fly-fishing equipment, English teas, and country tweeds—appeared to Gurney to be about as authentic a representation of rural life as a scented-candle catalog.

He took out his phone and called Hardwick for the third time that morning, and for the third time was shunted into voice mail. Then he called Esti's cell, also for the third time, but this time she picked up. "Dave?"

"Any news from Jack?"

"Yes and no. He called me at eleven forty-five last night. Didn't sound very happy. Apparently the shooter either had a trail bike or an ATV. Jack said he could hear him in the woods near the road at one point, but that was the closest he got. So, no progress there. I think he was going to spend time today trying to track down the guys who testified against Kay."

"What about the photos?"

"The Gurikos autopsy photos?"

"Well, those, too—but I meant the trail-cam photos. Remember the flashes we saw up in the woods after the shots hit the house?"

"According to Jack, the cameras were shattered. Apparently the shooter put a couple of bullets in each one. As for the Gurikos and the Mary Spalter autopsy stuff, I've got phone queries out. May have replies soon, fingers crossed."

The next call he made was to his own home landline number.

At first there was no answer, and the call went into voice mail. He was starting to leave a panicky *Where the hell are you?* message when Madeleine picked up. "Hi. I was outside, trying to figure out the electric thing."

"What electric thing?"

"Didn't we agree there'd have to be an electric line running out to the chicken house?"

He suppressed a sigh of exasperation. "Yeah, I guess. I mean, it's not . . . not something we need to deal with right now."

"Okay . . . but shouldn't we know where it's going to be, so we don't have a problem later?"

"Look, I can't focus on this now. I'm at Venus Lake, about to interview the victim's daughter. I need you to set up our phone to make a recording."

"I know. You told me. I just leave the line open and turn on the recorder."

"Right, that's pretty much it. Except, I thought of a better way to handle it."

She said nothing.

"You still there?"

"I'm still here."

"Okay. Here's what I need you to do. Call me exactly ten minutes from now. I'll say something to you—ignore whatever it is that I say—then I'll disconnect you. Call me back immediately. I'll say something else and disconnect you again. Call me a third time and, no matter what I say, leave the line open at that point and turn on the recorder. Okay?"

"Why the extra complication?" There was a rising note of anxiety in her voice.

"Alyssa may assume that I'm recording the interview on my phone or that I'm transmitting it to another recorder. I want to kill that idea in her head by creating a situation that will convince her I've turned it off completely."

"Okay. I'll call you in ten minutes. Ten minutes from right now?"

"Yes."

He slipped the phone into his shirt pocket and took a small digital recorder out of the car's console box and clipped it to a very visible position on his belt. Then he drove from Killington's Mercantile Emporium to the opposite end of Venus Lake—to the open wrought-iron gate and driveway that led up to the Spalter house. He passed slowly through the gate and parked where the driveway broadened in front of wide granite steps.

The front door appeared to be an antique salvaged from an older but equally prosperous home. On the wall beside it there was an intercom. He pressed the button.

A disembodied female voice said, "Come in, the door's unlocked."

He checked his watch. Just six minutes to Madeleine's call. He opened the door and stepped into a large entry hall illuminated by a series of antique sconces on each wall. An arched doorway on the left opened into a formal dining room; a similar one on the right opened into a well-furnished living room with a weathered-brick fireplace a man could stand in. At the rear of the hall a polished-mahogany staircase with elaborate banisters rose to a second-floor landing.

A half-naked young woman came out onto the landing, paused, smiled, and began to descend the stairs. She was wearing only two skimpy bits of clothing—clearly designed to emphasize what they nominally concealed—a pink cutoff T-shirt that barely covered her breasts, and white shorts that covered almost nothing. An unexplained acronym, FMAD, was printed in bold black letters across the stretched fabric of her shirt.

Her face looked fresher than Gurney had expected the face of a drug addict to look. Her shoulder-length ash-blond hair was disarrayed and damp-looking, as though she'd recently come from the shower. She was barefoot. As she descended farther, he noticed that her toenails were painted a pale pink, matching the hint of pink on her lips, which were small and delicately shaped, like a doll's.

When she reached the foot of the stairs, she paused, giving him the same sort of visual inspection he'd been giving her.

"Hi, Dave." Her voice, like her appearance, was both vain and absurdly seductive. Her eyes, he noted with interest, were not the dull, self-pitying eyes of the average junkie. They were sky blue, clear, bright. But the chilly substance sparkling in those eyes wasn't the innocence of youth. Far from it.

There is an interesting thing about eyes, thought Gurney. *They contain and reflect, even in the effort of concealment, the emotional sum of everything they've seen.*

He cleared his throat and asked a perfunctory but necessary question. "Are you Alyssa Spalter?"

Her pink lips parted slightly, showing a row of perfect teeth.

"That's the question cops on TV ask before they arrest somebody. Do you want to arrest me?" Her tone was playful, but her eyes weren't.

"That's not my plan."

"What *is* your plan?"

"No plan. I'm here because you called me."

"And because you're curious?"

"I'm curious about who killed your father. You told me you knew who it was. Do you?"

"Don't be in such a hurry. Come in and sit down." She turned at the foot of the stairs and walked through the archway into the living room, moving on her bare feet with a kind of silkiness, like a dancer. She didn't look back.

He followed her—thinking that he'd never before encountered such a remarkable combination of over-the-top sexuality and pure cyanide.

The room itself—with its enormous fireplace, leather-upholstered chairs, and English landscape paintings—provided a bizarre contrast to the Lolita-like figure who might soon inherit it. Or maybe not such a contrast after all, considering that the house was probably no older than Alyssa, and its outward appearance no more than a clever contrivance.

"Kinda like a museum," she said, "but the sofa is nice and soft. I love the way it feels on my legs. Try it."

Before he could choose a place to sit—anywhere but the sofa—his phone rang. He checked the ID. It was Madeleine, right on time. He stared at the screen with an expression of consternation, as though the caller were the last person he wanted to hear from, before pressing TALK.

"Yes?" He paused. "No." He paused again before repeating, angrily now, "I said no!" He pressed END CALL, put the phone back in his shirt pocket, looked at Alyssa and erased his frown. "Sorry for the interruption. Where were we?"

"We were about to get comfortable." She sat at one end of the sofa and gestured invitingly toward the cushion nearest her.

Instead he sat in a wing chair, separated from her by a coffee table.

She let a pouty little look come and go. "You want something to drink?"

He shook his head.

"Beer?"

"No."

"Champagne?"

"No, I'm fine."

"Martini? Negroni? Tequini? Margarita?"

"Nothing."

The pouty look again. "You don't drink?"

"Sometimes. Not now."

"You sound so tense. You need to—"

His phone rang again. He checked the ID, confirmed that it was Madeleine. He let it ring three more times, as though intending to let it go to his voice mail; then, in an apparent burst of impatience, he pressed TALK. "What is it?" He paused. "This is not the time . . . For Christ's sake . . ." He paused, looking increasingly annoyed. "Look. Please. I'm in the middle of something. Yes . . . No . . . NOT NOW!" He pressed END CALL and replaced the phone in his pocket.

Alyssa gave him a sly smile. "Girlfriend problems?"

He didn't answer, just stared at the coffee table.

"You need to relax. All that tension, I can feel it over here. Is there anything I can do?"

"It might help if you got dressed."

"Got dressed? I *am* dressed."

"Not noticeably."

Her lips parted in a slow, deliberate grin. "You're funny."

"Okay, Alyssa. Enough. Let's get to the point. Why did you want to see me?"

The grin was replaced by the pouty look. "No need to sound so unfriendly. I just want to help."

"How?"

"I want to help you understand the *reality* of the situation," she said earnestly, as though that answer clarified everything. When Gurney just stared at her and waited, she switched back to the grin. "You positive you don't want a drink? How about a tequila sunrise? I make a *fantastic* tequila sunrise."

He reached with obvious casualness to his hip, scratched a non-existent itch, and switched on the digital recorder affixed to his belt, awkwardly hiding the soft click under a loud cough.

Her grin broadened. "If you want to shut me up, sweetie, that's the way to do it."

"Beg pardon?"

"*Beg pardon?*" There was a glint of cold amusement in her eyes.

"What's wrong?" He projected as best he could the expression of a guilty man trying to appear innocent.

"What's that cute little thing on your belt?"

He glanced down at his side. "Oh, that's . . ." He cleared his throat. "That's actually a recorder."

"A recorder. No shit. Can I see it?"

He blinked. "Uh, sure." He unclipped it and held it out across the coffee table.

She took it, studied it, switched it off, and laid it on the sofa cushion next to her.

He put on an anxious frown. "May I have that back, please?"

"Come and get it."

He looked at her, at the recorder, back at her, cleared his throat again. "It's a routine thing. I make a point of recording all my meetings. It can be very helpful in avoiding disputes later about what was said or what was agreed to."

"That so? Wow. Why didn't I think of that?"

"So, if you don't mind, I'd like to record this meeting, too."

"Yeah? Well, like Santa said to the greedy little boy, fuck you."

He looked disconcerted. "Why is it such a big deal?"

"It's not a big deal. I just don't like being recorded."

"I think it would be better for both of us."

"I disagree."

Gurney shrugged. "Okay. Fine."

"What were you going to do with it?"

"Like I said, in case there was some dispute later . . ."

His phone rang for the third time. Madeleine on the ID. He pressed TALK.

"Jesus, what now?" he said into the phone, sounding thoroughly ticked off. Over the next ten seconds he imitated a man about to lose it completely. "I know . . . Right . . . Right . . . Jesus, can we talk about this LATER? . . . Right . . . Yes . . . I said YES." He took the phone from his ear, glared at it as though it were the source of nothing but problems, poked at a spot close to the END CALL button without breaking the connection, and put the still-transmitting phone back in his shirt pocket. He shook his head and shot Alyssa an embarrassed glance. "Jesus."

She yawned, as though there were nothing more boring on earth than a man thinking about something other than her. Then she arched her back. The movement raised what little there was of her shirt, exposing the bottom of her breasts. "Maybe we ought to start over," she said, nestling back into her corner of the sofa.

"Okay. But I'd like my recorder back."

"I'll hold on to it while you're here. You can have it when you leave."

"Fine. Okay." He gave a sigh of resignation. "Back to the beginning. You were saying that you wanted me to understand the *reality* of the situation. What reality?"

"The reality is that you're wasting your time, trying to turn everything upside down."

"Is that what you think I'm doing?"

"You're trying to turn the bitch loose, right?"

"I'm trying to find out who killed your father."

"Who killed him? His whore cunt bitch wife killed him. End of story."

"Kay Spalter, the supersniper?"

"She took lessons. It's true. It's *documented.*" She articulated the word reverently, as though it had magical powers of persuasion.

Gurney shrugged. "A lot of people take shooting lessons without killing anyone."

Alyssa shook her head—a quick, bitter movement. "You don't know what she's like."

"Tell me."

"She's a lying, greedy piece of shit."

"Anything else?"

"She married my father for his money. Period. Kay is a money-fucker. And a general slut. When this finally dawned on my father, he told her he wanted a divorce. Bitch figured that'd be the end of the good life for her, so she ended his life instead. BANG! Simple."

"So you think it was all about money?"

"It was all about that skeeve getting whatever she wanted. Did you know she was buying Darryl, the pool boy, presents with my father's money? She bought him a diamond earring for his birthday. You know how much she paid for that? Guess."

Gurney waited.

"No. Really. Guess how much."

"A thousand?"

"A thousand? I wish! Fucking *ten thousand*! Ten fucking thousand dollars of my fucking father's fucking money! For the fucking pool boy! You know why?"

Again Gurney waited.

"I'll tell you why. The disgusting bitch was paying him to fuck her. On my father's credit card. How disgusting is that? And speaking of disgusting, you should see her putting on her makeup . . . give you the fucking shakes watching it—like an undertaker putting a smiley face on a corpse."

This fury, this well of bile and hatred, struck Gurney as the most authentic part of Alyssa he'd seen so far. But even about that he wasn't absolutely sure. He wondered how extensive her acting talent might be.

She sat silently now, chewing at her thumb.

"Did she kill your grandmother, too?" he asked mildly.

She blinked in apparent confusion. "My . . . *who*?"

"Your father's mother."

"The hell are you talking about?"

"There's reason to believe Mary Spalter's death was no accident."

"What reason?"

"The day she was found dead, an individual was videotaped entering the Emmerling Oaks complex under false pretenses. The day your father was shot, that same individual was seen entering the apartment where the rifle was found."

"Is this some kind of bullshit invented by your scumbag lawyer?"

"Did you know, the same day your father was shot, a local mobster he was dealing with was killed? You think Kay did that, too?"

Gurney got the impression that Alyssa was rattled and trying not to show it.

"She could have. Why not? If she could kill her husband . . ." Her voice trailed off.

"She's a regular homicide factory, huh? Those lifers over in Bedford Hills better watch out." Even as he tossed in this sarcastic crack, he recalled the nickname Kay had acquired from her prison-mates, the Black Widow, and wondered if they saw something in her that he'd missed.

Alyssa made no reply, just sank a little deeper into the corner of the sofa and crossed her arms in front of her. Apart from her very adult figure, she looked for a passing instant like a troubled middle-schooler. Even when she finally spoke, it was with more angry bravado than confidence. "What a pile of bullshit! Anything to free that bitch, right?"

Gurney was weighing his options. He could leave things as they were, letting what he'd revealed fester in her mind, and see what developed. Or he could press on, use all his ammunition right now, try to provoke an explosion. There were sizable risks either way. He opted to press on. He hoped to Christ his phone was still transmitting.

He leaned toward her, elbows on his knees. "Listen carefully, Alyssa. Some of this you already know. In fact, most of it. But you better listen to all of it. I'll only say it once. Kay Spalter didn't kill anybody. She was convicted because Mick Klemper screwed up the investigation. On purpose. The only open question in my mind is whether that was his idea or yours. I'm thinking it was yours."

"You're funny."

"I'm thinking the idea was yours, because you're the one with the motive that makes the most sense. Get Kay put away for Carl's murder, and all the money goes to you. So you fucked Klemper—literally—into doing a frame job on Kay. Problem is, Klemper did a lousy job. So now the house of cards is collapsing. The prosecution's case is full of gaping holes, evidence problems, police misconduct. Kay's conviction is sure to be reversed on appeal. She'll be out in another month, maybe sooner. As soon as that happens, Carl's estate goes immediately to her. So you fucked that idiot Klemper for nothing. It'll be interesting to see what happens in court—which one of you ends up doing the most time."

"*Doing time?* For what?"

"Obstruction. Perjury. Suborning perjury. Conspiracy. And half a dozen other nasty legal offenses, with long prison sentences attached to them. Klemper will blame you, you'll blame Klemper. The jury probably won't care much for either one of you."

As he was speaking, she drew her knees up in front of her and wrapped her arms tightly around them. Her eyes appeared to be focused on some invisible road map.

After a long minute, she spoke in a small, even voice. "Suppose I told you he blackmailed me."

He worried whether her comment was loud enough for his phone to pick up. "Blackmailed you? How? Why?"

"He knew something about me."

"What did he know?"

She gave him a shrewd look. "You don't need to know that."

"Okay. He blackmailed you into doing what?"

"Having sex with him."

"And lying in court about things you heard Kay say on the phone?"

She hesitated. "No. I actually heard those things."

"So you admit having sex with Klemper but deny committing perjury?"

"That's right. Me fucking him was not a crime. But him *making me* fuck him was. So if anybody's got a problem, it's him, not me."

"Anything else you want to tell me?"

"No." She lowered her feet gracefully to the floor. "And you should really forget everything I just told you."

"Why is that?"

"It might not be true."

"Why bother telling me, then?"

"To help you understand. That stuff you were saying about me doing time? That's never going to happen." She moistened her lips with the tip of her tongue.

"Okay. Then I guess we're finished here."

"Unless you want to change your mind about my tequila sunrise. Believe me, it's worth changing your mind for."

Gurney stood up, pointed to his mini-recorder on the sofa cushion. "May I have that, please?"

She picked it up and jammed it into the pocket of her shorts, which were already about to burst a seam. She smiled. "I'll mail it to you. Or . . . you could try to take it now."

"Keep it."

"Aren't you even going to try? I bet you could take it if you really tried."

Gurney smiled. "Klemper didn't have a chance, did he?"

She smiled back. "I told you, he blackmailed me. Made me do things I never would have done willingly. Never. You can just imagine what kind of things."

Gurney walked around the far side of the coffee table and out of the living room, opened the front door, and stepped out onto the broad stone steps. Alyssa followed him to the doorway and put on her pouty look.

"Most men ask me what FMAD means."

He glanced at the big letters on the front of her tee. "I bet they do."

"Aren't you curious?"

"Okay, I'm curious. What does FMAD mean?"

She leaned toward him and whispered, "Fuck Me And Die."

Chapter 31

Another Black Widow

The red GTO was parked at his side door, as Gurney expected it would be. He'd called Hardwick on his way home from Venus Lake and left a message suggesting they get together ASAP, including Esti if possible. He felt the need for other perspectives on his Alyssa interview.

Hardwick had called Gurney back as he was nearing Walnut Crossing and offered to come right over. When Gurney entered the house, he found the man lounging in a chair at the breakfast table with the French doors open.

"Your lovely wife let me in as she was leaving. Said she was off to therapize the local nutcases at the clinic," he said in response to Gurney's unvoiced question.

"I doubt she put it that way."

"She might have put it in cuddlier words. Women love the fantasy that crazy fuckers can be de-crazed. As if the only thing Charlie Manson needed was a touch of TLC."

"Speaking of nice women getting involved with lunatics, what's the deal with you and Esti?"

"Hard to say."

"You serious about her?"

"Serious? Yeah, I guess, whatever 'serious' means. I'll tell you one thing. The sex is seriously good."

"Is she the reason you finally bought some furniture?"

"Women like furniture. Turns them on. Feathered nests trigger good feelings. The biological imperatives start kicking in. Beds,

couches, comfy chairs, cozy rugs—shit like that makes a difference."
He paused. "She's on her way. Did you know that?"

"On her way here?"

"I passed your invitation along to her. I thought she might've
called you."

"No, but I'm glad she's coming. The more heads on this subject the
better."

Hardwick made a skeptical face—his usual face—stood up from
the table and stepped over to the French doors. He gazed out curiously
for a while before asking, "Fuck are you up to out there?"

"What do you mean?"

"That pile of lumber."

Gurney came to the door. There was indeed a pile of lumber that
he'd missed on his way into the house. His view had been blocked by
the asparagus ferns. For a moment he was at a loss. There were stacks
of what appeared to be two-by-fours, four-by-fours, and two-by-sixes.

He took out his phone and entered Madeleine's number.

Surprisingly, she picked up on the first ring. "Yes?"

"What's this stuff out back?" Even as he was asking, he realized
the answer was obvious and calling her had probably been a mistake.

"Lumber. For the chicken house. I had it delivered this morning.
The things you said we'd be using first."

He started raising his shields. "I didn't say we'd be using them
today."

"Well, tomorrow, then? Don't worry about it. If you're too busy,
just point me in the right direction and I'll get started myself."

He felt cornered, but he remembered a wise man once saying that
feelings aren't facts. He decided it would be prudent to keep his irritation out of his voice. "Right."

"That's it? That's the reason you called?"

"Right."

"Okay, see you tonight. I'm on my way into a session."

He slipped the phone back in his pocket.

Hardwick was watching him with a sadistic grin. "Trouble in
paradise?"

"No trouble."

"Really? You looked like you were going to bite that phone."

"Madeleine is better at switching focus than I am."

"You mean she wants you to get involved in something you don't give a shit about?"

It was a comment, not a question, and like many of Hardwick's comments, it was rudely true.

"I hear a car," said Gurney.

"Got to be Esti."

"You recognize the sound of her Mini?"

"No. But who the hell else would be driving up that crappy little road of yours?"

A minute later, she was at the side door and Gurney was letting her in. She was dressed a lot more conservatively than at Hardwick's house—in dark slacks, white blouse, and dark blazer, looking like she'd come directly from the job. Her hair had lost some of the sheen it'd had the previous night. She had a manila envelope in her hand.

"You just coming off a shift?" Gurney asked.

"Yep. Midnight to noon. Pretty tiring after all that craziness last night. But I had to fill in for someone who filled in for me two weeks ago. Then I had to get my car inspected. Anyway, here I am." She followed Gurney into the kitchen, saw Hardwick standing at the table, and gave him a big smile. "Hi, sweetheart."

"Hey, peaches, how's things?"

"Good—now that I see you in one piece." She went to him, kissed him on the cheek, and ran her fingers down his arm, as if to confirm her observation. "You're really okay, right? There's nothing you're not telling me?"

"Babe, I am one hundred percent okay."

"I'm glad to hear that." She gave him a cute little wink. "So," she continued, suddenly all business, "I got some answers. You boys interested?"

Gurney gestured toward the dining table. "We can sit there."

Esti chose the end chair. The two men sat across from each other. She took her notepad out of the envelope. "Simple things first. Yes, according to the autopsy—pretty basic one—Mary Spalter's injuries *could* have been intentionally inflicted, but that option was never seriously considered. Falls, even fatal falls, happen enough in geriatric situations that the simplest explanation is usually accepted."

Hardwick grunted. "So there was no investigation at all?"

"Zero."

"Time of death?" asked Gurney.

"Estimated between three and five in the afternoon. How does that square with the floral delivery guy on the security video?"

"I'll double-check," said Gurney, "but I think he walked into Carol Blissy's office around three-fifteen. Any ViCAP hits on the MO elements?"

"Nothing yet."

"No witness reports of floral delivery vans at homicide scenes?"

"No, but that doesn't mean there weren't any such reports. It just means they didn't make it onto ViCAP forms."

"Right," said Gurney. "Anything on Fat Gus?"

"Time-of-death window between ten in the morning and one in the afternoon. And, yes, as you said it might, the word 'larynx' appears in the autopsy wound descriptions. Death, however, was not caused by the nails that were hammered into his head and neck. He was shot first—a .22 hollow point through the right eye into the brain."

"Interesting," said Gurney. "That would suggest that the nails weren't a form of torture."

"So what?" said Hardwick. "What's your point?"

"It supports the idea that the nails were a warning to someone, rather than a way of punishing the victim. The time of death is interesting, too. In the original incident report on Carl's shooting it gives the time of death as ten-twenty. The location of the Gurikos murder in his home near Utica would make it impossible for the shooter to have killed him at ten, gone through the nailing mess, cleaned himself up, driven to Long Falls, and gotten set up in time to hit Carl at ten-twenty. So it must have happened the other way around—Carl first, then Gus."

"Assuming only one shooter," said Hardwick.

"Right. But that's an assumption we ought to make, at least until there's evidence of more than one." He turned to Esti. "Anything yet on Gurikos?"

"My contact at OCTF is looking into it. She wasn't directly involved, so she has to tiptoe. She doesn't want to set off alarms that could prompt follow-up queries to the original investigator. Kind of a tricky situation."

"How about the Spalter MO?"

"That's different. Klemper never initiated any ViCAP or NCIC searches, because he'd already made his decision about Kay. So I can pursue that more safely."

"That's great. And, Jack, you're chasing after the prosecution witnesses—and whatever you can get from your Interpol friend?"

"Yeah. Nothing yet from Interpol. And none of the witnesses are still at the addresses listed in the case file—which may not be particularly significant, given their basic nature."

Esti stared at him. "Their basic nature?"

Hardwick's eyes lit up with the arch look that always got under Gurney's skin. "Their basic nature is that they lack upstanding qualities. They're fundamentally scumbags. It's a known fact that scumbags who lack upstanding qualities often lack permanent addresses. All I'm saying is that having difficulty in locating them does not signify much. But I will persevere. Even scumbags have to be somewhere." He turned to Gurney. "So how about telling us about your interview with the heiress."

"The *would-be* heiress—*if* Kay stays in prison."

"Which is becoming less likely each passing day. This turn of events must be having an interesting effect on Miss Alyssa, yes? You care to share your insights?"

Gurney smiled. "I'll do better than that. I have a recording. Might not be the greatest quality, but you'll get the gist."

"*F*uck me and die'? Did she really say 'Fuck me and die'?" Esti was leaning toward the recorder as they finished listening for the second time to the conversation at Venus Lake. "What was that all about?"

"Probably the name of her favorite rock band," suggested Hardwick.

"It could be a threat," said Esti.

"Or an invitation," said Hardwick. "You were there, Davey boy. What'd it sound like to you?"

"Like everything else she said and did—a combination of cartoon seduction and calculated bullshit."

Hardwick raised an eyebrow. "Sounds to me like a nasty little kid trying to shock the grown-ups. That FMAD T-shirt you described makes her seem kind of pathetic. Like inside she's about twelve."

"The T-shirt may have been harmless," replied Gurney, "but her eyes weren't."

Esti jumped in. "Maybe the shirt wasn't so harmless either. Suppose it was a literal statement of fact."

Hardwick ratcheted up his skeptical look. "What fact?"

"Maybe there's more than one 'black widow' in this case."

"You mean 'Fuck me and die' really means 'Fuck me and I'll kill you'? That's clever, but I don't get it. How does it——"

"She told Klemper her father coerced her into having sex with him. We have no proof of it, but it could be true."

"So you're saying that Alyssa killed her father as payback?"

"It's not impossible. And if she could rope a horny jerk like Klemper into bending the investigation to put Kay in the frame, the 'payback' would also include her ending up with her father's estate. That's two major motives—revenge and money."

Hardwick looked at Gurney. "What do you think, ace?"

"I'm sure Alyssa is guilty of something. She may have 'persuaded' or blackmailed Klemper into tailoring the evidence to make sure Kay was convicted. Or she may have masterminded the whole damn thing—the murder as well as the frame."

"Premeditated murder? You think she's capable of that?"

"There's something scary in those glittery blue eyes. But I have a hard time seeing her handling the executional details. Someone else smashed Mary's head on the side of that bathtub and hammered the nails into Fat Gus."

"You're saying she hired a pro?"

"I'm saying if she was the prime mover behind the three murders, she would've needed help—but none of that answers the basic question that's been eating at me from the beginning: *Why Carl's mother?* It really doesn't make sense."

Hardwick was drumming his fingertips on the table. "Neither does the Gus hit. Not unless you buy Donny Angel's story about Gus and Carl being hit by a guy they targeted. But if you buy that, and you also buy Alyssa as the prime mover, then you're stuck with the conclusion that she must have been Carl's original target—which never felt right to me, and it still doesn't."

"But it *would* give her a third motive," said Esti.

As Gurney considered the Angelidis scenario one more time, with Alyssa in the unnamed target position, it touched a nerve.

"What is it?" asked Esti, eyeing him curiously.

"Nothing very logical. In fact, nothing logical at all. Just a feeling and an image." He got up and went into the den to get that troubling photo of Carl Spalter from the case file. When he returned, he laid it on the table between Hardwick and Esti.

Hardwick stared at it, his expression tightening.

"I saw that once before," said Esti. "It's hard to look at for very long."

Hardwick glanced up at Gurney, who was still standing. "You have some point you want to make with this?"

"Like I said, nothing logical. Just an off-the-wall question."

"Christ, Davey boy, the suspense is killing me. Speak."

"Might that be the look of a man who's waiting to die—who knows he's about to die—as the final, twisted result of taking out a murder contract on his own child?"

They all stared at the photograph.

No one said anything for a while.

Hardwick finally leaned back in his chair and let out one of his barking laughs. "Holy Mary, Mother of God, wouldn't that be the ultimate fucking karma!"

Chapter 32

Another Missing Player

Hardwick suggested they listen to the Venus Lake recording one more time, which they did. He seemed especially interested in the section in which Alyssa claimed that Klemper had blackmailed her into having sex with him. "Beautiful! I love it! That fuckhead is done, cooked, finished!"

Now Gurney looked skeptical. "The recording of Alyssa won't be enough by itself. You heard her—she was all over the place, not exactly sounding like a solid citizen. You'll need a sworn statement from her—listing dates, places, details—which she's unlikely to supply. Because she's almost certainly lying. If anyone blackmailed anyone, I'm pretty sure it was the other way around. So she won't want—"

Esti broke in. "What do you mean, the other way around?"

"Suppose Alyssa seduced Klemper while he was still conducting an objective investigation of the original shooting. Suppose she video-recorded their . . . encounter. And suppose the price she demanded for keeping the recording out of the hands of the state police was Klemper's help in making the case turn out the way she wanted."

"It doesn't *matter* how they ended up in bed," said Hardwick. "Blackmail, seduction, whatever. Who gives a shit who was blackmailing who? Fucking a potential suspect is fucking a potential suspect. Klemper's career is going down the toilet."

Gurney sat back. "That's one way of looking at it."

"And the other way is . . . what?"

"It's a question of priorities. One way, we can pressure Alyssa to sink Klemper. The other way, we can pressure Klemper to sink Alyssa."

Esti looked interested. "You like number two better, right?"

Before Gurney could answer, Hardwick interjected, "You think Alyssa's the chief manipulator, but a minute ago you said she was all over the place, sounded less than solid—and I agree. She called you, she set up the meeting with you, but in that recording she comes across as pretty erratic—like she had no idea where the conversation might go, like she had no plan. This is a master manipulator?"

Esti spoke up with a knowing smile. "Maybe an overconfident manipulator. But she definitely had a plan."

"What plan?"

"Probably the same as she had for Klemper. Her plan today was to get Dave into bed, get it all on a hidden camera, and get him to change his approach to the case."

"Dave's retired. Pension guaranteed. Doesn't have a career to lose," said Hardwick. "Where's the leverage?"

"He has a wife." She looked at Gurney. "A video of you in bed with a nineteen-year-old could create a problem, right?"

That didn't require an answer.

Esti went on. "That was Alyssa's Plan A. When that little sweetheart makes it clear that she's available, I doubt many men turn her down. Dave not wanting to play her game probably came as a big surprise. She had no Plan B."

Hardwick shot a nasty grin in Gurney's direction. "Saint David here is full of surprises. But tell me something, ace. Why did she admit to you that she had sex with Klemper at all? Why not just deny the whole thing?"

Gurney shrugged. "Maybe someone else knows about it. Or she *thinks* someone knows about it. So she admits the fact, but lies about the reason. Common enough deception technique. Admit the external action but invent an exculpatory motive."

"My ex was big on exculpatory motives," said Esti to no one in particular. She checked her watch. "So what's the next step?"

"Maybe a little blackmail of our own," suggested Gurney. "Give Klemper a few shakes and see what comes loose."

That put a smile on her face. "Sounds good. Anything that rattles that son of a bitch . . ."

"You want backup?" asked Hardwick.

"Not necessary. Klemper may be an asshole, but he's not likely to pull a gun on me. Not in a public place, anyway. I just want to explain his situation to him, offer him an option or two."

Hardwick stared down at the table intently, as if the possible results of such a conversation were listed there. "I need to give Bincher a heads-up on this, see what he thinks."

"Go ahead," said Gurney. "Just don't make it sound like I'm asking for his permission."

Hardwick took out his phone and entered a number. Apparently it went to voice mail. He made a disgusted face. "Fuck! Where the hell are you, Lex? This is my third attempt. Get back to me for Christ's sake!"

He ended the call and made another.

"Abby, baby, where the hell is he? I left a message last night, another one first thing this morning, and another one thirty seconds ago." He listened for a few moments, his frown shifting from frustration to puzzlement. "Well, as soon as he gets back, we need to talk. Things are happening."

He listened again, longer this time, worry beginning to replace puzzlement. "You know anything more about that? . . . That was it, no explanation? . . . Nothing since? . . . I have no idea . . . The voice wasn't familiar to you? . . . You think it was intentional? . . . Yeah, kinda strange . . . Right . . . Please, the minute he checks in . . . No, no, I'm sure he's okay . . . Right . . . Yes . . . Good."

He ended the call, laid his phone on the table, and looked at Gurney. "Lex got a call yesterday afternoon. Somebody who claimed to have major information on the Carl Spalter murder case. After the call, Lex left the office in a hurry. Abby hasn't been able to reach him since. No answer on his cell, no answer at home. Fuck!"

"Abby is his assistant?"

"Yeah. Well, actually, his ex-wife. Don't know how that works, but it does."

"The caller was a man or woman?"

"That's the thing—Abby said she couldn't tell. At first she thought it was a kid, then a man, then a woman, some kind of foreign accent— didn't know who the hell she was talking to. Then Lex took the call. Couple of minutes later he left the office. All he said was that it was about the Long Falls murder case, could be a breakthrough, he'd be back in a couple of hours. But he never did come back—at least not to the office."

"Shit," said Esti. "She can't reach him anywhere?"

"She keeps getting his voice mail."

She stared at Hardwick. "You getting the feeling too many people are going missing?"

Chapter 33

Major Appointments

Action being the best antidote for anxiety, and information the only remedy for uncertainty, when they parted that afternoon, each had an assignment—along with a sense of urgency arising from the growing hazards and peculiarities of the case.

Esti would press her various contacts for OCTF data on Gurikos, NCIC data on the key players in the case, and MO data from ViCAP that might match elements of the murder scenes.

Gurney would have a frank discussion with Mick Klemper about his diminishing options, then try to set up a meeting with Jonah Spalter.

Hardwick would pay a visit to Lex Bincher's home in Cooperstown, track down the trial witnesses, and prod his pal at Interpol for anything on Gurikos and/or the Gurikos murder MO.

Like many cops, Mick Klemper had two cell phones, one personal and one job-related. Esti had both numbers from the time she'd worked closely, and miserably, with him. Before the meeting broke up, she gave both to Gurney.

Now, half an hour later, sitting at the desk in his den, he called the personal one.

Klemper picked up on the third ring, but evidently not before seeing Gurney's ID.

"How the hell did you get this private number?"

Gurney smiled, pleased at getting the reaction he'd expected. "Hello, Mick."

"I said, how the hell did you get this number?"

"It's all over the billboards on the Thruway."

"What?"

"There's just no privacy anymore, Mick. You ought to know that. Numbers get around."

"What the fuck are you talking about?"

"There's so much information floating around. Information overload. That's what they call it, right?"

"What? What the fuck is this?"

"I'm just thinking out loud. Thinking what a treacherous world we live in. A man might think he's engaging in a private activity, and next day on the Internet there's a video of him taking a crap."

"Yeah? You know what? That's disgusting. Disgusting! What do you want?"

"We need to talk."

"So talk."

"Face-to-face would be better. No intervening technology. Technology can be a problem. A violator of privacy."

Klemper hesitated—long enough to indicate a significant level of concern. "I still don't know what the hell you're talking about."

Gurney figured this was a cover-your-ass statement in the event the call was being taped, rather than pure thickheadedness. "What I'm talking about is that we should talk about some issues of mutual concern."

"Fine. Whatever the fuck that means. Let's get this bullshit over with. Where do you want to talk?"

"Up to you."

"I couldn't care less."

"How about Riverside Mall?"

Klemper hesitated again, longer this time. "Riverside? When?"

"Sooner the better. Things are happening."

"Where in the mall?"

"Main concourse? Lots of benches there. Usually empty."

Another hesitation. "When?"

Gurney knew from Esti that Klemper got off his shift at five. He checked the time on his cell screen—4:01 p.m. "How about five-thirty?"

"*Today?*"

"Definitely today. Tomorrow might be too late."

A final pause. "All right. Riverside. Five-thirty, sharp. You better make more sense there than you're making here. Because right now? Right now, this sounds like a pile of shit." He disconnected the call.

Gurney found the man's bravado encouraging. It sounded like fear.

Riverside Mall was a forty-minute drive from Walnut Crossing, giving Gurney about fifty minutes before he had to set out. It didn't allow him much time to prepare for a meeting that had the potential to give the investigation a dramatic shove in the right direction, if it was handled right. He got a yellow lined pad out of his desk drawer to help organize his thoughts.

He found it surprisingly difficult. His mind was unsettled, moving from one unresolved issue to another. The unreachability of Lex Bincher. The similar unreachability of the three key witnesses. The shots in the night eliminating Hardwick's lights and phone. The grotesque mutilation of Fat Gus—a warning that the killer's secret must be kept. But what secret? Was it his or her identity? Or something else?

And, of course, there was the central conundrum of the case from the beginning, the puzzle piece that Gurney felt would eventually make sense of all the others—the contradictory site of the shooting. On the one hand, there was the apartment with the silenced, tripod-fitted rifle and the fresh gunpowder residue with a chemical profile that linked it to a .220 Swift cartridge and the bullet fragments extracted from Carl Spalter's brain. On the other hand, there was the light pole that made the shot impossible.

It was possible that the killer used a different apartment in that building to make the shot and then transferred the weapon to the apartment where it was found, firing a second shot from that location to produce the powder residue. But that scenario was simpler in the saying than it would have been in the doing. It also involved a much-elevated risk of detection, requiring the shooter to carry the cumbersome combination of rifle, tripod, and suppressor through the public spaces of the building. And why bother? There were, after all, several unoccupied apartments from which the shot could have been fired successfully. So why move the weapon at all? Surely not to create an intellectual puzzle. Murderers are rarely that playful. And professional hitters never are.

That thought brought him full circle to the more immediate matter of Klemper. Was Mick the Dick the thuggish, horny clown that his nickname and general manner seemed to suggest? Or might the man be a darker, colder operator altogether?

Gurney hoped their meeting in the mall would provide some answers.

He needed to focus now on the broadest range of possibilities, think them through—angles, objectives. He straightened the yellow pad on his desk and picked up his pen. He tried to force his thoughts into a logical structure by drawing a branching diagram, beginning with four possibilities.

One posited Alyssa as the prime mover behind Carl's murder and Kay's conviction.

The second substituted Jonah Spalter for Alyssa.

The third posited an Unknown as Carl's murderer, with Alyssa and Klemper as opportunistic conspirators in Kay's conviction.

The fourth posited Kay as guilty.

He added a second level of branching possibilities under each of these.

"Hello?"

Gurney blinked.

"Hello?" It was Madeleine's voice calling from the opposite side of the house. From the mudroom, it sounded like.

Bringing his pad and pen with him, he went out to the kitchen. "I'm here."

She was just coming in from the side-door hallway, carrying two plastic supermarket bags. "I left the trunk open. Maybe you could bring in the cracked corn?"

"The what?"

"I read that chickens love cracked corn."

He sighed, then tried to regard this in the positive light of a momentary diversion from his darker duties. "Bring it in and put it where?"

"The mudroom would be fine."

He went out to Madeleine's car, hefted the fifty-pound bag out of the trunk, struggled for a few seconds with the side door of the house, came in, and dropped the bag in the nearest corner of the mudroom— the positive light fading quickly to a weak flicker.

"You bought a lifetime supply?" he asked when he returned to the kitchen.

"It's the only size they had. Sorry about that. Are you okay?"

"Fine. I guess I'm a little preoccupied—getting ready to go and meet with someone."

"Oh—that reminds me—before I forget . . ." Her tone was pleasantly even. "You have an appointment tomorrow morning with Malcolm."

"*Malcolm Claret?*"

"That's right."

"I don't understand."

"I called him before I left the clinic. He said he'd just gotten a cancellation and had an opening tomorrow at eleven."

"No . . . What I don't understand is *why.*"

"Because I'm afraid for you. We've discussed that."

"No, I mean why *you* made the appointment for *me.*"

"Because you hadn't made it yet, and it's important."

"So . . . you just . . . decided it was up to you?"

"It had to be up to somebody."

He turned his palms up in a pose of bewilderment. "I don't quite get that."

"What is there to *get?*"

"*I* wouldn't make an appointment for *you*—not unless you asked me to."

"Even if you thought it might save my life?"

He hesitated. "Don't you think that's a little dramatic?"

She met his gaze and answered softly. "No, I don't."

His voice was suddenly filled with exasperation. "You honestly believe an appointment with Malcolm Claret is going to *save my life?*"

Just as suddenly, her voice was filled with a weary sadness. "If you really don't want to see him, just cancel the appointment."

If she'd said that in any other tone, he could imagine himself launching into a grand debate over whose responsibility it was to cancel an appointment she had made, and then he might even segue to the lumber pile she'd ordered for the chicken-house project and how she had a way of starting things that he had to finish and how things always had to happen on her schedule.

But the emotion in her eyes short-circuited all of that.

Besides, it was beginning to dawn on him, strangely, that there might not be any harm in seeing Claret after all.

He was saved from going on with the discussion, however, by the ringing of the phone in his pocket. He pulled it out and checked the ID. *"Kyle Gurney"* was displayed for a second before the signal was lost. He was tempted to call him back, but figured his son was likely on the move somewhere, passing through a dead spot, and it would make more sense to wait a while.

He checked the clock. It was later than he'd guessed—4:44 p.m.

It was time to leave for the mall. For the crucial meeting for which he hadn't yet managed to prepare.

Chapter 34

A Gentlemen's Agreement

The parking lot at Riverside was, as usual, half empty.

In the mostly deserted expanse beside the T.J. Maxx that anchored one end of the mall, an incongruous flock of seagulls stood silently on the tarmac.

Entering the lot, Gurney slowed for a better look. He estimated the number of birds at fifty or sixty. From his perspective in the car, they appeared motionless, all standing in the same orientation, their backs to the setting sun.

As he drove past them to a parking spot closer to the main concourse, he couldn't help wondering about this increasingly commonplace migration of seagulls to inland malls—drawn, no doubt, by the droppings of fast-food gobblers. Were these transposed birds developing clogged arteries like their benefactors, making them sedentary, infrequent fliers? Food for thought. But not now. The urgency of his mission returned him to reality. He locked his car and walked through the entrance arch, an oddly festive structure with the words RIVERSIDE CENTER curving over the top in colored lights.

The mall was not a large one. There was one main concourse, with minor offshoots. The bright promise of the entry gave way to a rather bleak interior, which appeared to have been designed decades earlier with little refreshment since. Halfway along one side of the concourse, he sat on a bench in front of an Alpine Sports shop with a window display devoted to shiny, body-clinging cycling attire. A salesperson was lounging in the doorway, frowning at the screen of her cell phone.

He checked his watch. It was 5:33.

He waited.

Klemper appeared at 5:45.

The world of law enforcement, like prison, changes the people who spend time in it. It does this by nourishing certain traits: skepticism, calculation, insularity, toughness. Those traits may develop along lines that are benign or malignant, depending on the character of the individual—on the fundamental orientation of his soul. One cop might end up street-smart, loyal to his fellows, and courageous—determined to do a good job in difficult circumstances. Another might end up poisonously cynical, judgmental, and cruel—determined to screw the world that was screwing him. Gurney figured that the look in Mick Klemper's eyes as he approached the bench put him squarely in the second category.

He sat at the far end of the bench, several feet from Gurney. He said nothing, just opened a small attaché case on his lap, angling the top to obstruct any view of the contents, and began fiddling with something.

Gurney assumed it was a scanner, probably the multi-function type that could indicate the presence of any transmitting or recording device.

After a minute or so, Klemper closed the case. He did a quick three-sixty visual check of the concourse, then spoke in a rough voice, half through his teeth, his gaze fixed on the floor. "So what the hell kind of game is this?" The man's truculence seemed a shield for raw nerves, and his massive physique nothing more than excess baggage, a burden responsible for the sheen of sweat on his face. But it would be a mistake to go the extra yard and consider him harmless.

"You can do something for me, and I can do something for you," said Gurney.

Klemper looked up from the floor with a little snort of a laugh, as if recognizing an interrogation trick.

The young woman in the doorway of Alpine Sports was still frowning at her phone.

"How's Alyssa?" asked Gurney casually—knowing he was taking a chance playing that card so quickly.

Klemper shot him a sideways glance. "What?"

"The suspect you got tangled up with in a way you shouldn't have." He paused. "You still friends?"

"What kind of bullshit is this?" The man's raw tone told him he'd hit a nerve.

"For you, very expensive bullshit."

Klemper shook his head, as if trying to convey incomprehension.

Gurney went on. "It's amazing what ends up getting recorded these days. Can be very embarrassing. But sometimes you get lucky and there's a way to control the damage. That's what I want to talk to you about—damage control."

"I don't get any of this." His denial was loud and clear, seemingly for the benefit of a recording device his briefcase scanner might have missed.

"I just wanted to bring you up-to-date on the Kay Spalter appeal." Gurney was speaking in a flat, matter-of-fact tone. "First, we have enough evidence of . . . let's call them flaws . . . in the original investigation to guarantee a reversal of her conviction. Second, we're now at a fork in the road, meaning we have a choice in how those flaws are presented to the appellate court. For example, the trial witness who ID'd Kay as a person present at the shooting site could have been coerced into perjury . . . or he could have been innocently mistaken, as eyewitnesses often are. The con who claimed at the trial that Kay tried to hire him as a hit man could have been coerced . . . or he could have made up that story on his own, as men in his position often do. Kay's lover could have been told that the only way to avoid being the prime suspect was to make sure Kay ended up in that position . . . or he could have arrived at that conclusion on his own. The CIO on the case could have concealed key video evidence and ignored other avenues of inquiry because of an improper relationship with the victim's daughter . . . or he could simply have zeroed in on the wrong suspect too soon, as detectives often do."

Klemper was again staring grimly at the floor. "This is all hypothetical nonsense."

"The thing of it is, Mick, every flaw in the investigation could be described in either criminal or innocent terms—so long as no definitive proof of that improper relationship falls into the wrong hands."

"Hypothetical bullshit."

"Okay. Hypothetically, let's say I have the definitive proof of that improper relationship—in a very persuasive digital form. And let's say I wanted something in return for keeping it to myself?"

"Why ask me?"

"Because it's your career, your pension, your freedom that are on the line."

"What the fuck are you saying?"

"I want the security video from the electronics store on Axton Avenue."

"I have no idea what you're talking about."

"If I were to receive that missing video from some anonymous sender, I would be willing to exclude a certain career-ending piece of evidence from the appeal process. I would also be willing to delay indefinitely my plan to provide that same item to the NYSP inspector general. That's the hypothetical deal. A simple gentlemen's agreement, based on mutual trust."

Klemper laughed, or maybe he just grunted and shuddered involuntarily. "This is crazy crap. You sound like some fucking psycho." He looked over in Gurney's direction but made no eye contact. "Fantasy bullshit. All fantasy bullshit." He stood up abruptly, unsteadily, and headed for the nearest exit.

He left in his wake an acrid odor of alcohol and sweat.

Chapter 35

A Mysterious Way

Gurney's drive home was a journey into anxiety. He attributed it to the emotional free fall that often followed an intense encounter.

As he headed up the final stretch of road toward his barn, however, it struck him that there might be another cause: the ricketiness of his assumptions, not only about Klemper but also about the case as a whole. If Klemper's failing had been wishful thinking about Kay's guilt, might not his own failing be wishful thinking about her innocence? Might he and Klemper be equally blind to some more complex scenario that involved Kay in way that hadn't occurred to either of them?

And what was the significance of Klemper's drinking? Had he been drinking earlier in the day on the job? Or had he picked up a bottle for a few quick belts in the car on his way to Riverside? Either possibility suggested terrible judgment, great strain, or a serious drinking problem. Any of those issues had the potential to make the man an unpredictable, even explosive piece of the puzzle.

The first thing he noticed after rounding the barn was that Madeleine's car was gone from its normal spot by the house, which jogged a half-formed memory that this was the evening for one of her board meetings, although he wasn't sure which one.

Entering the kitchen, he found her absence momentarily comforting—relieving him of the need to immediately decide how much or how little to reveal about his Klemper meeting. It also meant he'd have some undisturbed time to himself to sort the jumbled pieces of a long day into some kind of order.

He was heading into the den for the organizing assistance of a pad and pen when his cell phone rang. He pulled it out of his pocket and checked the ID. It was Kyle.

"Hey, Dad. Hope I'm not interrupting anything."

"Nothing that can't wait. What's up?"

"I made some calls, asking around about Jonah Spalter and/or the Cyberspace Cathedral. None of my own contacts knew anything, one thought maybe the name was familiar, thought something might be happening with it, but didn't know anything specific. I was going to send you an e-mail saying, 'Sorry, no grapes on the vine.' But then one of the guys called me back. Told me he'd checked around and discovered a friend of his had handled a venture capital search for Jonah Spalter, the venture being a huge expansion of Spalter's Cathedral."

"What kind of expansion?"

"He didn't get into that beyond the fact that it was going to cost plenty."

"Interesting."

"The *really* interesting part is that Spalter ended the capital search the day after his brother died. Called up the guy who'd been working on it, took him to lunch, cut off the whole process—"

Gurney broke in. "That doesn't surprise me. I mean, the way that corporation was set up by their father, Carl's share of Spalter Realty would go directly to Jonah—entirely separate from the rest of his assets, which were covered by his will. So Jonah would have come into some big real estate holdings that he'd be free to sell or mortgage. So he wouldn't need to raise venture capital to finance whatever expansion he had in mind."

"You didn't let me get to the really interesting part."

"Oh? Sorry. Tell me."

"Jonah Spalter showed up for lunch half drunk, then got really drunk. And he quoted that saying 'God works in a mysterious way, His wonders to perform.' And according to this guy, Spalter kept saying it and laughing, like he found it really funny. Kind of weirded the guy out."

Gurney was silent for a while, imagining the scene. "You said the Cathedral expansion was going to cost plenty. Any idea how much?"

"The capital search had to be for at least fifty million. The guy

Jonah was dealing with wouldn't touch any deal for an amount less than that."

"Meaning," said Gurney, mostly to himself, "that the assets of Spalter Realty must be worth at least that much, if Jonah was willing to cancel the search."

"So what are you thinking, Dad?" said Kyle conspiratorially. "That fifty million could be a pretty compelling motive for murder?"

"More compelling than most. Did your contact have anything else to say about Spalter?"

"Just that he was super smart, super ambitious—but that's nothing special, just the nature of the beast."

"Okay, thanks. That was very helpful."

"Really?"

"Absolutely. More I know, the better my brain works. And there's no other way I could have come upon that revealing little anecdote. So thank you again."

"Glad I could help. By the way, you planning to go to the Summer Mountain Fair?"

"Me? No. But Madeleine will be there. She's helping some friends of hers who have a farm over in Buck Ridge. They bring their alpacas to the fair every year and enter them in ... I don't know ... alpaca events, I guess."

"You don't sound too revved up about it."

"You could say that."

"You mean to say you're not impressed by the *biggest* agricultural fair in the Northeast? Tractor pulls, demolition derbies, butter sculptures, cotton candy, hog judging, sheep shearing, cheese making, country music, carnival rides, blue ribbons for biggest zucchini—how could you not be impressed by all that?"

"It's tough, but somehow I manage to control my enthusiasm."

After ending the call with Kyle, Gurney stayed at his desk for some time, letting the economic facts of the Spalter case sink in, and pondering the significance of those famous lines *God moves in a mysterious way / His wonders to perform.*

He took the thick case file out of his desk drawer and riffled through it until he came to an index of key names and addresses. There were two email addresses for "J. Spalter"—one a Google gmail account, the other connected to the Cyberspace Cathedral website domain. There was also a physical address in Florida, with a notation indicating that it existed to serve legal and tax purposes, that it was the location where Jonah's motor home was registered and where CyberCath was incorporated, but that the man did not actually live there. A further marginal note read, "Postal forwarding instructions redirect mail to changing series of P.O. boxes." Apparently Jonah was on the road most of the time, maybe all the time.

Gurney sent a message to both email addresses—a message saying that Kay's conviction was likely to be overturned and that he urgently needed Jonah's help in evaluating some new evidence.

Chapter 36

An Unusual Killer

G etting to sleep that night was more difficult than usual.

It was a persistent source of frustration—this business of trying to pursue an investigation without the investigatory apparatus that had been available to him in the NYPD. And the problem had been compounded by Hardwick's loss of access to NYSP files, information systems, and channels of inquiry. Being outsiders created a heavy reliance on insiders who might be willing to take a risk. Hardwick's recent experience was proof that the risk was substantial.

In the current situation, much depended not only on Esti, whose commitment seemed positive and unequivocal, but also on the willingness of her contacts to be both helpful and discreet. Similarly, much depended on Hardwick's contacts and how they might be feeling about the man and his motives. It would be impolitic to put pressure on any of these helpers since none of them *had* to provide any help at all.

It was a position Gurney hated being in—relying on the unpredictable generosity of others, hoping for some breakthrough piece of information to arrive from sources beyond his control.

T he call came just before five a.m.—barely two hours after his churning thoughts had loosened their grip and let him drift into an exhausted half-sleep. Fumbling in the dark, knocking over an empty water glass, provoking a murmur of protest from Madeleine, he finally located his phone on the night table. When he saw Hardwick's name on the screen, he took the phone into the den.

"Yes?"

"You might be thinking it's a little on the early side for a call, but it's seven hours later in Turkey. Noon over there, as a matter of fact. Must be hot as a steaming turd."

"Great news, Jack. Thanks for letting me know."

"My contact in Ankara woke me up. So I figured I'd wake you up. Time for Farmer Dave to scatter some cracked corn for the chickens. In fact, you probably should've been out there an hour ago, you lazy son of a bitch."

Gurney was accustomed to Hardwick's unusual approach to business conversations, and generally ignored the ritual abuse. "Your Ankara guy is with Interpol?"

"So he says."

"What did he have for you?"

"A few tidbits. We get what we get. Goodness of his heart."

"What did his good heart have for you?"

"You got time for this? You sure you don't need to go do something for those chickens?"

"Chickens are a lovely addition to the rural life, Jack. You ought to get yourself a few."

Embracing Hardwick's tangent had the odd effect of getting him back on point.

"Tidbit number one. About ten years ago, the forces of good had one of the top bad guys in Corsica by the short hairs—had him looking at a hard twenty in a shithole prison—and they managed to turn him. Deal was, if he put the finger on some business colleagues the forces of good would put him in witness protection instead of the shithole prison. This plan did not work out well. About a week into the deal, the head of the witness protection operation received a box in the mail. What to take a stab at what was in the box?"

"Depends on how big a box we're talking about."

"Yeah, well, let's say it was a lot bigger than would be needed if they were mailing his dick. So what do you think it was?"

"Just a wild guess, Jack, but I'd say if the box was big enough to hold a head, then it was probably his head in there. Am I right?"

The silence on the other end was answer enough.

Gurney went on. "And this is just another wild guess, but I'd say there were some nails hammered into his—"

"Yeah, yeah, all right, Sherlock. One for you. Let's go on to story number two. You ready? You don't need to piss or anything?"

"Ready."

"Eight years ago, a member of the Russian Duma, a very connected multimillionaire, former KGB, made a trip to Paris. For his mother's funeral. The mother lived in Paris because her third husband was French, she loved it there, she wanted to be buried there. And guess what happened?"

"The Duma guy got popped in the cemetery?"

"On his way out the door of the Russian Orthodox church next to the cemetery. Dead-on head shot—eye shot to be precise."

"Hmm."

"And there were a couple of other interesting details. Wanna guess?"

"Tell me."

"Cartridge was a .220 Swift."

"And?"

"And no one heard what direction the shot came from."

"A suppressor?"

"Probably."

Gurney smiled. "And firecrackers?"

"You got it, ace."

"But . . . how did Interpol put these two cases together? What link did they see?"

"They didn't see any link, and they never did put them together."

"Then what—?"

"Your questions—your search terms from the Gurikos and Spalter cases—those terms brought up the Corsican mob case and the Paris—"

"But the nails-in-the-head detail would've only brought up the file on the Corsican murder, and the cemetery/firecrackers details would've only brought up the Duma guy. So what are we talking about? Just based on those two facts, it could've been two different hit men, no?"

"It might've looked that way—except for one little thing. Both Interpol files contained lists of possibilities—likely professional hitters the local cops or the national agencies thought would be worth looking at. Four names for the Corsican case, five for the Russian-in-Paris case.

Far as I can see, the Corsican and French police never got to any of those guys, not even to talk to them. But that's not the point. The point is, there's one name that pops up on both lists."

Gurney didn't say anything. A link that loose might be meaningless.

As if responding to this doubt, Hardwick added, "I know it doesn't prove anything. But it's sure as hell worth a closer look."

"I agree. So who is this guy who likes firecrackers and hammering nails into people's eyes?"

"The one name that appears on both lists is Petros Panikos."

"So we may be looking for a Greek hit man?"

"Hit man for sure. With a Greek name for sure. But a name is only a name. Interpol says there's no passport issued by any member country to anyone by that name. So it looks like he has other names. But they do have an interesting file on him under the name Panikos, for what it's worth."

"What *is* it worth? How much do they really know about him?"

"Good question. My contact told me there's a lot in the file, but that it's a mix—some facts, some secondhand stuff, some wild under-world stories that might be true or might be pure horseshit."

"You have this fascinating mix in your hands right now?"

"What I have is bare bones—what my man could remember with-out pulling up the full document, which he said he would do as soon as he could. By the way, you may not have to take a piss, Sherlock, but I sure as hell do. Hold on."

Judging from the sound effects, Hardwick had not only taken his phone into the bathroom with him but also managed to amplify the transmission volume. Sometimes Gurney was amazed that the man had survived as long as he had in the stiff culture of the NYSP. He presented such a prickly amalgam of characteristics. A sharp mind and sound investigative instincts were concealed behind a relentless eager-ness to offend. His troubled NYSP career had foundered, like many a marriage, on irreconcilable differences and a mutual lack of respect. He had been a feisty iconoclast in an organization that revered confor-mity and respect for rank. Now this formidable but abrasive character was hell-bent on embarrassing the organization that had divorced him.

Wandering through these thoughts, Gurney found himself staring out the east window of the den as the first gray wash of dawn outlined the crest of the far ridge. The latest sound effects coming from the phone suggested that Hardwick had left the bathroom and was shuffling through a pile of papers.

Gurney pressed the speakerphone button on his own phone, laid it on his desk, and leaned back in his chair. His eyelids were heavy from lack of sleep, and he let them drift pleasantly shut. His brain went into free fall and for a few moments he felt blessedly relaxed, almost anesthetized. The brief intermission was ended by Hardwick's voice, made harsher by the phone's cheap speaker. "I'm back! Nothing like a good leak to clear the mind and free the soul. Hey, ace, you still among the living?"

"I think so."

"Okay, here's what he gave me. Petros Panikos. Also known as Peter Pan. Also known as the Magician. Also known by other names we don't know about. He must have at least one passport in a name other than Panikos. He gets around. Never arrested, never detained—at least not under the Panikos name. Bottom line, he's a free agent, and an odd one. Has gun, will travel, for a price—upwards of a hundred grand per pop, plus expenses. Reachable only through a small handful of people who know how to reach him."

"Hundred grand minimum definitely puts him at the high end of the hit world."

"Well, the little man is kind of a celebrity in his world. He also—"

Gurney interrupted. "The *little* man? How little?"

"He's supposedly like four-foot-ten. Maybe five-two at the most."

"Like the Flowers by Florence delivery guy in the Emmerling Oaks video?"

"Yeah, like that."

"Okay. Go on."

"Favors .22 caliber rounds in all cartridge shapes and sizes. But he'll use anything that's right for the job, anything from a knife to a bomb. Actually, he's very fond of bombs. Might have connections with Russian arms and explosives dealers. Might have connections with the Russian mob down in Brooklyn. Might have been involved in a series of car explosions that wiped out a prosecutor and his staff in Serbia. Lot of *mights*. By the way, those slugs in the side of my house? They were .35 caliber—a much better choice for wire cutting than a .22—so I guess he really is flexible, assuming we're dealing with one guy. Problem with flexibility is that there's no consistent MO across all his hits. Interpol thinks Panikos, or whatever his name is, could have been involved in over fifty murders in the past ten or fifteen years. But that's based on underworld rumors, prison talk, shit like that."

"Anything else?"

"I'm waiting on that. There seems to be some weird stuff in his background, might originally have come from some kind of traveling freak show circus family, then some ugly Eastern European orphanage stuff, all hearsay, but . . . we'll see. My guy had to get off the phone, had some urgent shit on his plate. Supposed to be getting back to me as soon as he can. Meantime, I'm heading for Bincher's house in Cooperstown. Probably a complete waste of time, but the fucker isn't answering my calls or Abby's calls, and he's got to be somewhere. I'll get back to you when the Ankara data arrives—if it ever does."

"One last question, Jack. 'The Magician'—what's that all about?"

"Simple. The little fucker likes to show off—prove that he can do the impossible. Probably made up the name himself. Just the kind of psycho opponent you live for, right, Sherlock?" Hardwick didn't say goodbye—no surprise in that—just broke the connection.

More information, in Gurney's opinion, was always a good thing—objectively. But it was also possible to lose one's bearings in it. Right then he had the feeling that the more he was discovering, the deeper the puzzle was becoming.

Carl Spalter apparently had been the victim not only of a professional gun-for-hire but also of an unusual one—and an unusual investment had been made to secure the outcome. However, considering what was at stake for the three people closest to him—his wife, his daughter, his brother—the high hit fee would have been a reasonable investment for any of them. At first glance, Jonah would seem to be the one with easiest access to that kind of cash, but Kay and Alyssa could have their own hidden sources, or allies willing to invest in a major payday. Then another possibility occurred to him—the possibility that *more than one* of them was involved. Why not all three? Or all three, plus Mick Klemper?

The sound of Madeleine's slippered feet padding toward the den door brought Gurney back from his speculations to his immediate surroundings.

"Good morning," she said sleepily. "How long have you been up?"

"Since five."

She rubbed her eyes and yawned. "You want some coffee?"

"Sure. How come *you're* up?"

"Early clinic shift. Seems unnecessary, really. Early mornings are dead there."

"Jesus, it's barely dawn. How early do they open?"

"Not until eight. I'm not going there right away. I want time to let the chickens out for a while before I leave. I love watching them. Have you noticed they do everything together?"

"Like what?"

"Everything. If one goes a few feet away to peck at something in the grass, as soon as the others notice, they all scurry over and join her. And Horace keeps an eye on them. If one walks a little too far away, he starts crowing. Or he'll run over and try to bring her back. Horace is the guard. Always on the alert. While the hens all have their heads down pecking, he keeps looking around. That's his job."

Gurney thought about this for a minute.

"Interesting how evolution arrives at a variety of survival strategies. Apparently the gene that supports high vigilance in the rooster produces behavior that results in a higher rate of hen survival, which in turn results in the rooster with that gene mating with more hens, which in turn propagates the vigilance gene more broadly into successive generations."

"I suppose," said Madeleine, yawning again and heading for the kitchen.

Chapter 37

Death Wish

Half believing that he would eventually get around to canceling with Malcolm Claret, Gurney kept deferring the call, until the time came—8:15 a.m.—when he was forced to make a decision: either set out on the long drive to his eleven o'clock appointment or pick up the phone and let the man know he wasn't coming.

For reasons not entirely clear to him, he decided at the final moment to keep the appointment after all.

The day was starting to warm up, with a promise of typical August heat and humidity to come. He took off the long-sleeved work shirt he'd been wearing around the house in the coolness of the mountain morning, put on a light polo shirt and a pair of chinos, shaved, combed his hair, picked up his car keys and wallet, and, barely ten minutes after making his decision, he was on his way.

Claret's office was in his home on City Island, a small appendage of the Bronx in Long Island Sound. The drive from Walnut Crossing to the Bronx, the northernmost borough of New York City, took about two and a half hours. Once there, getting to City Island meant traversing the width of the borough, west to east—a journey Gurney had never been able to complete without feeling the negative emotional residues of his childhood there.

The Bronx was fixed in his mind as a place where the essential grunginess had little redeeming charm or character. The faded urban topography was universally uninspiring. In his old neighborhood, the most constricted paycheck-to-paycheck lives and the most prosperous ones were not far apart. The spectrum of achievement was narrow.

The neighborhood of his childhood was by no means a slum, but that absence of a negative was as positive as it got. Whatever civic pride existed arose from successfully keeping undesirable minorities at bay. The shabby but safe status quo was tenaciously maintained.

In the mix of small apartment buildings, two-family houses, and modest private homes—crowded together with little sense of order or provision for open spaces—there were only two homes he remembered as standing out among the drab multitude, only two that seemed pleasant or inviting. The owner of one was a Catholic doctor. The owner of the other was a Catholic funeral director. Both were successful. It was a predominantly Catholic neighborhood, a place where religion still mattered—as an emblem of respectability, a structure of allegiance, and a criterion for choosing providers of professional services.

That constricted way of thinking, of feeling, of making decisions, seemed to grow out of the tense, cramped, colorless environment itself—and it had created in him a powerful urge to escape. It was an urge he'd felt as soon as he was old enough to realize that the Bronx and the world were not synonymous.

Escape. The word brought back an image, a sensation, an emotion from his early teens. The rare joy he would feel, pedaling as fast as he could on his ten-speed English racer, the wind in his face, the soft hiss of the tires on the asphalt—the subtle sense of freedom.

And now he was driving back across the Bronx to see Malcolm Claret.

He'd allowed himself to be talked into it. Curiously, his two previous experiences with Claret had been brought about in a similar way.

When he was twenty-four and his first marriage was dissolving, when Kyle was barely more than an infant, his wife had suggested they see a therapist. It wasn't to save the marriage. She'd already given up on that, seeing that he was determined to stick with the lowly police career that she considered a terrible waste of his intelligence and—perhaps more to the point, Gurney suspected—a waste of his potential for making more money in another field. No, the purpose of therapy from Karen's point of view was to smooth out the separation, to make the process more manageable. And, in a way, it had done just that. Claret had proved to be a rational, insightful, calming influence on the dissolution of a marriage that had been fatally flawed from the start.

Gurney's second exposure to the man came six years later, after the death of Danny, his and Madeleine's four-year-old son. Gurney's reaction to that terrible event in the months following it—sometimes quietly agonized, sometimes numb, never verbal—prompted Madeleine, whose dreadful grief had been more openly expressed, to coax him into therapy.

With neither hope nor resistance, he'd agreed to see Claret, and he met with him three times. He didn't feel that their meetings were resolving anything, and after those three he stopped going. But some of the observations Claret had made stayed with him over the years. One of the things about the man that Gurney appreciated was that he actually answered questions, spoke his mind openly, didn't play therapy games. He didn't belong to that maddening tribe of clinicians whose favorite response to a client's problem is "How do you feel about that?"

Now, as he crossed the little bridge that led out to the separate world of City Island, with its marinas and dry docks and seafood restaurants, as he was thinking of Claret and imagining how the passing years might have changed his appearance, a long-buried memory came vividly to mind.

The memory was of walking across this same bridge with his father on a summer Saturday long ago—in fact, more than forty years ago. There were men standing at the bridge railing at intervals along the pedestrian walkway, casting lines out into the tidal current—shirtless men, tanned and sweating in the August sun. He could hear their reels whining as the lines flew out, big baited hooks and sinkers drawing them out in long arcs over the water. The sun was glinting here and there—on the water, on the stainless-steel reels, on the chrome bumpers of passing cars. The men were serious, intent on their activity, adjusting their rods, taking the slack out of their lines, watching the currents. They had seemed to Gurney like creatures from another world, utterly mysterious and out of reach. His father wasn't ever shirtless or tanned, never stood in a row with other men, never engaged in any group activity. His father wasn't an outdoorsman in that sense, certainly not a fisherman.

Although Gurney could not have articulated it at the age of six or seven when they took those three-mile Saturday walks from their Bronx apartment out over the City Island Bridge, the problem was that he didn't feel that his father was *anything*. His father, even on those walks together, was an enigma—a quiet, secretive man with no overt interests—a man who never spoke of the past or revealed any interest in the future.

Parking in the narrow, shaded side street in front of Malcolm Claret's weathered clapboard house, Gurney felt the way he always felt when he'd been thinking about his father—empty and alone. He tried to shake the feeling as he approached the front door.

He naturally expected Claret to look older, perhaps a bit grayer or balder, than the image, nearly two decades out of date, that he carried in his memory. But he wasn't prepared for the shrunken physique of the man who greeted him in the unfurnished foyer. Only the eyes at first seemed the same—soft blue eyes with an even, unblinking gaze. And the gentle smile—that was the same too. In fact, if anything, those two defining elements of Claret's wise and peaceful presence seemed to have become more pronounced, more concentrated, with the passing of time.

"Come in, David." The frail man gestured toward the same office Gurney had visited years earlier—a space that gave the impression of having once been, along with the foyer, an enclosed sun porch.

Gurney went in and looked around, struck by the instant familiarity of the little room. Claret's brown leather chair, showing fewer signs of aging than the man himself, was in the same position Gurney remembered, facing two other small armchairs, both of which appeared to have been reupholstered in the intervening years. A short-legged table sat at the center of the rough triangle formed by the chairs.

They took the same seats they'd occupied for their conversations following Danny's death, Claret easing himself down with evident difficulty.

"Let's get to the point," he said in his direct but soft voice, bypassing any preamble or small talk. "I'll tell you what Madeleine told me. Then you can tell me whether you think it's true. Is that all right with you?"

"Sure."

"She told me that on three occasions in the past two years you walked into situations where you could easily have been killed. You did this knowingly. In all three, you ended up with a gun pointed at you. In one, you were shot multiple times and put in a coma. She thinks you've probably taken these extraordinary risks many times before, without telling her. She knows that police work is dangerous, but she thinks that for reasons of your own you welcome that danger." He paused, perhaps to observe Gurney's reaction, perhaps to await some response.

Gurney stared down at the low table between them, noting numerous scuff marks, which suggested clients often used it as a hassock. "Anything else?"

"She didn't say it, but she sounded confused and terrified."

"Terrified?"

"She thinks you want to be killed."

Gurney shook his head. "In each situation she's talking about, I've done everything possible to stay alive. I *am* alive. Isn't that prima facie evidence of a desire to survive?"

Claret's blue eyes seemed to be looking through him.

Gurney went on. "In every dangerous situation, I make every effort—"

Claret interrupted, almost in a whisper, "Once you're in it."

"Beg pardon?"

"Once you're in the situation, once you're fully exposed to the danger, then you try to stay alive."

"What are you saying?"

Claret said nothing for a long while. His tone when he finally spoke was mild and even. "Do you still feel responsible for Danny's death?"

"*What?* What's that got to do with anything?"

"Guilt has tremendous power."

"But I'm not . . . I'm not guilty of his death. Danny stepped into the street. He was following a goddamn pigeon, and he followed it off the curb into the street. He was killed by a hit-and-run driver, a drunk in a red sports car. A drunk who just came out of a bar. I'm not guilty of his death."

"Not of his death. But of something. Can you say what it is?"

Gurney took a deep breath, staring at the scuff marks on the table. He closed his eyes, then opened them and forced himself to look at Claret. "I should have been paying more attention. With a four-year-old . . . I should have paid more attention. I didn't notice where he was walking. When I looked ..." His voice trailed off, and his gaze descended again to the tabletop.

After a while, he looked up. "Madeleine insisted I see you, so I'm here. But I don't really understand why."

"Do you know what guilt is?"

Something in Gurney's psychological makeup welcomed the question, or at least welcomed the opportunity to escape into abstraction. "Guilt as a *fact* would be personal responsibility for wrongdoing. Guilt as a *feeling* would be the uncomfortable sense of having done something you shouldn't have done."

"That uncomfortable sense—what exactly do you think that is?"

"A troubled conscience."

"That's a term for it, but it doesn't explain what it really is."

"All right, Malcolm, you tell me."

"Guilt is a painful hunger for harmony—a need to compensate for one's violation, to restore balance, consistency."

"What consistency?"

"Between beliefs and behavior. When my actions are inconsistent with my values, I create a gap, a source of tension. Consciously or unconsciously, we seek to close the gap. We seek the peace of mind that closing the gap—making up for the violation—will provide."

Gurney shifted in his chair, feeling a surge of impatience. "Look, Malcolm, if your point is that I'm trying to get myself killed to make up for the death of my son, then why haven't I let it happen? It's pretty damn easy for a cop to get himself killed. But, like I said before, here I am. Very much alive. How could someone with a serious death wish manage to be in such good health? I mean, that's just plain nonsense!"

"I agree."

"You agree?"

"You didn't kill Danny. So getting yourself killed wouldn't be a rational goal." A subtle, almost playful smile appeared. "And you're a very rational man, aren't you, David?"

"You're losing me."

"You told me that your offense was lack of attention, that you let him wander into the street, where he was hit by a passing car. Listen to what I am about to say, and tell me if it describes the situation accurately." Claret paused before going on in a slow, deliberate way. "With no one protecting him, Danny was at the mercy of a blind, uncaring universe. Fate flipped the coin, a drunk driver appeared, and Danny lost."

Gurney heard the words the man was speaking, sensed the truth in them, yet felt nothing. It was like a beam of light passing through shatterproof glass.

The rest of what Claret said flowed with a similar directness. "The way you see it, your distraction—your focus on your own thoughts—put your son at the mercy of the moment, at the mercy of fate. That, you believe, was your offense. And every once in a while, a situation arises in which you see an opportunity to place yourself in the same peril in which you placed him. You feel that it's only fair that you should do so—only fair that you should expose yourself to the same flip of the coin—only fair that you should treat yourself as uncaringly as you treated him. This is your way of pursuing balance, justice, peace of mind. This is your search for harmony."

They sat for a while in silence—Gurney's mind blank, his feelings numb. Then Claret jarred him with a final twist: "Of course, your approach is a self-centered, tunnel-vision delusion."

Gurney blinked. "What delusion?"

"You're ignoring everything that matters."

"Such as?"

Claret began to answer, then stopped, closed his eyes, and began taking long, slow breaths. When he placed his hands carefully on his knees, their shocking frailty became obvious.

"Malcolm?"

Claret's right hand rose a few inches from his knee in a gesture that appeared designed to allay alarm. A minute or so later, his eyes opened. His voice was just above a whisper. "Sorry about that. My medication is less than perfect."

"What is it? What . . . ?"

"A nasty cancer."

"Treatable?"

Claret laughed quietly. "In theory, yes. In reality, no."

Gurney was silent.

"And reality is where we live. Until we die."

"You're in pain?"

"I would call it periodic discomfort." He looked amused. "You're wondering how long I have to live. The answer is a month, maybe two. We'll have to wait and see."

Gurney tried to say something appropriate. "God, Malcolm. I'm sorry."

"Thank you. Now, since our time is limited—yours as well as mine—let's talk about where we live. Or should be living."

"Meaning?"

"Reality. The place we need to live, in order to be alive. Tell me something. About Danny. Did you ever have a special name for him?"

Gurney was momentarily thrown by the question. "What do you mean, a special name?"

"Something other than his actual name. Maybe something you called him when you were putting him to bed, or holding him on your lap, or in your arms?"

He was about to say no when something came back to him, something he hadn't thought of in years. The memory blindsided him with sadness. He cleared his throat. "My little bear."

"Why did you call him that?"

"There was a look about him ... especially if he was unhappy about something ... that for some reason reminded me of a little bear. I'm not sure why."

"And you would hug him?"

"Yes."

"Because you loved him."

"Yes."

"And he loved you."

"I suppose so. Yes."

"Did you want him to die?'

"Of course not."

"Would he want you to die?"

"No."

"Does Madeleine want you to die?"

"No."

"Does Kyle want you to die?"

"No."

Claret looked into Gurney's eyes, as if assessing his understanding, before going on. "Everyone who loves you wants you to live."

"I suppose so."

"So this obsessive need of yours to atone for Danny's death, to deal with your guilt by exposing yourself to the risk of being killed . . . it's terribly selfish, isn't it?"

"Is it?" Gurney's own voice sounded lifeless to him, somehow disconnected, as though coming from someone else.

"You're the only one for whom it seems to make any sense."

"Danny's death was my fault."

"And the fault of the drunk driver who hit him. And his own fault for stepping off the sidewalk into the street, which you'd probably warned him a hundred times not to do. And the fault of the pigeon he was following. And the fault of whatever God made the pigeon and the street and the drunk and the car and every past event that brought them all together at that unfortunate moment. Who are you to imagine *you* made all that happen?"

Claret paused, as if to catch his breath, to gather his strength, then spoke in a rising voice. "Your arrogance is outrageous. Your disregard for the people who love you is outrageous. David, listen to me. You must not cause pain to those who love you. If your great sin was a failure to pay attention, then pay attention *now*. You have a wife. What right do you have to risk her husband's life? You have a son. What right do you have to risk his father's life?"

The emotional energy expended in this short speech seemed to exhaust him.

Gurney sat motionless, speechless, empty, waiting. The room seemed very small. He could hear a faint ringing in his ears.

Claret smiled, his voice softer now, the softness somehow conveying a greater conviction, the conviction of the dying. "Listen to me, David. There is nothing in life that matters but love. Nothing but love."

Chapter 38

A Fondness for Fire

Gurney had no clear recollection of leaving City Island, of making his way through the Bronx, or of crossing the George Washington Bridge. It wasn't until he was driving north on Palisades Parkway that he regained a sense of normalcy. Along with that normalcy came the discovery that he was too low on gas to make it back to Walnut Crossing.

Twenty minutes later, he was sitting in the parking lot of a large gas station with a food court where he was able to refuel both the car and himself. After a large coffee and a couple of bagels made him feel like he was reestablishing contact with his daily life, he took out his phone—which he'd switched off for his meeting with Claret—and checked his messages.

There were four. The voice on the first, originating from an unknown number, was Klemper's—rougher and more slurred than the day before. *"Following up on Rivermall ... Riverside. Our conversation. Check your mailbox. Remember what you said. Don't fuck with me. People who fuck with me ... is not a good idea. Don't fuck with me. A deal is a deal is a deal. Remember that. Don't fucking forget that. Check your mailbox."*

Gurney wondered if the man was really as drunk as he sounded. More important, he wondered if the item in the mailbox was in fact the missing security video he'd asked for. He couldn't help remembering that someone had once put a snake in his mailbox. It was also a natural spot for a bomb. But that seemed a step too far.

The message also reminded him that he needed to fill in Hardwick and Esti on the Riverside meeting and "deal" Klemper was referring to.

He went on to the second message, which was from Hardwick. *"Hey, Sherlock. Just got off the phone with Ankara. Seems the little man who shot out our lights is quite a piece of work. Call me back."*

The third message was also from Hardwick, more agitated. *"Where the fuck you hiding, Sherlock? I'm outside Cooperstown, heading for Bincher's place. Still no word from him. Getting a bad feeling about this. And we need to talk about our crazy shooter. And I mean* crazy. *Call me, for Christ's sake."*

The fourth and final message was from a grimmer, angrier Hardwick. *"Gurney, wherever you are,* answer your fucking phone. *I'm at Lex Bincher's house. Or what used to be his house. It burned down last night. Along with his neighbors' houses. Three fucking houses in a row. Down to the fucking ground. Big, fast, super-hot fires ... started in Lex's house ... apparently some kind of incendiary devices ... more than one. Call me!* Now!*"*

Gurney decided to call Madeleine first. He got bounced into voice mail, and left a message: "Do me a favor and don't open our mailbox today. I'm pretty sure there's no problem, but I got kind of an agitated call from Klemper, and I'd rather open it myself. Just a precaution. I'll explain later. I'm at the Sloatsburg rest stop. Love you. See you in a couple of hours."

Thinking about what he'd said, he wished he'd said it differently. It was too ominous, too obscure. It needed context, explanation. He was tempted to call back and leave a longer message, but he was afraid he'd end up making the situation worse.

He called Hardwick's number and got voice mail. He left a message saying that he was currently en route to Walnut Crossing. He asked if there'd been any casualties in the Cooperstown fires, or any sign of Bincher. And, regarding the *crazy* shooter, what had he found out? He ended the call, making sure his phone was still on, and went back into the food court for another coffee.

It wasn't until he was up into the rural hills above Barleyville that Hardwick finally got back to him. "We've got some seriously insane shit going on here, ace. Three big houses, three big piles of ashes. Lex's house, plus one on each side of it. Six people dead—none of them

Bincher. Two bodies in the house on his left, four in the house on his right, including two kids. All trapped in the fires. Guys on the scene are saying it happened sometime after midnight, went up real quick. The arson unit guy is saying probable SIDs—small incendiary devices— four of them, one at each corner of Bincher's house. No effort by the arsonist to make it seem like anything but arson."

"And the other two houses were just collateral damage? You sure?"

"I'm not *sure* about anything. I'm outside the yellow tape, blending in with the asshole gawkers—just picking up what the local cops are telling their buddies. But the word is that the gas chromatograph tests were positive for incendiary chemicals at Bincher's, not at the others."

"But Bincher's house was empty? I mean, there were no bodies in that one?"

"None so far. But I can see the techs still crawling around down there in the wet ashes. Quite the fucking mob scene. Fire department, BCI, arson unit, sheriff's department, troopers, local uniforms." He paused. "Christ, Davey, if this is supposed to be . . . to be a way of *warning* Lex off the case . . ." His voice trailed off.

Gurney said nothing.

Hardwick coughed, cleared his throat. "You still there?"

"Still here. Just thinking about your 'warning' comment." He paused. "I'd say that cutting your power lines was probably a warning. The mutilation of Gurikos's head was probably a warning. But this . . . this Bincher thing . . . this feels like something more. Like war. With zero concern for who gets killed."

"I agree. The little fucker has an appetite for serious destruction. And arson seems to be a recurrent theme."

"Recurrent theme?" Gurney slowed down, pulled onto a grassy bluff overlooking the reservoir, turned off the engine, and opened his windows. "What do you mean, *recurrent* theme? What did you get from Interpol?"

"Maybe a lot, or maybe a lot of nothing. Hard to say. The thing of it is, the information they've pieced together in their database may or may not refer to a single individual. The current stuff, from the past ten years or so, is probably accurate—most of it anyway. But before that—earlier than ten years ago—it gets shakier. Also more bizarre."

Gurney wondered how much more bizarre it could get than hammering nails into someone's head.

Hardwick explained. "The guy in Ankara decided to talk to me on the phone rather than create an e-mail trail, so I took notes. What he gave me amounts to two little stories. Depending on how you look at them, they can seem very connected, or maybe not connected at all. The stories go backwards in time, starting with the material assembled in the last decade or so on the assassin who goes by the name Petros Panikos. You ready for this?"

"All ears, Jack."

"The Panikos name, used as a primary search link, led back to an event that occurred twenty-five years ago in the village of Lykonos in southern Greece. There was a Panikos family there that owned a gift shop. There were four sons in the family, the youngest of whom was believed to have been adopted. The gift shop, along with the family home, was destroyed by a fire that killed both parents and three of the sons. The fourth son, the adopted one, disappeared. Arson was suspected but never proved. No formal birth certificate or adoption papers were ever found for the missing son. The family was very private, had no close relatives, and there was even some disagreement in the village about the missing son's name. But—get this—the two possible names mentioned were Pero and Petros."

"How old was he?"

"No one could say for sure. According to the old arson investigation file, his age at the time was estimated to be anywhere from twelve to sixteen."

"No information on his birth name or where he came from originally?"

"Nothing official. However, in the arson investigation file there's a statement from a priest in the village who thought the boy came from a Bulgarian orphanage."

"What made him think that?"

"There's no indication in the file that anyone bothered to ask. But the priest did give the name of the orphanage."

Gurney let out a short laugh. It had nothing to do with humor. If he had to explain it, he probably would have called it an overflow of energy. There was something about the tracking process, the movement from one bit of information to another, the steps across the stream, that charged the circuits of his brain. "And I'm guessing that the trail to the orphanage takes us to another relevant event?"

"Well, actually, it takes us to a bleak communist-era orphanage for which there are no extant records. Wanna guess why?"

"Another arson?"

"Yep. So all we know about its residents at the time of the fire—in which most of them died—comes from a skimpy old police file, actually from one interview in that file, with a staff nurse who survived the blaze. By the way, there was no problem establishing arson as the cause. Apart from the orphanage's four buildings going up in flames at the same time—and apart from gas cans being found in all four—the outer doors were jammed shut with wooden wedges."

"Meaning the goal was mass murder. But it sounds like the fire was the end of the story. What was the beginning?"

"According to the nurse's statement, a couple of years before the fire, a strange little kid was discovered one winter morning, literally on the front steps. The kid appeared to be mute and illiterate. But then they discovered that he was fluent not only in Bulgarian but also in Russian, German, and English. This nurse got the idea that the kid was some sort of idiot savant with languages—he was that good. So she got him some basic grammar books, and sure enough, during the two years he was there he learned French, Turkish, and God knows what else."

"Did he ever tell them where he came from?"

"He claimed total amnesia—no memory of anything prior to arriving there. His only link to the past was a chronic nightmare. Something involving a carnival and a clown. They ended up putting him in a separate room at night, away from the other kids, because of how often he'd wake up screaming. For some reason—maybe because of there being a clown in the dream—the nurse got the idea that his original mother had been in some kind of creepy little traveling circus."

"Sounds like quite the unusual child. Any big red flags pop up before the fire?"

"Oh, yeah. Big one." Hardwick paused dramatically.

It was one of his habits that Gurney had learned to live with. "You want to tell me about it?"

"A couple of kids made fun of him, something about the nightmares." Another pause.

"Jack, for Christ's sake—"

"They disappeared."

"The kids who made fun of him?"

"Right. Off the face of the earth. Same thing with an aide who didn't believe his amnesia story, kept taunting him about it. Gone. Zero trace."

"Anything else?"

"More weird shit. Nobody could tell how old he was, because in the two years he was there he never changed, never grew, never seemed to look any older than the day he arrived."

"Like Peter Pan."

"Right."

"Was he ever called by that nickname at the orphanage?"

"There's nothing about that in the Bulgarian file."

Gurney ran the story back through his mind quickly. "I'm missing something. How do we know this orphanage kid is the same kid the Panikos family adopted?"

"We don't know for sure. The nurse said he was adopted by a Greek family, but she didn't know the name. That was handled by a different department. But it was the day he left with his new parents that the place burned down and just about everyone else was trapped and killed."

Gurney was silent.

"What are you thinking, Sherlock?"

"I'm thinking that someone paid a hundred grand to turn this little monster loose on Carl Spalter."

"And on Mary Spalter and Gus Gurikos and Lex Bincher," added Hardwick.

"Peter Pan," mused Gurney. "The kid who never grew up."

"Very fanciful, ace, but where does this leave us?"

"I'd say it leaves us in the middle of nowhere, drifting into total confusion. We've got some colorful stories, but we *know* almost nothing. We're looking for a pro hitter whose name might be Petros Panikos or Peter Pan or something else. Birth name unknown. Passport name unknown. Date of birth unknown. Nationality unknown. Birth parents unknown. Current address unknown. Arrests and convictions unknown. In fact, just about everything that could lead us to him is unknown."

"I don't disagree. What now?"

"You need to go back to your Interpol guy and beg for whatever crumbs might still be lurking in the corners of their Panikos file— especially anything more about the Panikos family, their neighbors, anyone in that village who might have known anything about little Petros, or whatever the hell they named him—anything that might give us a better handle than we have now. The name of anyone we could talk to . . ."

"Fuck, man, that was twenty-five years ago. Nobody's going to remember anything, even if we could find them. Get real."

"You're probably right. But get in touch with your Interpol guy anyway. Who knows what he might come up with?"

After ending the call, Gurney sat with his notebook open on his lap, gazing out over the reservoir. The low water level was exposing the rocky slopes that extended from the water's edge up to the tree line. Driftwood littered the stones. Across a small inlet, in the deep afternoon shadows, a pair of gnarled branches reached up from the water onto the slope in a way that stirred a chilling memory of one of his first murder scenes as a rookie—the body of a naked child washed up against a stony outcropping on the shore of the Hudson River.

It wasn't a memory he wanted to dwell on. He picked up his notebook, where he'd jotted down most of what Hardwick had told him, and went over it one more time.

He was frustrated with himself. Frustrated with having gotten involved in the case to begin with. Frustrated with not having made more tangible progress. Frustrated with the lack of official standing. Frustrated with all the question marks.

He decided he needed another cup of coffee. He started the car and was about to head into Barleyville when Hardwick called again, sounding more shaken than before. "We've got a new situation. If what I just overheard is true, Lex Bincher may no longer be missing."

"Oh, Jesus. What now?"

"One of the troopers with the BCI boys found a body in the water under Lex's private dock. Just a body. A body with no head."

"Are they sure it's Bincher?"

"I didn't hang around to find out. I got a bad feeling about the missing head. I backed out of the crowd and came back to my car. I gotta get outta here before I puke, or before some BCI guy recognizes me and puts two and two together—with me and Bincher and the Spalter case—and I end up in an interview room for the next two weeks. I can't afford that. Not with this kind of shit going down. I got to be able to move, got to be able to do whatever the fuck we have to do. Gotta go. Call you later."

Gurney sat there by the reservoir for another few minutes, letting the new situation sink in. His gaze drifted back out over the water to the piece of driftwood that had reminded him of the body snagged on the rocks at the edge of the Hudson. As he stared now at the bare, twisted wood, the configuration reminded him not just of a body, but of a headless body.

He shivered, restarted the car, and headed for Walnut Crossing.

Chapter 39

Terrible Creatures

Thinking about Hardwick's anxious departure from the crime scene—in fear of being recognized and having the reason for his presence questioned—pushed to the front of Gurney's mind an issue he'd been avoiding: Where did the right to conduct a private investigation in the interest of a client end . . . and obstruction of justice begin?

At what point did he have an obligation to share with law enforcement what he'd learned about the hit man who called himself Petros Panikos and his probable involvement in the lengthening string of homicides associated with the Spalter case? Did the fact that Panikos's involvement was only "probable" rather than certain make a difference? Surely, Gurney concluded with a feeling an inch shy of comfort, he had no obligation to share speculative scenarios with the police, who no doubt had plenty of their own. But how honest was that argument, really?

This debate occupied him uneasily as he drove through bleak little Barleyville—finding the little café where he'd hoped to get coffee closed. He continued on over the forested hills that separated it from the village of Walnut Crossing, and on past that to his mountain road. His thoughts culminated in a chilling question: *What if the Cooperstown deaths were a sign of things to come?* How long could one keep confidential the fruits of a private investigation, if the war that apparently had been declared by Panikos continued to claim casualties?

The sight of his mailbox at the end of the road shifted his focus from Panikos to Klemper. Had the man delivered the requested security video, as his phone message had implied? Or did the mailbox contain a less pleasant surprise?

He drove past the mailbox, parked the car by the barn, and walked back.

He'd have bet a thousand dollars against the possibility of a bomb, but he wasn't ready to bet his life. He eyed the mailbox and decided on a relatively low-risk way of opening it. He first needed to find a fallen branch long enough to reach the drop-lid from a spot shielded by the trunk of a hemlock several feet from the box.

After a five-minute search and a number of awkward thrusts with a less-than-ideal branch, he managed to jar the drop-lid loose. It swung open with a clank. He waited a few seconds, then circled around to the front of the box and peered inside. All it contained was a single white envelope. He removed it, brushing off a tiny ant.

The envelope was addressed to him in rough block printing. It had no stamp or postmark. He could feel a small rectangular object through the paper, which he thought might be a USB drive. He opened the envelope cautiously and saw that he was right. He put the drive in his pocket, walked back to the car, and drove up to the house.

The clock on the dashboard read 4:18 p.m. Madeleine's car was in its regular spot, which reminded him that she'd been on her early shift that day and had likely gotten home around two. He expected she'd be inside reading—perhaps engaged in her Sisyphean assault on *War and Peace*. He went in through the side door and called out, "I'm home."

There was no answer.

Passing through the kitchen on his way to the den, he called out again, and again there was no answer. His next thought was that she was out on one of her walks.

In the den he tapped a key on his open laptop to bring it to life. He took the USB drive out of his pocket and stuck it in the appropriate slot. The icon that appeared was titled "02 DEC 2011 08:00AM–11:59AM"—the time window within which the Spalter shooting had occurred. He went to the GET INFO menu and discovered that the little thumb drive had a 64GB capacity, far more than enough to cover the specified hours, even at a high resolution.

He clicked on the drive icon, and a window opened immediately with four video file icons—titled "CAM A (INT)," "CAM B (EAST)," "CAM C (WEST)," and "CAM D (SOUTH)."

Interesting. A four-camera array was an unusual level of video security for a small electronics store in a small city. Gurney figured the array was either an active display for the purpose of selling security cameras—like having a wall of televisions, all on—or, a possibility that had crossed his mind earlier, Hairy Harry and his girlfriend were in a riskier business than consumer electronics.

Since the south-facing camera would have been the one facing the Willow Rest cemetery, that was the file Gurney chose first. When he clicked on the icon, a video window appeared with controls for PLAY, PAUSE, REVERSE, and CLOSE, plus a sliding bar linked to the file time code, for getting to specific points in the video. He clicked on PLAY.

What he saw then was what he'd hoped for. It was almost too good to be true. Not only was the file resolution superb, but the camera that had produced the file evidently included the latest motion-tracking and zoom-to-action technology. And, of course, like most security cameras, it was motion-activated—recording video only when something was happening—and had a real-time indicator at the bottom of the frame.

The motion-activation feature meant that the nominal four-hour period of coverage would occupy far less recorded time in the file, since intervals of inactivity in the camera's field of view would not be represented. So it was that the first hour of the period had produced less than ten minutes of digital footage—triggered mainly by hardy dog walkers and winter-suited joggers performing their morning rituals on a path that paralleled the low cemetery wall. The scene was brightened by pale winter sunlight and a light, patchy coating of snow.

It wasn't until a little after nine that the camera responded to activity *inside* Willow Rest. A panel truck was moving slowly across the frame. It came to a stop in front of what Gurney recognized as the Spalter family plot (or, to use Paulette Purley's term, "property"). Two men in bulky overalls emerged from the truck, opened its rear doors, and began unloading a number of dark, flat, rectangular objects. These were soon revealed to be folding chairs, which the men set up with evident care in two rows facing an elongated area of dark earth—the open grave intended for Mary Spalter. After making some adjustments in the position of the chairs, one of the men erected a portable podium at the end of the grave, while the other retrieved a large broom from the truck and began sweeping some of the snow away from the grassy space between the chairs and the grave.

As this work was progressing, a small white car pulled into view and stopped behind the truck. Although he couldn't be sure of the face, impossibly tiny in the video frame, Gurney had a feeling that the woman who got out of the car, bundled in a fur jacket and fur hat, gesturing as though she was giving instructions to the workmen, was Paulette Purley. After some more straightening of the chairs, the men got back in the truck and drove out of the frame.

The woman stood by herself, looking around the plot as if giving everything a final once-over, then got back in her car, drove it past the open grassy area, and parked next to some cold-withered rhododendrons. The video continued for another minute or so before stopping. It restarted at a point twenty-eight minutes later in real time—at 9:54 a.m.—with the arrival of a hearse and a number of other cars.

A man in a black overcoat came from the passenger side of the hearse, and the woman Gurney figured was Paulette Purley reemerged from her car. They met, shook hands, spoke briefly. The man walked back toward the hearse, gesturing as he went. Half a dozen dark-suited men got out of a limo, opened the rear door of the hearse, and slowly removed a casket, which they then carried with practiced smoothness to the open grave and placed on a supporting structure that held it at ground level.

At some signal Gurney did not detect, the mourners began coming out of the other cars parked in a row along the lane behind the hearse. Wrapped in winter coats and hats, they made their way to the two rows of chairs alongside the grave, gradually filling all but two of the sixteen seats. The two left vacant were those on either side of Mary Spalter's triplet cousins.

The tallish man in the black overcoat, presumably the funeral director, moved to a position behind the seated mourners. The six pallbearers, having made some adjustments to the position of the casket, stood shoulder to shoulder beside him. Paulette Purley stood a few feet off to the side of the last pallbearer.

Gurney's attention was fixed on the man in the end seat of the first row. The unsuspecting victim-to-be. The clock at the bottom of the video window indicated that the time in Willow Rest was 10:19 a.m. Meaning that at that moment Carl Spalter had just one minute left. One more minute of life as he'd known it.

Gurney's gaze went back and forth between Carl and the clock, feeling the erosion of time and life with a painful acuteness.

There was just half a minute left, before a .220 Swift bullet—the fastest, most accurate bullet in the world—would pierce the man's left temple, fragment in his brain, and put an end to whatever future he might have imagined.

In his long NYPD career, Gurney had witnessed countless crimes on security videos—including muggings, beatings, burglaries, homicides—at gas stations, liquor stores, convenience stores, Laundromats, ATMs.

But this one was different.

The human context, with its complex and strained family relationships, was deeper. The emotional context was more vivid. The sedate physical appearance of the scene—the seated participants, the suggestion of a formal group portrait—bore no resemblance to the content of typical security camera footage. And Gurney knew more about the man about to be shot—in just a few more seconds—than he'd known up front about any other on-tape victim.

Then the moment came.

Gurney leaned in toward his computer screen, literally on the edge of his chair.

Carl Spalter rose and turned toward the podium that had been set up at the far end of the open grave. He took a step in that direction, passing in front of Alyssa. Then, just as he began to take another step, he lurched forward in a kind of stumbling collapse that carried him the length of the front row. He hit the ground face-first and lay motionless on the snow-whitened grass between his mother's casket and his brother's chair.

Jonah and Alyssa were the first on their feet, followed by two Elder Force ladies from the the second row. The pallbearers came around from behind the chairs. Paulette rushed toward Carl, dropped to her knees, and bent over him. After that it was difficult to sort out what was happening, as more people crowded around the fallen man.

During the ensuing minutes, at least three people appeared to have their phones out, making calls.

Gurney noted that Carl was hit, as the incident report indicated, at exactly 10:20. The first responder arrived at 10:28—a local uniform in a Long Falls police cruiser. Within the next couple of minutes, two more arrived, followed shortly by a trooper cruiser. At 10:42, an EMT unit arrived in a large ambulance. Parking directly in front of the main activity at the scene, blocking the security camera's field of view, it rendered the remainder of the video useless to Gurney. Even the first unmarked car—presumably bringing Klemper—was obscured when it stopped on the far side of the ambulance.

After skimming through the rest of the video, sampling bits here and there and finding no important additional data, Gurney sat back in his desk chair to consider what he'd seen.

In addition to the unfortunate position of the ambulance, there was another problem with the material. Despite the high resolution of the camera, its formidable zoom lens, and its auto-framing capabilities, the sheer camera-to-subject distance resulted in a visual product with definite limitations. Although he'd understood what he saw happening, he knew that some of that understanding had been supplied by what he'd been told. He'd long ago accepted a major counterintuitive cognitive principle: We don't think what we think because we see what we see. We see what we see because we think what we think. Preconceptions can easily override optical data—even make us see things that aren't there.

What he wanted was stronger optical data—to make sure his preconceptions weren't leading him in the wrong direction. Ideally, he'd submit the digital file to a sophisticated computer lab for maximum enhancement, but part of the price of retirement was lack of free access to that kind of resource. It occurred to him that Esti might have a back door into the NYSP lab that would enable her to get the job done without an ID or tracking number that could come back to bite her, but he wasn't comfortable with nudging her into that position. At least, not until less risky options had been exhausted.

He picked up his phone and called Kyle—an avid storehouse of information on all things related to computers, the more complex the better. He was invited to leave a message, and he did. "Hi, son. I have a digital technology problem. Official support channels aren't available to deal with it. Here's the thing. I have a hi-def video file that might be more revealing if we could apply a digital zoom effect without diluting its sharpness. That's kind of a contradiction, but I think there's enhancement software with certain algorithms that have a way of addressing that issue . . . so maybe you could point me in the right direction? Thanks, son. I'm sure whatever you can tell me will be a lot more than I already know."

After ending the call, he decided to go back to the beginning of the video and view it again. But then he happened to notice the current time, displayed in the upper corner of his laptop screen. It was 5:48 p.m. Even if Madeleine had taken the longest of her usual trails through the woods—the one over the top of Carlson's Ridge—she should have returned by now.

It was dinnertime, and she never . . . *Oh, Christ! Of course!*

He felt like an idiot. This was the day she was supposed to leave for her stay at the Winklers'. Too much was happening too damn fast. It was as though his brain couldn't contain another speck of information, and every time something new got jammed in, it shoved something out the other side. It was kind of scary to think about. What else might he have forgotten?

That's when he remembered that on his way in he'd seen her car parked by the house.

If she's at the Winklers', why the hell is her car still here?

Baffled, with a fast-growing feeling of unease, he called her cell number.

He was surprised a few seconds later to hear her phone ringing in the kitchen. Had she not gone to the Winklers' after all? Was she somewhere around the house? He called out to her, but there was no answer. He went out from the den to the kitchen. Following the sound of the ring, he found her phone on the sideboard next to the stove. That was truly odd. As far as he knew, she never left the house without it. Perplexed, he gazed out the window, hoping that he might see her heading up through the pasture toward the house.

There was no sign or her. Just her car. Which meant she *had to be* somewhere in the general vicinity—unless she'd gone somewhere with a friend who'd picked her up. Or unless, God forbid, she'd had an accident and was taken away in an ambulance.

He strained to recall anything she might have said that would . . .

Just then a breeze caught the asparagus ferns, stirring them briefly apart, and something bright flashed at the corner of his eye.

Something pink, he thought.

Then the ferns settled back together, and he wondered whether he'd seen anything at all.

Curiosity drove him outside to check.

As soon as he reached the far side of the asparagus bed his question was answered—with a larger one. Madeleine was sitting on the grass in one of her pink T-shirts. Next to her on the ground were a few pieces of bluestone placed over what appeared to be freshly loosened earth. On the far side of the stones, a shovel, recently used, lay on the grass. With her right hand, Madeleine was gently patting down the dark earth around the edges of the stones.

At first she said nothing.

"Maddie?"

She looked up at him with her mouth in a tight, sad little line.

"What is it? What's the matter?"

"Horace."

"Horace?"

"One of those terrible creatures killed him."

"Our rooster?"

She nodded.

"What sort of terrible creature?" he asked.

"I don't know. I guess what Bruce said the other night when he was here. A weasel? A possum? I don't know. He warned us. I should have listened." She bit her lower lip.

"When did it happen?"

"This afternoon. When I got home, I let them out of the barn for some air. It was such a nice day. I had some cracked corn, which they love, so they followed me up to the house. They were right out here. Running around. Pecking in the grass. I went into the house for . . . something, I don't even know what. I just . . ." She stopped for a moment, shaking her head. "He was only four months old. He was just learning to crow. He looked so proud. Poor little Horace. Bruce warned us . . . he warned us . . . about what could happen."

"You buried him?"

"Yes." She reached over and smoothed the soil by the stones. "I couldn't let his little body just lie there." She sniffled, cleared her throat. "He was probably trying to protect the hens from the weasel. Don't you think?"

Gurney had no idea what to think. "I guess so."

After patting down the soil a few more times, she got up from the grass and they went into the house. The sun had already started to slide down behind the western ridge. The slope of the opposite hill was bathed in that ruddy-gold light that only ever lasted a minute or two.

I t was a strange evening. After they had a brief, quiet dinner of leftovers, Madeleine settled into one of the armchairs by the big empty fireplace at the far end of the long room, abstractedly holding one of her perennial knitting projects in her lap.

Gurney asked if she'd like him to turn on the floor lamp behind her chair. She shook her head almost imperceptibly. As he was about to ask if she had a revised timetable for going to the Winklers' farm, she asked about his meeting that morning with Malcolm Claret.

That morning?

So much had intervened, his trip to the Bronx felt like something that had happened a week ago. He was having a hard time focusing on it, fitting it into his grasp of the day. He began with the first aspect of it that came to mind.

"When you made my appointment, did Malcolm tell you he was dying?"

"Dying?"

"Yes. He's in the end stages of a fatal cancer."

"And he's still . . . Oh, God."

"What?"

"He didn't tell me, not directly, but . . . I remember he did say that your appointment needed to be very soon. I'd just assumed he had some major commitment coming up, and . . . Oh, God. How is he?"

"Mostly the same. I mean, he looks very old, very thin. But he's . . . very . . . very clear."

A silence passed between them.

Madeleine was the first to speak. "Is that what you spoke about? His sickness?"

"Oh, no, not at all. In fact, he didn't even refer to it until the end. We spoke mainly about . . . me . . . and you."

"Was it useful?"

"I think so."

"Are you still mad about my making the appointment for you?"

"No. It turned out to be a good thing." At least, he thought it was a good thing. He was still having trouble wrapping words around its effect on him.

After a brief silence she smiled softly and said, "Good."

After a longer silence, he wondered if he should circle back to the Winkler situation and get it resolved. He was still determined to get Madeleine away from the house. But he figured there'd be time enough to take care of that in the morning.

At eight o'clock, she went to bed.

A little while later, he followed her.

It wasn't that he felt particularly sleepy. In fact, he was having a hard time putting any label at all on what he was feeling. The day had left him confused and overloaded. To begin with, there was the visceral impact of Claret's message. And beyond that, the jarring immersion in the Bronx of his childhood, followed by the escalating horrors reported by Jack Hardwick from Cooperstown, and finally Madeleine's pain at the rooster's death—which he suspected had resonated unconsciously with another loss.

He went into the bedroom, took off his clothes, and slipped into bed beside her. He let his arm rest gently against hers, finding himself unable to conceive of any more articulate or appropriate communication.

Part Three
All the Evil
in the World

Chapter 40

The Morning After

Gurney awoke with a heavy emotional hangover.

Mired between thinking and dreaming, his sleep had been too shallow and fitful to perform its vital function of downloading the jumbled experiences of the day into the orderly cabinets of memory. Bits of yesterday's turmoil were still in the forefront of his mind, obstructing his view of the present moment. It wasn't until he'd showered, dressed, gotten his coffee, and joined Madeleine at the breakfast table that he finally noticed it was a bright, cloudless day.

But even that positive factor failed to have its normal elevating effect on his outlook.

A piece of music was playing on the NPR station, something orchestral. He hated music in the morning and in his present mood he found it especially grating.

Madeleine eyed him over the top of the book she had propped up in front of her. "What is it?"

"I feel a bit lost."

She lowered the book a couple of inches. "The Spalter case?"

"Mainly that . . . I guess."

"What about it?"

"It's not coming together. It just gets uglier and more chaotic." He told her about Hardwick's two calls from Cooperstown, leaving out the missing head, which he didn't have the stomach to mention. He concluded, "I'm not sure what the hell is going on. And I don't feel I have the resources to deal with it."

She closed the book. "Deal with it?"

"Figure it out—what's really happening, who's behind it, why."

She stared at him. "Haven't you already succeeded in what you were asked to do?"

"Succeeded?"

"I'd gotten the impression that you'd pretty much shredded the case against Kay Spalter."

"True."

"So her conviction will be reversed on appeal. That was the point, wasn't it?"

"It was, yes."

"Was?"

"It seems that all hell is breaking loose. These new arson-murders—"

She interrupted. "Which is why we have police departments."

"They didn't do such a great job the first time. And I don't think they have a clue what they're up against."

"And you do?"

"Not really."

"So nobody knows what's going on. Whose job is it to find out?"

"Officially, it's BCI's job."

She cocked her head challengingly. "Officially, legally, logically, and every other way."

"You're right."

"But?"

After an uncomfortable pause, he said, "But there's a crazy person loose out there."

"There are a lot of crazy people out there."

"This one's been killing people since he was about eight years old. He likes killing people. The more the better. Someone turned him loose on Carl Spalter, and now he doesn't seem to want to go back in his box."

Madeleine held his gaze. "So the danger is increasing. You said the other day there might be a one percent chance of his coming after you. Obviously, this horrible thing in Cooperstown changes all that."

"To some degree, but I still think—"

"David," she interrupted, "I have to say this—I know what your answer will be, but I have to say it anyway. You *do* have the option of backing away."

"If I back away from the investigation, he'll still be out there. There'll just be less chance of getting him."

"But if you're not going after him, maybe he won't go after you."

"His mind may not work that logically."

She looked anxious, confused. "From what you've told me about him, he sounds like a very logical, precise planner."

"A precise, logical planner driven by a homicidal rage. Funny thing about contract killers. They can appear cool and practical about actions that horrify most people, but there's nothing cool or practical about their motivation—and I don't mean the money they get paid to do what they do. That's secondary. I've met hit men. I've interrogated them. I've gotten to know a few of them fairly well. And you know what they are, for the most part? They're rage-driven serial killers who've managed to turn their insanity into a paying job. You want to hear something really nuts?"

Her expression was more wary than curious, but he went on anyway. "I used to tell Kyle when he was a kid that one key to a happy life, a happy career, was to find an activity you enjoyed enough that you'd be willing to do it without being paid—then find someone willing to pay you to do it. Well, not many people succeed in doing that. Pilots, musicians, actors, artists, and athletes, mainly. And hit men. I don't mean that professional killers end up happy. In fact, most of them die violently or die in prison. But they *like* what they do when they're doing it. Most of them would end up killing people whether they were paid for it or not."

As he was speaking, she was becoming more distressed. "David, what on earth is your point?"

He realized he'd worked himself farther out onto a limb than he'd intended. "Only that my withdrawing from the case now wouldn't accomplish anything positive."

She was making an apparent effort to remain calm. "Because you're already on his radar screen?"

"It's possible."

Her tone began to fray. "It's because of that vile *Criminal Conflict* program. Bincher using your name, tying you to Hardwick. That idiot Brian Bork created the problem. He needs to make it go away. He needs to announce that you're off the case. Gone."

"I'm not sure that would make any difference at this point."

"What are you telling me? That you've managed to set yourself up—once again—in front of some lunatic murderer? That there's nothing to do now but wait for some horrible confrontation?"

"That's what I'm trying to *avoid*—by getting to him before he can get to me."

"How?"

"By finding out everything I can about him. So I can predict his actions better than he can predict mine."

"That's the pattern, isn't it? *You and him.*"

"Pardon?"

"You and him. One on one. It's the same life-or-death contest you always seem to get yourself into. It's the reason I wanted you to see Malcolm."

He felt numb. "It's not the same this time. It's not just me. I have people on my side."

"Oh, really? Who? Jack Hardwick, who dragged you into this mess to begin with? The state police, whom your investigation is undermining? Those are your friends and allies?" She shook her head in a way that looked like a shudder, then went on. "Even if the whole world was willing to help you, it wouldn't matter. It would still be just *you against him*. It always comes down to that. High Noon at the O.K. Corral."

He said nothing.

Madeleine sat back in her chair, watching him. Gradually, a look of discovery changed her expression. "I just realized something."

"What?"

"You never really worked *for* the NYPD, did you? You never saw yourself as their employee, as a tool of the department. You saw the department as *your* tool—something to be used on *your* terms, if and when you felt like it, to achieve *your* goals."

"My goals were their goals. Catch the bad guys. Get the evidence. Lock 'em up."

She continued as though he hadn't spoken. "For you, the department was really just *backup*. The real contest was always between you and the bad guy. *You and the bad guy* on the way to the showdown. Sometimes you took advantage of department resources, sometimes you didn't. But you always saw it as *your* battle, *your* call."

He listened to what she was saying. Maybe she was right. Maybe his approach to things was too limited, too restricted to his own point of view. Maybe that was a big problem, maybe it wasn't. Maybe it was just the natural product of his brain chemistry, something over which he would never have any control. But whatever it was, he had no desire to keep talking about it. He suddenly found the whole topic exhausting.

He wasn't sure what to do next.

But he had to do something. Even if it led to nothing.

He decided to call Adonis Angelidis.

Chapter 41

A Cautionary Tale

Gurney's call to the cell number given him by Angelidis had been answered immediately by the man himself. Gurney's brief description of a rapidly developing situation that could be of mutual interest resulted in an agreement to get together at the Aegean Odyssey in two hours.

Not wanting to leave before making sure that Madeleine was ready to go to the Winkler farm in Buck Ridge, he was pleased to find her in the bedroom, packing a big nylon duffel bag.

She spoke as she stuffed a pair of socks into a sneaker. "The hens have enough of their regular food and plenty of water, so you don't have to bother with that. But maybe in the morning you could bring them some chopped strawberries?"

"Sure," he said vaguely, the request hardly registering. He was caught up in conflicting feelings about her whole involvement in this Winkler business at the fair. He found it both annoying and fortuitous. Annoying because he'd never much liked the Winklers, and liked them less now for their having talked Madeleine into spending a week as an unpaid alpaca wrangler to make their lives easier. But he had to admit it was fortuitous as well, since it provided a safe place for her at the very time it was needed. And, of course, the work with the animals was something she'd enjoy doing. She just plain *liked* to be helpful, especially if feathered or furry creatures were involved.

In the midst of these thoughts, he found her looking at him with one of her gentler, more impenetrable expressions.

Somehow it relaxed him and made him smile.

"I love you," she said. "Please be careful."

She put out her arms, and they embraced—so long and so tightly, it seemed to leave nothing that needed to be put into words.

When he arrived in Long Falls, the restaurant block was deserted. Inside the restaurant there was only one employee in sight, a muscular waiter with expressionless eyes. There were no diners. No one at the unlit bar. Of course, it was barely ten-thirty, and it was highly unlikely that the Aegean Odyssey served breakfast. It occurred to him that the place might be open that morning only as a convenience to Angelidis.

The waiter led Gurney through the bar down a dim hallway, past two restrooms and two unmarked doors, to a heavy steel exit door. He gave it a hard shove with his shoulder, and it swung open with a metallic screech. He stepped to the side and motioned Gurney into a colorful walled garden.

The garden was the same width as the building, forty or fifty feet, and extended out at least twice that distance in length. The only break in the redbrick walls enclosing it was a set of large double doors in the far end. They were wide open, framing a view of the river, the jogging path, and the manicured tranquillity of Willow Rest. The view from here was similar to the view from the problematic apartment three blocks away. Only the angle was different.

The garden itself was a pleasant combination of grass paths, vegetable beds, and herbaceous borders. The waiter pointed to a shaded corner, to a small white café table with two wrought-iron chairs. Adonis Angelidis was sitting in one of them.

When Gurney arrived at the table, Angelidis nodded toward the empty chair. "Please."

A second waiter materialized and placed a tray in the center of the table. There were two demitasse cups of black coffee, two cordial glasses, and an almost full bottle of ouzo, the anise-flavored Greek liqueur.

"You like strong coffee?" Angelidis's voice was low and rough—like the purring of a large cat.

"Yes."

"You might like it with ouzo. Better than sugar."

"Perhaps I'll try some."

"You have an okay drive here, yes?"

"No problem."

Angelidis nodded. "Beautiful day."

"Beautiful garden."

"Yes. Fresh garlic. Mint. Oregano. Very good." Angelidis shifted slightly in his seat. "What can I do for you?"

Gurney took the cup of coffee closest to him and sipped it thoughtfully. On the drive up from Walnut Crossing he'd concocted an opening gambit that now, as he sat facing this man who might well be one of the cleverest mobsters in America, struck him as rather feeble. But he decided to give it a shot anyway. Sometimes a Hail Mary pass is all you've got left.

"Some information came my way that might interest you."

Angelidis's gaze was mildly curious.

Gurney went on. "Just a rumor, of course."

"Of course."

"About the Organized Crime Task Force."

"Rotten shits. No principles."

"What I heard," said Gurney, taking another sip of his coffee, "is that they're looking to pin Spalter on you."

"*Carl?* You see what I mean? Bunch of shits! Why would I want to lose Carl? I told you before, like a son to me. Why would I think to do such a thing? Disgusting!" Angelidis's big boxer's hands had closed into fists.

"The scenario they're putting together is that you and Carl had a falling-out, and—"

"Bullshit!"

"Like I said, the scenario they're putting together—"

"What the fuck's a *scenario?*"

"The hypothesis, the story they're making up."

"Making it up, all right. Slimy shits!"

"Their hypothesis is that you and Carl had a falling-out, you hired a hit on him through Fat Gus, and then you got nervous and decided to cover your tracks by getting rid of Gus—maybe doing that one yourself."

"*Myself?* They think I hammered nails into his head?"

"I'm just telling you what I hear."

Angelidis sat back in his chair, a shrewd look replacing the anger in his eyes. "This is coming from where?"

"The plan to hang the murder on you?"

"Yeah. This coming from the top of OCTF?"

Something about his tone gave Gurney the idea that Angelidis might have a line to someone inside the task force. Someone who would be aware of the major initiatives.

"Not the way I hear it. I get the impression that the move against you is a little off-center. Unofficial. Couple of guys who've got a bug up their ass about you. That ring any bells?"

Angelidis didn't answer. His jaw muscles tightened. He remained quiet for a long minute. When he spoke, his tone was flat. "You drove up here from Walnuts just to bring me this information?"

"Something else, too. I found out who the hitter was."

Angelidis became very still.

Gurney watched him carefully. "Petros Panikos."

Something changed in Angelidis's eyes. If Gurney had to guess, he'd say the man was trying to conceal a stab of fear. "How do you know this?"

Gurney shook his head and smiled. "Better not to say how I know."

For the first time since Gurney arrived, Angelidis looked around at the garden and its brick walls, his eyes stopping at the doors that were open to the view of the river and cemetery. "Why are you bringing this to me?"

"I thought you might want to help me."

"Help you do what?"

"I want to find Panikos. I want to bring him in. To cut a deal, he may be willing to tell us who bought the Spalter hit. Since that wasn't you, OCTF can go fuck themselves. You'd like that, right?"

Angelidis rested his burly forearms on the table and shook his head. "What's the problem?"

"The problem?" Angelidis emitted a short, humorless laugh. "The part about you bringing him in. That don't happen. Trust me. That don't happen. You got no idea who you're dealing with."

Again Gurney shrugged, turning up his palms. "Maybe I need to know a little more."

"Maybe a lot more."

"Tell me what I'm missing."

"Like what?"

"How does Panikos work?"

"He shoots people. Mostly in the head. Mostly in the right eye. Or he blows them up."

"How about his contracts? How are they set up?"

"Through a fixer. An arranger."

"A guy like Fat Gus?"

"Like Fat Gus. Top shelf for Panikos. Only a handful of guys in the world he deals with. They do the transaction. They transfer the payment."

"He gets his instructions from them?"

"Instructions?" Angelidis let out a guttural laugh. "He takes the name, the deadline, the money. The rest is up to him."

"I'm not sure I understand."

"Let's say you want a certain target whacked. Theoretically. For the sake of argument. You pay Peter Pan's price. The target gets whacked. End of story. *How* he gets whacked is Peter's business. He don't take *instructions*."

"Let me get this straight. The nails in Fat Gus's head—that wouldn't have been part of the deal?"

The point seemed to interest Angelidis. "No ... that would *not* have been part of the deal. Not if the hitter was Peter."

"So that would have been his own initiative, not an order from the client?"

"I'm telling you, he don't take orders—just names and cash."

"So the nasty shit he did to Gus—that would have been *his* idea?"

"You hear me? He don't take orders."

"So why would he do what he did?"

"I got no idea. That's the problem here. Knowing Panikos and Gurikos, it makes no sense."

"No sense that Panikos would worry that Gurikos might know something damaging? Or that he might talk? Or that he might already have talked?"

"You gotta understand something here. Gus did *time*—a *lot* of time. Twelve fucking years in that Attica prison shithole, when he could've been out in two. All he had to do was give up a name. But he didn't. And the guy couldn't have touched him. There wasn't gonna be no retribution. So it wasn't fear. You know what it was?"

Gurney had heard stories like this before, and he knew the punch line. "Principles?"

"You bet your fucking ass, principles! Steel balls!"

Gurney nodded. "Which leaves me wondering—why on earth did Panikos do what he did? None of this hangs together."

"I told you, it don't make no sense. Gus was like Switzerland. Quiet. Didn't talk to nobody about nobody. This was a known and respected fact. Secret of his success. Principles."

"Okay. Gus was a rock. What about Panikos? What's he all about?"

"Peter? Peter is . . . special. Only takes jobs that look impossible. Lot of determination. High success rate."

"And yet . . . ?"

"Yet what?"

"I'm hearing a reservation in your voice."

"A reservation?" Angelidis paused before going on with evident care. "Peter . . . is used only in . . . in *very* difficult situations."

"Why?"

"Because along with his skills . . . there's some risks."

"Like what?"

Angelidis made a face as if he were regurgitating yesterday's ouzo. "The KGB used to assassinate people by putting radioactive poison in their food. Tremendously effective. But you got to be very, very, careful using that shit. That's like Peter."

"Panikos is that scary?"

"Get on his wrong side, could maybe be a problem."

Gurney thought about that. The notion that getting on the wrong side of a determined, crazy killer *could* be a problem made him want to laugh out loud. "Did you ever hear that he liked to set fires?"

"I might've heard that. Part of the package you're dealing with. Which I don't think you really understand."

"I've faced some difficult people over the years."

"*Difficult?* That's pretty funny. Let me tell you a story about Peter—so you know about *difficult.*" Angelidis leaned forward, extending his palms on the tabletop. "There were these two towns, not far apart. A strong man in each town. This created problems—mainly, who had rights to various things between the two towns. As the towns got bigger, closer together, the problems got bigger. Lot of shit happened. *Escalation.*" He articulated the word carefully. "*Escalation,* back and forth. Finally, there is no possibility of peace. No possibility of *agreement.* So one of these men decides that the other one has to go. He decides to hire little Peter to take care of it. Peter at that time is just getting into the business."

"The hit business?" asked Gurney blandly.

"Yeah. His profession. Anyway, he does the job. Clean, quick, no problems. Then he shows up at the man's place of business to get paid. The man he did the job for. The man tells him he has to wait—a cash-flow problem. Peter says, 'No, you pay me now.' Man says, 'No, you gotta wait.' Peter says this makes him unhappy. Man laughs at him. So Peter shoots him. Bang. Just like that."

Gurney shrugged. "Never a good idea to stiff a hitter."

Angelidis's mouth twitched into what might have been a split-second grin. "Never a good idea. True. But the story don't end there. Peter goes to the man's house and shoots his wife and two kids. Then he goes around town, shoots the man's brother and five cousins, wives, kills the whole fucking family. Twenty-one people. Twenty-one shots to the head."

"That's quite a reaction."

Angelidis's mouth widened, showing a row of glistening capped teeth. Then he uttered an eruptive growling sound that Gurney thought was probably the most unnerving laugh he'd ever heard.

"Yeah. 'Quite a reaction.' You're a funny guy, Gurney. 'Quite a reaction.' I got to remember that."

"Seems like a chancy thing to do, though—from a business point of view."

"What do you mean, 'chancy'?"

"I would think, after that—after killing twenty-one people because of an overdue payment—potential customers might worry about dealing with him. They might want to deal with someone less . . . touchy."

"'Touchy'? I'm telling you, Gurney, you're a fucking riot. 'Touchy'—that's good! But what you don't understand is that Peter has a special advantage. Peter is *unique.*"

"How so?"

"Peter takes the *impossible* jobs. The ones other guys say can't be done—too risky, the target is too protected, shit like that. That's where Peter comes in. Likes to prove he's better than anyone else. You see what I mean? Peter is a unique resource. Highly motivated. High determination. Nine times out of ten he gets the job done. But the thing is ... there's always the possibility of some collateral damage."

"Can you give me an example?"

"Example? Like maybe the time he was hired to hit a target on one of them high-speed Greek island ferries, but he didn't know what the guy looked like, only that he was going to be on the boat at a particular time. So what did he do? He blew the fucking thing out of the water, killed about a hundred people. But I'll tell you something else. It ain't just that he produces collateral damage—the word is he likes it. Fires. Explosions. Bigger the better."

That started Gurney wondering about a lot of things. But he kept coming back to one central question: Exactly what was it that made Panikos seem like the right choice for the Spalter hit? What made that job seem impossible?

Angelidis interrupted his train of thought. "Hey, I almost forgot, one more thing—the thing everyone who was there still talks about. The thing that really got to them. You ready for this?" It wasn't really a question. "While little Peter was going around the town, wiping that whole fucking family off the face of the earth—guess what he was doing." He paused, real excitement in his eyes. "Guess."

Gurney shook his head. "I don't guess."

"Don't matter. You couldn't guess it anyway." He leaned forward another inch. "He was singing."

Before Gurney left the restaurant garden, he looked out again through the open doors in the back wall. He could see the Spalter plot clearly—all of it, with no light pole obstructing any part of it.

He heard Angelidis's fingers tapping restlessly on the tabletop.

Gurney turned toward him and asked, "Do you ever think about Carl when you look over at Willow Rest?"

"Sure. I think about him."

Watching Angelidis's fingers drumming on the metal surface, Gurney asked, "Does knowing that Panikos was the paid hitter tell you anything about the buyer?"

"Sure." The drumming stopped. "It tells me that he knew his way around. You don't go to your phone book, look up 'Panikos,' and say, 'Hey, I got a job for you.' It don't work that way."

Gurney nodded. "Very few people would know how to get in touch with him," he said, sounding like he was talking to himself.

"Peter accepts contracts through maybe half a dozen guys in the world. You have to be well placed to know who those guys are."

Gurney let a silence build between them before asking, "Would you say that Kay Spalter was well placed?"

Angelidis stared at him. He appeared to find the suggestion surprising, but his only answer was a shrug.

Turning to leave, Gurney had a final question.

"What was he singing?"

Angelidis looked confused.

"Panikos, while he was shooting everybody."

"Oh, yeah. Some little kid song. Whaddya call 'em—nursery rhymes?"

"Do you know which one?"

"How would I know that? Something about roses, flowers, some shit like that."

"He was singing a nursery rhyme about flowers? While he was walking around shooting people in the head?"

"You got it. Smiling like an angel and singing his little song in a little-girl voice. The people who heard that—they never forgot it." Angelidis paused. "The thing you got to know about him—most important thing—I'll tell you what it is. He's two people. One—precise, exact, everything a certain way. The other—very fucking crazy."

Chapter 42

The Missing Head

Gurney stopped at the first gas station he came to on the route from Long Falls to Walnut Crossing—for gas, for coffee (having barely touched the cup at the Aegean Odyssey), and to send another email to Jonah Spalter. He decided to take care of the last item first.

He checked the wording and tone of his previous message and purposely made this one more jagged, definitely unsettling, less clear, with an amped-up level of urgency—more like a harried text message than an email:

> *Increasing flow of new data, obvious corruption. Conviction reversal and aggressive new investigation to come. Family dynamics key issue? Could it be as simple as FOLLOW THE MONEY? How might CyberCath financial stress play into the investigation? Should meet ASAP for frank discussion of new facts.*

He read it over twice. If its edginess and ambiguity didn't provoke some communication from Jonah, he had no idea what would. Then he went into the shabby little convenience store for his coffee and a plain bagel, which turned out to be stale and hard. He was hungry enough to eat it anyway. The coffee, however, was surprisingly fresh, giving him a fleeting sense of okayness.

He was about to pull over to the gas pumps when he realized that he still hadn't told Hardwick about his meeting with Mick Klemper at

Riverside Mall and the subsequent arrival in his mailbox of the Long Falls security video. He decided to take care of that immediately.

The call went into voice mail, and he left a message. "Jack, I need to fill you in on some developments with Klemper. We had a little discussion about the various ways the story could end, some less painful for him than others, and, magically, the missing video turned up in my mailbox. The man may be trying to cushion his fall, and we need to talk about the implications. Also, you'll want to see the video. No obvious inconsistencies with the witness reports, but it's sure as hell worth a look. Get back to me as soon as you can."

This reminded him of another urgent task that had been sidelined—viewing the video segments from the other three cameras in the four-camera array, particularly the two labeled EAST and WEST, since they would have captured images of individuals approaching or leaving the building. Pondering the potential boost such evidence might give the investigation pushed Gurney's driving speed well above the posted limits for the rest of the trip home.

He was surprised, then confused, then worried to find Madeleine's car still parked where it was when he'd left that morning for Long Falls, expecting that she would be leaving moments after him for the Winkler farm.

Entering the house with an anxious frown, he found her at the kitchen sink, washing dishes.

"What are you still doing here?" There was an edge of accusation in his voice, which she ignored.

"Right after you left, as I was getting in my car, Mena arrived in her minivan."

"Mena?"

"From Yoga Club? Remember? You just had dinner with her."

"Ah. That Mena."

"Yes, *that* Mena—not any of the multitude of other Menas we know."

"Right. So she arrived in her minivan? For what?"

"Well, ostensibly to bring us the bounty of her garden. Take a look in the mudroom—yellow squash, garlic, tomatoes, peppers."

"I'll take your word for it. But that was hours ago. And you're still—"

"It was hours ago when she arrived, but only forty-five minutes ago when she departed."

"Jesus."

"Mena likes to talk. You might have noticed that at dinner. But, to be fair, she has some serious difficulties in her life, family problems, things she had to get off her chest. She needed someone to talk to. I didn't feel I could cut her off."

"What kind of problems?"

"Oh, Lord, everything from parents with Alzheimer's, to a brother in prison for drug dealing, to nieces and nephews with every known psychiatric disorder—I don't know ... do you really want to hear about this?"

"Maybe not."

"Anyway, I made her some lunch, tea, more tea. I didn't want to leave the dirty dishes for you, so that's what I'm doing now. And you? You look like you're in a hurry to do something."

"I was planning on reviewing the Long Falls security videos."

"Security videos? Oh, God, I almost forgot! Did you know Jack Hardwick was on RAM-TV last night?"

"He was *where*?"

"RAM-TV. On that dreadful *Criminal Conflict* thing with Brian Bork."

"How did you—?"

"Kyle called an hour ago to find out if you'd seen it."

"Last time Hardwick spoke to me was from Cooperstown ... midday yesterday? He didn't tell me he had any plan to—"

She cut him off. "You'd better take a look at it. It's in the current archive section of their website."

"You watched it?"

"I took a quick look at it after Mena left. Kyle said we needed to see it ASAP."

"It's ... a problem?"

She pointed to the den. "The RAM website is open on the computer. You watch it, then you tell me if it's a problem." Her troubled expression told him she'd already reached her own conclusion.

A minute later he was at his desk, gazing at the practiced concern and gelled hair of Brian Bork. The *Criminal Conflict* host occupied one of two chairs positioned on opposite sides of a small table. He was leaning forward as though the importance of what he was about to say made it impossible to relax. The second chair was empty.

He addressed the camera directly. "Good evening, my friends. Welcome to the real-life drama of *Criminal Conflict.* Tonight, we had intended to bring you a follow-up visit with Lex Bincher, the controversial attorney who stunned us just a few days ago with his no-holds-barred attack on the Bureau of Criminal Investigation—an attack designed to dismantle what he characterized as the fatally flawed conviction of Kay Spalter for the murder of her husband. Since then there have been some shocking new developments in this already sensational case. The latest is the breaking story of mayhem and tragedy in the idyllic village of Cooperstown, New York. It involves arson, multiple homicides, and the ominous disappearance of Lex Bincher himself, who was scheduled to be with us this evening. Instead, we'll be hearing from Jack Hardwick—a private investigator who's been working with Bincher. Investigator Hardwick is joining us from our RAM-TV affiliate in Albany."

A split-screen visual appeared, with Bork on the left and Hardwick, in a similar studio set, on the right. Hardwick, in one of his ubiquitous black polo shirts, appeared relaxed, which Gurney recognized as the oddly inverse public face the man sometimes put on his anger. The likely fury he felt at what had happened at Cooperstown and his personal contempt for Bork and RAM-TV were well concealed.

Gurney had one question in mind: Why had Hardwick agreed to appear on a media outlet he hated?

Bork continued, "First of all, thank you for accepting my invitation to join us on such short notice at such a stressful time. I understand you just came from that terrible scene by Otsego Lake."

"That's correct."

"Can you describe it to us?"

"Three lakeside homes burned to the ground. Six people burned to death, including two small children. A seventh victim was found in the lake under a small dock."

"Has that final victim been identified?"

"That may take some time," said Hardwick evenly. "His head is missing."

"Did you say *his head is missing*?"

"That's what I said."

"The killer cut off the victim's head? And then what? Is there any indication what might have happened to it?"

"Maybe he hid it somewhere. Or dumped it somewhere. Or took it with him. Investigation is under way."

Bork shook his head—the gesture of a man who just can't understand what the world is coming to. "That's really appalling. Investigator Hardwick, I have to ask the obvious question. Are you thinking the mutilated body could belong to Lex Bincher?"

"It could, yes."

"The obvious next question: What on earth is going on? Do you have an explanation you can share with our viewers?"

"It's pretty simple, Brian. Kay Spalter was framed for her husband's murder by a thoroughly corrupt detective. She's the victim of gross evidence tampering, gross witness tampering, and a grossly incompetent defense. Her conviction, of course, delighted the real murderer. It left him free to go about his deadly business."

Bork started to ask another question, but Hardwick cut him off. "The people involved in this case—not only the dishonest detective who railroaded an innocent woman into prison, but the whole team who condoned that farcical trial and conviction—they're the ones who are ultimately responsible for the massacre today in Cooperstown."

Bork paused, as though taken aback by what he'd just heard. "That's a *very* serious accusation. In fact, it's the kind of accusation that's likely to spark outrage in the law enforcement community. Are you concerned about that?"

"I'm not accusing the general law enforcement *community* of anything. I'm calling out the specific *members* of that community who falsified evidence and colluded in the wrongful arrest and prosecution of Kay Spalter."

"Do you have the evidence you need to prove those charges?"

Hardwick's answer was immediate, calm, and unblinking. "Yes."

"Can you share that evidence with us?"

"We'll share it when the time comes."

Bork directed several more questions to Hardwick, trying without success to get him to be more specific. Then he suddenly switched gears and raised what he obviously considered the most provocative question of all. "What if you prevail? What if you thoroughly embarrass everyone who you claim was in the wrong? What if you win and succeed in setting Kay Spalter free—and later discover that she was guilty of murder after all? How would you feel about that?"

For the first time in the interview, Hardwick's contempt for Bork began to seep into his expression. "How would I *feel* about it? *Feeling* has nothing to do with it. What I would *know* would be exactly the same as what I *know* now: that the legal process was rotten. Rotten from start to finish. And the people responsible know who they are."

Bork looked up as if checking the time, then gazed into the camera. "Okay, my friends, you heard it here." The half of the split screen devoted to him expanded to the full screen. Putting on the face of a brave witness to dire events, he invited his viewers to pay close attention to some important messages from his sponsors. He concluded, "Stay with us. We'll be back in two minutes with news of a nasty new reproductive rights clash headed for a Supreme Court showdown. In the meantime, this is Brian Bork for *Criminal Conflict,* your nightly ringside seat at today's most explosive legal battles."

Gurney closed the video window, shut down the computer, and sat back in his chair.

"So what do you think of that?" Madeleine's voice, close behind his chair, startled him.

He turned to face her. "I'm trying to figure it out."

"Figure what out?"

"Why he appeared on that program."

"You mean, apart from the fact that it offered him a big platform to take a free swing at his enemies—the folks who bounced him out of his job?"

"Yes, apart from that."

"I guess, if all those accusations had a purpose beyond venting, it might be to attract maximum media attention—drag in as many investigative reporters as he can, get them all digging into the Spalter case and keeping it in the headlines as long as possible. You think that's what it was all about?"

"Or he might want to provoke a lawsuit for slander, defamation, libel—a lawsuit he's confident he could win. Or put the NYSP in a corner—knowing the individuals involved can't sue him because he *would* win—and his *real* goal is to force the organization to toss Klemper to the wolves to cut their losses."

Madeleine looked skeptical. "I wouldn't have thought his motives would be that subtle. You're sure it's not just plain old anger looking for something to smash?"

Gurney shook his head. "Jack likes presenting himself as a blunt instrument. But there's nothing blunt about the mind wielding the baseball bat."

Madeleine still looked skeptical.

Gurney went on. "I'm not saying that he isn't motivated by resentment. He is, clearly. He can't stand the idea that he was forced out of a career he loved by people he despised. Now he despises them even more. He's mad as hell, he wants revenge—that's all true. I'm just saying that he isn't stupid, and his tactics can be smarter than they appear to be."

That comment produced a brief silence, broken by Madeleine. "By the way, you didn't tell me about . . . that . . . final little horror."

He looked at her quizzically.

She mimicked the look. "I think you know what I'm talking about."

"Oh. The thing about the missing head? No . . . I didn't tell you about that."

"Why not?"

"It seemed . . . too grisly."

"You were afraid I might find it upsetting?"

"Something like that."

"Information management?"

"Pardon?"

"I remember an oily politician once explaining that he never engaged in deception; he merely managed the flow of information in an orderly manner to avoid confusing the public."

Gurney was tempted to argue that this was a different situation altogether, that his motive was truly noble and caring, but she upset his balance with a surprising little wink, as if to let him off the hook—and immediately another temptation took its place.

Smart women tended to have an erotic effect on him, and Madeleine was a very smart woman indeed.

Chapter 43

Video Evidence

Every so often in his life as a detective, Gurney got the feeling that he was juggling hand grenades.

He knew he had no one to blame but himself for his current situation. From the beginning, it was evident that the mission was likely to be warped in unpredictable ways by Hardwick's personal agenda. But he'd signed on anyway, driven by his own obsessive motives—motives that Madeleine had seen clearly enough, while he had chosen to insist he was only returning a favor owed. Having tricked himself into participating in a three-ring circus with no ringmaster, he was now experiencing the inevitable disarray built into that arrangement.

He tried telling himself that his unwillingness to walk away from it—now that the reversal of Kay's conviction was all but certain and thus his ostensible duty to Hardwick was done—arose from a noble truth-seeking trait. But he couldn't make himself believe it. He knew his addiction to his profession had roots deeper than anything noble.

He also tried telling himself that the discomfort he was feeling over Hardwick's excoriation of Mick Klemper (not named but easily identified) on *Criminal Conflict* arose from another high-minded notion—that all agreements, even with conniving creeps, are sacred. He suspected, however, that his unease actually arose from his belated realization that he had promised Klemper more than he could deliver. The idea that he'd be able to cushion the man's fall by characterizing his lapses as the products of foolish error rather than felonious intent now seemed like little more than a convenient fantasy.

He saw that he had unconsciously maneuvered himself once again into a dangerous and untenable position with no direction out—except forward. Madeleine was right. The pattern was undeniable. Clearly, there was something wrong with him. Simply understanding that, however, opened no new doors. The only path he could see was still straight ahead, hand grenades and all.

He woke up his computer and went to the video files from the Long Falls security cameras.

It took him almost an hour to find what he'd hoped would be there—an image of a rather diminutive individual coming along Axton Avenue toward the camera. As Gurney watched, he, or conceivably *she*, disappeared into the building entrance. Gender identification was stymied by a puffy winter jacket; a wide skier's headband that covered ears, forehead, and hairline; oversized sunglasses; and a thick winter scarf that concealed not only the neck but much of the chin and jawline. What remained of the face to be seen—a sharp, slightly hooked nose and a smallish mouth—appeared consistent with the face of the Flowers by Florence delivery person Gurney had seen on the security video at Emmerling Oaks. In fact, the headband, sunglasses, and scarf appeared identical to those in the earlier video.

Gurney reversed the video, backing it up a minute or so, and replayed the individual's progress along the street and entry into the building. Unlike the Emmerling Oaks video, there were no flowers. But there was a package. A narrow package, between three and four feet long, wrapped in red and green Christmas paper with a big decorative bow in the middle. Gurney smiled. It was probably the most innocent-looking way one could transport a sniper rifle on a city street in the holiday shopping season.

He made a note of the actual clock time embedded in the frame as the individual turned into the building. It was 10:03 a.m. Just seventeen minutes before the shot that felled Carl Spalter.

The same individual emerged onto the street at 10:22 a.m.—just two minutes after the shot was fired—turned and walked calmly away, continuing along Axton Avenue until passing out of the camera's field of view.

Gurney sat back in his chair, contemplating the significance of what he'd just seen.

First, it suggested strongly that the shot was indeed fired from the apartment where the gun was later found. The timing of the likely shooter's exit would make other scenarios difficult if not impossible—which underscored the light pole problem.

Second, the individual in the video was clearly not Kay Spalter. Gurney felt a welcome surge of anger at Klemper, as well as the evaporation of any bad feeling over breaking their "agreement." That video alone would have ended the case against Kay Spalter. If nothing else, it would have ensured the presence of *reasonable doubt* by supporting a credible alternative theory of the case and by showing a credible alternative suspect. It would have prevented her conviction and incarceration. Klemper's willful suppression of that evidence—apparently in return for the sexual favors of Alyssa Spalter—was not only criminal but unforgivable.

Third, it was time to stop thinking of the individual in the Axton Avenue and the retirement village videos simply as "the individual." It was time to start calling him by his chosen name: Petros Panikos.

It wasn't easy. Something in the mind rebelled at connecting the slight, almost dainty figure, carrying bouquets of chrysanthemums in the one instance and a colorful Christmas box in the other, with the violent psychopath described by Interpol and Adonis Angelidis. The psychopath who hammered the nails into Gus Gurikos's eyes, ears, and throat. The psychopath who firebombed Bincher's home in Cooperstown, burned six innocent people to death, and cut off a man's head.

Oh, Jesus, was he singing when he did that, too? That was something Gurney didn't want to think about. That was the stuff of nightmares. It was time for more practical thoughts. It was time for a meeting of the minds with Hardwick and Esti. Time to agree on next steps.

He took out his phone and called Hardwick first. He was intending to leave a message and was surprised when the phone was answered immediately—and defensively.

"You calling to give me some shit about my bit with Bork?"

Gurney decided to postpone that discussion for another time. "I'm thinking we need to get together."

"For what?"

"Planning? Coordination? Cooperation?"

There was a short pause. "Sure. No problem. When?"

"Soon as possible. Like tomorrow morning. You, me, Esti if she can make it. We need to put the facts, questions, hypotheses on the table. With everything we have in one place, we may be able to see what's missing."

"Okay." Hardwick sounded skeptical, as usual. "Where do you want to do this?"

"My house."

"Any reason for that?"

The honest reason was that Gurney wanted to recapture some semblance of control, some sense of his hand being on the tiller. But what he said was "Your house has bullet holes in it. Mine doesn't."

After agreeing, with little enthusiasm, to meet at nine the following morning at Gurney's, Hardwick volunteered to pass the word to Esti, since he was about to talk to her about something else anyway. Something personal. Gurney would have preferred to call her himself—again, for that elusive hand-on-tiller feeling—but he could think of no reasonable way to insist on it.

They ended the call without either of them bringing up the matter of the "deal" with Mick Klemper or Gurney's allusion to it in his last phone message.

As Gurney emerged from the den, Madeleine emerged from the bedroom. She took the duffel bag she'd packed that morning out to her car, then came back in to remind him once again about the strawberries for the hens.

"You know," he replied, "Ozzie Baggott down the road just tosses his chickens a pail of table scraps once a day, and they seem to survive quite nicely."

"Ozzie Baggott is a disgusting lunatic. He'd be tossing garbage out into his backyard whether he had chickens there or not."

Upon reflection, he found he couldn't honestly argue with that.

They hugged and kissed, and she was on her way.

As her car passed out of sight below the barn, the last sliver of the setting sun disappeared behind the western ridge.

Chapter 44

The Thrill of the Chase

Gurney retreated again into the den. The deepening dusk had changed the color of the forested ridge above it from a dozen shades of green and gold to a monochromatic greenish gray. It made him think of the hillside opposite Jack Hardwick's house, the hillside the shots had come from that had severed the power and phone lines.

Soon his thoughts began to coalesce around the bits and pieces of the Spalter case, especially its incongruous elements. That made him think of a maxim one of his academy instructors had emphasized in an advanced course on the interpretation of crime scene evidence: The pieces that don't seem to fit are the ones that end up revealing the most.

He took a yellow legal pad out of his desk drawer and started writing. Twenty minutes later he reviewed the results, which he'd organized into a list of eight issues:

1. Eyewitnesses placed the victim at the moment he was shot in a position that would have made it impossible for a bullet to reach him from the apartment where the murder weapon and gunpowder residue were found.
2. Killing the victim's mother to ensure the presence of the victim at the cemetery plot seems needlessly elaborate. Might the mother have been killed for another reason?
3. The pro who executed the hit was known to accept only the most difficult assignments. What might have put the Carl Spalter hit in that category?

4. If Kay Spalter herself was not the shooter, could she have hired the shooter?
5. Could Jonah have hired the shooter to gain control of Spalter Realty assets?
6. Could Alyssa have hired the shooter—in addition to conspiring with Klemper after the shooting to frame Kay—in order to inherit her father's estate?
7. What secret was Gurikos killed and maimed to protect?
8. Was Carl killed in retaliation for trying to have someone else killed?

Going through the eight items, pondering each in turn, Gurney was disgusted with his lack of progress.

One positive aspect, however, of a case with multiple peculiarities was that once you had a theory that was consistent with *all* the peculiarities you could be sure that the theory was right. A single oddity in an investigation could often be explained in a variety of ways. But it was unlikely that there could be more than one theory that could explain the line-of-sight problem with the apartment *and* the grotesque mutilation of Gus Gurikos *and* Mary Spalter's oddly timed death.

When he looked out through the north window of the den some minutes later, the high forest appeared devoid of any green at all. The trees and the ridge they covered were now a uniformly dark mass against the gray slate of the sky. The night descending on the hillside brought to mind the attack on Hardwick's house and the escape of the motorized shooter through the forest paths.

At that moment he heard the sound of a motorcycle engine, which for a second he interpreted as the product of his imagination. Then the sound grew louder and its direction clearer. He went from the den to the kitchen to look out the window, sure now that he was hearing a very real motorcycle coming up the road. Half a minute later the machine's single headlight rounded the barn and began ascending the rough pasture path.

He went to the bedroom, got his .32 Beretta from the night table, chambered a round, slipped the gun in his pocket, and went to the side door. He waited until the motorcycle came to a stop by his car, then switched on the outside lights.

An athletic-looking figure in black riding leathers and a black helmet with a full face visor dismounted, removed a slim black briefcase from one of the saddlebags, and approached the door. He knocked firmly with a black-gloved hand.

That was when Gurney, about to ease the gun from his pocket, recognized the helmet.

It was his own, from his motorcycling days nearly three decades earlier. It was the helmet he'd given to Kyle a few months ago.

He flipped on the inside lights and opened the door.

"Hey, Dad!" Kyle handed him the briefcase, lifted off the helmet with one hand, and ran the other back through the short dark hair that was a mirror image of his father's.

They exchanged matching smiles, although in Gurney's there was a touch of bafflement. "Did I miss an email or a phone message?"

"About my coming up? No. It was a spur-of-the-moment kind of thing. Thought I could take care of your video enhancement easier up here than at home—so you can see what I'm doing and we can get it the way you want it. That's the main reason I came. But there's a second reason, too."

"Oh?"

"Cow-shit bingo."

"Excuse me?"

"Cow-shit bingo—at your Summer Mountain Fair. Did you know that was an actual thing? And deep-fried cheese. And on Sunday afternoon, a ladies-only demolition derby event. And a giant zucchini hurling contest."

"A what?"

"I made that last one up. But what the hell, it's not as weird as the real stuff. I've never been to a real country fair. With real cow shit. Figured it was time. Where's Madeleine?"

"Long story. She's staying with a couple of her friends. Involves the fair and . . . sort of a precaution. I'll tell you all about it later." He stepped back, holding the door open. "Come in, come in, take off the bike suit and get comfortable. Have you had any dinner?"

"A burger and a yogurt at the Sloatsburg rest stop."

"That was over a hundred miles ago. You want to have an omelet with me?"

"Cool. Thanks. I'll get my other bag and change."

"So, what's this 'precaution' thing you mentioned?" No surprise to Gurney, that was the first question Kyle asked when they sat down to eat twenty minutes later.

Instead of downplaying the threat, which would be his natural inclination, Gurney recounted the attack on Hardwick's house and the atrocity in Cooperstown in straightforward terms. If he was going to have to persuade Kyle to leave—for home or another safe place, at least by the following morning—it would make no sense to soft-pedal the peril now.

As Gurney spoke, his son listened with silent concern—as well as the visible excitement that a hint of danger often arouses in young men.

After they ate, Kyle set up his laptop on the dining table and Gurney gave him the USB drive with the Axton Avenue video files. They located the two short segments Gurney wanted enhanced. The first was the portion of the cemetery sequence beginning with Carl rising from his chair and ending with him sprawled face-down with a bullet in his brain. The second was the portion of the street sequence that showed the diminutive figure Gurney believed to be Petros Panikos entering the building with the gift-wrapped box that presumably contained the rifle later found upstairs in the apartment.

Kyle was studying the images on his computer screen. "You want these blown up for max detail with minimum software interpolation?"

"Say that again?"

"When you blow stuff up, you spread out the actual digital data. The image gets bigger but also fuzzier, because there's less hard information per square inch. Software can compensate for that by making assumptions, filling in the data gaps, sharpening, smoothing. But that introduces an element of unreliability in the image because not everything in the enhancement is present in the original pixels. In order to de-fuzz the enlargement, the software makes calculated guesses based more on probability than on hard data."

"So what are you recommending?"

"I'd recommend picking a point of reasonable compromise between the sharpness of the enlargement and the reliability of the data composing it."

"Fine. Aim for whatever balance you think is right." Gurney smiled not only at his son's grasp of the process but also at the excitement in his voice. He seemed the happy archetype of that under-thirty generation born and bred with a natural affinity for all things digital.

"Just give me a little time to mess around with a few test runs. I'll let you know when I have something worth looking at." Kyle opened the program's toolbar, clicked on one of the zoom icons, then stopped. He looked over at Gurney, who was carrying their omelet dishes to the sink island, and asked a question that seemed to come out of nowhere.

"Apart from dealing with sensational murders and things, how're you guys doing up here?"

"How are we doing? Okay, I guess. Why do you ask?"

"Seems like you're involved in *your* stuff, and Madeleine's involved in *her* stuff."

Gurney nodded slowly. "I guess you could say that. My stuff and her stuff. Generally separate, but mostly compatible."

"You like it that way?"

He found the question oddly difficult to answer. He finally said, "It works." But he was uncomfortable with the mechanical tone of that. "I don't mean it to sound so gray and pragmatic. We love each other. We still find each other attractive. We enjoy living together. But our minds work differently. I get into something and just sort of *stay* in it. Madeleine has a way of changing her focus, of paying total attention to whatever's in front of her—adapting to the moment. She's always *present*, if you know what I mean. And, of course, she's a hell of a lot more outgoing than I am."

"Most people are." Kyle took the negative edge off the comment with a big grin.

"True. So, most of the time, we end up doing different things. Or she ends up doing things and I end up thinking about things."

"You mean she's outside feeding the chickens while you're sitting in here figuring out who chopped up the body in the town dumpster?"

Gurney laughed. "That's not exactly it. When she's at the clinic she deals with what's *there*—some pretty horrific stuff—and when she's here she deals with what's *here*. I tend to be inside my head, obsessed with some ongoing problem, regardless of where I am. That's one difference between us. Also, Madeleine spends a lot of time looking, learning, doing. I spend a lot of time wondering, hypothesizing, analyzing." He paused, shrugged. "I suppose each of us does what makes us feel most alive."

Kyle sat for a while with a thoughtful frown, as if trying to align his mind with his father's to better understand his thoughts. Finally he turned back to his computer screen. "I better get started on this, in case it turns out to be harder than I thought."

"Good luck." Gurney went into the den and opened his email. His eye ran down through the two dozen or so items that had arrived since that morning. One item caught his attention. The sender was identified simply as "Jonah."

The email text appeared to be a personal response to Gurney's request for a meeting to discuss the status of the investigation.

> *I would be interested in having the proposed discussion as soon as possible. My location, however, would make a physical meeting at this time impractical. My suggestion is that we meet via Internet video-phone tomorrow morning at 8:00 a.m. If you would like to proceed this way, please email me your video-phone service name. If you do not already have this in place, you can download the software from Skype. I look forward to your response.*

Gurney accepted Jonah's invitation immediately. They already had the Skype program. At the request of her sister in Ridgewood, Madeleine had installed it on their computer when they'd first moved to the mountains. As he hit SEND, he felt a little rush of adrenaline—a sense that something was about to change.

He needed to prepare. That eight a.m. conversation was less than twelve hours away. And then at nine he, Hardwick, and hopefully Esti would be getting together to bring one another up-to-date.

He went to the Cyberspace Cathedral website and immersed

himself for the next forty-five minutes in the bland, smiley-positive philosophy of Jonah Spalter.

He was in the process of concluding that the man was a kind of saccharine genius—a Walt Disney of self-improvement—when Kyle called to him from the other room. "Hey, Dad? I think I've got this video stuff about as good as I can get it."

Gurney went out to the dining table and sat next to his son. Kyle clicked on an icon, and an enhanced version of the cemetery sequence began—enlarged, sharpened, and slowed to half speed. Everything was as Gurney remembered it from his first viewing—just clearer and bigger. Carl was seated at the far right side of the first row of chairs. He rose and turned toward the podium at the other end of the grave. He took a step forward in front of Alyssa, began to take a second step, and lurched forward in the direction he'd been moving, coming to rest face-down just past the last seat at the far end of the row. Jonah, Alyssa, and the Elder Force ladies got to their feet. Paulette rushed forward. The pallbearers and undertaker came around the chairs.

Gurney leaned closer to the screen, asking Kyle to pause the video, trying to discern the expressions on the faces of Jonah and Alyssa, but the detail just wasn't there. Similarly, even at this enlargement level, Carl's face against the ground was little more than a generic profile. There was a dark speck along the hairline of the temple that might have been the bullet's entry wound—or it could have been a bit of dirt, a tiny shadow, or an artifact of the software itself.

He asked Kyle to play the segment through again, hoping for some revelation to emerge.

None did. He asked for it a third time, peering intently at the side of Carl's head as he turned toward the podium, took a step, began to take another, pitched forward into a rapidly staggering collapse. Either some breeze at the site or Carl's own jerky movement had disarranged his hair, making it impossible to see that subtle little dark spot until his head hit the ground and stopped moving, just beyond Jonah's feet.

"I'm sure the FBI has software that could give you an upgraded image," said Kyle apologetically. "I've pushed this program about as far as I can without producing a picture that's essentially fictional."

"What you've given me is a lot better than what I started with. Let's take a look at the street scene."

Kyle closed a few windows, opened a new one, and hit a play icon. Starting with a subject much closer to the camera, filling a larger portion of the frame to begin with, the enlargement in this instance was clearer and more detailed. The likely killer of Mary Spalter, Carl Spalter, Gus Gurikos, and Lex Bincher came walking along Axton Avenue and entered the apartment building. Gurney wished the little man had left more of his face uncovered. But, of course, the obscuration had been intentional.

Apparently Kyle was thinking along the same lines. "Didn't give us much for a Wanted poster, did he?"

"Not much for a Wanted poster and not much for a facial recognition program either."

"Because his eyes are hidden by the huge sunglasses?"

"Right. The shape of the eyes, position of the pupils, corners of the eyes. The scarf hides the jawline and the tip of the chin. The headband hides the ears and the position of the hairline. There's nothing left for the measurement algorithms to work with."

"Still, if I saw it again, I think I could recognize that face—just by the mouth."

Gurney nodded. "The mouth, and what I can see of the nose."

"Yeah, that too. He looks like a fucking little bird—excuse my language."

They sat back in their chairs and gazed at the screen. At the half-hidden face of one of the world's strangest killers. Petros Panikos. Peter Pan. The Magician.

And, of course, there was Donny Angel's final description of him: "very fucking crazy."

Chapter 45

Out of Harm's Way

"So what do you think?" Kyle, a questioning look on his face, was holding a mug of hot black coffee in both hands, elbows propped on the breakfast table.

"What do I think about the videos?" Gurney sat on the other side of the round pine table, holding his own mug in a similar way, appreciating the warmth on his palms. The temperature had dropped nearly twenty degrees overnight, from the low seventies to the low fifties, not an unusual thing in the northwestern Catskills, where autumn often arrived in August. The sky was overcast, hiding the sun, which normally would be visible above the eastern ridge at that time—a quarter past seven.

"Do you think they'll help you achieve ... what you want to achieve?"

Gurney took a slow sip from his mug. "The cemetery sequence will do a couple of things. It establishes the point at which Carl was hit, and the obstructed angle from the apartment window to that position will undermine the police scenario for the source of the shot. And the fact that the video was in police hands from the beginning—Klemper's hands—will support a charge of evidence suppression." He fell silent, unsettled for a moment by the memory of his conversation with Klemper at Riverside Mall.

He saw Kyle watching him curiously and went on. "The street sequence is useful in a couple of ways—for what it shows and what it doesn't show. The simple fact that it *doesn't* show Kay Spalter entering the building would have made it an important piece of exculpatory evidence for the defense. So, at the very least, it supports serious charges of evidence suppression and police misconduct."

"So . . . how come you don't sound happier?"

"Happier?" Gurney hesitated. "I guess I'll be happier when we get closer to the end point."

"What *is* the end point?"

"I'd like to know what really happened."

"You mean, find out who killed Carl?"

"Yes. That's the thing that really matters. If Kay is innocent, then someone else wanted Carl dead, planned it, and hired Panikos to accomplish it. I want to know who that was. And the little assassin who pulled the trigger? So far he's managed to kill nine other people in the process—not counting the scores of people he's killed before, always managing to walk away and do it again. I'd rather he didn't walk away this time."

"How close do you think you are to stopping him?"

"Hard to say."

Kyle's intelligent, inquisitive gaze remained fixed on him, in evident expectation of a better answer. As Gurney was reaching for one and finding it elusive, he was reprieved by the ring of his cell phone.

It was Hardwick. As usual, the man didn't waste time saying hello. "Got your message about the video-phone thing with Jonah Spalter. Where the hell is he?"

"I have no idea. But his willingness to have a conversation this way is better than nothing. You want to come here at eight instead of nine, be part of it?"

"Nine's the best I can do. Same with Esti. But we both have a deep and abiding faith in your interview skills. You have the software to record the call?"

"No, but I can download it. You have any specific questions you'd like me to ask?"

"Yeah. Ask him if he hired the hit on his brother."

"Great idea. Any other advice?"

"Yeah. Don't fuck it up. See you at nine."

Gurney slipped the phone back in his pocket.

Kyle cocked his head curiously. "What do you need to download?"

"A piece of audio-video recording software that's compatible with Skype. You think you could do that for me?"

"Give me your Skype name and password. I'll take care of it right now."

As the young man headed into the den armed with the information he needed, Gurney smiled at his eagerness to help, smiled also at the simple pleasure of his being in the house. It made him wonder, yet again, why their times together were so few and far between.

There was a period when he thought he knew the reason—a period peaking a couple of years earlier when Kyle was making an obscene amount of money on Wall Street, in a job he'd stepped into through a door opened by a college friend. Gurney was convinced that the yellow Porsche accompanying that job was proof positive that the money-mad genes of his real estate broker ex-wife, Kyle's mother, had taken over. But now he suspected that this had been nothing more than a rationalization that absolved him of a deeper and less explainable failure to reach out to his son. He used to tell himself that it was because Kyle reminded him of his ex-wife in other unpleasant ways as well—certain gestures, intonations, facial expressions. But that too was a questionable excuse. There were many more differences than similarities between mother and son, and even if there weren't, it would be petulant and unfair to equate one person with the other.

He would sometimes think that the real explanation was nothing more complicated than the defense of his own peculiar comfort zone. That comfort zone did not include other people. That was the point his college girlfriend, Geraldine, had hammered home the day she left him so many years ago. When he viewed the issue in that light, he saw his apparent avoidance of his son as just one more symptom of his innate introversion. Not such a big deal. Case closed. But as soon as he would settle on this, a tiny doubt would begin to nibble at the edge of his certainty. Did simple introversion *fully* explain how little he saw of Kyle? And the nibble would grow into a gnawing question: Did the presence of *one* son inevitably remind him that he'd once had *two* sons and would still have two sons if only . . .

Kyle reappeared at the kitchen door. "You're all set up. I left the screen open for you. It's totally simple."

"Oh. Great. Thank you."

Kyle was watching him with a curious smile.

It reminded Gurney of a look he sometimes saw on Madeleine's face. "What are you thinking?"

"About how you like to figure stuff out. How important it is to you. While that software was downloading, I was thinking . . . if Madeleine was a detective, she'd want to solve the puzzle so she could catch the bad guy. But I think you want to catch the bad guy so you can solve the puzzle."

Gurney was pleased, not by his own position in the comparison— which didn't strike him as especially laudable—but by Kyle's perception in noting it. The young man had a good mind, a fact that meant a lot to Gurney. He felt a little surge of camaraderie. "You know what I'm thinking? I'm thinking that you use the word 'think' almost as much as I do."

As he was speaking, the house phone was ringing. He went into the den to answer it. As if summoned by Kyle's reference to her, it was Madeleine.

"Good morning!" She sounded cheerful. "How are things going?"

"Fine. What are you up to?"

"Deirdre and Dennis and I just finished breakfast. Orange juice, blueberries, French toast, and . . . *bacon!*" The final item was voiced with the faux guilt of having committed a faux sin. "We'll be going out in a few minutes to check on all the animals and get them ready to transport to the fairgrounds. In fact, Dennis is out there by the little corral already, waving to us to come out."

"Sounds like fun," he replied in a not very fun-filled voice, marveling once again at her ability to find compartments of pure enjoyment within a larger landscape of serious problems.

"It *is* fun! How are our little hens this morning?"

"Fine, I assume. I was just about to go down to the barn."

She paused, then in a more subdued tone stepped tentatively into the larger landscape, the one in which he was so deeply mired. "Any developments?"

"Well, Kyle showed up here at the house."

"What? Why?"

"I asked him for some computer software advice, and he just decided to come up and do what needed to be done. Actually, it was very helpful."

"Did you send him home?"

"I'm going to."

She paused. "Please be careful."

"I will."

"I mean it."

"I know."

"Okay. Well ... Dennis is waving more urgently, so I better go. Love you!"

"Love you too." He replaced the handset, then sat staring at the phone unseeingly, his mind drifting back to Panikos's face on the video and the words "very fucking crazy."

"Did I hear you say your video call was at eight?" Kyle's voice from the den doorway pulled Gurney back to the moment. He glanced at the time in the corner of his computer screen—7:56 a.m.

"Thanks. Which reminds me—I wanted to ask you to stay out of the camera's field of view during the call. Okay?"

"No problem. As a matter of fact, what I was thinking of doing, since you've got your other meeting here at nine, and it's an ideal day for it ... I thought I'd take a little ride on the bike up to Syracuse."

"*Syracuse?*" There was a time when the name of that gray snow-belt city meant little to Gurney, but now it had become a mental repository for all the terrible events of the recent Good Shepherd case.

Obviously, it had a more positive association for Kyle. "Yeah, I thought I'd take a ride up, as long as I was this far upstate, maybe have lunch with Kim."

"Kim Corazon? You stayed in touch with her?"

"A little. By email mostly. She came down to the city once. I let her know last week that I planned to be up here with you for a few days, halfway to Syracuse, thought it might be a good time to get together with her." He paused, eyeing his father warily. "You look kind of shocked."

" 'Surprised' would be the word. You never mentioned Kim after ... after the case was wrapped up."

"I figured you wouldn't want to be reminded of that whole mess she dragged you into. Not that she meant to. But it ended up being pretty traumatic stuff."

It was true that it wasn't a case he enjoyed talking about. Or thinking about. Very few were. In fact, he rarely considered the past at all, unless it was a past case with loose ends that demanded resolution. But the Good Shepherd case wasn't one of those. The Good Shepherd case was solved. The puzzle pieces, in the end, were all in place. It could be argued, however, that the price had been too high. And his own position in the final act of that drama had become one of Madeleine's chief exhibits in her argument that he exposed himself too willingly to unreasonable levels of danger.

Kyle was watching him now with a worried look. "Does it bother you that I'm visiting her?"

In other circumstances, the honest answer would have been yes. He'd found Kim to be very ambitious, very emotional, very naive—a combination more troublesome than he would wish for in any girlfriend for his son. But in the current circumstances, Kyle's plan struck him as a convenient coincidence—in the same category as Madeleine's plan to help the Winklers.

"Actually," said Gurney, "it seems like a pretty good idea at the moment—a bit safer, anyway."

"Jeez, Dad, you really think something bad's going to happen here?"

"I think the chance is very, very slight. But I wouldn't want you to be exposed to it."

"What about *you*?" It was Madeleine's question, repeated in the same tone.

"It's part of the job—part of what I signed on for when I agreed to help with the case."

"Is there anything I can do for you?"

"No, son, there isn't anything right now. But thank you."

"Okay," he said doubtfully. For a minute he looked lost, as if hoping for some other option, some other plan of action, to occur to him.

Gurney said nothing, just waited.

"Okay," Kyle repeated. "Let me get some of my things and I'll be on my way. When I get to Syracuse I'll check in with you." He retreated from the den with a worried frown.

A musical computer tone announced the start of Gurney's eight a.m. video call.

Chapter 46

The Spalter Brothers

A medium shot of a man sitting in a comfortable-looking armchair filled most of the laptop screen. Gurney recognized Jonah Spalter from his photograph on the Cyberspace Cathedral website. He was illuminated clearly, expertly, with no extraneous elements in the video framing to distract from the strong bone structure of his face. His expression was one of practiced calm seasoned with mild concern. He was gazing directly into the camera with the effect of gazing directly into Gurney's eyes.

"Hello, David. I'm Jonah." If his voice were a color, it would have been a pastel. "Is it all right if I call you David? Or would you prefer Detective Gurney?"

"David is fine. Thank you for getting in touch with me."

There was a tiny nod, a tiny smile, the hint of a social worker's concern in the eyes. "Your email had an urgent tone, along with some rather alarming phrases. How can I help you?"

"How much do you know about the effort to get your sister-in-law's conviction overturned?"

"I know that the effort resulted in her lead attorney being killed, along with six of his neighbors."

"Anything else?"

"I know that Mr. Bincher had made some serious allegations of police corruption. Your email to me also referred to corruption, as well as 'family dynamics.' That could mean just about anything. Perhaps you could explain it."

"It's an area that the official investigation is likely to pursue."

"Official investigation?"

"Lex Bincher's murder will force BCI to take a new look at your brother's murder. Not only BCI, but probably the AG's office as well, since the corruption charges in Kay's appeal are aimed at BCI. At that point, we'll be turning over the new evidence we've uncovered—evidence indicating that Kay was framed. So, whichever agencies are involved, they'll be asking who, besides Kay, stood to benefit from Carl's death."

"Well," said Jonah, with wide-eyed chagrin, "that would certainly include me."

"Is it true that you and your brother didn't get along?"

"Didn't get along?" He laughed softly, ruefully. "That would be an understatement." He closed his eyes for a moment, shaking his head, as though overwhelmed by the thoughts this subject raised. When he spoke again his tone was sharper. "Do you know where I am right now?"

"I have no idea."

"No one does. That's the point."

"What point?"

"Carl and I never did get along. When we were younger it didn't matter that much. He had his friends and I had mine. We went our own ways. Then, as you may know—it's no secret—our father yoked us together in the monstrosity known as Spalter Realty. That's when 'not getting along' turned into something poisonous. When I was forced to work with Carl on a daily basis ... I realized I was dealing with something more than a difficult brother. I was dealing with a *monster.*" Jonah paused, as if to give that term room to expand in Gurney's imagination.

It sounded to Gurney like a speech Jonah might have delivered before—an oft-repeated explanation of a terrible relationship.

"I watched Carl evolve from a selfish, aggressive businessman into a complete sociopath. As his political ambition grew, on the outside he became more charming, more magnetic, more charismatic. On the inside, he was rotting away to nothing—a black hole of greed and ambition. In biblical terms, he was the ultimate 'whitewashed sepulchre.' He got in bed with like-minded people. Ruthless people. Major criminals. Mob figures like Donny Angel. Murderers. Carl wanted to pull enormous amounts of money out of Spalter Realty to finance his megalomaniac schemes with those people, as well as his supremely hypocritical gubernatorial candidacy. He kept pressuring me to agree to unethical transactions that I wouldn't—*couldn't*—agree to. 'Ethics,' 'morality,' 'legality'—none of those words meant anything to him. He began to frighten me. Actually, that's not a strong enough word. The truth is, he *terrified* me. I came to believe there was nothing—*nothing*—he wouldn't do to get what he wanted. Sometimes . . . the look in his eyes . . . it was positively satanic. As though all the evil in the world were concentrated in that gaze."

"How did you deal with it?"

"Deal with it?" Again, the small smile and rueful laugh, followed by a lowered voice, almost confessional. "I ran away."

"How?"

"I kept moving. Literally moving. One of the blessings of current technology is that you can do just about anything from anywhere. I bought a motor home, outfitted it with the appropriate communications equipment, and made it the rolling headquarters of the Cyberspace Cathedral. A process in which I have come to see the hand of Providence. Good can come out of evil, if good is our objective."

"The good in this case being . . . ?"

"Having no fixed geographical location, of being in a sense *nowhere*. My sole location has become the Internet, and the Internet is *everywhere*. Which has turned out to be the ideal 'place' for the Cathedral. The ubiquitous, worldwide Cyberspace Cathedral. Do you see what I mean, David? The need to get away from my brother and his deadly associates has been transformed into a gift. God does indeed work in a mysterious way, His wonders to perform. This is a truth we encounter again and again. All that is required is an open mind and an open heart." Jonah was looking increasingly radiant.

Gurney wondered if a delicate shift had been made in the lighting. He felt the urge to dull the glow. "Then you got a second gift, a large one, with Carl's death."

Jonah's smile grew cooler. "That's true. Once more, out of evil came good."

"Apparently, quite a lot of good. I've heard that Spalter Realty's assets are worth over fifty million dollars. Is that true?"

The man's forehead frowned while his mouth continued to smile.

"In today's market, it's impossible to say." He paused, shrugged. "But I suppose, give or take a significant amount, it's as good as any other guess."

"Is it true that before Carl's death you couldn't touch that money, but now it all goes to you?"

"Nominally to me, but ultimately to the Cathedral. I'm merely a conduit. The Cathedral is of supreme importance. It's far more important than any individual. The work of the Cathedral is the only thing that matters. The *only* thing."

Gurney wondered if he was hearing a not-so-subtle threat in this emphatic priority. Rather than take that issue head-on, however, he decided to change direction. "Were you surprised by Carl's murder?"

That question triggered Jonah's first noticeable hesitation. He steepled his fingers in front of his chest. "Yes and no. *Yes*, because one is always initially startled by that ultimate form of violence. *No*, because murder was not a surprising end to the kind of life Carl led. And I could easily imagine someone close to him being driven to that extreme."

"Even someone like Kay?"

"Even someone like Kay."

"Or someone like yourself?"

Jonah wrapped his answer in an earnest frown. "Or someone like myself." Then he glanced, not quite surreptitiously, at his watch.

Gurney smiled. "Just a couple more questions."

"I do have a live webcast scheduled in ten minutes, but go ahead, please."

"What did you think of Mick Klemper?"

"Who?"

"The chief investigator at Carl's shooting."

"Ah. Yes. What did I think of him? I thought he might have a drinking problem."

"Did he interview you?"

"I wouldn't call it an interview. He asked a few basic questions at the cemetery that day. He took down my contact information, but he never followed up. He didn't strike me as particularly thorough . . . or trustworthy."

"Would you be surprised if you heard that he was guilty of evidence tampering?"

"I can't say it would be a shock." He cocked his head curiously. "Are you saying that he used illegal means to get Kay convicted? Why?"

"Again, that's confidential within the appeal process at this point. But it does raise an important point. Assuming that Kay didn't kill Carl, obviously someone else did. Does the fact that the real killer is out there roaming around free worry you?"

"For my own safety? Not at all. Carl and I were on the opposite sides of every business decision, every proposed action of Spalter Realty—as well as every personal matter that ever came up between us. We never had the same friends, the same goals, the same anything. It's highly unlikely that we'd have the same enemy."

"One last question." Gurney paused, more for dramatic effect than because of any indecision. "What would you say if I told you that your mother's death may not have been accidental?"

"What do you mean?" He blinked, appeared stunned.

"Evidence has come to light that connects her death with Carl's."

"What evidence?"

"I can't go into that. But it seems persuasive. Can you think of any reason that the person who targeted Carl would also have targeted your mother?"

Jonah's expression was a frozen mix of emotions. The most recognizable one was fear. But was it the fear of the unknown? Or was it fear of the *unknown becoming known?* He shook his head. "I . . . I don't know what to say. Look, I need to know what . . . I mean, what kind of *evidence* are you talking about?"

"Right now that's a confidential part of the appeals case. I'll see that you're informed as soon as possible."

"What you're saying is . . . absolutely bizarre."

"It must seem that way. But if any explanation occurs to you, any scenario that you think might connect the two deaths, please let me know right away."

The man's only visible response was a small nod.

Gurney decided on another abrupt change of direction. "What do you think of Carl's daughter?"

Jonah swallowed, shifted in his chair. "Are you asking me if she could . . . could have killed her father? And her grandmother too?" He looked lost. "I have no idea. Alyssa is . . . not a healthy person, but . . . *her father? Her grandmother?*"

"Not healthy in what way? Can you be more specific?"

"No. Not now." He looked at his watch, as if baffled by the data it conveyed. "I really have to go. Really. Sorry."

"Last question. Who else might have wanted to kill Carl?"

He turned up his palms in a gesture that conveyed frustration with the question. "Anyone. Anyone who got close enough to see the rot behind the smile."

"Thank you for your help, Jonah. I hope we can speak again. By the way, what's the topic of your webcast?"

"Sorry, my what?"

"Your webcast."

"Oh." He looked sick. "Today's topic is 'Our Path to Joy.'"

Chapter 47

Still Missing

Gurney used the quarter hour prior to Hardwick's and Esti's scheduled arrival at nine o'clock to type and print out three copies of what he'd jotted down the day before on a legal pad—the case's key points.

Esti was the first to arrive but only by a minute. As she was parking her hot blue Mini Cooper by the asparagus bed, Hardwick's red GTO was rumbling up past the barn.

She stepped out of the little car, and her T-shirt, cutoff jeans, and relaxed smile all proclaimed a day off from the job. Her caramel skin glowed in the morning sunlight. As she approached the side door, she cast a curious glance at the flat stones marking the rooster's grave.

Gurney opened the screen door and shook hands with her.

"Hey," she said, "it's so gorgeous today, we should stay out here."

Gurney returned the smile. "That'd be nice. Problem is, I have some videos inside I want you and Jack to see."

"Just a thought. The sun feels good on my skin."

Hardwick pulled his car in next to hers, got out, and swung the heavy door shut. Without bothering to acknowledge her or Gurney, he shaded his eyes with his hand and began scanning the surrounding fields and wooded hillsides.

She gave him a sideways glance. "You looking for somebody?"

He didn't answer, just continued what he was doing.

Gurney followed his gaze until it reached Barrow Hill, realizing then what was on the man's mind. "That's the most likely spot," said Gurney.

Hardwick nodded. "At the top of that narrow trail?"

"It's actually an overgrown quarry road."

Hardwick stayed focused on the hill. "Pretty good distance from here. He'd need to be really good. Maybe twelve hundred feet?"

"Maybe a little more. Not too different from Long Falls."

Esti looked alarmed. "You guys talking about a sniper?"

"A possible location for one," said Gurney. "There's a place near the top of that hill that would be my choice if I were targeting someone who lived in this house. Clear view of the side door, clear view of the cars."

She turned to Hardwick. "Every place you go now, that's what you're checking out? Sniper spots?"

"With two rounds in the side of my house, it's on my mind these days. Areas surrounded by good cover concern me."

Her eyes widened. "So maybe instead of standing here like sitting ducks, staring at a place we could be shot from, we should go inside, yes?"

Hardwick looked like he was about to make a wiseass comment about her standing/sitting remark, but he just grinned and followed her into the house. After another glance up the hill, Gurney joined them.

He got his laptop and list of issues from the den, and they all settled down at the dining table. "Why don't we start by getting up-to-date?" suggested Gurney. "You and Esti were going to make some calls. Do we have any new facts?"

Esti went first. "This Greek mob guy, Adonis Angelidis? According to my friend at OCTF, he's a big deal. Low profile, compared to the Italians and the Russians, but a lot of influence. Works with all the families. It was the same with Gurikos, the guy who got his head nailed. He arranged big hits for big players. Major connections. Very trusted."

"So why was he hit?" asked Hardwick. "Your task force buddy got any clue?"

"None. According to OCTF, Gurikos kept everybody happy. Smooth as silk. A *resource*."

"Yeah, well, somebody didn't agree."

She nodded. "It could have happened the way Angelidis told Dave: Carl went to Gurikos to set up a hit on someone, then that someone found out about it and hired Panikos to kill them both. Makes sense, no?"

Hardwick turned his palms up in a gesture of uncertainty.

Esti looked at Gurney. "Dave?"

"In a way, I'd like the Angelidis version to be true. But it doesn't feel quite right. Like it *almost* makes sense. The problem is, it doesn't account for the nails in Gus's head. A practical, preemptive hit on Carl and Gus is one thing. A gruesome warning about keeping secrets is something else. The two don't fit together."

"I've got the same problem with the mother," said Esti. "I don't get why she had to be killed."

Hardwick sounded restless. "It's not that big a mystery. To put Carl at the funeral, exposed, delivering a eulogy."

"So why didn't Panikos wait until he was actually standing at the podium? Why shoot him before he got there?"

"Who the hell knows? Maybe to stop him from revealing something."

Gurney couldn't see the logic in that. Why go to elaborate lengths to set up a situation in which someone would be scheduled to make a speech if you were afraid of what they might say?

"I've got one last thing," said Esti. "About the Cooperstown fires? I found out something interesting, but strange. The four incendiary devices used on Bincher's house were all different types and sizes." She looked from Hardwick to Gurney and back again. "Does that say anything to you?"

Hardwick sucked at his teeth and shrugged. "Maybe that's what little Peter happened to have in his toy box at the time."

"Or maybe what his supplier had available? Any ideas, Dave?"

"Just an off-the-wall possibility: that he was experimenting."

"*Experimenting?* For what purpose?"

"I don't know. Maybe evaluating different devices with some future use in mind?"

She made a face. "Let's hope that's not the reason."

Hardwick shifted in his chair. "You got anything else, sweetheart?"

"Yes. The headless body recovered at the scene has been positively ID'd." She paused for one dramatic beat. "Lex Bincher. For sure."

Hardwick was staring warily at her.

She went on slowly, "The head . . . is still missing."

Hardwick's jaw muscle twitched. "Christ! This is like some shit in a horror movie."

Esti screwed up her face. "I don't understand how this gets to you so much. That story about how you and Dave met—that incident involved a woman who got cut in half, right? I heard you laugh about that, tell sick jokes, right?"

"Right."

"So how come when this head thing comes up, you get all disturbed-like?"

"Look, for Christ's sake . . ." He raised his hands in surrender, shaking his head. "It's one thing to find a chopped-up body. A body in ten pieces. You're a cop long enough, you work the inner city long enough, that kind of thing is going to happen. It just is. But there's a big difference between finding a cut-off head and *not* finding it. You get what I mean? The fucking thing is *missing*! Which means somebody is keeping it somewhere. For some reason. For some God-awful use he has for it. Believe me, that fucking thing is going to turn up when we least expect it."

" 'When we least expect it'? I think you see too much Netflix." She gave him one of her affectionate little winks. "Anyway, that's all the new stuff I have for now. How about you? You have anything?"

Hardwick rubbed his face hard with his palms, as though he were erasing a bad dream, trying to give his day a fresh start. "I managed to locate one of the missing witnesses—Freddie, the one whose testimony put Kay in the Axton Avenue apartment house at the time of the shooting. Officially, Frederico Javier Rosales." He shot a glance at Gurney. "Any chance of getting some coffee?"

"No problem." Gurney went to the machine on the sink island to get a fresh pot going.

Hardwick continued. "We had a friendly talk, me and Freddie. We focused on the interesting little gap between what he actually saw and what Mick the Dick told him he saw."

Esti's eyes widened. "He admitted that Klemper told him what to say on the stand?"

"Not only did Klemper tell him what to say, but he told him he damn well better say it."

"Or else what?"

"Freddie had a drug problem. Small dealer supporting a big addiction. One more conviction would give him an automatic hard twenty, no parole. When a skell's in that kind of spot, a prick like Mick has a lot of leverage."

"So why'd he open up to you?"

Hardwick grinned unpleasantly. "Boy like Freddie has a short attention span. Always sees the biggest threat as the one that's standing in front of him, and that was me. But don't get the wrong idea. I was very civilized. I explained that the only way for him to avoid the substantial penalties for having committed perjury in a murder case would be for him to un-perjure himself."

Esti looked incredulous. "*Un-perjure* himself?"

"Nice concept, don't you think? I told him he could get out from under the avalanche of shit that was about to come down on him if he described how his original testimony was concocted entirely by Mick the Dick."

"He spelled all that out on paper?"

"And signed it. I even got his fucking thumbprint on it."

Esti looked cautiously pleased. "Does Freddie think you're with BCI?"

"It's possible he may have formed the impression that my connection with the bureau is more current than it actually is. I don't really give a shit what he thinks. Do you?"

She shook her head. "Not if it helps put Klemper away. You have any leads on the other two witnesses who dropped out of sight—Jimmy Flats and Kay's boyfriend, Darryl?"

"Not yet. But Freddie's statement, along with the recording of Dave's conversation with Alyssa, should absolutely seal the deal on the police misconduct issue—which in turn should seal the deal on Kay's appeal."

Hardwick's happy little rhyme scraped Gurney's brain like nails on a blackboard. But then it occurred to him that his edginess might be coming from another direction—from the unresolved question of Kay's guilt, an issue quite apart from the fairness or unfairness of her trial. There was little doubt about the evidence tampering and witness tampering. But none of those illegalities made Kay Spalter *innocent.* As long as the identity of the person who hired Petros Panikos to kill Carl Spalter remained a mystery, Kay Spalter remained a viable suspect.

Esti's voice broke into Gurney's train of thought. "You said something about showing us some videos?"

"Yes. Right. In addition to my Skype conversation with Jonah, I have a couple of security camera sequences from Axton Avenue—a close-up view of someone entering the apartment building before the shooting, and a long-distance view of Carl getting hit and going down." He looked at Hardwick. "Did you fill Esti in on how I got the videos?"

"Things were moving a little too fast. And there wasn't much information in that thirty-second voice mail you left me."

"And what information there was you decided to ignore, right?"

"The hell's that supposed to mean?"

"My message to you was clear on the key point. I had told Klemper things would go better for him if the missing video material was to end up in my hands. Well, it did. But then you made your no-holds-barred appearance on *Criminal Conflict*—and bashed the 'thoroughly corrupt' detective on the case for framing Kay with perjured testimony. Everyone in the criminal justice system up here knows that the detective on the case was Mick Klemper—so you essentially named him and blamed him, and totally ignored my situation with him."

Hardwick's expression was darkening. "Like I said, things were moving fast. I'd just come from the arson by the lake—seven dead people, Davey, *seven*—and I was a fuckload more focused on the main battle than with the niceties of your tête-à-tête with Mick the Dick." Hardwick went on, reminding Gurney that ambiguous promises and expedient lies were the hidden foundation stones of the criminal justice system. He wound up with a semi-rhetorical question. "Why the hell would you worry about a piece of shit like Klemper?"

Gurney opted for a practical and simplistic response, prompted by his memory of the odor of alcohol on the man and the almost incoherent message he left on Gurney's voice mail the next day. "My concern is that Mick Klemper is an angry drunk being backed into a corner, and that he might be desperate enough to do something stupid."

When Hardwick said nothing, Gurney continued. "So I'm keeping my Beretta a little closer than usual, just in case. In the meantime, Esti asked about the videos. So let's take a look. I'll run the street-view sequence first, then the long shot of the cemetery."

Chapter 48

Montell Jones

After they watched the security camera videos twice, Hardwick asked, "Can we prove that Klemper had these in his possession at the time of the trial?"

"I'm not sure we can prove he ever had them. The electronics store owner might be talked into providing an affidavit, saying he turned the videos over, but he's shadier than Klemper. And besides—"

Esti broke in. "But you asked Klemper for the recordings and he gave them to you."

"I told him if I got the recordings, things might go better for him. And the next day they appeared in my mailbox. You and I know what that means. But legally, it's a yard or two short of proving possession. In any event, who had the recordings or when they had them isn't the important thing. What's important is what's on them."

Hardwick looked ready to object, but Gurney pressed on. "The importance of the long-distance cemetery sequence is that it shows Carl being shot in the exact spot where everyone said he was shot—which essentially confirms the impossibility of the shot having come from the window that Klemper's team claims it came from."

Esti looked troubled. "This is like the fourth time I've heard you talk about the bullet thing—the contradiction in where it came from. What do you think is the answer?"

"Honestly, Esti? I'm going around in circles on that one. The physical and chemical evidence in the apartment where the murder weapon was found says that's where the bullet must have been fired. The line of sight to the victim says it couldn't have been."

"This reminds me of the Montell Jones mess over in Schenectady. You remember that one, Jack? Five, six years ago?"

"Drug dealer? Big controversy over whether it was a righteous kill?"

"Right." She turned to Gurney. "Young officer in a cruiser is making his rounds in a druggy neighborhood—bright, sunny day—when he gets a 'shots fired' call, location about two blocks from where he is. Ten seconds, he's there, out of the car. People on the street point him to a broad alley between two warehouses, say that's where they heard two shots a couple of minutes earlier. He's first on the scene, should wait for backup, but he doesn't. Instead, he pulls out his nine-millimeter, steps into the alley. Facing him, about fifty feet away, is Montell Jones, local bad guy, violent drug dealer, super-long rap sheet. The way the officer tells it, he sees that Montell's got his own nine. In his hand. He raises it slowly in the officer's direction. Officer shouts at him to drop it. The nine keeps coming up. Officer fires one round. Montell goes down. Other cruisers start arriving. Montell's bleeding out through a hole in his stomach. Ambulance comes, takes him away, he's pronounced dead on arrival at the hospital. Everything seems totally righteous. Young officer is a hero for about twenty-four hours. Then everything goes to hell. Internal Affairs calls him in and gets his account of the shooting. He has no doubt about anything. All crystal-clear—facing Montell, sunny, perfect visibility, Montell's nine rising toward him. Officer fires, Montell goes down. End of story. The IA interviewer asks him again. He goes through it again. And again. They have it all on tape. They have the whole thing transcribed, printed out, he signs it. Then they drop the bombshell. 'We have a problem here. The ME says the stomach wound was an exit wound, not an entry wound.' The officer is speechless, he can't grasp what he just heard. He asks them what the hell they're talking about. They tell him it's simple. He shot Montell in the back. And now they'd like to know why."

"Sounds like every cop's worst nightmare," said Gurney. "But at least this Montell guy had a loaded weapon, right?"

"He did. That much was okay. But the bullet in the back was a big problem."

"Did the cop try to use the old 'He turned away just as I pulled the trigger' explanation?"

"No. He kept saying that the shooting went down exactly the way he described it. He even insisted that Montell absolutely did *not* turn away, that he was facing him straight on from start to finish."

"Interesting," said Gurney, a thoughtful light in his eyes. "What's the punch line?"

"Montell had actually been shot in the back a couple of minutes *earlier* by an unknown assailant—hence the original report of shots fired to which the officer was responding. After being left to die in the alley, Montell managed to get back up on his feet—just in time for our hero to arrive. Montell was probably in a state of shock, didn't know what the hell he was doing with his gun. Officer fires—*misses Montell completely*—and Montell collapses again."

"How did IA finally put it all together?"

"A thorough second search of the area turned up a slug in the gutter outside the alley with a trace of Montell's DNA on it—the gutter *behind* where the officer had been standing, meaning the original round had come from the opposite direction."

"Lucky find," said Gurney. "Could have turned out differently."

"Don't knock it," said Esti. "Sometimes luck is all you got."

Hardwick was drumming his fingertips on the table. "How does this alley thing relate to the Spalter shooting?"

"I don't know. But for some reason it came to mind. So maybe it does relate somehow," Esti said.

"How? You think Carl was shot from a different direction? Not from the apartment house?"

"I don't know, Jack. The story happened to come to mind. I can't explain it. What do *you* think, Dave?"

Gurney answered hesitatingly. "It's an interesting example of two things occurring in a way that everyone assumes are connected but aren't."

"What two things?"

"The officer shooting at Montell, and Montell getting shot."

Chapter 49

Positively Satanic

While they were finishing their second round of coffee, Gurney played the recording of his Skype conversation with Jonah Spalter.

When it ended, Hardwick was the first to react. "I don't know who's the bigger piece of shit—Mick the Dick or this asshole."

Gurney smiled. "Paulette Purley, resident manager of Willow Rest, is convinced Jonah's a saint, out to save the world."

"All those saints out to save the world ought to be ground up for fertilizer. Bullshit is good for the soil."

"Better for the soil than the soul, right, Jack?"

"You can say that again, brother."

"He got fifty million dollars as a result of his brother's death?" asked Esti. "Is that true?"

"He didn't deny it," said Gurney.

"Hell of a motive," said Hardwick.

"In fact," Gurney went on, "he didn't seem interested in denying anything. Seemed comfortable admitting that he profited enormously from Carl's death. No problem admitting that he hated the man. Happy to reel off all the reasons everyone should have hated him."

Esti nodded. "Called him 'monster,' 'sociopath,' 'megalomaniac'..."

"Also called him 'positively satanic,'" added Hardwick. "As opposed to himself, who he'd like us to see as positively angelic."

Esti continued. "He admitted he'd do *anything* for that Cathedral thing of his. *Anything*. Actually sounded like he was bragging." She paused. "It's strange. He admitted to all these motives for murder like it didn't matter. Like he felt we couldn't touch him."

"Like a man with powerful connections," added Hardwick.

"Except at the end," said Gurney.

Esti frowned. "You mean the thing about his mother?"

"Unless he's the world's greatest actor, I believe he was truly disturbed at that point. But I'm not sure whether he was disturbed by the fact that she might have been murdered, or by the fact that we knew about it. I also find it peculiar that he was eager to know what evidence we had but never asked the more basic question: 'Why would someone kill my mother?' "

Hardwick showed his teeth in a humorless grin. "Kinda gives you the impression that the warm and wonderful Jonah in reality might not give a fuck about anyone. Including his mother."

Esti looked confused. "So where do we go from here?"

Hardwick's chilly grin widened. He pointed at Gurney's list of unresolved issues lying on the table next to the open laptop. "That's easy. We follow the ace detective's road map of clues and clever questions."

They each took one of the copies Gurney had printed out. They read through the eight points silently.

The further down the list Esti read, the more worried her expression became. "This list is ... depressing."

Gurney asked what gave her that feeling.

"It makes it painfully clear that we don't know much at this point. Don't you agree?"

"Yes and no," said Gurney. "It enumerates a lot of unanswered questions, but I'm convinced that discovering the answer to any one of them could make all the others fall into place."

She offered a grudging nod but appeared unconvinced. "I hear what you're saying, but ... where do we start? If we could coordinate the efforts of the relevant agencies—BCI, FBI, OCTF, Interpol, Homeland Security, DMV, et cetera—and throw some major manpower against the case, tracking down this Panikos character might be feasible. But, as it is ... what are we supposed to do? Panikos aside, we just don't have the hands and feet and hours to look into all the other relationships and conflicts in the lives of Carl, Jonah, Kay, Alyssa—not to mention Angelidis and Gurikos and God knows who else." She shook her head in a gesture of helplessness.

Her comments produced the longest silence of the meeting.

At first, Hardwick showed no reaction at all. He appeared to be comparing his thumbs, studying their relative size and shape.

Esti stared at him. "Jack, you have any feeling about this?"

He looked up and cleared his throat. "Sure. We have two separate situations. One is Kay's appeal process, which Lex's partner tells me is in great shape. The other is the effort to answer the 'Who killed Carl?' question, which is a trickier deal altogether. But yon crafty Sherlock has an optimistic look in his eye."

Her anxious gaze moved to Gurney. "Optimism? You feel that?"

"Actually, yes, a bit."

Even as he was saying this, he was struck by the rapid change in his attitude in the short time since he'd first put his list of issues together and reacted to it with frustration at the complexity of the project and lack of law enforcement resources he'd once taken for granted—exactly what Esti was just complaining about.

Neither the complexity nor the resource problem had gone away. But he'd finally realized that he didn't need answers to an endless series of perplexing questions to unlock the solution.

Esti looked skeptical. "How can you be optimistic when there are so many things we don't know?"

"We may not have a lot of answers yet, but . . . we do have a person."

"We have a *person*? What person?"

"Peter Pan."

"What do you mean, we *have* him?"

"I mean he's here. In this area. Something about our investigation is keeping him here."

"What's this 'something'?"

"I think he's afraid that we'll discover his secret."

"The secret behind the nails in Fat Gus's head?"

"Yes."

Hardwick began tapping his fingers on the table. "What makes you think it's Panikos's secret and not the secret of whoever hired him?"

"Something Angelidis told me. He said Panikos only accepts pure hit contracts. No restrictions. No special instructions. You want somebody dead, you give him the money and chances are they end up dead. But he handles all the details his own way. So if a message was being sent with the nails in Fat Gus's head, it was Panikos's message—something that mattered to *him*."

Hardwick produced his acid-reflux grimace. "Sounds like you're putting a shitload of trust in what Angelidis told you—a mobster who lies, cheats, and steals for a living."

"There'd be no advantage to him in lying about the way Panikos does business. And everything else we've learned about Panikos, especially from your friend at Interpol, supports what Angelidis said. Peter Pan operates by his own rules. Nobody gets to tell him what to do."

"You're suggesting the boy may be a bit of a control freak?"

Gurney smiled at the understatement. "No one ordered him to shoot out the lights in your house, Jack. He doesn't take orders like that. I don't believe anyone ordered him to burn down those houses in Cooperstown, or to walk away with Lex Bincher's head in a tote bag."

"You suddenly sound awful goddamn sure about this shit."

"I've been thinking about it long enough. It's about time I started to see at least one piece of it clearly."

Esti threw up her hands in bafflement. "I'm sorry, maybe I'm being dense here, but what is it you see so clearly?"

"The open door that's been right there in front of us all along."

"What open door?"

"Peter Pan himself."

"What are you talking about?"

"He's responding to our actions, to our investigation of Carl's murder. A response equals a connection. A connection equals an open door."

"Responding to our actions?" Esti appeared incredulous, almost angry. "You mean by shooting at Jack's house? By killing Lex and his neighbors in Cooperstown?"

"He's trying to stop what we're doing."

"So we investigate, and his response is to shoot and burn and kill. That's what you're calling an open door?"

"It proves he's paying attention. It proves he's still *here*. He hasn't left the country. He hasn't slipped back into his hole in the ground. It proves we can reach him. We just have to figure out how to reach him in a way that provokes a reaction we can work with."

Esti's eyes narrowed, her expression shifting from disbelief to speculation. "You mean, like, use the media—maybe that asshole Bork—to offer Panikos some kind of deal to reveal who hired him?"

"Bork could play a role, but not to offer that kind of deal. I think our little Peter Pan operates on a different wavelength."

"What wavelength?"

"Well . . . just look at what we know about him."

Esti shrugged. "We know he's a professional killer."

Gurney nodded. "What else?"

"He's an expensive one, specializing in difficult contracts."

"Impossible jobs that no one else will take—that's the way Donny Angel put it. What else?"

"A psychopath, yes?"

Hardwick chimed in. "The psychopath from hell. With bad dreams. The way I see it, this wee fucker is one highly motivated murder machine—angry, crazy, bloodthirsty, and not about to change his ways any time soon. How about you, Sherlock? You got any other insights for us?"

Gurney swallowed the last mouthful of his lukewarm coffee. "I've just been trying to put all this together to see what it adds up to. His absolute insistence on doing everything his own way, his high intelligence combined with a total lack of empathy, his pathological rage, his killing skills, his appetite for mass murder—all that combined would seem to make little Peter the ultimate control freak from hell. Then there's the final explosive element—the loose end, the secret, whatever it is that he's desperate to conceal and afraid we may discover. Oh, and one more thing Angelidis told me—I almost forgot to mention it—little Peter likes to *sing* while he's shooting people. Put all that together and it looks like a recipe for an interesting endgame."

"Or a fucking world-class disaster," said Hardwick.

"I guess that would be the downside."

Chapter 50

Jabbing the Madman

"Is there an upside?" Hope and apprehension were vying with each other in Esti's expression. Apprehension was winning.

"I think so." Gurney's tone was matter of fact. "My sense of Panikos is that his ultimate motivation is hatred, probably directed at every human being on earth. But his tactics, his planning—those aspects are steady and well thought out. His success in his profession depends on maintaining a delicate balance between his hot appetite for killing and his cold planning process. It's evident in the behavior we're seeing, and Donny Angel told me as much. On the outside Panikos is a reliable businessman who accepts difficult assignments with equanimity. And inside there's a fierce little monster whose main pleasure—maybe *only* pleasure—is murder."

Hardwick let out his harsh bark of a laugh. "The wee Peter could be quite the eye-opening experience for an 'inner child' therapist."

Gurney uttered a small laugh, despite himself.

Esti turned to him. "So he's part planner, part psycho. The motive is crazy, but the method is rational. Let's say you're right. Where does it take us?"

"Since that delicate balance between madness and logic seems to work well for him, we need to upset it."

"How?"

"By attacking its most accessible weak point."

"Which is?"

"The secret he's trying to protect. That's our way in. Our way into his thinking. And our way into understanding Carl's murder, and who ordered it."

"Be nice if we knew what the precious fucking secret was," inter-jected Hardwick.

Gurney shrugged. "All we have to do is make him *think* we know, or that we're about to find out. It's a game we need to play—inside his head."

"And the point of this game?" asked Esti.

"To disrupt the careful calculation he relies on for his success and survival. We need to hammer a wedge between the core lunatic and his rational support system."

"You're losing me."

"We apply pressure in a way that threatens his sense of control. If control is his most intense obsession, it's also his greatest weakness. Take away a control freak's feeling of control, and the result is panic-driven decisions."

"You hear what the man is saying?" interjected Hardwick. "He plans to poke a mass murderer in the eye with a sharp stick to see what might happen."

It was a way of putting it that seemed to resonate with Esti's grow-ing anxiety. She turned to Gurney. "Suppose what happens after we apply this 'pressure' is that Panikos kills another six or seven people. What then? We apply *more* pressure? And if he slaughters another dozen victims at random? What then?"

"I'm not saying there's no risk. But the alternative is to let him fade back into the shadows. Right now we've pulled him up close to the surface. Almost within reach. I want to keep him there, stir up his fear, make him do something stupid. As for his potential slaughter of innocent people, we can take the random factor out of his decision. We'll feed him a specific target and use it to trap him."

"Target?" Esti's chocolate-brown eyes widened.

"We have to get him focused where we want him. It's not enough to just ratchet up the threat level and push him over the edge. We have to be able to contain the response we provoke—keep it aimed in a manageable direction, within a manageable time frame."

She looked unconvinced.

Gurney went on. "We set him up, generate the reaction we want, then reel him in—at a time and place of *our* choosing."

"You say it so easily. But it's very risky, no?"

"Yes—but not as risky as the alternative. Jack described Peter Pan as a murder machine. I agree. That's what he does. Always has. Ever since he was a child. Always will, if he gets his way. He's like a fatal disease that no one has figured out how to stop. I don't see any risk-free options. We either let the murder machine keep running, keep converting people into corpses, or we do what we can to jam it up."

"Or," Esti offered hesitantly, "we could turn over everything we have to BCI right now and let them deal with it. They've got the resources. We don't. And those resources could—"

"Fuck BCI!" growled Hardwick.

Esti emitted a small sigh and turned to Gurney. "Dave? What do you say?"

Gurney said nothing. His mind had been ambushed by too vivid a memory. A sickening thump. A red BMW speeding away from the scene ... down a long city street ... turning a corner with squealing tires ... disappearing ... forever. Except in his memory. The victim of the hit-and-run lying twisted in the gutter. The little four-year-old boy. His own Danny. And the pigeon Danny had followed, unthinking, into the street—the pigeon rising on a flurry of wings, alarmed but untouched, flying away.

Why hadn't he commandeered a car right there on the street?

Why hadn't he pursued the killer, right then and there, to the gates of hell?

Sometimes the memory triggered tears. Sometimes just an aching in his throat. And sometimes a terrible anger.

The anger was what he felt now.

"Dave?"

"Yes?"

"Do you think it might be time to hand the case over to BCI?"

"Hand it over? And stop doing what we're doing?"

She nodded. "It's really within their—"

He cut her off. "No. Not yet."

"What do you mean, not *yet*?"

"I don't think we should let Panikos escape. And if we stop, that's what will happen."

Whatever remaining desire she might have had to argue the point seemed to melt away. Perhaps it was the granite in Gurney's voice. Or the determination in his eyes. The message was clear. He wasn't about to hand anything over to anyone.

Not while the killer was still within reach.

Not while the red BMW was still within sight.

After they took a break to check and respond to texts and voice mail, Gurney put on a third pot of coffee and opened the double doors to let in the balmy August air. As usual, he was surprised by the fragrances of warm earth, grass, wildflowers. It was as if he were incapable of remembering what nature smelled like.

When they were all resettled at the big table, Esti's gaze met Gurney's. "You're the one who seems sure about how we should proceed. You have some specific steps in mind?"

"First we need to decide on the content of our message to Panikos. Then the channel of communication, the identity of the target we want him to zero in on, timing, necessary preparation, and—"

"Slow down, please, one thing at a time. The content of the message? You mean telling him we know something about this secret he's protecting?"

"Right. And that we're about to reveal it at some specific time."

"And the channel? You mean how we actually get this message to him?"

"You said it yourself this morning. *Criminal Conflict.* Brian Bork. I'd bet that Panikos saw Bork's interview with Lex, and he probably also saw Bork's interview with Jack after the Cooperstown fires."

Esti made a face. "I know I mentioned Bork—but now when I think about it, I can't imagine our psycho assassin sitting around watching TV."

"He may have a search engine alert set for certain names—Spalter, Gurikos, Bincher—so if there's a promotion for an upcoming news program or anything else related to the case in the media, he'd be aware of it."

She responded with an uneasy little nod.

There was a glint of excitement in Hardwick's eyes. "I have an open invite from Asshole Bork to provide updates on the case. So I can plant whatever message we want."

Esti turned toward Gurney. "Which brings us to the part of what you said that I don't like the sound of. 'The target.' What did you mean by that?"

Hardwick interrupted. "Simple, babe. He wants to sic the wee Peter on *us*."

She blinked. "Dave? That's what you meant?"

"Only if we're confident that we can maintain control of the situation—and that he'd be falling into our trap, not us into his."

Her expression was a picture of worry.

"But," Gurney added quickly, "I'm not really making 'us' the target."

She stared at him. "Who, then?"

He smiled. "Me."

Hardwick shook his head. "It would make more sense for *me* to be the target. I was the one who appeared on *Criminal Conflict*. He'll see me as enemy number one."

"More like an enemy of the state police, if I recall your rant."

Hardwick ignored the criticism and leaned forward, raising a forefinger to emphasize what he was about to say. "You know, there's another angle here. I've been thinking about the shots that cut my power and phone lines. In addition to the possible warning—'see no evil, hear no evil, speak no evil'—there might have been a second purpose. Something more practical." He paused, making sure he had their full attention.

Gurney had a feeling he knew what was coming.

"That Bolo guy you talked to claimed that Panikos visited the Axton Avenue apartment building almost a week before he whacked Carl. The question is, *Why?* Well, one reason occurred to me. An obsessive-compulsive hit man might want to zero in his rifle scope ahead of time—at the actual location. What do you think?"

Gurney nodded admiringly. He liked being reassured from time to time that beneath Hardwick's irritating shell there lurked a solid, insightful detective.

Esti frowned. "What's that got to do with the shots at your house?"

"If he could put my power lines in the crosshairs of his infrared scope and cut them cleanly, he'd know he could put a bullet between my eyes at that same range any time I stepped onto my front porch."

Esti looked like she was trying not to appear shaken. "On-site practice? Preparation? You think that was the purpose of those shots from the hill?"

It was clear from the speculative excitement in Hardwick's eyes that that's exactly what he thought.

Then Esti said something.

And Hardwick answered her.

Then she said something else.

And he responded to that as well.

But none of their words registered in Gurney's consciousness—not a single syllable after Esti's use of the phrase "those shots from the hill."

Because his mind had made a leap from Hardwick's property to his own. And all he could think about now was what one possible shot from Barrow Hill might have done.

Twenty minutes later, his freshly soiled garden shovel propped in the corner, Gurney stood at the utility sink in the mudroom. He was gazing down in tense concentration at the roughly washed carcass of the rooster he'd just unearthed from its stone-covered grave. On the muddy drain board next to the sink lay one of Madeleine's silk scarves, now dirty and bloodstained, which she'd used to wrap Horace's body.

Esti and Hardwick, having received no answers to their repeated questions, stood at the doorway, watching with growing concern. Gurney, holding his breath intermittently to avoid the rotten odor, bent over the dead bird, studying as closely as he could the damage that had ended its life. When he was satisfied that his informal postmortem had told him as much as it was going to, he straightened up and turned around, explaining.

"Madeleine had four chickens. One was a rooster. She named him Horace." He felt a little stab of sadness at saying the name. "When she found him out on the grass the other day, she thought a weasel had gotten him and bitten his head off. Someone told us weasels will do that." He felt his lips growing stiff with anger as he spoke. "She was right, in a way. It was a weasel with a sniper rifle."

At first, Esti's expression showed only bafflement. Then the significance of Gurney's comment struck her. "Oh, dear Jesus!"

"Fuck!" said Hardwick.

"I don't know whether this was about sighting-in his scope for future reference or just sending me a back-off message," said Gurney. "But whichever it was, I'm apparently on the little bastard's mind."

Chapter 51

The Plan

The dead rooster, the apparent method of its execution, and the possible motives behind it had further darkened the mood of the meeting.

Even Hardwick seemed subdued, standing now at the open French doors, gazing across the western field at Barrow Hill. He glanced back at Gurney, who was at the table with Esti. "You figure the shot came from that spot you pointed out before, at the top of the trail?"

"That'd be my guess."

"The position of things—house, hill, woods, trails—is kind of similar to the situation at my place. Only difference is that he hit my house at night, your rooster in the daylight."

"Right."

"Can you think of any reason for that?"

Gurney shrugged. "Only the obvious one. Night's the most dramatic time to cut a power line. But if you want to shoot one of our chickens, you need to do it in the daytime. They're locked up in the barn at night."

As Hardwick appeared to be mulling this over, a silence fell—broken by Esti.

"So you guys are figuring Panikos has given you both the same warning—to get off the case because he's got you in his sights?"

"Something like that," said Gurney.

"Well, let me ask the big question. How long before he moves from shooting your chickens to . . . ?" She let her voice trail off meaningfully.

"If he really wants us to back off, then our backing off might prevent any further action. If we don't back off, then further action might come quickly."

She took a couple of seconds to absorb this. "Okay. What do we do? Or not do?"

"We proceed." Had Gurney been expressing his intention to refill the saltshaker, his tone could not have been more matter of fact. "We proceed by giving him a compelling reason to kill me. Plus an urgent deadline. We don't have to pick a location—he's already picked it."

"You mean . . . here, at your house?"

"Yes."

"How do you imagine he would . . . ?"

"There are lots of possibilities. Best guess? He'll try to set fire to the house, with me in it. Probably with a remotely detonated incendiary device, like the ones he used at Cooperstown. Then shoot me when I come out."

She was getting wide-eyed again. "How do you know he'll go after *you* first and not Jack? Or even me?"

"With the help of Brian Bork, we can point him in the right direction."

As Gurney expected, Hardwick objected—reiterating his argument that he'd already established himself as a threat to Panikos, so it would be easy to set himself up as a credible target—but the argument now seemed to lack both foundation and conviction.

The rooster, it seemed, had tilted the game toward Gurney.

All that remained to be discussed were details, responsibilities, and logistics.

An hour later, with a mix of determination and misgiving, they'd agreed on a plan.

Esti, who'd been jotting down notes during the discussion, appeared the least comfortable at its conclusion. When Gurney asked about her concerns, she hesitated. "Maybe . . . you could just run through the thing one more time? If you wouldn't mind?"

"*Mind*, hell," growled Hardwick. "Sherlock *loves* this strategic shit." He stood up from the table. "While you're running through it one more time, I'll be doing something useful, like making the necessary phone calls. We need to get Bork on board ASAP, and we need to make sure SSS has the stuff we need in stock."

Scranton Surveillance & Survival was a kind of technology and weaponry supermarket catering to a mixed clientele of security firms, survivalists, serious militia guys, and garden-variety gun lovers. Its "SSS" logo was composed of three rattlesnakes, fangs bared. The salesclerks wore commando-style berets and fatigues. Gurney had visited the place once out of curiosity and gotten an uncomfortable feeling about it. It was, however, the most convenient source for the kind of electronic equipment they needed.

Hardwick had volunteered to make the trip. But first he wanted to make sure the stuff was in stock. He turned to Gurney. "Where do you get your strongest cell signal up here?"

After directing him out the side door to the far edge of the patio, Gurney returned to Esti, who was still sitting at the table, looking uneasy.

He sat across from her and recounted the plan they'd spent the previous hour putting together. "The objective is to give Panikos the impression that I'll be appearing on the Monday evening segment of *Criminal Conflict*, where I'll be revealing everything I've discovered about the Spalter murder, including the explosive secret Panikos has been trying to keep hidden. Jack is sure he can persuade Brian Bork and RAM-TV to run announcements promoting this revelation all day Sunday."

"But what do you do Monday, when you're supposed to appear on the show? What are you actually going to reveal?"

Gurney evaded the question. "If we're lucky, the game will be over by then and we won't have to deal with the actual show. The whole point is the *promotion* of our supposed revelation and the threat Panikos will feel—the deadline pressure he'll feel to silence me before showtime on Monday."

Esti did not look reassured. "What are these promotion ads actually going to say?"

"We'll work out the wording later, but the key will be making Panikos believe that I know something *big* about the Spalter case that no one else knows."

"Won't he assume that you'd have shared whatever you discovered with Jack and me?"

"He probably *would* assume that." Gurney smiled. "That's why I'm thinking that you and Jack might need to be killed in an auto accident. Bork'll love making that part of the promotion. Tragedy, controversy, drama—all magic words at RAM-TV."

"*Auto accident?* What the hell are you talking about?"

"I just made it up. But I like it. And it definitely narrows Panikos's target possibilities."

She gave him a long skeptical look. "To me, that sounds way over the top. You're sure the people at RAM-TV will go along with that kind of bullshit?"

"Like flies on that very substance. You're forgetting that RAM-TV thrives on bullshit. Bullshit boosts ratings. Bullshit is their business."

She nodded. "So all this is like a funnel. Everything is designed to channel Panikos toward one decision, one person, one location."

"Exactly."

"But it's a pretty shaky funnel. And the container the funnel goes into—maybe it's got holes in it?"

"What holes?"

"Let's say your funnel works: Panikos hears the promotion ads on Sunday, believes the bullshit, believes you know his secret, believes Jack and I are out of the picture—auto accident or whatever—believes it would be a good idea to eliminate you, comes here to do it . . . when? Sunday night? Monday morning?"

"My bet would be on Sunday night."

"Okay. Let's say he comes after you Sunday night. Maybe sneaking through the woods on foot, maybe on an ATV. Maybe with firebombs, maybe with a gun, maybe both. You with me?"

Gurney nodded.

"And our defense against this is what? Cameras in the fields? Cameras in the woods? Transmitters sending images back here to the house? Jack with a Glock, me with a SIG, you with that little Beretta of yours? Am I getting this right?"

He nodded again.

"I haven't left out anything?"

"Like what?"

"Like calling in the cavalry to save our asses! Have you and Jack forgotten what happened in Cooperstown? Three huge houses incinerated, seven people dead, one head missing. You have amnesia?"

"No need for the cavalry, babe," interrupted Hardwick, coming back in from the patio, grinning. "Just a good positive attitude and the best infrared surveillance equipment on the market. I just got us a short-term rental contract on everything we need. Plus total cooperation from our buddies at RAM-TV. So Davey boy's batshit plan to sucker the leopard into attacking the lamb might actually work."

She was looking at him like he was crazy.

He turned to Gurney and went on, as though he'd been asked to elaborate. "Scranton Surveillance and Survival will have everything ready for pickup tomorrow afternoon at four."

"Meaning you'll be getting back here around the time it's getting dark," said Gurney. "Not a great time to be setting stuff up in the woods."

"No matter. We'll have early Sunday morning to deploy everything. And then get ourselves in position. Bork's producer told me they'll start running the promos during the Sunday-morning talk shows, then all day, right into the late-night news."

"They'll do it?" Esti's tone was sour. "Just like that?"

"Just like that, babe."

"They really don't care that it's all made-up nonsense?"

Hardwick's grin became positively incandescent. "Not one goddamn bit. Why should they? Bork *loves* the feeling of crisis the whole thing generates."

Esti nodded slightly—the gesture conveying more resignation than agreement.

"By the way, Davey," said Hardwick, "I'd get that dead chicken out of the mudroom sink if I were you. Fucking thing really stinks."

"Right. I'll take care of that. But first—I'm glad you reminded me—we've got a little add-on for the RAM-TV announcements. An unfortunate auto accident."

Chapter 52

Florence in Flames

After Hardwick and Esti were gone—after her agile little Mini and his rumbling GTO had turned past the barn and headed down the mountain road—Gurney sat gazing out at the pile of lumber and pondering the henhouse project it represented.

Then his mind proceeded from the henhouse to Horace. He forced himself out of his chair and through the side hallway to the mudroom.

Back in the house a little while later after reburying the rooster, Gurney found that whatever sense of organization and control he'd experienced during the meeting with Hardwick and Esti had evaporated, and he was taken aback by the improvisational sketchiness of what he had boldly been calling a "plan." Now the whole caroming enterprise felt downright amateurish—driven more by anger, pride, and optimistic assumptions than by facts or real capabilities on the ground.

What they "knew" about Petros Panikos, after all, was little more than a hodgepodge of rumors and anecdotes from sources of widely varying credibility. The uncertain provenance of the data opened the door to an unsettling range of possibilities.

What, he asked himself, was he sure of?

In truth, very little. Very little beyond the implacable nature of the enemy—his proven willingness to do *anything* to achieve a goal or make a point. If evil was, as one of Gurney's philosophy professors had once insisted, "intellect in the service of appetite, unrestrained by empathy," then Peter Pan was evil incarnate.

What else was he sure of?

Well, there could be no doubt about the risk to Esti's career. She'd put everything at stake to join the crew of what was feeling increasingly like a runaway train.

And there was at least one other undeniable fact. He was again putting himself in the crosshairs of a killer. He was tempted to believe that this occasion was different—that the circumstances demanded it, that their precautions permitted it—but he knew he wouldn't be able to convince anyone else of that. Certainly not Madeleine. Certainly not Malcolm Claret.

There is nothing in life that matters but love.

That's what Claret had said as Gurney was leaving his little sun porch office.

As he reflected on the statement now, he realized two things. It was absolutely true. And it was absolutely impossible to keep it in the forefront of his mind. The contradiction struck him as yet another nasty trick played on human beings by human nature.

He was saved from sliding further into a pit of pointless speculation and depression by the ringing of the landline in the den.

The ID screen announced it was Hardwick.

"Yes, Jack?"

"Ten minutes after leaving your house I got a call from my Interpol guy, probably the last one we're going to get, from the tone of his voice. I've been pushing him pretty hard for every damn detail he could find in their old files on the Panikos family. Made a real pain in the ass of myself—which isn't my true nature—but you wanted more information, and I live to be of service to my betters."

"A very positive quality. And you found out what?"

"Remember the fire that destroyed the family gift shop in the village of Lykonos? Burned everyone to death, except the adopted firebug? Well, turns out it wasn't just a gift shop. It had a little annex, a second business, run by the mother." He paused. "Need I say more?"

"Let me guess. The annex was a flower shop. And the mother's name was Florence."

"Florencia, to be precise."

"She died with the rest of the family, right?"

"Up in flames, one and all. And now little Peter likes riding around in a van with a sign that says FLOWERS BY FLORENCE. Any ideas about that, ace? You figure he just likes thinking about his mom while he's killing people?"

Gurney didn't answer right away. For the second time that day, someone's use of a short phrase—earlier it was Esti's comment on "those shots from the hill"—sent him off on a mental tangent. This time it was Hardwick's "up in flames."

The words brought to mind an old case involving a flaming auto wreck. It was one of the instructive examples he'd used in an academy seminar called "The Investigative Mind-set." The odd thing was that this was the third time in as many days that something had brought that case to mind. In this instance, hearing "up in flames" seemed a simple enough trigger, but nothing so obvious had occurred on the two previous occasions.

Gurney considered himself as far from superstitious as a man could be, but when something like that—a specific case—kept intruding into his consciousness, he'd learned not to ignore it. The question was, what was he supposed to make of it?

"Hey, you still there, ace?"

"I'm here. Just got caught up thinking about something you said."

"You thinking like me that our little maniac might have some mommy problems?"

"A lot of serial killers do."

"That's a fact. Maternal magic. Anyway, that's it for now. Just thought you'd want to know about Florencia."

Hardwick broke the connection, which was fine with Gurney, whose mind had been taken over by the flaming auto wreck case. He recalled that the previous event triggering the same memory had been Esti's story about the shooting in the alley. Was there some similarity between the incidents? Was it possible that they both related in some way to the Spalter case? He couldn't see any connection at all. But maybe Esti could.

He called her cell number, got her voice mail, and left a brief message.

Three minutes later, she called him back. "Hi. Something wrong?" Her voice still carried some of the anxiety she'd expressed at their morning meeting.

"Nothing wrong. I may be just wasting your time. But my mind seems to be making some kind of connection between two cases—your alley case and an old NYPD case—and maybe between them and the Spalter case."

"What kind of connection?"

"I don't know. Maybe if I told you the NYPD story you'd see something I'm missing."

"Sure. Why not? I don't know if I can help, but go ahead."

Half apologetically, he told her the story.

"The accident scene at first seemed easy enough to explain. A middle-aged man on his way home from work one night was driving down a hill. At the bottom of the hill, the road made a turn. His car, however, proceeded straight ahead through the guardrail, coming to rest nose-down in a ravine. The gas tank exploded. There was an intense fire, but enough remained of the driver to perform an autopsy and conclude that he had suffered a massive coronary. This was listed as the precipitating cause of his loss of control and the subsequent fatal accident. That would have been the end of the story, if it weren't for the fact that the investigating officer had an uncomfortable feeling about it that wouldn't go away. He went to the location where the vehicle had been towed, and went over it one more time. That's when he noticed that the areas of the most severe impact and fire damage inside the car didn't quite coincide with those outside. At that point, he ordered a complete forensic workup on the vehicle."

"Wait a second," said Esti. "The inside and outside didn't *coincide*?"

"He noticed that there was heat and concussive damage inside the passenger compartment that didn't seem to line up directly with similar points of damage to the exterior. The explanation, discovered by the forensic lab, was that there'd been *two* explosions. Before the gas tank blew up, there was a smaller explosion *inside* the vehicle—under the driver's seat. It was that first explosion that resulted in the driver's loss of control, as well as his coronary. Further chemical tests revealed that both the initial blast and the gas tank blast had been remotely detonated."

"From where?"

"Possibly from a vehicle following the target vehicle."

"Hmm. Interesting. But what point are you making?"

"I don't know. Maybe none. But the case keeps coming to mind. It came to mind immediately when you told your story about the shooting in the alley. I know a psychologist who talks about something called pattern resonance—how things remind us of other things because they share a structural similarity. And this can occur without our conscious knowledge of what the similarity is."

Beyond a barely audible "Hmm," she didn't respond.

He felt uneasy, even a bit embarrassed. He didn't mind sharing his ideas, concerns, hypotheses. He was a lot less comfortable sharing his confusion, his failure to grasp some connection he hoped might be present.

When she finally did speak, her voice was tentative. "I guess I can see what you're saying. Let me sleep on it, okay?"

Chapter 53

A Terrible Calm

The feeling that he'd dumped his quandary unfairly in Esti's lap was still with him that evening. Finding significant patterns in situations and relating one to another was supposedly *his* strength.

The sun had set, and colors were fading from the hills and fields around the house. It was past dinnertime, but he had no appetite. He made himself a cup of coffee and drank it black, his only concession to his need for nourishment being the addition of an extra spoonful of sugar.

Perhaps he'd been staring too hard, too directly, at the problem. Perhaps it was another example of the dim-star phenomenon, which he'd discovered one night lying in a hammock gazing up at the sky. There are some stars so distant that their faint pinpricks of light will not register at the center of the retina, which by some slight measure is less sensitive than the rest of the retinal surface. The only way to see one of these stars is to look several degrees to one side of it or the other. To direct scrutiny the star is invisible. But look away, and there it is.

A frustrating puzzle was often like that. Let go of it for a bit and the answer might suddenly appear. A name or a word one was struggling to remember might surface only when the struggle had been abandoned. He knew all this, but his tenacity—Madeleine called it stubbornness—made it difficult for him to put anything aside.

Sometimes the decision was made for him by simple exhaustion. Or by an external intervention, like getting a phone call—which is what happened now.

The call was from Kyle.

"Hey, Dad, how's everything?"

"Fine. Are you still up in Syracuse?"

"Yeah, still here. In fact, I think I'm going to stay over. There's a giant art show at the university this weekend and Kim has some stuff in it, some art videos. So I figured I'd stay up here, like maybe through lunch, then . . . then I'm not sure what. Originally, on my trip up to see you, I'd been thinking of going to the fair, but now . . . with your situation . . ."

"There's no reason for you not to go to the fair. I was only concerned about your being right here at the house—and even that concern is probably way out of proportion to the chance of any real problem. If you want to go to the fair, go."

Kyle sighed—a sound of uncertainty.

"Really. Go. There's no reason not to."

There was another sigh, followed by a pause. "Saturday night is the big night, right? With all the main events?"

"Far as I know."

"Well, maybe I'll drop by for a quick look on my way back to the city. Maybe for the demolition derby. I'll check in with you again when I figure out what I'm doing."

"Great. And don't worry about anything here. Everything'll be fine."

"Okay, Dad. Just be careful."

Although the call had lasted less than two minutes, it rearranged Gurney's thoughts for the next half hour—overlaying his murder case concerns with paternal worries.

Telling himself finally that Kyle's possible involvement with Kim Corazon was none of his business, he tried to steer his mind back to the conundrums surrounding the Spalter case and Peter Pan.

This time, rather than the phone, it was exhaustion that intervened—the kind of exhaustion that made linear thought impossible.

It was then, sitting by the still open double doors, watching the dusk darken into night, that he heard that familiar eerie sound in the woods—that quavering wail—followed by a profound silence that was stranger than the sound itself. To his deeply weary state of mind, it was the silence of emptiness and isolation.

The silence was interrupted by a low, directionless rumble that seemed to come from the earth itself. Or was it from the sky? Surely it must be thunder from some miles distant, echoed and muffled by the surrounding hills and valleys. When it faded away like the growl of an old dog, it left behind a disquieting stillness, a terrible calm that by some errant-crosscurrent in the brain brought to mind a childhood memory of the desolate no-man's-land between his parents.

It was that disconcerting twist in his stream of consciousness that finally convinced him of his dire need for sleep and sent him to bed— but not before locking the doors and windows, cleaning and loading his .32 Beretta, and placing the reliable little pistol within easy reach on the night table.

Part Four

Perfect
Justice

The Growling of
the Tiger

*T*he blackbirds are shrieking.

He looks up from the cell phone into which he has been entering the special list of numbers. He knows that the shrieking of the blackbirds is a territorial defense, a red alert to their kind, a call to arms against the trespasser.

None of his own electronic alarms are flashing, however, meaning that there is no human encroachment. But he peers out anyway through each of the four small windows in the sides of the little cinder-block building, scanning the hummocky beaver pond and boggy woods.

There are crows perching in the tops of three dead, root-drowned trees. The crows, he concludes, are the interlopers who have upset the blackbirds, provoking their high-pitched screeches. He finds the protection they afford comforting. Like the creaking treads on a staircase might alert him to an intruder.

Or like the dismal little structure itself, in the midst of a hundred acres of low-lying forest and swamp, is comforting. Nearly inaccessible, uninviting in the extreme, it is his ideal home away from home. He has many homes away from home. Places to stay while he conducts his business. Fulfills his contracts. This particular place, with no visible trail in from the public road, has always felt more secure than most.

Fat Gus had represented another kind of trail. A trail of sensitive information. Information that could be ruinous. But that had been eradicated at its source. Which made this business with Bincher and Hardwick and Gurney so incomprehensible. So infuriating.

At the thought of Bincher, his gaze drifts to a shadowy corner of the garage-like room. To a blue and white plastic picnic cooler. He smiles. But the smile quickly fades.

The smile fades because the nightmare keeps returning to his mind, more vividly than ever. The nightmare's images are with him almost continually now—ever since he caught sight of that Ferris wheel at the fairgrounds.

The Ferris wheel has insinuated itself into his nightmare—enmeshed with the merry-go-round music, the terrible laughter. The hideous, stinking, wheezing clown. The low, vibrating growl of the tiger.

And now Hardwick and Gurney.

Swirling around him, closing in.

The spiral tightening, the final confrontation inevitable.

It would be a great risk, but there could be a great reward. A great relief.

The nightmare might at last be extinguished.

He goes to the darkest corner of the room, to a small table. On the table are a large candle and a pack of matches. He picks up the matches and lights the candle.

He lifts the candle and gazes at the flame. He loves its shape, its purity, its power.

He imagines the confrontation—the conflagration. His smile returns.

He goes back to his cell phone—goes back to entering the special numbers.

The blackbirds are shrieking. The crows are perching uneasily on the dead black treetops.

Chapter 54

Cornered

Gurney put no stock in dreams. If he did, that night's marathon could have occupied a week of nonstop analysis. But he held a solidly pragmatic view—and generally low opinion—of these outlandish processions of images and events.

He'd long believed they were nothing more than by-products of the nightly filing and indexing process the brain employs in the movement of recorded experience from short-term to long-term memory. Bits of visual and aural data are stirred up and mashed together, narrative strings are triggered, vignettes are constructed—but with no more meaning than a suitcase of old photos, love letters, or term papers shredded and reassembled by a monkey.

The one practical effect of a night of discomfiting dreams was a lingering need for more sleep—which resulted in Gurney's rising an hour later than usual, with a mild headache. When he was finally taking his first sip of coffee, the sun, rendered pallid by a thin overcast, had already risen well above the eastern ridge. The sense he'd had the night before of an unsettling quietness after the eerie sound in the woods was still with him.

He felt cornered. Cornered by his unwillingness to drop out of the game in time. Cornered by his appetite for control, coherence, completion. Cornered by his own "plan" to break the case open by provoking the shooter into taking a foolish and fatal risk. Pulled forward and backward by alternating currents that seemed one minute to lead to success and the next to defeat, Gurney decided to seek the comfort that came with taking action.

Hardwick would be returning that evening from Scranton Surveillance & Survival with the video cameras they needed, and they would have the following morning, Sunday, to install the units in a way to ensure that anyone approaching within half a mile of Gurney's house would be detected. Strategic placement was a crucial factor, and pre-selection of the sites would save precious time Sunday morning.

He went to the mudroom and pulled on a pair of knee-high rubber boots—protection against thistles, brambles, and wild raspberry thorns. Noticing a remnant of odor from the rooster carcass, he opened the mudroom window to let in fresh air, then went out to the pile of henhouse construction materials, from which he borrowed a metal tape measure, a ball of yellow cord, and a jackknife. With these items in hand he set off for the woods on the far side of the pond to begin identifying and marking key video locations.

The goal was to select the spots from which an array of motion-activated cameras and wireless transmitters could provide full coverage of the woods and fields around his home. According to Hardwick, each camera would generate its own GPS coordinates, displaying this information along with its video on a receiving monitor inside the house, so the location of Peter Pan—or any intruder—would be known immediately.

Contemplating the technical capability of the equipment, Gurney experienced if not quite optimism at least some relief from the fear that the plan was too flimsy to succeed. The logical process of measuring angles and distances also had a positive effect. With a fair degree of discipline and determination, he completed his site-selection project in a little more than four hours.

He'd arranged his progress around his fifty-acre property and the relevant sections of his neighbors' properties so that he would complete his circuit at the top of Barrow Hill. He was convinced that this was the spot Panikos would choose. Therefore, this was the place, with its various trails and access points, that he wanted to commit most carefully to memory.

When he finally made his way back to the house, it was mid-afternoon and the morning overcast had thickened into a featureless gray sky. There was no movement in the air, but there was no peace in this stillness. As he stopped in the mudroom to remove his boots, the sight of the sink brought to mind the question of how and when to let Madeleine know about the cause of the rooster's death. *Whether* to tell her was not the issue. She had an innate preference for candor over evasion, and significant omissions could have a high price. After considering the *when* and *how* options, he decided to tell her as soon as possible and in person.

The half-hour drive to the Winkler mini-farm was filled with a low-level foreboding. Although the need to reveal the truth was clear, that reality did not change how he felt.

A quarter mile from his destination, it occurred to him that he should have called ahead. What if they were all at the fairgrounds? Or what if the Winklers were at the house and Madeleine was at the fairgrounds? But as soon as he pulled into their driveway he saw Madeleine. She was standing in a fenced pen, gazing down at a small goat.

He parked next to the house. As he approached the pen, she showed no surprise at his arrival—just gave him a brief smile and a longer assessing gaze.

"Communing with the goat?" he asked.

"They're supposedly quite intelligent."

"I've heard that rumor."

"What's on your mind?"

"You mean, what am I doing here?"

"No, I mean, you look like you have something on your mind. I'm wondering what it is."

He sighed, tried to relax. "The Spalter case."

She was petting the goat's head gently. "Anything in particular about it?"

"Couple of things." He chose to speak about what seemed a less fraught issue first. "The case keeps bringing to mind an old auto crash investigation."

"Is there a connection?"

"I don't know." He made a face. "Jesus."

"What's the matter?"

"This place stinks of manure."

She nodded. "I kind of like it."

"You *like* it?"

"It's a natural farm smell. Nothing wrong with it."

"Jesus."

"So what about this auto crash?"

"Do we have to stand here with the goat?"

She looked around, then gestured in the direction of a weathered picnic table in a grassy area behind the house. "Over there?"

"Fine."

She gave the goat a few more little strokes on the head, then left the pen, secured the gate, and led the way to the table.

They sat across from each other, and he told her the story of the explosive crash—the initial mistaken impression of what had happened and the subsequent discoveries—just as he had related it all to Esti.

When he'd come to the end, Madeleine gave him a quizzical look. "So?"

"It just keeps coming to mind, and I don't know why. Any ideas?"

"Ideas?"

"Does anything about the case strike you as especially significant?"

"No, not really. Nothing beyond the obvious."

"The obvious being . . . ?"

"The sequence."

"What about it?"

"The assumption that the heart attack came before the crash and the crash came before the explosion, instead of the explosion coming first and causing everything else. It was a reasonable assumption, though. Middle-aged man has heart attack, loses control, drives off the road, car crashes and the gas tank explodes. Makes total sense."

"Total sense, yes, except that it was all wrong. That was the point I'd make when I talked about the case in one of my academy seminars—that something can make perfect sense and be perfectly wrong. Our brains are so fond of coherence that they confuse 'making sense' with the truth."

She cocked her head curiously. "If you know all this, why are you asking me about it?"

"Just in case you saw something that I was missing."

"You drove all the way over here to ask me about that story?"

"Not just that." He hesitated, then forced out the words. "I discovered something about the rooster."

She blinked. "Horace?"

"I discovered what killed him."

She sat motionless, waiting.

"It wasn't another animal." He hesitated again. "Someone shot him."

Her eyes widened. "Someone ... ?"

"I don't know for sure who it was."

"David, don't ..." There was an edge of warning in her voice.

"I don't know for sure who it was, but it's possible that it was Panikos."

The rhythm of her breathing changed and her face filled slowly with a barely contained fury. "The crazy assassin you're after? He ... killed Horace?"

"I don't know that for sure. I said it's possible."

"Possible." She repeated the word as though it were a sound without a meaning. Her eyes were fixed intently on his. "Why did you come here and tell me this?"

"I thought it was the right thing to do."

"That's the only reason?"

"What else?"

"You tell me."

"I don't what you're getting at. I just thought I should tell you."

"How did you find out?"

"That he was shot? By examining the body."

"You dug him up?"

"Yes."

"Why?"

"Because ... because something came up in our discussion yesterday that gave me the idea that it could have been a gunshot that killed him."

"Yesterday?"

"In my meeting with Hardwick and Esti."

"So you thought I needed to know today? But I didn't need to know yesterday?"

"I told you as soon as it was clear to me that I should tell you. Maybe I should have told you yesterday. What's your point?"

"It's *your* point I'm wondering about."

"I don't get it."

Her mouth formed a small ironic smile. "What's next on your agenda?"

"My agenda?" It began to dawn on him what she was getting at—and that, as usual, with relatively little evidence, she had moved quickly to the finish line. "We need to capture Panikos before he slips back into whatever dark hole he inhabits between jobs."

She nodded, communicating nothing.

"As long as he believes we can damage him, he'll hang around and . . . try to stop us. His attempt to do that will make him vulnerable to capture."

"*Vulnerable to capture.*" She articulated the phrase slowly, musingly—as though it summed up all the misleading jargon in the world. "And you want me to stay here, so you can risk your life without worrying about me?"

She didn't really seem to be asking a question, so he offered no response.

"You'll be the bait in the game once again. Right?"

That wasn't really a question either.

A long silence fell between them. The overcast sky was heavy now, slatey and dusklike. A phone began ringing inside the house, but Madeleine made no move to answer it. It rang seven times.

"I asked Dennis about that bird," she said.

"What bird?"

"The strange one we sometimes hear at dusk. Dennis and Deirdre have heard it too. He checked it out with the Mountain Wildlife Council. They told him it's a rare type of mourning dove that's found only in upstate New York and parts of New England, and only above certain elevations in the mountains. The local Native Americans considered it sacred. They called it 'Spirit Who Speaks for the Dead.' The shaman would interpret its cries. Sometimes they were accusations, sometimes they were messages of forgiveness."

Gurney wondered about the chain of associations that led Madeleine to her mourning dove story. Sometimes when it would seem to him that she'd changed the subject, he'd discover that she hadn't changed it at all.

Chapter 55

Ring Around the Rosies

On his drive home from the Winkler farm Gurney felt alternately free and trapped.

Free to proceed according to his plan. And trapped by its limitations, by the rickety assumptions on which it rested, and by his own compulsion to press forward. He suspected that Malcolm Claret and Madeleine were right—that there was something pathological in his appetite for risk. But self-knowledge is not a therapeutic panacea. Knowing who you are doesn't automatically convey the power to change who you are.

The fact that mattered most to him at the moment was that Madeleine intended to stay at the Winklers' at least through Tuesday, the final day of the fair, safely out of the way. It was still only Saturday. The promotion ads for his Monday-night *Criminal Conflict* tell-all revelations would start running the next morning on the Sunday talk shows. The ads would be touting not only the revelation of the shooter's identity in the Spalter case but also the disclosure of the sensitive secret that the shooter was trying to protect. If Panikos wanted to keep that from happening, he had a very narrow window of opportunity—from Sunday morning to Monday evening—to make his move. And Gurney intended to be ready for him.

Driving up the darkening road to his property, he tried to hang on to a reasonable sense of confidence. But Madeleine's enigmatic story about that damn spirit-bird kept undermining whatever pragmatic thoughts he was able to muster.

As he passed the barn and the house came into view, he noticed that the light over the side door was on, as well as the light in the mudroom. He felt a quick stab of fight-or-flight adrenaline—which subsided into an uneasy curiosity when he saw a glint of light reflecting off the chrome of Kyle's BSA. He continued up through the pasture and parked next to the motorcycle.

Inside the house, he heard the shower running upstairs. When he found the hall light on and all the kitchen lights, too, his uneasiness was replaced by a little surge of déjà vu—perhaps arising from memories of how when Kyle was a young teenager living with his mother and visiting Gurney on weekends, he'd seemed incapable of remembering to turn off the lights when he left a room.

He went into the den to check for messages on the landline and on his cell, which he'd neglected to bring with him on his trip to see Madeleine. There was nothing on the landline. There were three messages on his cell. The first was from Esti, but the transmission was too broken up to understand anything.

The second was from Hardwick, who, through a profusion of obscenities, managed to convey that he was stuck on I-81 in a mammoth traffic jam due to roadwork in progress, "except there isn't any fucking work actually in progress, just miles of fucking orange cones blocking two of the three fucking lanes"—so he wouldn't be delivering the camera equipment from SSS to Walnut Crossing until "bloody fucking midnight. Or bloody fucking whenever."

The logistics delay was an inconvenience for Hardwick but not really a problem, since they hadn't planned to set out the cameras until the following morning anyway. Gurney listened to the third message, another from Esti, broken up and finally fading away altogether, as though her battery was dying.

He was about to call her back when he heard a sound in the hallway. Kyle appeared at the den doorway in jeans and a T-shirt, his hair wet from the shower.

"Hey, Dad, what's up?"

"I was out for a while. Went to see Madeleine. I was surprised to see your bike outside. I didn't expect you back here at the house. Did I miss a message?"

"No, sorry about that. My plan was to go straight to the fair. Then, when I was passing through the village, I got the idea to stop for a quick shower and change my clothes. Hope you don't mind."

"It was just . . . unexpected. I'm more focused than usual on anything out of the ordinary."

"Hey, speaking of that, is your neighbor down the road some kind of hunter or something?"

"Hunter?"

"When I was coming up the road, there was a guy down in the pines by the next house, maybe half a mile down from your barn—with a rifle, I think?"

"When was this?"

"Maybe half an hour ago?" Kyle's eyes widened as he spoke. "Shit, you don't think . . ."

"How big a guy?"

"How big? I don't know . . . maybe bigger than average. I mean, he was way back from the road, so I'm not sure. And he was definitely down on your neighbor's property, not yours."

"With a rifle?"

"Or maybe a shotgun. I only saw it for a second, as I was riding by."

"You didn't notice anything special about the gun? Anything unusual about the barrel?"

"Jesus, Dad, I don't know. I should have paid more attention. I guess I figured everyone up here in the country is some kind of hunter." He paused, looking increasingly like he was in pain. "You don't think it was your neighbor?"

Gurney pointed to the light switch by the doorway. "Turn that off for a second."

With the light off, Gurney lowered the blinds on both of the den windows. "Okay, you can switch it back on."

"Jesus. What's going on?"

"Just another precaution."

"Against what?"

"Probably nothing tonight. Don't worry about it."

"So, who . . . who was that guy in the woods?"

"Most likely my neighbor, like you said."

"But this isn't hunting season, is it?"

"No, but if someone is having coyote problems, or woodchuck problems, or possum problems, or porcupine problems, the season doesn't matter."

"A second ago you said there probably would be nothing to worry about *tonight*. When are you thinking there *will* be something to worry about?"

Gurney hadn't intended to do this, but explaining the whole situation seemed now to be the only honest approach. "It's a complicated story. Have a seat."

They sat together on the den couch and Gurney spent the next twenty minutes filling Kyle in on the parts of the Spalter case background he wasn't yet aware of, the current status of things, and the plan being launched the following day.

As he listened, Kyle's expression grew confused. "Wait a second. What do you mean when you say that RAM-TV is going to run these program announcements starting *tomorrow morning*?"

"Just that. Starting with the Sunday-morning talk shows, and running through the day."

"You mean the announcements saying that you're going to be making big revelations about the case and about the shooter?"

"Right."

"They're supposed to run *tomorrow*?"

"Yes. Why are you—"

"You don't know? You don't know that those announcements started running *yesterday afternoon*? And that they've been running *all day today*?"

"*What?*"

"The announcements you're describing—they've been on RAM-TV for at least the past twenty-four hours."

"How do you know this?"

"Kim has her friggin' TV on all the time. Jeez, I didn't realize . . . I'm sorry . . . I didn't know it wasn't supposed to be happening. I should've called you."

"There's no way you could have known." Gurney felt sick, absorbing the shock, thinking his way through the implications.

Then he called Hardwick and told him what he'd just learned.

Hardwick, still stuck in his traffic jam, made a sound between gagging and growling. "*Yesterday?* They started running the fucking thing *yesterday?*"

"Yesterday, and last night, and all day today."

"That fucking Bork! That scum-sucking fuck! That rotten piece of shit! I'll tear that putrid little fucker's head off and shove it up his ass!"

"Sounds good to me, Jack, but we need to deal with a few practical issues first."

"I told that little Bork bastard that the timing of the plan was crucial—that people's lives were at stake—that the timing was a fucking life-or-death issue! I made that perfectly clear to that shit-eating slimebag!"

"Glad to hear it. But right now we need to make some adjustments in the plan."

"First thing you need to do is adjust yourself the fuck out of there. Go! Like, now!"

"I agree the situation requires urgent action. But before we jump overboard—"

"GET THE FUCK OUT OF THERE! Or at least do what Esti wanted to do from the start—call in the fucking cavalry!"

"It sounds to me like we're about to do what we want Panikos to do—panic and make a mistake."

"Look, I admire all this cool-under-pressure shit, but it's time to admit that the plan is fucked, toss in the cards, and leave the table."

"Where are you?"

"What?"

"Where are you, exactly?"

"Where am I? I'm still in Pennsylvania, maybe thirty miles from Hancock. What the hell difference does it make where I am?"

"I don't know yet. I just want to give this whole thing a little more thought before I go screaming down the hill."

"Davey, for Christ's sake, either go down that goddamn hill now, or call in the fucking troops."

"I appreciate the concern, Jack. I really do. Do me a favor and let Esti know about our new situation. I'll get back to you in a little while." Gurney ended the call over a final shouted objection. Thirty seconds later, his phone rang, but he let it go into voice mail.

Kyle was staring at him, wide-eyed. "That was that Hardwick guy on the phone, right?"

"Yes."

"He was shouting so loud at you, I could hear everything he said."

Gurney nodded. "He was a little disturbed."

"You're not?"

"Of course I am. But going nuts over it is a waste of time. Like most situations in life, there's only one question that matters: *What do we do now?*"

Kyle watched him, waiting for him to go on.

"I guess one thing we could do now is turn off as many inside lights as we can, and lower the blinds in any room where we want to keep a light on. I'll check the bathrooms and bedrooms. You turn off the kitchen and mudroom lights."

Kyle went out through the kitchen to the mudroom, while Gurney headed for the staircase. Before he got to it, Kyle called to him.

"Hey, Dad, come here a minute."

"What is it?"

"Come here, look at this."

Gurney found Kyle in the hallway by the side door, pointing through the glass at something outside.

"You have a flat tire. Did you know that?"

Gurney looked out. Even in the dim light cast by the forty-watt bulb over the door, there was no doubt that the front tire on the driver's side was dead flat. And there was no doubt in his mind that the tire had been perfectly okay when he drove up to the house half an hour earlier.

"You have a jack and a spare in the trunk?" Kyle asked.

"Yes, but we're not going to use them."

"Why not?"

"Why do you think the tire is flat?"

"Because you ran over a nail?"

"That's possible. Another possibility is that it was punctured by a bullet while it was parked there. And if that's the case, the question is *why?*"

Kyle's eyes widened again. "To keep us from driving away?"

"Maybe. But if I were a sniper and my goal was to keep someone from driving away, I'd shoot out as many tires as I could—not just one."

"Then why ... ?"

"Maybe because one flat can be dealt with—with a jack and a spare, like you said."

"So . . . ?"

"A jack, a spare, and one of us kneeling out there for five or ten minutes to do the job."

"You mean, like a sitting duck?"

"Yes. Speaking of which, let's kill the mudroom light and get away from the door."

Kyle swallowed. "Because that weird little hit man you just told me about might be out there . . . waiting?"

"It's possible."

"The guy I saw with the rifle down in the pine woods—he wasn't that small. Maybe it was your neighbor after all?"

"I'm not sure. What I do know is that a very provocative message has been running on TV, a message designed to get Peter Pan to come after me. I have to assume that it might have worked. It would also be smart to assume—"

He was interrupted by his cell phone ringing in the den.

It was Esti. She sounded stressed. "Where are you?"

He told her.

"Why are you still there? You better get the hell out before something happens."

"You sound like Jack."

"I sound like Jack because he's right. You have to get out now. I called you twice today after I found out about the screwup on TV. I called to tell you to get out."

"It might be a little late for that now."

"Why?"

"Someone may have put a bullet in my front tire."

"Oh, shit. This is true? If this is true, you got to bring in some help. Right now. You want me to come, I can be there in maybe forty-five minutes."

"That's not a good idea."

"Okay, then call 911."

"Like I said, you sound like Jack."

"Who the hell cares what I sound like? The point is, you need help *now*."

"I need to think it through."

"*Think?* That's what you're going to do? *Think?* While somebody's shooting at you?"

"At my tire."

"David, you are a crazy person. Do you know that? Crazy! The man is *shooting,* and you're *thinking.*"

"I have to go, Esti. I'll call you back in a little while." He ended the call the same way as he had with Hardwick—breaking the connection in the middle of a cry of protest.

That's when he remembered the message that had come in right after he'd broken off his conversation with Hardwick. He'd assumed it was the man trying to finish what he had to say, but now, as he checked, he saw that the call's origin wasn't Hardwick's phone but an unknown number.

He played the message back.

As he listened to it, a chill crept up his back, raising the hairs on his neck.

A falsetto voice, shrill and metallic, a voice not quite human, was singing the most bizarre and least-understood of all children's nursery rhymes—an inanely lilting allusion to the roseate skin sores, the flowers used to stifle the stench of rotting flesh, and the ashes of burnt corpses during one of Europe's deadliest plagues.

> *Ring around the rosies,*
> *Pocket full of posies.*
> *Ashes, ashes,*
> *All fall down.*

Chapter 56

A Fatal Rage

"Dad?"

Kyle and his father were standing uneasily near the fireplace end of the living room—the end farthest from the kitchen area, and well away from the doors. The blinds were lowered at all the windows. The only light came from a small table lamp.

"Yes?"

"Before the phone rang, you were starting to say that we should assume that the Peter Pan guy might be out there somewhere?" Kyle shot a nervous glance at the glass doors.

Gurney took a long moment to answer. His mind kept going back to the creepy, singsong nursery-rhyme message—and how its words reflected not only its grotesque bubonic plague origins but also the Flowers by Florence and arson elements, Panikos's own MO.

"He *might* be out there, yes."

"You have any idea *where* out there?"

"If I'm right about the flat tire, he'd be on the west side of us, and Barrow Hill would be his likely choice."

"You think maybe he'll sneak down here by the house?"

"I doubt it. If I'm right about the tire, he has a sniper rifle with him. In that game, distance gives him a major advantage. My best guess is that he'll stay—"

There was a startling flash of light, a sharp explosion, and something came smashing through one of the kitchen windows, flinging shards of glass everywhere.

Kyle cried out, "What the fuck . . . ?"

Gurney grabbed him and pulled him to the floor, then drew the

Beretta from his ankle holster, extinguished the lamp by yanking the cord out of the wall socket, and scrambled across the floor to the nearest window. He waited a moment, listening, then parted the bottom two slats of the blinds and peered out. It took him several seconds to comprehend what he was looking at. Scattered over a broad area out beyond the patio were the remains of the henhouse materials, many of the pieces burning.

Kyle's voice behind him was a rasping whisper. "What the hell . . . ?"

"The lumber pile . . . it's . . . blown up."

"*Blown . . . what . . . how?*"

"Some kind of . . . I don't know . . . incendiary device?"

"*Incendiary?* What the hell . . . ?"

Gurney was absorbed in scanning the area as best he could in the near-darkness.

"Dad?"

"Just a minute." Adrenaline surging, he was squinting out at the perimeter of the area, checking for any movement. Also checking the little fires, many of which now seemed to be dying out in the damp treated lumber almost as quickly as they were ignited.

"*Why?*" There was a desperation in Kyle's question that made Gurney respond.

"I don't know. Same purpose as the flat tire, maybe? He wants me out there? He seems to be in a hurry."

"Jesus! You mean he was just . . . *just out there himself . . . planting a bomb?*"

"Maybe earlier, while I was at the Winklers', before you got back from Syracuse."

"Jesus. A bomb? With a timer?"

"More likely a cell phone detonator. More controllable, more precise."

"So . . . what now?"

"Where are the keys to your motorcycle?"

"In the ignition. Why?"

"Follow me."

Crawling, he led Kyle across the floor and out of the room—now flickeringly illuminated through the glass doors by the burning lumber strewn outside—down the back hallway into the dark den. He felt his way around the furniture to the north window, lifted the blinds, opened it, and, with the Beretta still in his hand, eased himself carefully out onto the ground.

Kyle did the same.

Fifty feet ahead of them, between the house and the high pasture, there was a small hardwood thicket, just barely visible at the outer edge of the faint light cast by the fire, where Gurney sometimes parked his rider mower. He pointed at the black bulk of a giant oak. "Directly behind that tree there are two boulders, with some space between them. Slip into that space and stay there until I call you."

"What are you going to do?"

"I'm going to neutralize the problem."

"*What?*"

"No time to explain. Just do as I say. Please." He pointed again, more urgently. "Over there. Behind the tree. Between the boulders. We're running out of time. Now!"

Kyle hurried toward the thicket and disappeared out of the wavering firelight into the darkness. Then Gurney made his way around to the corner of the house where the BSA was parked. He was fairly sure that in that position it would be out of sight from the top of Barrow Hill. He hoped Kyle was right about the key. If it wasn't in the ignition ... But it was.

He slipped the Beretta back in his ankle holster and straddled the bike. It had been more than twenty-five years since he'd been on a similar motorcycle—the old Triumph 650 he rode in his college days. He quickly familiarized himself with the positions of brakes, clutch, shift lever. Looking down at the gas tank, the handlebars, the chrome headlight, the front fender, the front tire—it all began to come back to him. Even the physical sensation, the recollection of balance and momentum—it was all there, as though it had been preserved in some airtight container of memory, alive and undiminished.

He grasped the throttle ends of the handlebars and started easing the bike up from its leaning position, when a momentary surge of flame from the burning lumber illuminated something dark and bulky on the ground by the asparagus patch. He let the bike settle back on its kickstand, slowly reached down and got the pistol back in his hand. As best he could tell in the fluctuating light, the object on the ground wasn't moving. It was about the right size for a human body. Something on the near side looked like it might be an extended arm.

Gurney raised his weapon, stepped carefully off the bike, and moved forward as far as the corner of the house. He was sure now that he was looking at the prone body of a man, and at the end of that putative outstretched arm he could make out roughly the shape of a rifle.

He got down on his knees and took a quick glance around the side of the house—confirming that his car was blocking the line of sight between Barrow Hill and the space he'd have to cross to reach the figure on the ground. Without any further delay, he crept quickly ahead, Beretta ready, eyes fixed on the rifle. With about three feet to go, his free hand landed on a wet, sticky patch of earth.

By its subtle but distinctive odor, he realized he was crawling into a pool of blood.

"Ach!" His whispered exclamation was as reflexive as his recoiling from the contact. Having begun his NYPD career at the height of the AIDS terror, he'd been indoctrinated to regard blood as a deadly toxin until proven otherwise. That feeling was still with him. Miserably regretting the lack of gloves, but desperately needing to understand the situation, he forced himself forward. On a scale of zero to ten, the dying light from the scattered debris still burning near the asparagus patch was varying from zero to two.

He reached the rifle first, grasping it tightly and pulling it from the hand that held it. It was a common lever-action deer rifle. But deer season was four months away. Sliding the rifle behind him, he moved closer to the body, close enough to see that the source of the blood on the ground was an ugly wound in the side of the neck—a wound so deep, ripping completely through the carotid artery, that death would have occurred within seconds.

The object that had caused it was still embedded there. It looked like two knife blades joined at one end to form a strange U-shaped weapon. Then he recognized what it actually was. It was one of the sharp metal joist hangers that had been delivered with the lumber. The obvious explanation was that the explosion had propelled that nasty piece of hardware with terrific force at the man with the rifle, cutting his throat. But that led to other questions.

Did the man set off the explosion himself, then suffer this unintended consequence? But it seemed unlikely that he would have detonated the device while he was still within range of the debris. Perhaps he detonated it by accident? Or in ignorance of the strength of the explosive charge? Or was he the unfortunate accomplice of a second individual who acted too soon? But questions like these begged a more fundamental question.

Who the hell was he?

Violating crime scene protocol, Gurney grasped the man's heavily muscled shoulder and, with some effort, rolled him over for a better view of his face.

His first conclusion was that the man was definitely not his neighbor. His second conclusion, delayed by the lack of light and by the man's spectacularly broken nose, probably caused by falling on his face, was that he'd seen that face before. It took a few moments for the identity to register.

It was Mick Klemper.

That's when Gurney noted a second odor, not as subtle as the blood itself. Alcohol. And that led him to a third conclusion—one that was assumption-ridden but plausible.

Klemper, possibly like Panikos, had seen—or been told about—the *Criminal Conflict* program teaser, with its promises of sensational revelations, and it had provoked him to take action. Drunk and enraged—perhaps in a crazed effort at damage control, or driven by fury at what he surely would have perceived as a broken promise—he'd come after the man who was betraying him, the man who was ending his career and his life as he knew it.

Drunk and enraged, he'd come gunning for Gurney, skulking around the woods, sneaking up to the house as darkness fell. Drunk and enraged, he hadn't given a second thought to what a dangerous place that might be.

Chapter 57

Pocket Full of Posies

Once again Gurney faced the simple, urgent question: *What now?*

In a less pressured position, he might have chosen the sanest and safest option—an immediate call to 911. A state police officer, however demented his motive might have been for being on the scene, had been killed. Though perhaps unintended, his death was hardly accidental. Occurring as the direct result of a felony—the reckless detonation of the explosive—it was murder. Failure to report this, along with the pertinent background information, to the appropriate authorities in a timely fashion could be construed as obstruction of justice.

On the other hand, much could be excused by the immediate pursuit of a suspect.

And perhaps there was a way to bring the local police to the scene without entrapping himself in the prolonged questioning that was sure to occur and thus losing what might be his last real chance to catch Panikos and untangle the Spalter knot.

After turning Klemper's body back over to its original position—hoping that the techs summoned to the scene wouldn't be sharp enough to discern any evidence of the interference—Gurney scrambled back behind the corner of the house and called out in a low voice to Kyle.

Less than half a minute later the young man was standing next to him. "Jeez, is that ... is that ... somebody ... over there on the ground?"

"Yes. But forget about it for now. You didn't see it. Do you have your phone?"

"Yes, sure. But what—?"

"Call 911. Tell them everything that happened here up to the point when we climbed out the window—the flat tire, the explosion, my belief that the tire had been shot out. Tell them that I'm ex-NYPD, that after the explosion I saw some movement on Barrow Hill, that I told you to hide in the thicket, that I took your motorcycle and went in pursuit of whoever I thought was up there. And that's all you know."

Kyle's gaze was still on Klemper's body. "But . . . what about . . . ?"

"Our lights were out, it's dark, your father sent you up to that thicket to hide. You never saw the body. Let the 911 responders find it themselves. You can be as surprised and disturbed by it as they'll be."

"Surprised and disturbed—that should be easy enough."

"Stay in the thicket until you see the first cruiser coming up through the pasture. Then come out slowly and let them see you. Let them see your hands."

"You still haven't told me what happened . . . to him."

"The less you know, the less you'll need to forget, and the easier it'll be to be surprised and confused."

"What are *you* going to do?"

"That depends on the situation on the hill. I'll give it some thought on my way up there. But whatever it is, it needs to happen now." He got back on the bike, started it as quietly as he could, turned it around, and headed slowly around the back of the house. Confident that the structure was providing sufficient cover, he switched the headlight on and guided the softly rumbling bike slowly toward the old cow path that led to the large field separating his property from Barrow Hill.

He was pretty sure that the roundabout arc he was taking would prevent anyone on the top of the hill from seeing the headlight of the bike approaching. Then he could make his way up the north-side trail, a switchback with no direct visibility from the top.

All this sounded fine, as far as it went. But it didn't go far enough. Too much was unknown. Gurney couldn't escape the feeling that he was heading into a situation where the guy on the other side of the table had not only higher cards, but a better seat and a bigger gun. Not to mention a history of winning.

Gurney was tempted to blame everything on the cynical, duplicitous creeps at RAM-TV whose timing "mistake" with the *Criminal*

Conflict promotion announcements was almost certainly a deliberate decision. More promotional exposure meant a bigger audience, and a bigger audience was their number one goal. In fact, it was their only goal. If someone should die as a result of that decision, well ... that could create the biggest ratings boost of all.

But the difficulty with blaming it all on them, vile and venal as they were, was that he knew that he owned a piece of the problem. His piece had been his pretending, mostly to himself, that the plan made sense. It was hard to maintain that illusion now—as he struggled to keep the BSA upright, negotiating a tortuous route through clumps of briars, waist-high aspen saplings, and groundhog burrows that would have made the outer edge of the unmowed field a challenge even with perfect visibility. On a murky night it was a nightmare.

As he neared the foot of the hill, the terrain grew rougher and the jouncing movements of the headlight beam through the bushy weeds filled the area out in front of him with erratic shadows. Gurney had faced tough conditions before in the endgame of a battle with a dangerous opponent, but this was worse. Without time to think, to evaluate pros and cons and levels of risk, he felt forced to act.

Forced was not too strong a word for it. Now that he was within striking distance of Panikos, letting him get away was unthinkable. When he was this near his quarry, the gravitational field of the chase grew stronger and the rational assessment of risk began to fade.

And there was something else. Something very specific.

The echo of the past—stirring a force within him far stronger than reason.

That searing memory of an escaping car, Danny sprawled dead on the pavement. A memory that gave birth to an iron conviction that never again—*never again, no matter the danger*—would a killer so close get away from him.

This was something far beyond the niceties of rationality. This was something burned by unbearable loss into the circuits of his brain.

Having reached the opening to the north trail, he needed to make an immediate decision, and none of the options was encouraging. Since Panikos would probably be equipped with an infrared scope and infrared binoculars, any effort to get to the top of the hill would likely be fatal long before Gurney could get within Beretta range. The only way he could think of to neutralize the man's technological advantage was to put him on the run. And the only way he could think of to make him run was to give him the impression that he was outnumbered and outgunned—not an easy impression to create in the absence of backup. For a few moments, Gurney considered roaring full throttle up the switchback trail, shouting orders to imaginary cohorts, shouting replies in other voices. But he dismissed it as too transparent a ploy.

Then it occurred to him that a solution was at hand. Although he'd have no actual backup, the *appearance* of backup might be enough— and a very solid appearance of backup would soon be on the scene. A police cruiser or two, maybe three, hopefully with all their lights flashing, should be driving up any minute now through the pasture in response to Kyle's 911 call. Their arrival would be clearly visible from Panikos's likely position up by the tarn—and the sight of them should create a sufficient impression of manpower to dislodge Panikos and persuade him to retreat down the back trail to Beaver Cross Road.

That would all be for nothing, however, if Panikos established a large enough lead on Gurney to slip away into the night—or, worse, to pull off the trail unobserved and wait in ambush. To avoid that possibility Gurney decided to maneuver the BSA as quietly as he could to a location about three quarters of the way up the switchback, wait for the arrival of the cruisers in the pasture, and then play it by ear, depending on Panikos's reaction.

He didn't have to wait long. No more than a minute or two after he'd reached his intended position on the trail—within striking distance of the hilltop—he saw the oscillating colored lights through the trees at the far side of the field. And almost immediately he heard the sound he was hoping for—an ATV, loud at first, then beginning to recede—meaning that Panikos was, at least for the moment, behaving as anticipated.

Gurney revved up the idling BSA and maneuvered as fast as he dared through the remaining switchback segments. When he reached the small open area by the tarn, he turned the throttle back to idle for a moment to listen for the ATV and judge its position and speed. He guessed it was no more than a hundred yards down the back trail.

As he turned toward the trailhead and his headlight swept across the clearing, his eye caught first one oddity and then another. Resting on the flat rock that offered the best view of Gurney's house was a bouquet of flowers. The stems were wrapped in yellow tissue. The blossoms were a deep brownish red, a color typical of dried blood—and also the most common color of the local August mums.

He couldn't help wondering if the bouquet—or "posies" in the words of the nursery rhyme—had been intended for delivery to him, perhaps as a final message to be left on his dead body.

The second oddity was a black metal object, half the size of a carton of cigarettes, on the ground between Gurney and the bouquet. His reaction to that was sudden and physical, yanking the handlebars to the right and twisting the throttle. The bike pivoted sharply, propelling a shower of dirt and pebbles into the darkness and accelerating along the edge of the tarn.

Had he failed to get out of the way as quickly as he did, the explosion that followed would have killed him. As it was, the only negative effect was a painful blast of dirt and small stones against his back.

In response to this attempt on his life, he called out in his best team-leader voice. "All units converge, back slope, Barrow Hill. Remote explosive. No casualties." The idea was to increase the pressure. Make Panikos get reckless, make mistakes, lose control. Maybe hit a tree, flip into a ditch. The goal was to stop him, one way or another.

The unforgivable thing would be to let him get away.

To let the red BMW race off into the distance and disappear forever.

No. That wasn't going to happen. *No matter what, that wasn't going to happen again.*

He couldn't let Panikos get too far ahead. At two hundred yards, for example, he might have the space and time he'd need to come to a sudden stop, turn, steady his weapon, and get off a good shot while Gurney was still too far away to have a chance with the Beretta.

With his attention alternating rapidly now between the ATV taillights and the rutted trail, Gurney was neither gaining nor losing ground. But with every passing second on the bike, he could feel his physical motorcycle memory returning. Like skiing after a long layoff, heading down that trail was bringing back his timing and coordination. By the time they emerged onto the paved surface of Beaver Cross, the ATV still about a hundred yards ahead of him, Gurney felt confident enough to open up the throttle all the way.

The ATV seemed unusually fast—apparently built or modified for racing—but the BSA was faster. Within a mile, Gurney had reduced the gap between them to fifty, maybe forty yards—still too far for a pistol shot from a motorcycle. He figured he'd be close enough in another half mile or so.

Perhaps sensing the same possibility from the opposing point of view, Panikos veered off the paved road onto a roughly parallel farm track that ran along the verge of a long cornfield. Gurney did the same, in case the little man decided to head off into the cornfield itself.

Even more rutted than the Barrow Hill trail, the farm track imposed its own speed limit of twenty to thirty miles per hour, taking away the BSA's open-road advantage and preserving Panikos's lead—even widening it a bit, since the forks and shocks of his machine were more suited to the surface than Gurney's.

The track and its adjacent cornfield sloped down to the relatively flatter but still severely uneven terrain of the river valley. At the end of the track, Panikos continued on into the abandoned pasture of what Gurney had been told was once the region's largest dairy farm. Now a patchwork of large grassy hummocks and muddy rivulets, it gave the ATV a distinct advantage over the BSA, widening Panikos's lead to the original hundred yards and then some, impelling Gurney to push the BSA at insane speeds through the equivalent of an unlit slalom course. There was a primal simplicity in hot pursuit that anesthetized fear and suppressed any reasonable calculation of risk.

In addition to the red taillights that he was zeroing in on, he began catching glimpses of other lights farther down the valley. Colored lights, white lights, some seemingly fixed in place, some moving. These at first had a disorienting effect on him. Where the hell was he? Bright arrays of lights were as uncommon in Walnut Crossing as meadowlarks in Manhattan. Then, when he saw an arc of orange lights slowly rotating, it came to him.

It was the Ferris wheel at the Summer Mountain Fair.

Panikos was still widening his lead through a wet depression of boggy land that separated the former pasture from the higher and drier square-mile field that was home to the fair and its parking areas. For a few desperate seconds, Gurney thought he'd lost Panikos in the sea of vehicles surrounding the perimeter fence of the fair itself. But then he caught sight of the familiar taillights moving along an outer parking lane in the direction of the exhibitors' entrance.

By the time he reached that entrance himself, the ATV had already passed through it. Three young women wearing FAIR SECURITY armbands, evidently in charge of controlling that admission point, looked disconcerted. One was on a walkie-talkie, the other on a cell phone. Gurney pulled up next to the third. Straddling the bike, he flashed his NYPD-Retired credentials at her as he spoke. "Did an ATV just run this gate?"

"Damn right! Kid on a camo four-by-four. You after him?"

He hesitated for half a second at the word "kid" before realizing that, seen fleetingly, Panikos would give that exact impression.

"Yes, I am. What was he wearing?"

"Wearing? Jeez … I … maybe some kind of shiny black jacket? Like one of those nylon windbreaker things? I'm not really sure."

"Okay. Did you see which way he went?"

"Yeah, freakin' little creep! Right through there." She pointed at a makeshift alleyway between one of the main tents and a long row of RVs and motor homes.

Gurney passed through the gate, headed into narrow passage, and proceeded to the far end of it, where it connected with one of the fair's main concourses. The carefree look of the ambling crowd seemed to preclude any recent encounter with a speeding ATV—meaning that Panikos had probably slipped through one of the many spaces between the motor homes and could now be anywhere in the fairgrounds.

Gurney pivoted the BSA and sped back up the alley to the gate area, where he saw that the three young women had now been joined in their consternation by a sour-faced cop—no doubt one of the locals moonlighting in the security detail.

Gray-haired and paunchy, stretching a uniform that might have fit him ten years earlier, he eyed the BSA with a blatant combination of envy and contempt.

"What's the problem here?"

Gurney showed his ID. "The guy who ran your gate a couple of minutes ago is armed and dangerous. I have reason to believe he shot out a tire on my car."

The cop was eyeing the ID like it was a North Korean passport. "You carrying?"

"Yes."

"That card says you're retired. You got your carry permit on you?"

Gurney flipped quickly to the section of his wallet that displayed the permit. "There's a time factor here, Officer. The guy on the ATV is a serious—"

The cop cut him off. "Remove that from your wallet and hand it to me."

Gurney did so, his voice rising. "Listen to me. The guy on the ATV is a fugitive murder suspect. Losing him now would not be a good thing."

The cop examined the permit. "Slow down ... *Detective.* You're a long way from the Rotten Apple." He wrinkled his nose unpleasantly. "This fugitive of yours have a name?"

This was not a can of worms Gurney had planned to open, but now he saw no alternative. "His name is Petros Panikos. He's a professional killer."

"He's a *what?*"

The three young women assigned to mind the gate were standing in a row behind the cop, wide-eyed.

Gurney was straining to maintain his patience. "Petros Panikos killed seven people in Cooperstown this week. He may have caused the death of a police officer half an hour ago. He's in your fairgrounds right now. Is this getting through to you?"

The cop put his hand on the butt of his holstered gun. "Who the hell are you?"

"My ID told you exactly who I am—David Gurney, Detective First Grade, NYPD-Retired. I also told you I'm in pursuit of a murder suspect. Now I'm going to tell you something else. You're creating an unnecessary obstruction to his capture. If your obstruction results in his escape, your career is over. You hear what I'm saying, Officer?"

The muddy hostility in the cop's eyes was sharpening into something more dangerous. His lips drew back, revealing the tips of clenched yellow teeth. He took a slow step backward. With his hand tightening on his gun, the movement was far more threatening than a step forward. "That's it. Get off the bike."

Gurney looked past him and spoke to the row of gaping young women in a loud, deliberate voice. "Call your head of security! Get him out here to this gate—NOW!"

The cop turned around, raising his free hand in a *stop* gesture. "You don't need to call anybody. Nobody. No call. I'm taking care of this myself."

It struck Gurney that this might be his only chance. Risk be damned—losing Panikos was not an acceptable option. He gave the throttle a quick twist, pulled the handlebars down to the right, spun the machine in a one-eighty, and, with the rear tire smoking, shot back down into the alleyway behind the motor homes. Halfway to the main concourse, he made a sharp turn in between two of the big vehicles and found himself threading his way through a maze of RVs of all shapes and sizes. He soon emerged onto one of the fair's narrower concourses, along which exhibitor tents displayed everything from wildly colored Peruvian hats to chain-sawed bear sculptures. He abandoned the BSA in a half-hidden space between two of the tents, one selling Walnut Crossing sweatshirts and the other straw cowboy hats.

On an impulse, he bought one of each, then stopped in a restroom farther along on the same concourse to cover the dark, short-sleeved shirt he was wearing with the light gray sweatshirt. He moved the Beretta from his ankle holster to the sweatshirt pocket, and checked his appearance in the restroom mirror. The change, along with the brim of the cowboy hat shielding his eyes, convinced him he'd be less recognizable, at least at a distance, either by Panikos or the troublesome cop.

It occurred to him then that Panikos might be taking similar steps to blend in with his surroundings—and that raised an obvious question. As Gurney began searching the crowd for the little man, what characteristics was he looking for?

His height—which had been estimated at between four-ten and five-two—would put him in the range of most middle-schoolers. Unfortunately, middle-schoolers probably comprised at least several hundred of the approximately ten thousand visitors at the fair. Were there other criteria that could narrow the profile? The security videos had been useful in establishing certain facts, but for the purpose of generating a likeness independent of the original context, their value was limited—since so much of Panikos's hair and face had been covered with sunglasses, headband, scarf. His nose had been visible and distinctive, as well as his mouth, but little else—little that would facilitate the quick scanning of faces in a moving crowd.

The stressed security girl at the gate said she thought he was wearing a black jacket, but Gurney gave that little weight. She hadn't sounded sure, and even if she had, pressured eyewitness reports like that were more often dead wrong than anywhere near right. And whatever he might have been wearing when he ran the gate, Panikos could have altered his appearance as quickly and easily as Gurney just had. So, for the moment at least, he was looking for a short, thin person with a sharp nose and a childlike mouth.

As if to underscore the insufficiency of that description, an excited cluster of at least a dozen kids—ten-year-olds, eleven-year-olds, maybe twelve-year-olds—crossed the concourse just ahead of him. Perhaps half of them would fall outside the size parameters either because of their height or pudginess, but Panikos could easily blend in with the other half.

In fact, suppose he *had* blended in. Suppose Panikos was among them, right there in front of him. How could Gurney pick him out?

It was a discouraging challenge—particularly since the whole group had evidently visited one of the fair's face painters, obscuring their features under the visages of what Gurney assumed were comic-book superheroes. And how many similar little groups might there be—all circulating through the fairgrounds at that moment, with Panikos as a potential hanger-on?

It was then that he noticed what the members of this particular group were doing. They were approaching other fairgoers, adults primarily, with bunches of flowers. He picked up his pace and followed them onto the larger concourse to observe more closely what was happening.

They were selling the flowers—or, more accurately, giving a free bunch to anyone who would make a minimum ten-dollar donation to the Walnut Crossing Flood Relief Fund. But the thing that captured his attention—one hundred percent of his attention—was the appearance of these bouquets.

The flowers were rust-red mums, and the stems were wrapped in yellow tissue—seemingly identical to those left by Panikos on the rock by the tarn.

What did this mean? Processing the implications, Gurney came quickly to the conclusion that the flowers by the tarn had most likely come from the fair, which meant that Panikos had been there prior to his visit to Barrow Hill, which raised an interesting question:

Why?

Surely he hadn't gone to the fair originally for the purpose of acquiring a bouquet to bring to Gurney's property—since he would've had no way of knowing such a thing would be available there and a local florist would have been a more obvious source in any event. No, he'd gone to the fair for some other reason, and the mums had been secondary.

So what was the primary reason? It sure as hell wasn't for the rustic amusement, cotton candy, and cow-flop bingo. Then why on earth . . . ?

The ringing of his phone interrupted his train of thought.

It was Hardwick, highly agitated. "Shit, man! Are you all right?"

"I think so. What's going on?"

"That's what I want to know! Where the fuck are you?"

"I'm at the fair. So is Panikos."

"Then what the hell's happening at your place?"

"How do you know—?"

"I'm out on the county route, approaching your turnoff, and there's a fucking convoy—two trooper cruisers, a sheriff's car, and a BCI SUV—all heading up your road. Fuck's going on?"

"Klemper's up there by my house. Dead. Long story. Looks like the first responders found the body and called for help. The convoy you see would be the second wave."

"Dead? Mick the Dick? Dead how?"

Gurney gave him the fastest run-through he could—from the flat tire to the lumber explosion to the fatal joist hanger in Klemper's neck to the flowers on Barrow Hill to the flowers at the fair.

Reviewing it all underscored in his own mind his need to call Kyle ASAP.

Hardwick listened in complete silence to the narration of events.

"What you need to do," said Gurney, "is get over here to the fairgrounds. You've seen the same videos I have, so your chance of recognizing Panikos is as good as mine."

"Which is close to zero."

"I know that. But we're got to try. He's here, somewhere. He came here for a reason."

"What reason?"

"I have no idea. But he was here earlier today, and now he's here again. It's not a coincidence."

"Look, I know you think that getting Panikos is the key to everything, but don't forget that somebody hired him, and I'm thinking it's Jonah."

"You find out something new?"

"Just what my gut tells me, that's all. There's something off about that slimy bastard."

"Something beyond a fifty-million-dollar motive?"

"Yeah. I think so. I think he's way too smiley, way too cool."

"Maybe it's just the charming Spalter gene pool."

Hardwick produced a phlegmy laugh. "Not a pool I'd want to swim in."

Gurney was getting antsy to check in with Kyle, antsy to start looking for Panikos. "Okay, Jack. Hurry up. Call me when you get here."

As he was ending the call, he heard the first explosion.

Chapter 58

Ashes, Ashes

H e'd recognized the sound as the muffled *whump* of a small incendiary device.

As soon as he reached the scene, two concourses over, his impression was confirmed. A small booth was engulfed in flames and smoke, but already two men with FAIR SECURITY armbands were hurrying toward it with fire extinguishers and shouting at the onlookers to step back out of the way. Two female security people arrived and began working their way around to the rear of the booth, repeatedly calling out, "Anyone inside? Anyone inside?" An emergency vehicle with lights flashing and siren blaring was making its way down the middle of the concourse.

Seeing there was no immediate contribution he could make to the effort, Gurney focused instead on the crowd within sight of the fire. Arsonists have a well-known proclivity for observing their handiwork, but whatever hope he might have had of spotting someone matching even the most general description of Peter Pan soon evaporated. But then he noticed something else. The half-burnt sign above the booth said WALNUT CROSSING FLOOD RELIEF. And amid the debris the explosion had scattered onto the concourse were charred bouquets of rust-red mums.

It seemed that Panikos had a love-hate relationship with chrysanthemums, or maybe with all flowers, or with anything that reminded him of Florencia. But that alone couldn't explain his presence at the fair. There was another possibility, of course. A more frightening one. Major public events were attractive venues for the making of memorable statements.

Was it conceivable that the purpose of Panikos's earlier visit to the fair that day was to lay the groundwork for such a statement? Specifically, might he have mined the place with explosives? Was the destruction of the flower stand only the opening sentence of his message?

Was this possible scenario something Gurney needed to share immediately with Fair Security? With the Walnut Crossing PD? With BCI? Or would an attempt to explain such a scenario take more time than it was worth? After all, if it was true, if that was the reality they were facing, by the time the story was told and believed, it would be too late to stop the event.

As crazy as the conclusion seemed, Gurney decided that going it alone was the only feasible route. It was a route that depended on the successful identification of Peter Pan—a task that he realized was close to impossible. But there were no other options on the table.

So he started doing the only thing he could do. He started making his way through the crowd, using height as the first screen, weight as the second, facial structure as the third.

As he made his way through the next concourse, checking not only the individuals in the flowing crowd but also the customers at each booth and each exhibitor's tent, an ironic thought came to mind: The upside of the worst-case scenario—that Peter Pan had come to the fair to blow it up piece by piece—was that he'd be there for a while. And as long as he was there, it was possible to catch him. Before Gurney could wrestle with the edgy moral question of how much human and material destruction he'd be willing to trade to get his hands on Peter Pan, Hardwick called—announcing that he'd arrived at the main gate and asking where they should get together.

"We don't need to get together," said Gurney. "We can cover more ground separately."

"Fine. So what do I do—just start searching for the midget?"

"As best you can, based on your memory of the images on the security videos. You might want to pay special attention to groups of kids."

"The purpose being . . . ?"

"He'd want to be as inconspicuous as possible. A five-foot-tall male adult is attention-getting, but a kid that size isn't, so there's a good chance he's made himself look like a kid. Facial skin can be an age giveaway, so I'd expect he'd find a way to obscure that. A lot of kids tonight have their faces painted, and that would be an obvious solution."

"I get that, but why would he be in a group?"

"Again, inconspicuousness. A kid alone attracts more attention than one with other kids."

Hardwick uttered a sigh, making it sound like the ultimate expression of skepticism. "Sounds like a lot of guesswork to me."

"I won't argue with that. One more thing. Assume that he's armed, and don't underestimate him. Remember, he's alive and well, and a hell of a lot of people who crossed paths with him are dead."

"What's the drill if I think I have him ID'd?"

"Keep him in sight and call me. I'll do the same. That's the point when we need to back each other up. By the way, he blew up a flower stand here right after your last call."

"*Blew it up?*"

"Sounded like a low-impact incendiary. Probably like the ones at Cooperstown."

"Why a flower stand?"

"I'm not a psychoanalyst, Jack, but flowers—especially mums—seem to mean something to him."

"You know 'mum' is the Brit word for 'mom,' right?"

"Sure, but—"

A series of rapid-fire explosions cut off his reply—propelling him down into an instinctive crouch. He sensed that the blasts had come from somewhere above him.

Quickly scanning the area around him, he got the phone back up to his ear in time to hear Hardwick yell, "Christ! What did he blow up now?"

The answer came in a second series of similar explosions—with geometric lines of light and bursts of colored sparks streaking across the night sky. Gurney's tension was released in a sharp single-syllable laugh. "Fireworks! It's just the summer-fair fireworks."

"Fireworks? What the fuck for? Fourth of July was a month ago."

"Who the hell knows? It's a tradition at the fair. They do it every year."

A third series went off—louder and gaudier.

"Assholes," muttered Hardwick.

"Right. Anyway. We have work to do."

Hardwick was silent for a few seconds, then switched directions abruptly. "So what do you think about Jonah? You didn't react when I brought it up. You think I'm right?"

"Right about him being the mastermind behind Carl's murder?"

"It's all to his advantage. All of it. And you gotta admit, he's one oily operator."

"Where does Esti come out on this? She agree with you?"

"Hell, no. She's all zeroed in on Alyssa. She's convinced the whole thing was payback for Carl raping her—even though there was no real evidence for that. It was all hearsay, through Klemper. Which reminds me, I have to let her know about Mick the Dick's demise. I guarantee she'll do a happy dance."

It took Gurney a few seconds to get that image out of his mind. "Okay, Jack, we need to get to the job at hand. Panikos is here. With us. Within reach. Let's go find him." As he ended the call, a final deafening display of fireworks lit up the sky. It made him think, for the twelfth time in the past two days, of the case of the exploding car. That made him think of the events in the alley shooting described by Esti. Which made him wonder yet again what revealing element they might have in common with the Spalter case. As important as that question seemed, however, he couldn't let it divert his attention now.

He resumed his progress through the fairgrounds, fixating on the face of every short, thin person he came upon. Better to study too many than too few. If someone of the right size happened to be looking away, or if their features were obscured by glasses, a beard, the brim of a hat, he followed them discreetly, angling for a better view.

With a rising sense of possibility, he followed one tiny, ageless, genderless creature in loose black jeans and a baggy sweater until a wiry, sunburned man in a John Deere hat greeted her warmly in a tent sponsored by the Evangelical Church of the Risen Christ, called her Eleanor, and asked about the condition of her cows.

Two more such "possibilities"—discovered in the next two concourses and collapsing in similar absurdities—were draining the hope out of his search, while the nasal country lyrics blaring from the giant four-sided screen at the fair's central intersection were saturating the atmosphere with a disorienting sentimentality. There was a similarly disorienting combination of odors, dominated by popcorn, French fries, and manure.

As Gurney rounded the corner where a room-sized refrigeration unit with a glass front was displaying a huge bovine butter sculpture, he caught sight of the same roving band of a dozen or so face-painted kids he'd seen before. He picked up his pace to get closer.

Apparently they'd been successful in their flowers-for-donations pitches. Only two members of the group were still carrying bouquets, and they seemed in no hurry to give them away. As he was watching them, he spotted the cop from the exhibitors' gate coming along the concourse from the opposite direction with what looked like two plain-clothes colleagues.

Gurney ducked through a doorway and found himself in the 4-H Club exhibit hall, surrounded by displays of large, shiny vegetables.

As soon as the search party had passed, he stepped back outside. He was closing in again on the face-painted kids when he was startled by another explosion, not far away. It was a powerful *whump*—incendiary style—with maybe twice the force of the one that had destroyed the flower stand. But it had little immediate effect on the meandering mass of fairgoers, probably because the fireworks had been louder.

It did, however, get the attention of the face-painted kids. They stopped and gaped at one another—as if the explosion had awakened their appetite for disaster—then turned and hurried back along the concourse toward the origin of the sound.

Gurney caught up with them two concourses later. They had drawn together at the edge of a larger crowd, staring. Smoke was billowing from the arena that was home to the nightly demolition-derby events. Some people were running toward the arena. Some were backing away from it, clutching small children. Some were questioning one another, wide-eyed with anxiety. Some were pulling out cell phones, tapping in numbers. A siren began wailing in the background.

And then, barely discernible above the general din, there was another *whump*.

Only a few members of the little posse Gurney was focused on showed any immediate reaction, but the ones who did then appeared to be passing the news of it to their companions. It also appeared that this was breaking the group apart—that there were those who'd heard the latest explosion and those who hadn't (or who had, but considered the commotion in front of them more interesting). In any event, three individuals separated themselves from the larger group and headed off in the direction of the latest scene of destruction.

Curious himself about the pattern of Panikos's attack, Gurney decided to follow the splinter group. As he passed those who were remaining at the periphery of the unsettled crowd of onlookers, he tried to get a good enough look at each little face to judge its compatibility with the mental images he carried from the videos.

Failing to see any resemblance convincing enough to demand a closer examination, he continued after the departing threesome.

His progress was slowed by people beginning to flow out of the arena. From what he overheard of their comments to one another, he concluded that the audience in the stands hadn't come close to grasping the significance of what they'd just witnessed—the massive, fiery explosion of one of the cars in the final event of the derby, the horrifying immolation of the driver, and multiple injuries to other drivers. They seemed to be attributing all this to some sort of gas-tank malfunction or the use of a prohibited fuel. The darkest suggestion was that there might have been some sort of sabotage arising from a family feud.

So, two firebombs within a twenty-minute period, and still no panic. That was the good news. The bad news was that the only reason there was no panic was that no one understood what was happening. Gurney wondered if that third *whump* he'd heard would change things.

A couple of hundred yards ahead of him, a fire engine was trying to clear a right-of-way through the throng with repeated blasts of its air horn. Overhead, smoke was blowing in the wind—coming from the area toward which the fire engine was heading. It was a cloudy, moonless night, and the smoke was weirdly illuminated by the concourse lights below it.

People were starting to show signs of unease. Many were proceeding in the same direction as the fire engine—some walking fast beside it, some running ahead of it. The expressions on faces ran the gamut from apprehension to excitement. The three small figures he'd been following had been swallowed up in the moving mass of bodies.

Turning the corner into the intersecting concourse about a hundred yards behind the engine, he could see flames against the black sky. They were coming from the roof of a long, single-story wooden structure, which he recognized as the main shelter for the animals entered in the various demonstrations and competitions. As he drew closer, he saw a few cows and horses being led out of the building's main doors by their young handlers.

Then others, unattended and skittish, began coming out through other doors—some hesitating uncertainly and stamping on the ground, some bolting into the crowd, generating cries of alarm.

One overwrought individual with an unfortunate sense of drama shouted "Stampede!" A sense of panic, the absence of which Gurney had noted minutes earlier, now appeared to be infecting pockets of the crowd. People were jostling one another to get to what they probably imagined were positions of greater safety. The noise level was rising. So was the wind. The flames on the barn roof were being lashed sideways. Loose canvas panels on the exhibition tents along the concourse were flapping sharply.

It appeared that a sudden summer storm might be blowing in. A flash of light in the clouds and a rumble in the hills confirmed it. Moments later the lightning flashed more brightly, and the rumble grew louder.

Chapter 59

All Fall Down

More security people were rushing to the scene now. Some were trying to get the fairgoers away from the barn and the engine, out of the way of the fire crew deploying the hoses. Others were struggling to regain control of escaping horses, cows, hogs, sheep, as well as a pair of giant oxen.

Gurney observed that word of the two earlier fire explosions was spreading, producing a rising level of fear and confusion. At least a third of the people were now glued to their phones—talking, texting, and photographing the fire and the turmoil around them.

Scanning the shifting mass of faces for the trio who'd slipped out of sight, or for anyone else who might resemble Panikos, Gurney was taken aback to catch a glimpse of Madeleine emerging from the barn. Angling for a less obstructed view, he saw that she was leading two alpacas by their halters, one in each hand. And Dennis Winkler was right behind her, leading two more the same way.

As soon as they were out of the immediate area occupied by the fire crew, they stopped to confer about something—Winkler doing most of the talking, Madeleine nodding earnestly. Then they continued on, Winkler now in front, following a kind of passageway through the crowd opened by some security people for the evacuation of the animals.

This brought them within a few feet of Gurney.

Winkler noticed him first. "Hey, David—you want to make yourself useful?"

"Sorry. I can't help you right now."

Winkler looked offended. "I've got a significant emergency here."

"We all do."

Winkler stared at him, then moved on with a muttered comment that got lost under a peal of thunder.

Madeleine stopped and eyed Gurney curiously. "What are you doing here?"

"What are *you* doing here?" Even as he was speaking, the harshness in his voice was warning him to be quiet.

"Helping Dennis and Deirdre. As I told you I would be."

"You need to get out of here. Now."

"*What?* What's the matter with you?" The wind was blowing her hair forward, around her face. With both hands on the halters, she was shaking her head to keep the hair out of her eyes.

"It's not safe here."

She blinked uncomprehendingly. "Because of the fire in the barn?"

"The fire in the barn, the fire in the arena, the fire in the flower booth ..."

"What are you talking about?"

"The man I'm chasing ... the man who burned down the houses in Cooperstown ..."

There was flash of lightning and the loudest thunderclap yet. She flinched and raised her voice. "What are you telling me?"

"He's here. Petros Panikos. Here, tonight, now. I think he may have seeded the whole fairgrounds with explosives."

Her hair was still blowing in her face, but now she was making no effort to control it. "How do you know he's here?"

"I followed him here."

"From where?"

Another lightning flash, another thunderclap.

"Barrow Hill. I chased him here on Kyle's motorcycle."

"What happened? Why—"

"He killed Mick Klemper."

"Madeleine!" Dennis Winkler's impatient voice reached them from the place where he was standing, waiting, about thirty feet away. "Madeleine! Come on! We need to keep moving along."

"*Klemper?* Where?"

"By our house. I don't have time to explain it. *Panikos is here.* He's blowing things up, he's burning things down, I need you to get the hell out of here."

"What about the animals?"

"Maddie, for Godsake . . ."

"They're terrified of fire." She glanced back in distress at her oddly thoughtful-looking pair of alpacas.

"Maddie . . ."

"All right, all right . . . let me just get these two to a safe place. Then I'll leave." She was obviously finding the decision a difficult one. "What about you? What are you doing?"

"I'm trying to find him and stop him."

Outright fear finally filled her eyes, and she started to object, but he cut her off.

"I *have* to do this! And *you* have to get the hell out of here— *please*—now!"

She appeared for a moment immobilized by her own frightening thoughts, then she dropped the halters, stepped toward him, hugged him with something like desperation, turned away without another word, and led her charges along the concourse to where Winkler was waiting for her. They exchanged a few words, then moved on quickly, side by side, through the corridor that had been cleared through the crowd.

Watching them for the few seconds until they were out of sight, Gurney felt the stab of an emotion he couldn't name. They looked so goddamn domestic, so bloody compatible, like caring parents of little children, hurrying to find shelter from the storm.

He closed his eyes, hoping for a way up and out of the acid pit.

When he opened them a moment later, the strange little face-painted threesome had reappeared, seemingly out of nowhere. They were walking past him in the same direction taken by Madeleine and Winkler. Gurney had the unsettling impression—it could have been his imagination—that one of the painted faces was smiling.

He let them get about fifty feet farther along before he set out after them. The concourse ahead was a jumble of conflicting currents. Curiosity was pulling droves of the mindless toward the burning barn, while the security staff were doing their utmost to turn them back and to keep a channel open for the displaced animals and their handlers moving in the opposite direction to a series of corrals on the far side of the fairgrounds.

Beyond the radius of the fire's visibility and primitive power of attraction, the threat of a downpour was persuading swarms of fairgoers to abandon the pedestrian concourses in favor of the exhibitor tents or their own cars. The reduced density was making it easier for Gurney to keep the trio in sight.

At the end of a massive thunderclap that reverberated through the valley, he realized his phone was ringing.

It was Hardwick. "You spot the fucker yet?"

"Maybe a possibility or two, nothing firm. What area have you covered so far?"

There was no answer.

"Jack?"

"Hold on a sec."

As the seconds passed, Gurney found himself dividing his attention between the trio he was following and the giant video cube that dominated the center of the fairgrounds and provided an incessant country-music accompaniment to the nightmare in progress. As he listened for Hardwick's return to the phone, he couldn't quite tune out the Oedipal-creepy chorus of a song called "Mother's Day"—about a hard-workin', hard-drinkin', pickup-drivin' guy who'd never met a lady as lovin' as his mama.

"I'm back." It was Hardwick's voice on the phone.

"What's happening?"

"I've been tailing a rat pack, didn't want to lose them. Dressed in scumbag couture. Couple of them got that paint shit on their faces."

"Anything special about them?"

"There seems to be a core group, and then there's sort of an outlier."

"An outlier?"

"Yeah. Like he's with the pack but not really part of them."

"That's interesting."

"Right, but don't get carried away. There's always some kid in a group who's a little *out* of the group. Don't necessarily mean shit."

"Can you see what's painted on his face?"

"Got to wait till he turns around."

"Where are you?"

"Passing in front of a booth selling taxidermied squirrels."

"Jesus. Any bigger landmarks?"

"There's a building down the concourse with a picture of a humongous pumpkin on the door, next to a video arcade. In fact, the mini-scumbags just went into the arcade."

"What about the outlier?"

"Yeah, him too. They're all inside. You want me to go in?"

"I don't think so. Not yet. Just make sure there's only one door, so you don't lose them."

"Hold on, they just came back out. On the move again."

"All of them? The outlier, too?"

"Yeah. Just counting . . . eight, nine . . . yeah, all of them."

"Which way are they heading?"

"Past the pumpkin building toward the end of the concourse."

"That means we're going to converge. I'm one concourse over from you, moving in the same direction—following a procession of animals and a face-painted troupe of my own."

"Animals?"

"The animals that were in the barn are being moved to the corrals behind the Ferris wheel. The barn is on fire."

"Shit! I heard someone talking about a burning barn. I thought they were just confused about the fire in the arena. Okay, let me hang up. I got to pay attention here—but wait! You got any news on what's happening up at your house?"

"I need to call my son and find out."

"Let me know."

As he ended the call, Madeleine and Winkler were turning onto a kind of rotary concourse that encircled the carnival rides and the corrals. A minute later Gurney's target threesome went the same way, and by the time he reached the intersection, they were meeting up with the group of nine Hardwick had been following.

Moving among the animals and those clutches of fairgoers who remained ignorant of the unfolding disaster and undaunted by the threatening storm, the dozen little bodies defied Gurney's efforts to identify any conspicuous outsider—any monstrous mini-adult in the guise of a child. As he watched, they gravitated toward the waist-high railing that separated the curving concourse from the rides.

Madeleine and Dennis and the alpacas were moving along past the rides toward the corrals. Gurney placed himself where he could see as far as possible in the direction of the corrals while still maintaining a clear view of the group gathering at the railing. He spotted Hardwick taking up a position where the second straight concourse fed into the circular one. Rather than reveal their connection by walking over and conferring with Hardwick directly, he took out his phone and called him.

When he answered, Hardwick was looking over at Gurney. "What's with the redneck hat?"

"Ad hoc camouflage. Long story for another time. Tell me—have you spotted anyone else of interest, or are our prime candidates right here in front of us?"

"That's them. And you can knock out about half on the basis of the pudge factor."

"What factor?"

"Some of these kids are way too fat. From what I could see on the videos, our little Peter has a lean and hungry look."

"So that leaves us with maybe six possibles?"

"I'd say more like two or three. In addition to the pudge factor, there's the height factor, and the basic facial structure factor. Which leaves maybe one of your group, two of mine. And even those seem a bit of a stretch."

"Which three are you talking about?"

"The one closest to you—idiot baseball hat, hand on the railing. The one next to him, in the black hoodie, hands in his pockets. And the one closest to me, wearing the blue satin basketball uniform three sizes too big. You got any better choices?"

"Let me take a closer look. I'll call you back."

He slipped the phone in his pocket, studying the twelve little bodies at the railing, with particular attention to the three highlighted by Hardwick. But there was a phrase the man had used that hit a nerve: *a bit of a stretch.*

A bit of a stretch, indeed. In fact, Gurney had a sick, sinking feeling that there was something preposterous about the whole notion—the notion that one of these restless, absurdly dressed middle-schoolers might actually be Peter Pan. As he changed his position in order to see more of their faces, he was tempted to abandon the whole endeavor, to accept the probability that Peter Pan had escaped the fairgrounds and was at that moment bound for places unknown, far from Walnut Crossing. Surely that was a saner position than believing that one of the little people at that railing—seemingly enthralled by the roar and clatter of the "amusements"—was a ruthless executioner.

Was it conceivable that the man whom Interpol credited with more than fifty hits, who cracked Mary Spalter's skull on the edge of her bathtub, who hammered nails into Gus Gurikos's eyes, who burned seven people to death in Cooperstown, who cut off Lex Bincher's head, was now passing himself off as one of these children? As Gurney ambled past them as if he were trying to get a better view of the huge Ferris wheel, he found it mind-boggling to imagine any of them as a professional murderer—and not only a murderer but also a man who specialized in contracts others considered impossible.

That final thought pulled Gurney sideways to an issue he'd wondered about several times in the last few days but had spent no real time examining. It was probably the most perplexing question of all:

What was so hard about the hit on Carl Spalter?

What was the "impossible" aspect? What made it a job for Panikos in the first place?

Perhaps the answer to that one question would unravel all the other secrets in the case. Gurney decided then and there to think his way through it until the truth emerged. The simplicity of the question persuaded him that it was the right question. It even restored in him a modest sense of optimism. He felt that he was on the right track.

Then something startling happened.

An answer occurred to him that was as simple as the question.

At first he was afraid to breathe—as though the solution were as fragile as smoke and breathing might blow it away. But the more he examined it, the more he tested its solidity, the more convinced he became that it was right. And if it was right, then the Spalter murder case was finally solved.

As he stared at the staggeringly simple explanation taking shape in his mind, he felt the tingling excitement that always accompanied a dawning truth.

He repeated the key question to himself. *What was so hard about the hit on Carl Spalter? What had made it seem so impossible?*

Then he laughed out loud.

Because the answer was, quite simply, nothing.

Nothing at all had made it seem impossible.

As he walked back past the figures at the railing, he double-checked the validity of his insight and all its implications by asking himself what light it cast into the remaining dark corners of the case. His feeling of excitement intensified as one mystery after another dissolved.

Now he understood why Mary Spalter had to die.

He knew who had ordered the shot that ended Carl Spalter's life. The motive was as plain as day. And darker than a night in hell.

He knew what the terrible secret was, what the nails in Gus's head were all about, and what the slaughter in Cooperstown was supposed to accomplish.

He could see how Alyssa and Klemper and Jonah all fit in the puzzle.

The mystery of the shot that came from a place it couldn't have come from was no longer a mystery.

In fact, everything about the Spalter murder case was suddenly simple. Nauseatingly simple.

And it all underscored one inescapable truth. Peter Pan had to be stopped.

As Gurney pondered that final challenge, his accelerating thoughts were interrupted by another *whump.*

Chapter 60

Perfect Little
Peter Pan

Some of the fairgoers who were wandering by stopped, cocked their heads, looked at one another with anxious frowns. But no one at the railing gave any sign of noticing anything out of the ordinary. Perhaps, Gurney thought, they were too wrapped up in the racket of the amusements and the happy cries of the amused. And if someone at the railing was responsible for this latest in the series of muffled explosions—if he'd rigged the incendiary with a timer or had sent an electronic signal with a remote detonator—he was certainly doing nothing to advertise the fact.

Recognizing that this was likely his best, and maybe last, opportunity to decide for himself if any of these individuals merited further attention—or if he'd hit a dead end in his "hot pursuit" of Panikos—Gurney moved to the railing, to a position that afforded a reasonably good view of their profiles.

Putting Hardwick's stated selections and exclusions aside, he studied each partial face and body shape in turn. Of the twelve, he was able to see nine clearly enough to make a confident judgment, and all those judgments were for exclusion. Among the nine were the three he himself had been following earlier, which gave him a brief feeling of regret for time wasted—even though he well knew that investigative work was as much about exclusion as inclusion.

In any event, only three individuals remained to be assessed. They happened to be the three closest to him, but all were turned away from him. All three were wearing the wretched uniform of the rebellious young.

Like many other little upstate towns that for years had lingered in a kind of *Leave It to Beaver* time warp of old-fashioned manners and appearances, Walnut Crossing was slowly being infiltrated—as Long Falls already had been—by the toxic culture of rap crap, gangsta clothes, and cheap heroin. The three young men that Gurney was watching seemed to exemplify the trend. He was hoping, however, that two of them were merely idiots and that the third . . .

Bizarre as the thought might seem, he was hoping that the third was evil incarnate.

He was also hoping that he'd have no doubt about it. It would be nice if it was all in the eyes—if he could with one good look identify evil as easily as he could exclude it. But he feared that would not be the case, that more than simple observation would be required to verify so crucial a judgment. He would almost certainly have to rely on some form of interview, some way of generating a series of challenges demanding a series of responses. Responses come in many forms— words, tones, expressions, body language. The truth is cumulative.

The question before him now, of course, was how to get from here to there.

The options were simplified when one of the three individuals who'd been looking away turned sufficiently in Gurney's direction to reveal a facial structure quite inconsistent with the one appearing on the security videos. He said something to the other two about the Ferris wheel, at first seemed to be cajoling, then taunting them to come with him. In fact, it seemed, he was taunting them to come with him and the other nine, who were now pouring excitedly through the opening in the railing that led directly to the Ferris wheel line. Eventually he abandoned the two holdouts, after shouting that they were fucking pussies, and joined the line.

That's when one of the two, the one nearest Gurney, finally turned his head in Gurney's direction. He was wearing a black hoodie that concealed his hair and much of his forehead and shadowed his eyes. His face was painted a bilious yellow. A painted rust-colored smile obscured the contours of his mouth. Only one feature was plainly discernible. But that one riveted Gurney's attention.

It was the nose—small, sharp, slightly hooked.

He couldn't swear it was a perfect match with what he'd seen on the videos, but he felt the similarity was close enough to qualify this individual as a definite *possible*. More would be needed, however, to move the needle to *probable*. And he still hadn't had gotten a decent view of Black Hoodie's companion at the rail.

As Gurney was about to shift his position, that young man simplified the situation by turning his head sufficiently to eliminate himself (and his broad, flat face) from further consideration. He was saying something to Black Hoodie, which Gurney only partially overheard. He wasn't sure, but it sounded like "You got any more shit?"

Black Hoodie's response was inaudible, but there was nothing ambiguous about the disappointment on the other's face. "You got any more coming?"

Again the answer was inaudible, but its tone was not pleasant. The questioner was obviously taken aback, and after an awkward hesitation, he backed away, then turned and hurried into the concourse nearest Hardwick. After a brief hesitation, Hardwick followed him, and they were soon both out of sight.

Black Hoodie was alone at the railing. He had turned back toward the carnival rides and was gazing now, with a kind of dreamy speculation, at the gaudy array of Ferris wheel lights. There had been a measured smoothness in his movement, and now there was a stillness about him that Gurney deemed far more adult than childlike.

Black Hoodie (as Gurney mentally called him, unwilling to give him the assassin's name prematurely) was keeping his hands in the front pockets of his sweatshirt—which could be a convenient way for him to keep his hands hidden, as the skin on one's hands is a powerful revealer of age, without the oddity of wearing gloves in August. His height—no more than five feet—was consistent with Peter Pan's, and he appeared to have the same sort of slim body that left its gender an open question. There were specks of mud on his black sweatpants and sneakers, consistent with racing an ATV down Barrow Hill and across the soggy pasture bordering the fairgrounds. The suggestion in that snippet of overheard conversation with his companion at the rail that he may have been supplying drugs that evening would explain how a stranger might have been accepted instantly into the shabby little circle.

As Gurney was eyeing the black-clad figure and weighing this circumstantial evidence, the background strumming and twanging

of country music that had filled the fairgrounds abruptly ceased—
and was followed by several seconds of loud static and finally an
announcement:

> *Ladies and gentlemen, may I have your attention, please.*
> *This is an emergency announcement. Please remain calm. This*
> *is an emergency announcement. We are currently responding*
> *to several fires of unknown origin. For everyone's safety, we are*
> *discontinuing this evening's scheduled events. We will be evacu-*
> *ating the fairgrounds in a safe and orderly fashion. Any rides*
> *now in progress will be the last ones this evening. We ask that*
> *all exhibitors begin closing down their booths and displays. We*
> *ask that everyone follow the instructions of security, fire, medi-*
> *cal, and safety personnel. This is an emergency announcement.*
> *All fair visitors should begin proceeding in an orderly fashion*
> *toward the exits and the parking areas. I repeat, we are respond-*
> *ing to several fires of unknown origin. For everyone's safety at*
> *this time we must begin an orderly evacuation of the—*

The announcement was truncated by the loudest explosion yet.

Panic was spreading widely. Shouts. Mothers screaming for their
children. People looking around wildly, some struck motionless, some
moving erratically.

Black Hoodie, standing at the rail, gazing up at the colossal Ferris
wheel, showed no reaction at all. No shock, no curiosity. This, in Gurney's estimation, was the most damning evidence so far. How could this
person not react—unless what was happening was no surprise to him?

As was often the case in Gurney's mental life, though, growing
conviction brought with it a growing caution. He was all too aware of
how one's perceptions can start lining up to support a particular conclusion. Once a pattern begins to take shape, however erroneous it might
be, the mind unconsciously favors any data points that support it and
discounts any that don't. The results can be disastrous and, particularly
in law enforcement, fatal.

Suppose Black Hoodie was just another pathetic waster, stoned out
of his mind, more absorbed by the carnival lights than by any real danger. Suppose he was just another one of a million people on the planet

with a small hooked nose. Suppose the spattered mud on his pants had been there for the past week?

Suppose what seemed like an increasingly obvious pattern wasn't a pattern at all?

Gurney had to do something, anything, to resolve the issue. And he had to do it alone. And quickly. There was no time left for subtlety. Or teamwork. God only knew where Hardwick had gotten to at that point. And there was no chance of gaining the cooperation of the local police, who were probably already in over their heads trying to deal with the incipient pandemonium—not to mention the obstacle of his having made an enemy of one of their own. If he approached them now, he'd be more likely to get himself arrested than to get their help in settling the Black Hoodie question.

The amusement rides were still roaring and screeching around their mechanical confinements. The Ferris wheel was slowly rotating, its size and the relative silence of its motion endowing it with a peculiar majesty among the lesser and noisier carnival contraptions. People were still moving in both directions on the circular concourse. Anxious parents were beginning to congregate at the railing, presumably to gather up their children as soon as they disembarked from the rides.

Gurney couldn't wait any longer.

He gripped the Beretta in his loose sweatshirt pocket, released the safety, and made his way along the railing to a position a few feet behind Black Hoodie. Running now on little more than instinct and impulse, he began to sing softly.

> *Ring around the rosies,*
> *Pocket full of posies.*
> *Ashes, ashes,*
> *All fall down.*

A man and woman standing together near Gurney gave him a couple of odd glances. Black Hoodie didn't move.

A ride called Wild Spinner rolled to a halt with the sound of gigantic nails on a blackboard. It disgorged a few dozen giddy kids, many of whom were hustled away by waiting adults—with the effect of clearing the area around Gurney.

With his hidden Beretta aimed at the back of the figure in front of him, he resumed his barely audible singing, maintaining the inanely lilting tune of the nursery rhyme as best he could, while adding his own words.

Perfect little Peter Pan
had the perfect murder plan—
till it all turned upside down.
Peter, Peter, perfect clown.
Ashes, ashes, all fall down.

Black Hoodie turned his head slightly, enough perhaps to get a peripheral glimpse of the size and position of whoever was behind him, but said nothing.

Gurney could now see several dark red circular marks about the diameter of small peas painted on the side of his cheekbone in a way that reminded him of the tear-shaped tattoos gang members often displayed in that same place—sometimes as memorials to murdered friends, sometimes as advertisements of murders they themselves had committed.

Then he felt a small frisson—as he realized that they weren't just little red marks, or even red tears.

They were tiny red flowers.

Black Hoodie's hands moved slightly inside his garment's bulky front pockets.

In his own pocket, Gurney's right forefinger slipped over the trigger of the Beretta.

In the concourse behind him, at a distance he estimated at no more than a hundred yards, there was another explosion—followed by shouts, screams, curses, the sharp clamor of several fire alarms going off at once, more screams, someone wailing the name "Joseph," the sound of many running feet.

Black Hoodie stood perfectly still.

Gurney felt a rising anger as he imagined the scene behind him, the scene that was provoking those cries of pain and terror. He let that anger drive his next words. "You're a dead man, Panikos."

"You talking to me?" The tone of the question was conspicuous for its lack of concern. The accent was vaguely urban, with a scruffy attitude. The voice was ageless—childlike in an odd way—its gender no more certain than that of the body it came from.

Gurney studied what little he could see of the yellow painted face in the black cowl. The garish carnival ride lights, the cries of dismay and confusion welling up from the explosion sites, and the acrid odor of smoke blowing in the wind were transforming the creature before him into something unearthly. A miniature image of the Grim Reaper. A child actor playing the role of a demon.

Gurney replied evenly. "I'm talking to perfect Peter Pan, who shot the wrong man."

The face in the cowl turned slowly toward him. Then the body began to follow.

"Stop where you are," said Gurney. "Don't move."

"Gotta move, man." A whiny distress had entered Black Hoodie's voice. "How can I not move?"

"Stop now!"

The movement stopped. The unblinking eyes in the yellow face were focused now on the pocket where Gurney held the Beretta, ready to fire. "What are you gonna do, man?"

Gurney said nothing.

"You gonna shoot me?" The style of his speech, its cadence, its accent, all sounded about right for a tough street kid.

But, somehow, thought Gurney, not quite right enough. For a moment he couldn't identify the problem. Then he realized what it was. It sounded to him like the intonation of some sort of generic street kid, not specific to any particular part of any particular city. It was like the deficiency in the speech of British actors playing New Yorkers. Their accents wandered from borough to borough. Ultimately, they were from nowhere.

"Am I going to shoot you?" Gurney frowned thoughtfully. "I'm going to shoot you if you don't do exactly as I say."

"Like what, man?" As he spoke, he began turning again as if to face Gurney head-on.

"Stop!" Gurney thrust the Beretta forward in his sweatshirt pocket, making its presence more obvious.

"I don't know who you are, man, but you are fucking nuts." He turned another few degrees.

"One more inch, Panikos, and I pull the trigger."

"Who the hell is Panikos?" The tone was suddenly full of bafflement and indignation. Perhaps too full.

"You want to know who Panikos is?" Gurney smiled. "He's the biggest fuck-up in the business."

At that moment he noted a fleeting change in those cold eyes—something that appeared and disappeared in less than a second. If he had to label it, he'd say it was a glint of pure hatred.

It was replaced by a display of disgust. "You're gone, man. You're completely gone."

"Maybe," said Gurney calmly. "Maybe I'm crazy. Maybe, like you, I'm going to shoot the wrong man too. Maybe you're going to catch a bullet just because you ended up in the wrong place at the wrong time. That kind of thing happens, right?"

"This is bullshit, man! You're not going to shoot me in cold blood in front of a thousand people at this fucking fair. You do that, that's the end of your life, man. No escape. Picture the fucking headline, man—'Crazy Cop Shoots Defenseless Kid.' That's what you want your family to see in the paper, man?"

Gurney's smile broadened. "I see what you mean. That's very interesting. Tell me something. How'd you know I was a cop?"

For the second time something happened in those eyes. Not hatred this time, more like a one-second hiccough in a video before normal play resumed. "You gotta be a cop, right? You gotta be a cop. Obvious, right?"

"What makes it obvious?"

Black Hoodie shook his head. "It's just obvious, man." He laughed humorlessly, revealing small, sharp teeth. "You want to know something? I'll tell you something. This conversation is bullshit. You're too fucking nuts, man. This conversation is over." In a quick sweeping movement, he turned the rest of the way toward Gurney, his elbows rising at the same time like the wings of a bird, his eyes wide and wild, both hands still hidden in the folds of his oversized black shirt.

Gurney pulled out his Beretta and fired.

Chapter 61

Perfect Chaos

After the pistol's sharp report, as the slight black-clad figure fell to the ground, the first sound Gurney was aware of was Madeleine's cry of anguish.

She was standing no more than twenty feet away, evidently on her way back from the corrals. Her expression reflected not only the natural shock of witnessing a shooting, but the dreadful incomprehensibility of her husband being the shooter and the victim being, to all appearances, a child. Hand to her mouth, she seemed frozen in place, as if the effort to make sense of what she was seeing occupied her so completely that no motion was possible.

Other people on the concourse were in a state of confusion, some backing away, some angling for a better view, asking one another what had happened.

Shouting "Police!" several times, Gurney pulled out his wallet and flipped it open with his free hand, raising it over his head to display his NYPD credentials and reduce the possibility of an armed citizen intervening.

As he was approaching the body on the ground to confirm the neutralization of any danger and to check vital signs, a harsh voice behind him broke through the anxious jabbering of the onlookers. "Hold it right there!"

He stopped immediately. That tone was one he'd heard too many times on the job—a brittle layer of anger enclosing a jittery attitude. The safest path was to do absolutely nothing except comply with all instructions quickly and accurately.

An obvious cop in plain clothes came up on Gurney's right side, gripped his right forearm tightly, and removed the pistol from his hand. At the same time, someone behind him took the wallet from his raised left hand.

A few moments later, presumably after examining the ID, the edgy voice announced, "Goddamn—the man we've been looking for." Gurney recognized it now as the voice of the uniformed cop moonlighting in the fair security operation.

He walked around in front of Gurney, looked at him, looked down at the body on the ground, looked back at Gurney. "What the hell is this? You shot this kid?"

"He's not a kid. He's the fugitive I told you about at the gate." He was speaking loudly and clearly, wanting as many witnesses to his description of the situation as possible. "You better check his vitals. The wound should be between the right shoulder and right pleural cavity. Have the EMT check ASAP for arterial bleeding."

"Who the fuck are you?" The cop looked down at the body again. Bewilderment was creeping into his hostility without diminishing it. "He's a kid. No weapon. Why'd you shoot him?"

"He's not a kid. His name is Petros Panikos. You need to contact BCI in Sasparilla and FBI Regional in Albany. He was the hit man in the Carl Spalter murder."

"Hit man? Him? You fucking kidding me? Why'd you shoot him?"

Gurney gave him the only acceptable legal answer. It also happened to be true. "Because I believed my life was in imminent danger."

"From who? From what?"

"If you take his hands out of his pockets, you'll find a weapon in one of them."

"Is that a fact?" He looked around for the plainclothes guy, who seemed to be concluding a triage dispute with someone on his walkietalkie. "Dwayne? Hey, Dwayne! You want to pull the boy's hands out of his pockets? So we can see what he's got? Man here says you're gonna find a gun."

Dwayne said a few final words into the walkie-talkie, clipped it back on his belt. "Yes, sir. No problem." He knelt by the body. Black Hoodie's eyes were still open. He appeared to be conscious. "You got a gun, boy?"

There was no response.

"We don't want nobody to get hurt now, right? So I'm just going to check here, see if maybe you have a gun here you might've forgot." As he patted the front pocket area of the thick black sweatshirt, he frowned. "Feels like you might have something in there, boy. You want to tell me what it is, so nobody gets hurt?"

Black Hoodie's eyes were on Dwayne's face now, but he said nothing. Dwayne reached into both pockets simultaneously, grasped the concealed hands, and slowly pulled them both out into the light.

The left hand was empty. The right hand held an incongruously girlish pink cell phone.

The uniformed cop gave Gurney an exaggerated look of mock sympathy. "Oooh, that's not good. You went and shot that little boy because he had a phone in his pocket. A harmless little phone. That's not good at all. We got a serious 'imminent danger' question here. Hey, Dwayne, check the kid's vitals, get a call in for the EMTs." He looked back at Gurney, shaking his head. "Not good, mister, not good at all."

"He's carrying. I'm sure of it. You need to do a closer check."

"*Sure* of it? How the hell could you be *sure* of it?"

"You work inner-city homicide for twenty-plus years, you get a good sense for who's carrying."

"That a fact? I'm impressed. Well, I guess he was carrying, all right. Just wasn't carrying a gun," he added with an ugly grin. "Which kinda changes the lay of the land in an unfavorable way for you. Be hard to call this shooting righteous, even if you were still a police officer—which, of course, you're not. I'm afraid you're going to need to come with us, Mr. Gurney."

Gurney noticed that Hardwick had returned and positioned himself at the inside edge of the growing circle of gawkers, not far from Madeleine, who now appeared less frozen but no less fearful. Hardwick's eyes had taken on an icy malamute stillness that signaled danger—the particular danger that arises from indifference to danger. Gurney got the feeling that if he were to give a small nod in the direction of the antagonistic cop, Hardwick would calmly put a nine-millimeter round in the man's sternum.

It was then that a sound of humming caught Gurney's attention—a humming barely audible amid the growing clamor of the fire and medical equipment moving in all directions through the fairgrounds.

As he strained to make out the source of this incongruous sound, it grew stronger, with a more noticeable pattern. And then the pattern became recognizable.

It was "Ring Around the Rosies."

Gurney recognized the melody first, its source second. It was coming from the slightly parted lips of the wounded person on the ground—the slightly parted lips in the center of the painted rust-red smile. Blood, just a bit redder than the smile, was beginning to soak through the shoulder area of the black hooded sweatshirt and stain the dusty pavement. As everyone who could hear it stood staring, the humming was gradually transformed into the actual words:

> *Ring around the rosies,*
> *Pocket full of posies,*
> *Ashes, ashes,*
> *All fall down.*

As he sang, he slowly raised the pink cell phone that had been left in his hand.

"Jesus!" cried Gurney to the two cops as the truth hit him. "The phone! Grab it! That's the detonator! Grab it!"

When neither of them seemed to understand what he was saying, he hurled himself forward, taking a wild kick at the phone—as the two cops launched themselves at him. His foot reached the phone, sending it skittering across the concrete, just as he was tackled.

But Peter Pan had already pushed the SEND button.

Three seconds later there was a rapid-fire series of six powerful explosions—sharp, near-deafening blasts—not the muffled reports of the earlier incendiaries.

Gurney's ears were ringing—to the exclusion of all other sounds. As the cops who'd tackled him were struggling to their feet, there was a tremendous impact on the ground very close by. Gurney looked around wildly for Madeleine, saw her grasping the railing, evidently stunned. He ran toward her, extending his arms. Just as he reached her, she screamed, pointing over his shoulder to something behind him.

He turned, stared, blinking, not registering for a moment what his eyes were seeing.

The Ferris wheel was unmoored from its supports.

But it was still turning.

Still turning. Not rotating in place on its axle—the steel supports of which appeared to have been blasted away—but rolling ponderously forward in a cloud of gagging dust, away from its cracked concrete base.

Then the lights went out—everywhere—and the sudden darkness immediately amplified and multiplied the screams of terror all around, near and far.

Gurney and Madeleine grabbed each other as the monstrous wheel rolled by, smashing the railing that had enclosed it, silhouetted by a lightning flash in the low clouds, its wobbling structure emitting not only the shrieks of its riders but also the awful sounds of metal twisting against metal, scraping, snapping like steel whips.

The only illumination Gurney could see in the fairgrounds now was being provided by the intermittent lightning and the scattered fires, fanned and spread by the wind. In a Fellini-esque scene of hell on earth, the untethered Ferris wheel was rolling in a kind of nightmarish slow motion toward the central concourse—mostly in darkness, except when it was caught in the blue-white strobe of a lightning flash.

Madeleine's fingers were digging into Gurney's arm. Her voice was breaking. "What in the name of God is happening?"

"It's a power failure," he said.

The absurdity of the understatement struck them both at the same instant, provoking a shared burst of crazy laughter.

"Panikos . . . he . . . he mined the place with explosives," Gurney managed to add, looking around wildly. The darkness was filled with acrid smoke and screams.

"You killed him?" cried Madeleine, as one might ask in desperation if the rattlesnake in front of them was safely dead.

"I shot him." He looked toward the place where it happened. He waited for a flash of lightning to direct him to the black form on the ground, realizing as he did so that the spot was in the path the Ferris wheel had followed. The thought of what he might see gave him a surge of nausea. The first flash got him fairly close, with Madeleine still glued to his arm. The second flash revealed what he didn't want to see.

"My God!" cried Madeleine. "Oh my God!"

Evidently, one of the Ferris wheel's huge structural circles of steel had rolled over the middle of the body—essentially cutting it in half.

As they stood there in the darkness between the split-second flashes of light and blasts of thunder, the rain started, and soon it was a downpour. The lightning strobes showed a shifting, stumbling mass of people. It was probable that only the darkness and the deluge were keeping them from stampeding and trampling one another.

Dwayne and the uniformed cop had apparently been driven back from Panikos's body by the progress of the rolling Ferris wheel—which they were now following into the main concourse, seemingly drawn helplessly along after it by the terrible screams of its trapped riders.

It was a measure of the staggering hellishness of the scene—with all its sensory, mental, and emotional overload—that they could abandon a fresh homicide like that with hardly a backward glance.

Madeleine sounded like she was straining desperately to speak calmly. "My God, David, what should we do?"

Gurney didn't answer. He was looking down, waiting for the next flash to show him the face in the black cowl. By the time the flash came, the pelting rain had washed much of the yellow paint away.

He saw what he was waiting to see. All doubt was erased. He was certain that the delicate heart-shaped mouth was the same mouth he'd seen in the security videos.

The mangled body at his feet was indeed that of Petros Panikos.

The fabled executioner no longer existed.

Peter Pan was now nothing but a pathetic bag of broken bones.

Madeleine pulled Gurney back out of the pool of spreading blood and rainwater he was standing in, kept pulling him back until they reached the crushed railing. The flashes of lightning and thunder—punctuating the terrifying thumps and rattles and metallic screeches and human wails from the still-rolling Ferris wheel—were making rational thought nearly impossible.

Madeleine's efforts at self-control were collapsing, her voice starting to break. "God, David, God, people are *dying*—they're *dying*—what can we *do*?"

"Christ only knows—whatever we can—but first—right now—I need to get ahold of that phone—that phone Panikos used—the detonator—before it gets lost—before it sets off something else."

A familiar voice, raised almost in a shout amid the din, caught Gurney off-balance. "Stay with her. I'll get it."

Behind him, behind the remains of the railing, back where the Ferris wheel had been mounted, the wooden platform riders used for entering and exiting their seats suddenly burst into flames. In the uneven orangey light cast by the new fire, he caught sight of Hardwick making his way through the slanting rain toward the body on the ground.

When he got to it, he hesitated before bending down to reach for the gleaming pink phone, which was still in Panikos's hand. It was too soon for rigor mortis to have stiffened the finger joints, so extricating the phone should have posed no problem. But when Hardwick tried to lift it away, Panikos's hand and arm rose up with it.

Even in the dim firelight, Gurney could see why. One end of a short lanyard was attached to the phone, and the other end was looped around Panikos's wrist. Hardwick grasped the phone firmly, pulling the lanyard loose. The motion raised Panikos's arm higher. The instant the arm was fully extended, there was a loud pistol report.

Gurney heard a sharp grunt from Hardwick—as he toppled face-down onto the little corpse.

A sheriff's deputy had been half running with the help of a flash-light along the curved concourse in the direction of the ponderously rolling Ferris wheel. At the sound of the shot he stopped abruptly, his free hand on the butt of his holstered gun, his gaze moving in a dangerously overloaded state from Gurney to the crossed bodies on the ground and back again.

"What the hell is this?"

The answer came from Hardwick himself, straining to push himself up off Panikos, his voice a hissing mix of agony and fury, forced out through clenched teeth. "This dead fucker just shot me."

The deputy stared in understandable bewilderment. Then, as he stepped closer, the emotion went beyond simple bewilderment. "Jack?"

The answer was an indecipherable growl.

He looked over at Gurney. "Is that . . . is that Jack Hardwick?"

Chapter 62

A Trick of the Mind

Sometimes in the midst of a battlefield apocalypse, when the assault on Gurney's mental resources seemed most devastating, a possible path to safety would suddenly present itself. This time it appeared in the form of Deputy J. Olzewski.

Olzewski recognized Hardwick from a multiagency law enforcement seminar on special provisions of the Patriot Act. He was unaware of Hardwick's separation from BCI, which made gaining his cooperation easier than it might have been otherwise.

In a highly abbreviated manner appropriate to the emergency, Gurney gave the deputy an outline of the situation and got his agreement to secure the immediate area around Panikos's body, to take official custody of Panikos's cell phone, to summon his own department's supervisory personnel rather than the local police, to personally conduct the search for the concealed weapon that had discharged when Panikos's arm had been raised, and to ensure that the weapon passed into the custody of the Sheriff's Department.

Although moving Hardwick would be risky, they all agreed that waiting for an ambulance to reach him under the circumstances would be riskier.

Despite the bleeding bullet wound in his side, Hardwick himself was hell-bent to get back on his feet—which he managed to accomplish with the help of Gurney and Olzewski and an explosion of curses—and head for the gate where the emergency vehicles would be entering. As if to endorse this decision, a generator kicked in and some of the concourse lights came back on—although only at a small fraction of their normal brightness. At least the change made movement possible beyond the illumination limits of fires and lightning flashes.

Hardwick was hobbling and grimacing, supported by Gurney on one side and Madeleine on the other, when the Ferris wheel—its upper half visible over the top of the main tent in the next concourse—began to shudder and wobble with the sounds of snapping metal and heavy objects smashing against the pavement. Then, in a kind of surreal slow motion, the huge circular structure tilted away out of sight beyond the tent—followed a second later by an earth-shaking crash.

Gurney felt nauseous. Madeleine began to cry. Hardwick uttered a guttural sound that might have been expressing emotional horror or physical pain. It was hard to tell how much of the surrounding calamity he was absorbing.

As they pressed on toward the vehicle gate, however, something changed his mind about finding a place in an ambulance. "Too many people here hurt, too much pressure on the medics, don't want to take anybody's place, keep anyone from getting help, don't want to do that." His voice was low, no more than a rough whisper.

Gurney leaned in to make sure he was hearing right. "What do you want to do, Jack?"

"Hospital. Out of the radius. Everything here'll be swamped. Can't handle it. Cooperstown. Cooperstown'll be better. Straight to the ER. How about it, ace? Think you can drive my car?"

It struck Gurney as a terrible idea—transporting a man with a bullet wound fifty-five miles over winding two-lane country roads in a vehicle with no first-aid equipment. But he agreed to do it. Because entrusting Hardwick to the mercies of a crushingly overburdened emergency system in the middle of a cataclysm unlike anything the local EMTs had ever faced before seemed like an even more terrible idea. God only knew how many mangled, barely alive Ferris wheel victims, not to mention victims of the several previous explosions and fires, would have to be treated before him.

So they plodded on through the vehicle gate—which also functioned as the exhibitor's gate—outside of which, at the edge of the entry road, Hardwick had parked his old Pontiac muscle car. Before they got into it, Gurney took off the shirt he was wearing under his sweatshirt and tore it in three pieces. Two he folded into bulky wads and placed over the front entry wound and the rear exit wound in Hardwick's side. He tied the third tightly around Hardwick's waist to hold the wads in place. He and Madeleine eased him into the front passenger seat, reclining it as far as it would go.

As soon as Hardwick recovered sufficiently from the pain of the process, he took his cell phone from his belt, pressed a speed dial number, waited, and left a message in an utterly exhausted but smiling voice, presumably for Esti. "Hi, babe. Little problem. Got sloppy, got shot. Embarrassing. Got shot by a dead guy. Hard to explain. On my way to Cooperstown ER. Sherlock's the chauffeur. I love you, Peaches. Talk later."

It reminded Gurney to call Kyle. That call also went into voice mail. "Hey, son. Checking in. I followed our man to the fair. All hell broke loose. Jack Hardwick got shot. I'm about to drive him to the hospital in Cooperstown. Hope everything there is okay. Give me a call and fill me in as soon as you can. Love you."

As soon as he ended the call, Madeleine got into the back seat, he got into the driver's seat, and they were on their way.

The mass of vehicles fleeing the immediate area of the fairgrounds created a kind of high-pressure traffic that felt surreal in a place where cows as a rule far outnumbered cars, and the rare moments of obstruction were caused by slow-moving hay wagons.

By the time they reached the county route, the line of thunderstorms had passed to the east in the direction of Albany, and media helicopters were moving in, raking the valley with their searchlights—evidently hunting for the most photogenic bits of catastrophe they could find. Gurney could almost hear the breathlessly creative RAM-TV news report on "the panicky flight into the night from what some suspect may have been a terrorist attack."

Once free of the temporary congestion, Gurney drove as fast as he dared, and then some. With the speedometer reading between fifty and a hundred most of the way, he made it to the Cooperstown ER in about forty-five minutes. Amazingly, along the way not one word was spoken. The harrowing combination of the excessive speed, Gurney's aggressive approach to curves, and the barely muffled roar of the big V8 seemed to freeze out any possibility of conversation en route—no matter how large and urgent the open issues and unanswered questions.

T wo hours later, the situation was quite different.

Hardwick had been examined, probed, scanned, needled, stitched, bandaged, and transfused; put on an IV drip of antibiotics, painkillers, and electrolytes; and admitted to the general hospital for further observation. Kyle had arrived unexpectedly and had joined Gurney and Madeleine in Hardwick's room. The three of them were sitting in chairs by Hardwick's bed.

Kyle filled everyone in on everything that had occurred from the arrival of the police at the house up to the removal of Klemper's body and the abrupt suspension of the initial investigatory process when they, along with all other police and emergency personnel in a fifty-mile radius, had been called to the fairgrounds—leaving a large area outside the house taped off as a designated crime scene. At that point, having overheard enough of the police communications to have a sense of the disaster in progress, Kyle had replaced the flat on the car with the spare and headed for the fairgrounds himself. It was then that he checked his phone and found his father's message about driving to the Cooperstown hospital.

When he finished his narrative, Madeleine let out a nervous laugh. "I guess you figured if a madman was blowing up the fair, that's where your father would be?"

Kyle looked uncomfortable, glanced at Gurney, said nothing.

Madeleine smiled and shrugged. "I'd have made the same assumption." Then she asked a question of no one in particular in a deceptively casual tone. "First it was Lex Bincher. Then Horace. Then Mick Klemper. Who was supposed to be next?"

Kyle looked again at his father.

Hardwick was lying back against a pile of pillows, restful but alert.

Gurney finally offered a reply so oblique, it was hardly a reply at all. "Well, the main thing, the important thing, the only thing that matters, is that it's all over."

Now they all stared at him—Kyle curious, Hardwick skeptical, Madeleine baffled.

Hardwick spoke slowly—as though speaking faster might hurt. "You gotta be fucking kidding."

"Not really. The pattern is finally clear," said Gurney. "Your client, Kay, will win her appeal. The shooter is dead. The danger has been neutralized. The case is over."

"Over? You forget about the corpse on your lawn? And that we have no proof that the midget you shot is really Peter Pan? And that those promotion ads on RAM-TV promising your big Spalter case revelations are going to have every cop involved in it out for your ass?"

Gurney smiled. "I said the *case* was over. The complications and conflicts will take time to resolve. The resentments will fester. The recriminations will linger. It will take time for the facts to be accepted. But too much of the truth has come out at this point for anyone to rebury it."

Madeleine was gazing at him intently. "Are you saying that you're done with the Spalter murder case?"

"That's exactly what I'm saying."

"You're walking away from it?"

"Yes."

"Just like that?"

"Just like that."

"I don't understand."

"What don't you understand?"

"You've never walked away from a puzzle with a major piece still missing."

"That's right."

"But you're doing it now?"

"No, I'm not. Quite the opposite."

"You mean it's over because you've solved it? You know who hired Peter Pan to kill Carl Spalter?"

"The fact is, nobody hired him to kill Carl."

"What on earth do you mean?"

"Carl wasn't supposed to be killed. This whole case has been a comedy—or tragedy—of errors from the very beginning. It's going to end up being a great teaching tool. The chapter in the criminal investigation textbook will be titled 'The Fatal Consequences of Accepting Reasonable Assumptions.'"

Kyle was leaning forward in his chair. "*Carl wasn't supposed to be killed?* How'd you figure that out?"

"By banging my head against all the other pieces of the case that made no sense with Carl as the bull's-eye. The prosecution's wife-shoots-husband scenario fell apart almost as soon as I looked closely at it. It seemed far more likely that Kay, or maybe someone else, had hired a pro to hit Carl. But even that scenario had awkward aspects—like where the shot actually came from and the general complexity of the hit and the peculiarity of bringing in an expensive but uncontrollable pro like Peter Pan for what should have been a fairly straightforward job. It just never felt right. And then there were some old cases that kept coming to mind—a shooting in an alley, an exploding car."

Kyle's eyes were widening. "Those cases were connected to Carl's murder?"

"Not directly. But they both involved faulty assumptions about timing and sequence. Maybe I sensed those same assumptions might be lurking in the Spalter case."

"What assumptions?"

"In the alley shooting, two big ones. That the shot the officer fired actually struck the suspect and killed him. And that the officer was lying about which way the suspect was facing when he shot him. Both assumptions were quite reasonable. But they were wrong. The bullet wound that ended up killing the suspect had been incurred *before* the officer arrived on the scene. And the officer was telling the truth. With the car, the assumption was that it exploded because the driver lost control of it and drove it into a ravine. In fact, the driver lost control and drove it into a ravine because it exploded."

Kyle nodded thoughtfully.

Hardwick made one of his distressed faces. "So what's this got to do with Carl?"

"Everything—sequence, timing, assumptions."

"How about spelling that out in the simple language of a peasant like me?"

"Everyone assumed that Carl stumbled and fell because he was shot. But suppose he was shot because he stumbled and fell."

Hardwick blinked, his eyes revealing a rapid rethinking of the possibilities. "You mean stumbled and fell in front of the intended victim?"

Madeleine looked unconvinced. "Isn't that a bit of a stretch? That he was *accidentally* shot because he stumbled in front of the person the hit man was actually aiming at?"

"But that's exactly what everyone *saw* happen, but then they all changed their minds—because their minds immediately reconnected the dots in a more conventional way."

Kyle looked perplexed. "What do you mean, 'That's exactly what everyone saw happen'?"

"Everyone at the funeral who was interviewed claimed they thought at first that Carl had stumbled—maybe tripped over something or turned his ankle and lost his balance. A little while later, when the bullet wound was discovered, they all automatically revised their original perceptions. Essentially, their brains unconsciously were evaluating the relative likelihood of two possible sequences and favoring the one that normally would have had the greater chance of occurring."

"Isn't that what our brains are supposed to do?"

"Up to a point. The problem is, once we accept a certain sequence—in this case, 'was shot, stumbled, and fell' rather than 'stumbled, was shot, and fell'—we tend to dismiss and forget the other. Our *new* version becomes the *only* version. The mind is built to resolve ambiguities and move on. In practice this often means leaping from reasonable assumption to assumed truth, and not looking back. Of course, if the reasonable assumption happens to be inaccurate, everything built on it later is nonsense and eventually collapses."

Madeleine was exhibiting the impatient frown with which she greeted most of Gurney's psychological theorizing. "So who was Panikos aiming at when Carl got in the way?"

"The answer is easy enough to get to. It would be the person whose role as a victim makes all the other oddities of the case make sense."

Kyle's eyes were fastened on his father. "You already know who it is, don't you?"

"I have a pretty good idea."

Madeleine spoke up excitedly. "The thing I keep hearing you talk about, the 'oddity' that bothers you the most, is the involvement of

Peter Pan—who supposedly only accepted really difficult contracts. So there are just two questions. First, 'Who at the Mary Spalter funeral would be the most difficult to kill?' And second, 'Did Carl pass in front of that person as he was heading for the podium?' "

Hardwick's interjected response sounded certain, despite his speech being somewhat blurred. "Answer to the first is Jonah. Answer to the second is yes."

Gurney had come to the same conclusion nearly four hours earlier on the concourse by the Ferris wheel, but it was reassuring to see another mind arrive at the same place. With Jonah as the intended victim, all the twisted pieces of the case straightened out. Jonah was somewhere between difficult and impossible to locate physically, which made him the perfect challenge for Panikos. In fact, his mother's funeral may well have been the only event that was capable of guaranteeing his presence in a predictable place at a predictable time, which is why Panikos killed her. Jonah's seated position at graveside solved the line-of-sight problem from the Axton Avenue apartment. Carl couldn't have been hit as he stepped past Alyssa, but he could easily have been hit by a bullet intended for Jonah as he stumbled to the ground in front of him. That scenario also explained the inconsistency that had troubled Gurney from the outset: How did Carl manage to travel ten or twelve feet *after* a bullet had destroyed the motor center of his brain? The simple answer was that he didn't. And finally, the absurd outcome—in which "the Magician" shot the wrong man, making a potential laughingstock of himself in the very circles where his reputation mattered—explained his subsequent deadly efforts to keep that ruinous fact a secret.

The next question followed naturally.

Kyle asked it, uneasily. "If Jonah was the real target, who hired Panikos to kill him?"

From a simple cui bono perspective, it seemed to Gurney that the answer was obvious. Only one person would have benefited significantly from Jonah's death, and he would have benefited *very* significantly indeed.

The expressions on their faces showed that the answer was equally obvious to everyone in the room.

"Slimy piece of shit," muttered Hardwick.

"Oh, God." Madeleine looked as if her view of human nature had absorbed a body blow.

They all stared at one another, as if wondering if there could be an alternative explanation.

But it seemed that there was no escaping the loathsome truth.

The man who'd bought the hit that killed Carl Spalter must have been none other than Carl Spalter himself. In his effort to do away with his brother, he'd brought about his own terrible demise—slow death in full knowledge of his full responsibility.

It was both horrifying and ludicrous.

But it had about it a terrible, undeniably satisfying symmetry.

It was karma with a vengeance.

And it finally provided an adequate explanation of that look of dread and despair on the face of the dying man in the courtroom—a man already in hell.

For the next quarter of an hour, the conversation veered between bleak observations on fratricide and efforts to come to terms with the harrowing practicalities of the situation in which they were entangled.

As Hardwick put it slowly but determinedly, "Tragic Cain-and-Abel shit aside, we need to figure out where we stand. A giant law enforcement clusterfuck is about to begin, with every participant doing his best to be a fucker, not a fuckee."

Gurney nodded his agreement. "Where do you want to start?"

Before Hardwick could answer, Esti appeared at the door—out of breath and looking fearful, relieved, and curious in rapid succession.

"Hey! Peaches!" Hardwick's rough whisper was accompanied by a soft smile. "How'd you manage to get away down there with all hell breaking loose?"

She ignored the question, just hurried over to the side of his bed and squeezed his hand. "How are you doing?"

He gave her a twisted little smile. "No problem. Slippery bullet. Went right through me without hitting anything that matters."

"Good!" She sounded alarmed and happy at the same time.

"So tell me, how'd you get away?"

"I didn't really *get away*—not officially—just took a detour on my way to a traffic assignment. Would you believe it—we have more idiots coming into the area now than trying to get out of it. Disaster lovers, gawkers, jerks!"

"So they're putting investigators on traffic assignments?"

"They're putting everybody on everything. You can't believe what a mess it is down there. And lots of rumors flying around." She looked significantly over at Gurney, who was sitting at the foot of the bed. "There's talk about a crazy hit man blowing everything up. There's talk about an NYPD detective shooting a kid. Or maybe shooting the crazy hit man? Or some unidentified midget?" She looked back at Hardwick. "One of the deputies told me that the midget was Panikos, and that he's the one who shot you—and somehow he did this after he was already dead. You see what I mean? Everybody's talking, nobody's making sense. And on top of all that, there's a jurisdictional pissing match between the county-level sheriff's people, the local people, the state people, maybe soon the feds. Why not? More the merrier, right? And this is all happening while crazy people in the parking lot are ramming one another, every asshole trying to get out first. And even crazier assholes trying to get in, maybe take pictures, put them on Facebook. So that's the way it is down there." She looked back and forth between Hardwick and Gurney. "You guys were there. What's with the kid? You shot him? He shot you? What on earth were you doing there to begin with?"

Hardwick looked at Gurney. "Be my guest. Talking's getting rough for me right now."

"Okay. I'll make it fast, but I need to start at the beginning."

Esti listened in anxious amazement to Gurney's rapid recounting of the key events of the evening—from the lumber pile explosion and death of Klemper by the asparagus patch right up to the motorcycle chase and the death of Peter Pan in the midst of the rampant destruction at the fair.

After a stunned silence, her first question was a big one. "Can you prove that the person you shot is actually Panikos?"

"Yes and no. We can definitely prove that the person I shot is the same person who set off the series of explosions—and whose concealed gun discharged and shot Jack. The sheriff's people have custody of his body, his gun, and his cell phone—which he was using as a remote det-onator. The nearest cell tower records will show that he called a series of numbers in that same location. And I have no doubt that the times of those calls will relate precisely to the times of the explosions—which can be verified through fairgrounds security recordings. If we have any luck, the bomb fragments at the fair will include bits of cell phone detonation systems, and the systems will match those that were used at Bincher's house. And we'll almost certainly get a match between the incendiary chemical formulas used at the fair and at Bincher's. If the concealed weapon on Panikos's body was used elsewhere, that could open another door. Linking the body and its DNA back to the Panikos identity in Europe will be a job for Interpol and their interested part-ners. In the meantime, pre-autopsy photos of his face, which was intact at last sight, can be compared to the features captured on the security videos from Axton Avenue and Emmerling Oaks."

As Esti was nodding slowly in an evident effort to absorb and remember all of this, Gurney concluded, "I'm one hundred percent convinced that the body belongs to Panikos. But from a purely practi-cal cover-my-ass legal perspective, it doesn't matter. We can prove that the body belongs to an individual who was willfully responsible for the deaths of God only knows how many people in just the past couple of hours."

"Actually, it's not only God who knows. The latest count is between fifty and a hundred."

"What?"

"That's the latest as I was leaving for my traffic assignment. The number is expected to rise. Severe burns, two collapsed buildings, a fatal dispute in the parking lot, kids who got trampled. And the big one was the collapsing Ferris wheel."

"Fifty to a hundred?" whispered Madeleine, horrified.

"Christ." Gurney leaned back in his chair, closing his eyes. He could see the Ferris wheel tipping, slowly falling, disappearing behind the tent. He could hear the shocking crash, the screams piercing the awful din.

There was a prolonged silence in the room, broken by Hardwick. "Could have been even worse, maybe a lot worse," he growled, coming back to life, "if Dave didn't stop the little bastard when he did."

To this observation there were somber nods of agreement.

"Plus," added Hardwick, "in the middle of all that horrible shit, he managed to solve the Spalter murder case."

Esti looked startled. "Solved . . . how?"

"Tell her, Sherlock."

Gurney ran through the scenario with Carl as the tragic villain who initiated the plot that fatally backfired.

"So his plan was to eliminate his brother, take control of Spalter Realty, liquidate the assets for his own use?"

Gurney nodded. "That's how I see it."

Hardwick added his own nod. "Fifty million bucks. Just about right to buy the governor's mansion."

"And he figured we'd never get him for the hit? God, what an arrogant bastard!" She glanced curiously at Gurney. "You have a strange look on your face. What's that about?"

"Just thinking that a hit on his brother could've been a major plus in Carl's campaign. He could've positioned it as the mob's effort to scare him out of politics—their effort to keep a man of integrity from taking over the state government. I wonder if that might have been part of his plan all along—to position his brother's murder as proof of his own virtue?"

"I like it," said Hardwick, with a cynical glint in his eyes. "Ride that fucking corpse like a white horse—straight to his inauguration!"

Gurney smiled. He regarded the resurgence of Hardwick's vulgarity as a positive health indicator.

Esti changed the subject. "So Klemper and Alyssa were just rotten little vultures trying to cash in, after the fact, at Kay's expense?"

"You could say that," said Gurney.

"Actually," added Hardwick with some relish, "more like one rotten little vulture named Alyssa and one idiotic vulture-fucker named Mick the Dick."

After gazing at him for several long seconds with the pained fondness one might have for a charmingly incorrigible child, Esti took his hand again and squeezed it. "I better get going. I'm supposed to be intercepting and diverting traffic—idiots heading toward the fairgrounds from the interstate."

"Shoot the bastards," he suggested helpfully.

There was some more discussion after she left, discussion that drifted into theories of guilt and self-destruction, all of which appeared to be putting Hardwick to sleep.

Kyle brought up something he'd remembered from a college psychology class, Freud's theory of accidents—the idea that these events may not really be "accidental" at all but have a purpose: to prevent or punish an action about which the person is conflicted. "I wonder, could something like that have been behind Carl's stumbling the way he did in front of his brother?"

No one seemed inclined to take up the issue.

As if groping for some organizing structure into which he could fit the chaotic events, he raised the subject of karma. "It wasn't just Carl whose evil actions came flying back at him. I mean, think about it. The same thing happened to Panikos when he was crushed by the Ferris wheel that *he* blew up. And look what happened to Mick Klemper when he came after Dad. Even Lex Bincher—he kind of went wild with that big ego trip on RAM-TV, claiming credit for the whole investigation, and it got him killed. Man, like, this karma thing is *real*."

Kyle sounded so earnest, so excited by this idea, so *young*—sounding and looking so much like he did in his enthusiastic moments as a teenager—that Gurney felt an urge to hug him. But to act on so spontaneous an impulse, especially in public, wasn't in his nature.

A short while later two aides came to take Hardwick back to Radiology for some additional scans. As they settled him on the rolling stretcher, he turned to Gurney. "Thanks, Davey. I'm . . . I'm thinking you might have saved my life . . . getting me here so quickly." A rare thing for Hardwick, he said it without any ironic twist.

"Well . . ." Gurney muttered awkwardly, never comfortable with being thanked, "you've got a fast car."

Hardwick uttered a small laugh—which ended in a stifled yelp at the pain it produced—and they wheeled him out.

Madeleine, Kyle, and Gurney were left in the room, standing around the vacated bed. All perhaps finally on the verge of collapse, all with nothing to say.

The silence was broken by the ringing of a phone, which turned out to be Kyle's. He glanced at the ID screen. "Jeez," he said to no one in particular, then looked at his father. "It's Kim. I told her I'd call her, but with everything ..." After a moment of indecision, he added, "I should talk to her." He stepped out into the corridor and, speaking softly, moved out of sight and hearing.

Madeleine was gazing at Gurney with an expression that was at once full of great relief and great weariness—the same qualities that were in her voice. "You came through it all right," she said. Then added, "That's the main thing."

"Yes."

"And you figured it all out. Once again."

"Yes. At least, I think so."

"Oh, there's no doubt about it." On her face was a gentle, indecipherable smile.

A silence fell between them.

In addition to a deep wave of emotional and physical exhaustion, Gurney began to feel a widespread soreness and stiffness setting in—which, after some puzzlement, he attributed to being tackled by the two cops during his efforts to knock the pink cell phone out of Panikos's hands.

He was suddenly too tired to think, too tired to stand.

For a moment, standing there in the hospital room, Gurney closes his eyes. When he does, he sees Peter Pan—all in black, with his back to him. The little man begins turning. His face is a bilious yellow, his smile blood red. Turning. Turning toward him, raising his arms like the wings of a predatory bird.

The eyes in the bilious face are the eyes of Carl Spalter. Full of horror and hate and despair. The eyes of a man who wished he'd never been born.

Gurney recoils at the vision, tries to focus on Madeleine.

She suggests that he lie down on the hospital bed. She offers to massage his neck and shoulders and back.

He agrees and soon finds himself in a drifting state of consciousness, feeling only the warmth and gentle pressure of her hands.

Her voice, soft and soothing, is the only other reality he is aware of.

In the place between exhaustion and sleep there is a locale of deep disengagement, simplicity, and clarity where he often found a kind of serenity he found nowhere else. He imagined it might be similar to the heroin addict's rush—a surge of pure, impervious peace.

It normally was a state of isolation from all sensory stimuli—bringing with it a blessed inability to tell where his body ended and the rest of the world began—but tonight it is different. Tonight the sound of Madeleine's voice and the penetrating warmth of her hands has been incorporated into the cocoon.

She is talking about walking on the coast of Cornwall, about the sloping green fields, the stone walls, the cliffs high above the sea . . .

Kayaking on a turquoise lake in Canada . . .

Cycling in Catskill valleys . . .

Picking blueberries . . .

Erecting bluebird houses along the border of the high pasture . . .

Crossing a stile on a footpath through a Scottish Highlands farm . . .

Her voice is as gentle and warm as the touch of her hands on his shoulders.

He can see her on a bicycle in white sneakers, yellow socks, fuchsia shorts, and a lavender nylon jacket shimmering in the sun.

Her smile is the smile of Malcolm Claret. Her voice and his voice are one.

"There is nothing in life that matters but love. Nothing but love."

Acknowledgments

The Dave Gurney series continues to benefit enormously from the crucial guidance and support of the best agent in the world, Molly Friedrich—along with her remarkable associates Lucy Carson and Nichole LeFebvre, who have done so much to make the series an international success. And I am once again indebted to my great editor, Rick Horgan, whose incisive comments and suggestions make everything I write so much better. Finally, a special thank-you to my good friend Porter Kirkwood for taking the time to read an early outline of this novel and to set me straight on some of the general legal issues involved in the plot. He's responsible for whatever I managed to get right. Any errors in the final version of the story are mine alone.